Everything I Understand

LUX CUNNINGHAM

This is a work of fiction. All of the characters, organizations, and events portrayed in this novel are either products of the author's imagination or used fictitiously.

For Lucy Margaret Keen and Merlin Lorene Cunningham Shaffer.

Cast of Characters

<u>Comparative Literature Department, The University of New York</u>
ANNIE FAY CAMPBELL - student

BRANDI BLUMENTHAL - student, best friend of Annie

GRETEL MILLER - student, Annie's first friend in the department

WINIFRED MACGREGOR - professor, joint appointment with the
French department, Annie's mentor

<u>Religion Department, The University of New York</u>
NICHOLAS ÓLAFUR IVERSSEN - student, ex-boyfriend and close friend
of Annie

CHRISTIA THOMPSON - sought-after professor of religion, well-known
author, Nicholas' adviser

ABDUS SYED - student, close friend of Nicholas and Kirpal

KIRPAL ANAND SINGH - student, close friend of Nicholas and Abdus

3

TOMÁS BAUTISTA - student, Annie's crush

IBRAHIM HEYREDDIN ("Ibo") - former student, adjunct faculty member, friend of Nicholas, Abdus, and Kirpal

BRENDA FUJIKI - women's studies graduate student, work-study administrative assistant for the religion department

RICHARD REDMUND ("Guru Rich") - popular professor of Eastern religions and Sanskrit studies

CYRUS WILSON - Chair of the religion department

Miscellaneous

PHILIPPE PEREZ-THROGMORTON - poet, husband of Christia

THEODORA HARMON - interdisciplinary scholar, successful writer and guest lecturer, friend to Christia

MOTTE DUPREE THOMPSON - brother of Christia

ANDY TOMASINO - Detective in charge of case

KALINKA - lapsed student in the history department, Abdus' girlfriend

I can't abide the sound of blood pounding in my ear when I'm trying to sleep.

Amidst the rustle of the pillowcase and the soft crunch of hair, the throb of the ear's pulse – cupped just-so – is amplified. Exaggerated, as a hollow shell will seem to capture the roar of the sea. You turn and turn, trying this side, then that, one position, another...

You cannot escape the rhythmic beating: mor-tal, mor-tal, mor-tal.

This is the story of an ill-starred series of events that kept me awake nights for a very long time, tossing and turning to tune out the relentless sound of my own heart.

-- A.F.C.

Prologue (Bitter)

He'd asked her to read his manuscript. Again. She couldn't get past the cover page:

Marionette: A Selection of Formal Poetic Explorations
(unpublished manuscript)
        By Philippe Perez-Throgmorton

Marionette
Silence, then shaking.
Whipped around by he-who-is.
Sap. Heart. Blood from wood.

Christia's shoulders shook with laughter. The haiku was so awful, she mused. How to respond? Well, yes, Philippe, we do feel that way, I suppose.

Leave it to a man to make it all seem so – striking.

Her mood fell as she took in the intent of her husband's words. Yes, blood…but not from wood, from tender flesh, she mused, mine and every woman's…Despite the cozy warmth of her comfortable, well-appointed office, she shivered, and swallowed a big mouthful of brandy.

She considered the woman she'd spent much of her life studying: Jeanne Marie Bouvier de la Motte Guyon, founder of the mystical Quietists in France in the 17ᵗʰ century. She'd been incarcerated for her writings, her strong and unique spirit ultimately broken, forced to fit the confines of the Roman Catholic Church.

Somehow – a miracle! -- de la Motte Guyon's interpretation of the Song of Songs, *Le cantique des cantiques interprete selon le sens mystique*, had survived – and it surpassed by far any others in its revelation of the hidden riddles and alchemies in that confusing text; as well, in its relatively overt eroticism. Yet it had been almost completely unknown until Christia's well-received biography had come out…centuries too late to help its author.

At least de la Motte Guyon had been allowed to live following her surrender. Capitulation is the only real choice, Christia conceded to herself, under certain circumstances.

After all, a woman's alternative is often failure. Or worse. Think of only the most obvious examples: Virginia Woolf, Sylvia Plath, Anne Sexton…consumed by their own brilliance in a world that was not big enough to let them shine, a world that demanded they be housewives.

…Look at me.

But I must try to seem less strident, she resolved, and reached for the stereo remote. A recording of de la Motte Guyon's composition would be soothing.

There was a soft knock on her door.

*

"May I come in?"

"So formal," she joked.

She was standing behind her desk. Once she saw my face, she bent down and lifted a glass and a bottle from the floor under the desk. She had been drinking. Something amber-colored in a giant snifter. The bottle, half-full of the golden liquid, shone in the slanting late afternoon light.

"Come on, sit down. No, here, closer. I've made a great discovery. A breakthrough!" Her grip on her drink tightened and for a moment she looked away, shuddered slightly, took a sip. Was she, too, in need of courage?

I moved awkwardly around the chairs arranged for students in front of her desk. I was so close now to her, and still I was unsure how to proceed. I'd guessed that if I planned too much I'd never have the guts to follow through. My need, though, my lifelong all-consuming need, was what sustained me now. I forced myself to sit down near her, at the edge of her desk. I was so afraid she would touch me, and of how I might respond.

"Drink?" She offered me her bulbous glass. "I've only got one of these in here, but there's plenty more brandy."

I paused. Getting drunk might dull my wits. Then again, it might brace me for what I'd come here to do.

"Taste it." She licked her lips. "It burns, but it's so smooth, too. Come, darling. I won't bite." She grinned (nervously?) and swirled the brandy around.

She held out the glass again, and I took it. Feeling oddly detached, as if I were an observer of my own life, I let a big gulp flow into my mouth and swallowed quickly. I imagined a line of fire running into my belly and joining up with that ache which I'd felt every day of my life and neutralizing that ache, however temporarily. The vision was peculiarly satisfying.

Maybe we two could be this way too: we could combine our pain – surely she must be in pain like me? – and end up with a mutually satisfying resolution. Even though she had what I needed, I had something to offer her too. Something she could not refuse. Not, I hoped then, when we were getting so close.

The sun dropped lower and lower and we emptied the bottle of brandy and talked. She certainly wove a spell between us; but then she always did that with everyone she found attractive. She made you feel as if you were the only other person in the world. Sometimes. Then it was on to someone else, another willing victim of her seductions. She got her book contracts this way, I would bet on it. Maybe even her position at the university. She left quite a few people wanting more of this attention, too.

That day, I gave her a taste of her own medicine. I listened raptly as she revealed to me some, but not all, of her secrets and recent discoveries, her tongue rendered loose by the exquisite drink. Toward five or so, we were startled out of our reveries together by the tolling of the campus chapel bells. I venture we were both momentarily reminded of our mundane duties, and maybe even a little disappointed by the realization that our time together was finite. Then she stretched like a cat, languorously and with great pleasure. I could see through the thin Egyptian cotton of her shirt and willed my gaze away. I reminded myself to focus, and of why I was there. And, inevitably, she turned to me and looked into my eyes and sort of purred my name.

My whole life was distilled in the next moment, while in the background some generic Medieval chants droned on.

Everybody knows what happened; nobody knows why. Although, to tell the truth, I didn't expect things to unfold as they did. She knew a lot more about what was going on than I'd thought. Still, I never meant to hurt her. I only needed something from her.

Chapter One – Home

…lonely thing, twelve-fingered, out of mind…
…whining, rearranging the disaligned…
A woman like that is not ashamed to die.
      I have been her kind.

      Anne Sexton, "Her Kind"

Annie Campbell, your life is perfect, I thought happily as I settled into my favorite couch corner and took a deep breath. I told myself not to feel guilty about relaxing, but the midterm grading period had taken its toll on my sense of entitlement to peace and inactivity.

Beside me on the coffee table sat a steaming mug of peppermint tea with honey and a tall pile of books and magazines. This pile -- from which I now planned to choose at leisure: a serious novel? A trashy magazine? -- had been growing for several weeks and was my incentive for making it through the first half of the fall semester as a Teaching Assistant at the University of New York. I had also lined up several chocolates in order of preference, from least-delicious to most.

I was in the second year of my Ph.D. studies, but I'd barely had time to breathe since beginning the program. As soon as I'd finally gotten the hang of graduate school classes (lots of information to memorize, try not to be too original), I'd been honored by being chosen as a Fellow, with an attendant T.A. position. This honor came complete with frantic, grade-grubbing undergraduates and an overworked professor who was teaching Intro. Comp. Lit. for the eighth year in a row. So far, graduate school had been a period of hectic disillusionment, relieved only by an occasional glimmer of inspiration.

All the same, I was never without a sense of deep gratitude for my university-subsidized housing. In New York City, space is the greatest luxury, so while the salary of a T.A. barely covered food, I reveled daily in my housing-pool luck. Where most of my friends in the city lived in apartments with the spaciousness and sunlight of a humane mouse trap, I lived in an apartment with an actual bedroom, not to mention high ceilings, four tall windows and a walk-in closet. My living room/kitchen/dining room area was, admittedly, a bit overcrowded, with books on every available surface, a profusion of struggling plants, and colorful swaths of cloth, saris, and afghans covering my threadbare secondhand furniture. My bedroom, on the other hand, was a Zen retreat, with little in it but my futon and my ever-changing view of the tree outside my window and the building across the way.

I had strung multicolored Christmas lights around my windows just after Hallowe'en, and was admiring them as I sunk a little further in my cushiony lair, mulling over my myriad of possible indulgences. Pepita, my Boston Terrier, and my black cat, Merlin, snuggled in with me, careful to be simultaneously as far away from one another yet as close to me as possible. My infrequent breaks called for total shutdown and I was happy to be alone with my two non-human best friends.

Naturally, the doorbell rang, startling the three of us with several urgent-sounding staccato rings. I gave a sigh of resignation and got up to buzz the intruder in.

"Annie? It's Nicholas."

Into the sweet and calm glow of my apartment walked my sometimes lover/sometimes best friend Nicholas Iverssen. He was out of breath, but sartorially splendid as always in a herringbone topcoat with fake fur collar, a cashmere scarf draped jauntily around his neck, his cheeks bright from the chill outside. With his windswept, pale-blonde hair it was clear to me why he was regarded as one of the best-looking and best-dressed men on campus. He always took my breath away. Nicholas was also a brilliant Ph.D. student in the Department of Religion, studying some obscure 17th-century mystical texts and attempting to make them relevant to contemporary experience.

Just then his expression was one of shock. He stood in the doorway, ignoring Pepita's frantic greeting. Not for the first time, I completely misread his demeanor.

Nicholas would never read trashy magazines and my pile, I should say tower, of magazines was prominently displayed for my personal delectation.

"You know, I find that when one does a great deal of intense intellectual work the brain needs some sort of release," I explained sheepishly…

His expression was unchanged. He said nothing.

"I suppose you think I sit around all day eating bonbons," I added.

"Christia is dead," he announced without further ado, in a tone self-consciously dramatic but sad, too. "Murdered."

I knew immediately that it was true, both because of the look of him and because he used "Christia" instead of "Kristi," our nickname for his advisor in the Department of Religion. Nicholas might've had an

13

extreme, even morbid fascination with the macabre, but that's not to say he'd be so cruel as to joke about someone's death.

Christia Thompson. We had not liked her, but she had fascinated us nonetheless. She had been one of those professors who made a point of her enduring hipness in the face of increasing entrenchment in the patriarchal faculty regime. She was remarkable for having been offered a tenure track position at a top university at the relatively young age of forty; but academic glory was never enough for her. In truth, with her flawless ivory skin and emerald green eyes, her sharply cut black hair and her expensive Japanese and French prêt-a-porter wardrobe, she was quite a striking woman.

She was also prone to frequent name-dropping to signal her connections to the downtown cognoscenti, a habit which made me want to extol to her the virtues of sitcoms and elevator music. One meets more than one's share of pompous people in academia as well as in the downtown art scene -- Christia had pompousness enough for both. People tended to listen to her, though, and reverently, because she was attractive, charismatic and intelligent.

We knew her well because Christia was Nicholas' thesis advisor. Like him, she specialized in the 17th century, specifically in the spiritual lives of Western European women mystics of that era. She'd recently written an acclaimed biography of a French woman who'd been sort of an early Quaker and had, naturally, endured a great deal of suffering at the hands of the religious establishment of her time. Unfortunately, this project hadn't done as well as her best-selling earlier books, the books which had gotten her the University job. Back then, critics had called her "the next Camille Paglia," for heaven's sake. Where could she go after that? The commercial failure of her latest book might have disappointed her, or it might have been a point of pride, as obscurity often is in the ivory tower. In any case, I'd never brought her recent book up in conversation. It didn't seem tactful.

I am not sure who had chosen whom—had Christia encouraged Nicholas to pursue his interests in the 17th-century, or had Nicholas' interest been piqued by one of the few non-geriatric females in the department?—in any case, I had long sensed a magnetism between them, one which had worn thin on his part by the time I came into the picture.

The ambiguous relationship Nicholas and I shared had clearly interested Christia, and made me an enticing target, especially as she had been known to date both men and women in her pre-partnered days. For my part, I had found her brilliant, but not kind. Even so, as Nicholas' advisor she was to be treated with respect (fawning obsequiousness was even better) by his putative significant other. Because she was unaware of the particulars of our relationship, I always thought she assumed flirting with either one of us would be a good power play in the scheme of things. And since negotiating power -- sexual, departmental, what-have-you -- seemed to be her main *modus operandi*, I guessed she figured her machinations would at least set us subtly against one another…but they never did. For various and complex reasons, I was not jealous. And Nicholas was simply too head-in-the-clouds to notice.

All this flashed through my mind as Nicholas, having finally noticed Pepita's slobbering hello, frolicked, albeit in a slightly subdued manner, with her on the floor.

"My little behemoth," he murmured tenderly, tickling her behind the ears.

I sighed. When we'd lived together he'd regularly forgotten to walk or feed her, preoccupied as he was with reading obscure texts in esoteric languages.

Nicholas was witty, urbane…a genius. And utterly unequipped for daily life. For example, despite his superficially natty appearance, his contempt for the lowly material world was manifested in significant ways. He would often forget to shower, never mind cut his toenails, unless told to do so, as he was too busy thinking lofty thoughts. Since I had a lofty thought or two of my own to think, I'd decided I couldn't afford to be someone's caretaker.

Still, a real love remained between us and it was because of this that I had - unbeknownst to Nicholas - written a note several days before. A note that suddenly grew in importance as the news of Christia's death began to sink in. My stomach churned as I realized just how much trouble I might be in.

The last time I saw Christia was in the foyer of her apartment building after one of those ever-so-rare — and thus remarkably delightful — academic soirées that is actually fun. Copious alcohol consumption is usually a key ingredient.

Christia and her husband, Philippe, and Nicholas and I, along with most of the teachers and graduate students of the religion department, had attended a guest lecture by Theadora Harmon, the author of the trade bestseller, *Chastity Belts and Temple Whores: Two Sides of the Same Coin.* The auditorium of Religion Hall was almost full by ten before the hour. Undergraduates with dreadlocks and piercings jostled distinguished faculty for places to sit. By the time Harmon arrived at the podium, the hall was standing-room-only. I chuckled to see several important university bigwigs standing at the back of the room. I saw a lot of folks from Womens' Studies, but I also recognized a fair number from African-American Studies, and from my own department.

Christia, as someone who shared similar scholarly interests, was in charge of entertaining the department's popular guest at a post-lecture dinner. Nicholas, as her most charming advisee, had been invited along. I'd decided to consider myself included in Christia's invitation. I'd chosen my look for the night with uncharacteristically

16

elaborate care: I'd knotted my hair in two rolls above my ears, Star Wars style, and brushed sparkling green eyeshadow on my top eyelids. Over a black bodysuit and lace-up boots I'd put on an almost-transparent, shimmery violet dress with rhinestone buttons running from the empire waist all the way up under my chin. The dress was floor length, with flared sleeves. Dramatic and provocative, if in actual coverage quite modest.

Just as I'd expected, there was a lot going on, sartorially speaking, at Theadora Harmon's talk. Along with the aforementioned wildly-attired undergraduates, Harmon herself stood out as even wilder. Her shoulder-length jet-black hair had been braided into an infinite number of tiny braids, with tiny red, gold, black and green beads at random points and at the ends. She was poured into what, with its extreme flared shoulders and blade-sharp pencil skirt of neon yellow, looked like a Thierry Mugler suit on acid—and, given her rumored million-dollar deal for her forthcoming book, it probably was. Moreover, her entire being exuded the health and passion of a woman who loves what she does. Word was, the success of her book had enabled her to give notice at her Harvard tenure-track position to travel and lecture, so perhaps she had good reason to look so happy!

"Just wait, Annie," Christia had confided to me before the lecture, "Theadora Harmon is one of those rare important scholars who are very cool at the same time. Her work is bombastic and won't necessarily hold up under intense scrutiny, but it certainly is piquant. This is going to be fun. The dinner, that is." Nicholas had evidently told her I was joining them. "All the junior faculty stiffs are just dying to have a heart-to-heart, or *something*, with the Harvard babe. Mind you don't keel over in jealousy."

I laughed. "Those pasty guys?" I inevitably found myself becoming more sarcastic around Christia and I didn't like it. I mentally shook myself. "I'm really looking forward to hearing her speak."

Christia looked at me a little condescendingly. "I'll just bet you are, Annie."

Christia'd worn a skin tight, 'forties-era, velvet jacket over a turtleneck and a supple leather skirt, all black, with seamed stockings and square-toed pumps. Her only jolt of color came from a blood-red long-stemmed rose woven through the buttonholes of her jacket, thorns and all.

Harmon was a dynamic speaker and the time passed quickly. The central point of her argument was a controversial one: that women in any position within religious institutions (including congregations), even so called honored or honorable ones, that is, priestesses and wives, were oppressed under the patriarchal religious hegemony. As might be expected, lively questioning followed her talk. I myself was moved to ask, referring to Frazer's *Golden Bough*, whether she included the European fire festival celebrants of the Middle Ages in her analysis. Women, I explained, were widely considered to be equal, even dominant, participants in these rites.

She replied that she did, because fire festival participants were forced to conduct their activities in secret. "Besides," she added, "who but would-be modern day witches reads Frazer anymore?"

The audience, consisting of approximately 25-percent would-be modern day witches, erupted in indignant chatter and was only becalmed once she'd pointed out that Frazer had probably been marginalized for his proto-feminist leanings, after which the question and answer period continued until after seven o'clock.

As people began to file out, Christia took Nicholas' arm and led him toward the front of the hall. Philippe and I were left to catch up. The aristocratic, fey Philippe always seemed henpecked to me, but Nicholas told me he was deeply important to Christia, or at least to her image. As we hurried to join the group milling about at the front of the

18

room I remember seeing a fleeting look of rage pass over Philippe's mild features.

With a sly wink at Nicholas, I took Philippe's arm. At once, I felt a current pass between us. I guessed it was a tremor from his uncharacteristic bout of anger; in any case, as anger can, it felt almost sexual. He was an attractive older man, but until then I'd never even considered that he might be attracted to me. Christia was so *riveting*. He'd always seemed consumed by her, his effeminacy notwithstanding.

The dinner had been held at Caffé Taci, a boisterous Italian place with delicious, simple Northern Italian fare. Our table was crammed with faculty from the religion department, most of whom were, most of the time, contemptuous of their peers' pop-cultural leanings. Popularity with coolness-obsessed undergraduates was also seen as slightly suspect. Moreover they were, to a man, either jealous or contemptuous of Christia herself, or so I'd heard.

These guys were willing to make an exception tonight. Theadora Harmon was just too compelling, not to mention famous, gorgeous and apparently single. The potential opportunity to hobnob with important figures in the world of academic publishing was also attractive, I'm sure. Even "Guru Rich," the enormously popular Eastern Religion specialist and Sanskrit scholar, who rarely attended university functions, was there, to my delight.

Over my asparagus and squash blossom risotto, I pondered how much more dynamic Harmon was as a speaker than almost every faculty member I'd had the dubious distinction of studying with thus far in my graduate career. I imagined that Christia might be one of the few to rival her. I wondered how Christia felt about their similarities as authors and teachers, and whether she would feel competition or sisterhood toward Harmon…and whether she'd use her wit to oh-so-subtly disparage Harmon's work or to express admiration. My money was on the former.

I'd ended up sitting next to Guru Rich and after I got my nerve up I'd brought up my latest dissertation idea, which loosely concerned contemporary female South Asian poets. I was thinking about doing some kind of comparative study, but didn't really know where to begin, since it was a fairly marginal topic, as, for better or worse, the focus of a dissertation must be.

Richard Redmund, Guru Rich, the Wallace Cudsworth Breathewaithe Professor of Religion, was one of the sadly few faculty at the university who really cared about students in general. I'd been told that if one could get ahold of him and get him to sit for a moment between his many duties, obligations, and investigations, he would happily share his knowledge and insights with any student who asked.

Just as I sensed he was about to give me the very insight that I was sure would inspire and shape my work for the next umpteen years, Nicholas cupped the back of my neck with his hand. "Annie, I'm sorry, I need to speak with you."

"Don't you see who I'm talking to?" I whispered angrily, looking back with a fleeting, and, I hoped, engaging, smile to my dinner companion.

"Oh, I'm sorry. Oh god, yes, please, we'll talk later, love. But I have to go see someone. I'll be back in an hour or so."

I gave his hand a squeeze and turned back to Guru Rich, but he was already on his way out the door, just behind Nicholas. I meandered to the bar, sipped my wine and, largely thanks to said wine, relaxed, chatting easily with various of the other guests who stopped by. Since the faculty weren't in my department (and I had nothing yet to offer the few publishing folk), I had nothing to lose by ignoring the politics and intrigues that were surely simmering just below the surface of the interactions around me.

At one point, about three glasses of Chianti into my dinner, Theadora Harmon sought me out and asked, with a dazzling smile, her

20

copper skin glowing, whether I thought Frazer's description of Beltane was an adequate one. Smiling back, and flushed with the heady feeling of good wine and food together, I answered that of course I did not— "After all, Frazer was a big prude. He barely even alludes to the wild sex that went on at the Beltane fires! The actual *point* of the fires?"

Her smile broke into a deep, throaty laugh. "You are *so* right," she said, through guffaws. "But seriously, he was essentially one of these patriarchs himself, anyway, even though he was trying to bust out with a whole bunch of 'primitive' and earthy matter, right? I can't picture someone who'd write so formally dancing around anywhere…"

"Speaking of someone it's hard to imagine dancing—" Theodora looked theatrically over at Christia with raised eyebrows and then looked at me. "What's with her, anyway?"

"In which sense?" I had to be careful.

"She just seems so shallow in this context. You know, she really is quite an artist. It must be hard for you to see where her intellectual sensitivity comes from." Theodora had probably had at least three Chiantis herself. Or maybe she was just refreshingly frank.

"I don't know. It's definitely something I've wondered about!" I admitted.

I'd thought more than a little about why so many academics seemed so cold and even, yes, shallow. My whole impetus for going into academia in the first place had to do with the sensitivity I'd imputed to all intellectuals. My reasoning went as follows: I was an oversensitive, high-strung child who poured herself into matters of the mind in order to have a sort of emotional outlet, a way of disciplining myself and ordering my emotions; therefore, all those who were involved with matters intellectual were sensitive souls; therefore, I should naturally surround myself with such individuals.

Ha. Most academics avoided emotion like a plague. I couldn't've counted the number of times a faculty member had snickered at me, or worse, for mentioning that one of the reasons I liked a certain teacher or student was his or her kindness.

Despite her snippy questions about Christia, Theadora Harmon struck me as fundamentally kind. I tried to respond to her questions honestly, while remaining kind myself. That's always a delicate balancing act.

"Maybe Christia is actually so sensitive underneath all of that attitude that she can't even show one iota of her, uh, soft underbelly. Because it would hurt too much? So she cultivates herself. You know, the whole vampire thing," I nodded toward her, as she stood a few yards away in her all-black clothes, faint circles under her eyes, pale skin, bloodless lips, "and her sophistication...I think most people are fooled by it though, don't you?"

"You're pretty smart for a grad student," she said. "Let me give you my card. Let's get together one of these days. I'm in town pretty often. You can see my schedule on my website or you can just email me. I think I'm in town a lot the next few months, and I've got family here, in Queens."

I was awed by her friendliness. "Thanks." With an exaggerated leer, I asked, "Are you going to be around for Mayday?" It might've been my imagination, but I thought she looked quite intently at me as my question hung in the air between us.

Before I could even begin to analyze Harmon's reaction (but having had just enough time to internally label myself a big dork), Christia came up behind us and put a hand on each of our shoulders. "Have you ever been to a Beltane fire, Annie?" she asked, winking at Theadora Harmon. "I have. Let's sit down and I'll tell you a story!"

She drew us back to our large round table, now littered with crusts of bread, crumpled napkins, cigarette butts, and half-drunk glasses of wine, and we took seats, joining the last few seated members of our group. Since Theadora, the guest of honor, was sitting again, people began to drift back to the table.

Christia was glad of the audience. She proceeded to describe, with relish, a ritual she'd participated in some years back during her year as a visiting scholar at Oxford, before she'd met Philippe— "Although, don't get me wrong," she added, "It's not as if Philippe would've objected…Or could've stopped me if he did!"

Philippe winced. I'd always thought of him as the sort of man who enjoys a good spanking, but that night I was beginning to change my mind.

I looked around the room as Christia held forth. All other conversation at the table had stopped as Christia described the twelve other people around the fire, the smoky smell, the quarts of homemade mead drunk, the increasingly charged air. Nicholas' friend Ibo, a hapless recent Ph.D. who'd been hired as an adjunct -- a recent favorite of Christia's -- was staring at her with his dark, now glittering eyes. He looked half-mad. Everyone else was listening with various degrees of attentiveness. Even Theadora Harmon was drawn in; her eyes were partially closed, as if she was imagining the scene herself. Only Nicholas, just back from his errand and probably hoping for dialogue rather than monologue, looked slightly bored. He later told me this was a tale he'd heard before.

"When people began to drift away from the fire I thought the party was over," Christia continued, "But I was very wrong. I couldn't find my friend Mary, so I decided to go back to the car by myself and as I walked out into these old, old woods where the glade was where we'd had the fire, I was drawn into the embrace of a bearded man I'd never met before."

*

Christia remembered that night with perfect clarity. Her one friend at Oxford, Mary, a mild, heretofore conventional-seeming woman, a woman who always kept her hair in a tight bun at the nape of her neck, that sort, had mentioned a few days before that she and some friends were looking for a thirteenth participant for a neo-Pagan ritual celebrating May Day. Christia wasn't sure why Mary'd considered her; except they'd been discussing the Isis (known as the Thames in London) river's flowing into the Cherwell river in Oxford, and how in India the confluence of two or more rivers was considered a place of great power. Christia had then mentioned her love of the Isis archetype and Mary had asked her if she'd like to see a real celebration of Goddess energy, "under the stars," on May 1st.

Christia had leapt at the chance. "Certainly. What should I bring?"

"Oh, just bring yourself," Mary had said with what Christia would've taken for an enticing grin if she hadn't known Mary as a humdrum gal.

Christia had looked forward to the event with great excitement. Her time at Oxford had so far been quiet, uneventful, solitary. She'd spent most of her time studying. She had a lot of catching up to do because the English educational system was so much more rigorous and tradition-laden than that back in the U.S. So most of her time was spent in striving -- at first to catch up, and, then, to excel.

She'd also been intrigued by the town of Oxford, and had spent hours and hours walking its streets alone, finding, at each turn, something that compelled her and drew her deeper into her dreams of another life. In Oxford, for the first time, she'd begun to feel free of her past. She'd felt as if she might be anyone -- she had only to invent herself.

As Christia probed the tender edges of her new freedom on Oxford's ancient streets, no one gave the slight, dark-haired American a second glance.

She and Mary had driven through Oxfordshire and north toward Coventry in Mary's sky-blue Mini, taking a long, two-laned country road that started just outside of their ancient university town. Christia had felt uncharacteristically languorous, and, as the sun sank over the horizon, she had allowed herself to doze off. She'd been startled awake when Mary stopped the car, opening her eyes just as the sun set over a lake that was already black as night on its near shore. Just to the north side of the lake was a large and dense deciduous forest that seemed to go on forever. A few other cars were already parked alongside the pastoral scene.

Mary's eyes shone. "We're here."

Christia opened her door and unfurled herself from the seat of the car. She stepped out onto the softest, spongiest grass she'd ever encountered. A brisk wind was blowing, and she took a full, long breath of the sweet, green-smelling air. She gave a big stretch, reaching her arms up to the sky where the first stars were just beginning to emerge.

"Come on, follow me," Mary beckoned. "There's a fire in the woods, not far." Christia noticed with surprise that her friend no longer looked mousy. She'd unbound her hair while Christia slept, and it hung, in shining milk-chocolate brown ripples, past her waist. There was an electricity to Mary now that animated and glamorized, in the old, magical sense of the word, her plain features.

Christia followed her friend, whose long hair was teased this way and that by the wind, to an opening in the ancient oak forest that had been invisible from the road. For the first time in more than a decade, Christia allowed herself to feel beautiful-- her surroundings would allow nothing less. To her one-item list of pleasures she permitted herself – "academic success" -- she added one more, the first since she'd begun her quest for accomplishment: "the power of beauty." The thought thrilled her. In the darkening night, she, too, was beginning to glow.

As Christia and Mary walked through the deep woods, whiffs of wood smoke beckoning them and saturating their hair, the soft grass gave way to soft moss, and the last light of the sun was quickly left behind. The light of the waxing gibbous moon was just enough to discern the path, and to show, as if in bas-relief, the gnarled roots of the old trees. Conifers now, too, intermingled with the oaks, all pressing in towards the path on either side.

After a few minutes, they reached a glade formed by a circle of giant pines that loomed protectively toward the center of the clearing. In the center of the space, a small fire was burning and half a dozen people stood gazing silently into the flames. A table just outside the group had been set with many candles in ornate silver candlesticks, trays of cakes, big bowls of fruit, and tarnished silver pitchers of wine. There was so much to smell and taste and touch and see. Christia's senses hummed with it all, like those of a wild animal.

Then, in the glade, the wind ceased its whistling. There was not a sound, and little movement save the flickering of firelight.

Many people would've been spooked, Christia thought, but she was not at all afraid. Her mind felt oddly still. She reached a hand to touch the bumpy, mottled bark of the nearest tree, pausing at the edge of the glade. A slow smile spread across her face. She didn't know a single person, and yet everything just felt right. For the first and last time in her adult life, she had forgotten her repressive vow to herself. Stepping into the clearing, she felt as if she were home.

Her mind returned abruptly to Caffé Taci, to her attentive audience -- and to her regrettably empty wine glass. A waft of smoke reached her from the restaurant's brick oven, though, and for a split-second her thoughts skittered back to that night in the woods: Why had she, the very Christia Thompson who'd blossomed that night and who still carried its glow, forgotten that feeling? Why hadn't she sought it out to anchor her life on her return to the states? Why had she aligned her central goals on this course of difficulty and ambition, instead of seeking peace? Oh yes, she remembered there in the café, surrounded by admirers (if not people who actually cared about her), because there would never, could never, be peace for someone like her. Someone who was not-innocent, and who was, above all, unwise. She had much to prove – through academic success, which was still the central axis of her being…and more for which to atone. No, she was not like other people: her background, her past…brought her only shame.

After that night, the only thing that had stayed with her consistently was that she'd become more attractive somehow, more compelling. Beauty's peace, she'd stamped out of herself; its power, she'd retained. It was useful. Before the Beltane fire, Christia had been as unnoticeable as Mary. Afterwards, she'd treated herself to a whole new wardrobe, filled with dark colors and sensuous fabrics. She'd cut her hair to frame her elfin face, and left her skin and full lips bare and pale. In a way, her appearance had been imbued with the magic of that night, though her spirit hadn't, at least not so as she could perceive it. Christia knew she was striking now, and did everything in her power to further the dramatic impression she made on people, but she never again felt at home. Anywhere.

With effort, Christia used the very solid sight of Theadora Harmon, head cocked, listening, to anchor herself in the present. She was recounting an entertaining anecdote, she reminded herself, and no more.

*

"Well…I ended up having quite the authentic Beltane celebration after all!" Her voice became softer. "…I've always thought of him as 'The Bear' – he was quite tall and hairy…Um…"

We collectively held our breath.

"Well, let's just say," she concluded, "That there was a lot more going on in those woods than you'd've thought. Very Olde, *Olde* England, don't you know."

The whole table full of people was silent, whether in awe or disgust it was hard to say, though I could've guessed in a few cases. Theadora Harmon looked pensive. Nicholas was back, and, from his expression, mildly appalled. Only Christia looked happy, and her wide smile became strained as she realized she might have gone too far for some of her audience. I should have smiled at her. She was quite a storyteller. I should have met her eyes.

"Cheers!" said Philippe, with a wry expression, and thereby broke the awkward moment. Was it only me who saw Christia's eyes dart his way, suffused with hatred? People seemed to shake themselves a little bit and some began to get ready to leave our gathering. But for our malingering group and a few waiters, Caffé Taci was empty. Nicholas told me he needed a book from Christia, but that he would walk me home after we stopped by her place. I replied that I would walk with him to Christia's but I would be fine walking home alone, that the streets of New York City, not some idyllic mossy forest, awaited us outside. His face fell, but only a little.

I was wary of going back to Christia and Philippe's place after her intimate tale, but she was cold and withdrawn on the brief walk to their doorman building, wan as her now-wilted rose. As well, Philippe was choosing, perhaps a bit too late, to keep his mouth shut. Nicholas and I were in a minor snit after his untimely disappearance. Nobody was arm in arm this end of the evening's festivities; nobody even seemed to be communicating at all.

Back in my apartment, days later, I marveled at the complex calculus by which we choose a course of action. Could I have changed the mood somehow? By taking Christia's arm, or by introducing a new

28

topic of conversation perhaps, thereby breaking the veil of gloom that seemed to cover us all at the end of that otherwise-fun night?

Guilt and shock vied for emotional preeminence as I rubbed the soft spot under Pepita's chin, trying to decide what I should say. "What should we do?" I asked finally, swallowing the bubble of anxiety that I felt rising in my throat.

"Ah, you're a good egg, Annie." Nicholas gave me the tiniest of sweet smiles. "I suppose I just needed to be somewhere safe – here –" he patted Pepita fondly, "to let this sink in."

For a few minutes, we sat quietly together. Nicholas was still in shock, I guessed, even grieving; whereas I was debating whether to tell him what I had done. My empathetic Pepita was very concerned and was looking at us with what I called her "undertaker" expression, as if to say, "Although I do not know exactly what your relationship is to this tragedy, nor, in fact, what the tragedy is, my demeanor is meant to convey tactful sympathy." To stall, I got up to put on some tea for Nicholas, and to concoct a snack. Food, like sex, is always so comforting, so life-affirming, in the face of death.

My kitchen was essentially *in* the living room, but the back of the couch served as a room divider. As Nicholas looked out the windows and I bustled about the kitchen, such as it was, we were free to think our own thoughts.

I thought of Christia, her shining, dark hair, always severely styled, her narrow, catlike green eyes and her mostly fine-featured face. I recalled various of her outré outfits which managed to nevertheless virtually reek of rarefied good taste. How much all this refinement contrasted with her full, generous mouth, which she always seemed to be holding tightly shut with a semi-smirk. Maybe she'd been trying to hide the real zest for life and love that a mouth like hers conveyed through her meticulously cultivated persona. Maybe she'd been hurt so badly once that all those mannerisms -- the coldness, the more-cool-than-thou attitude -- seemed imperative to her survival.

You didn't think these exculpatory things when she was alive, I chided myself. I felt my eyes fill with unspilled tears. To be sure, Christia was a domineering and not-necessarily-trustworthy woman, but that did not mean she deserved to die. I could think of plenty of people who probably did not like her, but hatred was another matter.

I set the tea, date nut bread with cream cheese (part of my day-off stash), and lemon squares (ditto) down on my rickety, now indisputably overloaded, coffee table. Christia would have been appalled by the sight.

Growing up in Greenwich, Connecticut, I'd babysat for people with impeccably-decorated, brittle-feeling homes, with huge expanses of empty space, usually inhabited by one small, angular, cushionless chair and a large abstract artwork. Some part of me always wanted to just mess something up, to desecrate the too-clean, shiny floor, if not for my sake then for the sakes of the children living in such cold perfection. At home I always heard these people referred to as "New Money"—but then maybe that was because we'd begun to run out of money by that time. Deep down, though, I guess I just believed that happy people, people who have nothing to prove, can tolerate the small decorative disjunctions of a life well- and fully-lived. I still believed this at the time of Christia's death. Still, someone can be happy and nonetheless have something to prove, no?

Despite all of her efforts to appear cultivated, or maybe because of them, Christia always seemed to Nicholas and me to be putting on airs. In the milieu in which we moved, education and a good working knowledge of varied cultural signifiers was taken for granted. Actual cultural activities, obviously, varied according to income: trips to the Hermitage versus books deconstructing the Hermitage, say. But people living on university fellowships without parental support, like me,

30

could, with a little ingenuity and legwork, furnish their homes and dress themselves perfectly well, often relying heavily on kitsch. We could go to the Film Forum, or the Miller Theater, or the latest ethnic restaurant in Queens for that matter, as well as the next person—just not as frequently. More importantly, we could saturate our minds with the highest currency of all: intellectual capital. In this way, although our circle of friends included a Pakistani aristocrat and a Turkish magnate's son, as well as a Mennonite farmgirl from Wisconsin, we could all enter as equal participants in the lively jostling for attention, affection and position that exists in any dynamic social group. Of course, we'd've never put it this way, we'd have said we were friends, more or less, but nothing is ever that simple.

In all of this signification, one never wanted to be seen to be trying too hard. And it did seem to us that Christia Thompson was doing just that. So Nicholas and I had, little by little, developed this whole mythology around our Christia. We'd begun by bringing a twang into our voices when we'd talked about her and, as the story got deeper, she became "Kristi-Bob Scrubbs" from "up a holler" in West Virginia. The more esoteric her references, the more highfalutin' her tastes, the more we became convinced that she was trying to hide her true roots, whatever they were. Christia was trying to prove herself, we reasoned, and we took our small pleasure in disbelief.

I admit, in retrospect, that this sounds snobbish, but in our defense I can only say that he and I would never have actually looked down on anyone for their ethnicity, roots, or socioeconomic background. It was Christia herself, it seemed to us, who would've been mortified to be discovered to be anything less than entirely top-shelf, someone who sprung whole-cloth from the pages of the bible of the high culture avant-garde.

From our perspective, not to put too fine a point on it, we felt Christia was full of crap. We didn't know what kind of crap *per se*, but we smelled something, and it might as well have been from up a hollar in West Virginia as from the next place.

This was harmless fun, so far, no?

I took a long, slow swallow of tea. I savored a bite of my lemon bar—the buttery shortcake crumbling and melting in my mouth, the creamy, sweet-sour lemon goo on top—as I considered how to tell Nicholas what I had done.

I looked out the window. I caressed Merlin's soft fur as she purred contentedly. Nicholas looked at me with shining eyes, then, after blinking rapidly for valiant moment, he dissolved into tears. I drew him into a big, long hug.

I decided not to tell Nicholas what I'd done.

At the time, my actions seemed harmless. Three days earlier, in the midst of midterm madness, I'd been daydreaming over cocoa at the Hungarian Pastry Shop. This hallowed and somewhat decrepit institution, where poets such as Jack Kerouac and Suzanne Vega had wiled away their undergraduate days at Columbia and Barnard, was my local coffee shop and I enjoyed breathing the stale air therein. It was necessary to engage in a lot of potentially flirtatious eye contact with other habitués in order to get through the endless hours of studying or grading drudgery. This was, mind you, the sort of coffee shop where "Is that Bourdieu's critique of Flaubert?" would be considered a suave pick-up line.

At the same time, one wanted to avoid attracting the "lifers"— people who'd perhaps once been students but who'd ended up mired in some graduate students' no man's land, spending years upon years studying or pretending to study more and more obscure theorems or texts. These pathetic souls could be identified by their yellowed piles of papers, often covered with scribbling in more than one color of ink, usually perused while muttering to themselves. "Lifers" were generally older and more pungent than the rest of us graduate students. There were more of them than one might imagine.

Anyway, on this particular day, the ratio of intriguing to "must avoid" people in the coffee shop was quite low. I'd been reduced to relying on my own fantasy life for a little intrigue. I was thinking of my current crush, Tomás, then of the subject of my penultimate crush, Nicholas, and then from there my mind wandered to Christia Thompson. My frustration over grading—original thought was not necessarily rewarded within the grading guidelines set up by the professor, while repetition of the course's party line *was*—spilled over into my extracurricular thoughts. I found myself going off on my usual riff about the unfairnesses of university life.

Christia, for instance, as Nicholas' advisor, used her power over him as currency in the social realm. She expected him to kowtow to her intellectually and to reaffirm her sexual attractiveness by responding in kind to her provocations. She often said to him, à propos his questioning of some required change in his dissertation, "Because I'm the mommy, that's why." This would be said with a knowing twinkle in her eye. Now that his crush on Christia had abated, behavior like this drove Nicholas crazy, and not in a good way.

I knew in the past, before we'd met, he'd probably enjoyed their relationship a great deal. After all, Christia was attractive in her own way—and for a female professor she was dazzling. And don't most men have some sort of mommy thing once in a while? But Christia was bad mommy, she was domineering and controlling, and whatever treat she'd promised baby was sure to be laced with something not so sweet.

Nicholas was not the only graduate student who'd been caught in her spell. She'd had a whole coterie of male and female students who encircled her with varying levels of sycophancy and real respect. After all, she was tops in her field, she was relatively young and attractive and hip, and she was giving of her time, within certain parameters. Any number of her advisees and hangers-on might've been thinking along the frustrated lines I was mentally treading...There were also faculty members who were in her web. All in all, she made of herself quite a target. The funny thing was, I'd bet she would've been just as gratified by the negative emotional attention as by the positive. Christia Thompson was, by her own design, a magnetic woman, both attractive and repellent -- sometimes in equal measure.

There was no one in my department like her. The Comparative Literature department at the University of New York was, first of all, inhabited primarily by elderly white men. We, the mostly female new generation of literary scholars, actually referred to them as "Dead White Men." There were legends about some of them in their heydays, but those would've been decades ago. Furthermore, the junior faculty were all too harried and overworked to interact too much with we (harried, overworked) graduate students, never mind to dazzle anyone. My own interactions with faculty were usually brief — and revolved around undergraduate grading issues, or whether I could cover their office hours, as usual.

That day at the coffee shop, all of my frustrations got tangled up in my head and, as I procrastinated, an idea began to emerge in my mind. Oh, it wasn't such a great idea, and if things had gone differently it probably wouldn't have amounted to anything, but it certainly seemed satisfying at the time. I decided to write Christia a little note, just one silly sentence: "The jig is up, Kristi." I would slide the note under her office door at school the next day. I tore a piece of paper out of my notebook and wrote in block letters, leaving the note unsigned.

What did I intend to accomplish? At the very least, I thought the note might give Christia the Pompous a moment's pause. At most, I hoped to give her just a smidge of paranoia in return for all the humiliation she'd brought dear Nicholas.

I was even laughing a little to myself as I folded the note in half and tucked it in my pocket. The lifer at the table next to me had asked me what was so funny and I'd been so self-satisfied as to say, "Me. I'm funny." I gave him a little wink just to be sure he knew I wasn't serious.

"Maybe you can help me inject a little humor in my work," he said, eyes full of semi-desperate hope.

"I don't think so," I replied, "considering I've got a serious load of work to do right now. You caught me in a major procrastination moment."

"Don't I know it." With that, to my relief, he turned back to his dog-eared pile of work materials, and I patted the note comfortingly, vowing to reward the next few hour's diligence with a secret note-delivery mission.

Now, of course, the significance of the note—slipped under her door without any witnesses the day before her death—was much greater. If she'd kept it, it would surely be taken in as major evidence. It would be subjected to tests both arcane and high-tech and a disgruntled, probably jealous, Comp. Lit. graduate student named Annie Fay Campbell would be found responsible. It was a short step from there to being found guilty of her murder, was it not? It figured that in death she was more dangerous to me than she was alive. That probably would've made her smile, too, in her vulpine way.

Poor Christia. Even when she was dead I was hard put to find something good to say about her. Let's say she was brilliant, and leave it at that.

Chapter Two – Lachrimosa

The more bonfires could be seen sparkling and flaring in the darkness, the more fruitful was the year expected to be.

Sir Richard George Frazer *The Golden Bough*

Nicholas waited for Annie in the foyer of her building, reminiscing over the days when it had been *their* building, before things had gotten confusing. The first time he had gone home with her, his anticipation had taken his breath away. She was such a funny mix, irreverent and elegant, and he'd noted right off that her surroundings suited her. Like here: the lovely dark, curved woods of the banister and railing leading up to her apartment contrasted sharply with the institutional linoleum floor. She'd explained that her building had once been a grand single-family residence. Until it had been taken over by the university's ever-spreading campaign of gentrification, it had been crumbling and abandoned for decades. Sensual and rich as the original fixtures of Annie's building were, the work the university had done to bring the building into the 20th-century was probably much more practical. The shifting graduate student population had no care for fine wood floors or stained glass – they had too little time and energy, and moved too often besides.

To Nicholas, though, it was jarring to see signs of renovation. He always preferred the antique, as a matter of principle. There remained a gigantic, gilt-framed mirror in the vestibule and he gazed at his reflection with approval: to be sure, he didn't wear bespoke suits like Philippe, Christia's husband, but who could tell the difference? Nicholas had in fact always been somewhat in awe of that older man, with his languid and droll upper crust British drawl, his Cambridge degrees (philosophy *and* economics, was it?), his apparent lack of interest in doing anything that might remotely resemble work, his impeccable style.

Nicholas was always trying to live down the fact that he came from California, where his stepfather was a rich, ambulance-chasing lawyer and his mother, married to Sam Green for his money alone, was a serial adult-education enthusiast. One week Janene Iverssen-Green was extolling the virtues of Ikebana flower arranging, then, the next, how to read vitamin deficiencies in the lines of the palm. Nicholas' sister Brooke was a miniature Janene. His family was rich only thanks to Sam's generosity to his stepchildren and second wife; and it was cultured only insofar as any suburban, social-climbing, first-generation wealthy family can be cultured, which was, as far as Nicholas was concerned, not cultured atall.

The Green family spent the majority of its time in Palm Springs, where they kept an impeccably green lawn and a turquoise jewel of a pool (with a pool house twice the size of the apartment Nicholas lived in now). They liked to think of the Palm Springs house, a 5,000 square-foot construction of glass, metal and slate, as a piece of history, since it was rumored that Rat Pack members had stayed there in their heyday. The slate and glass motif continued inside of the very open and spacious house, which had ceilings high enough to accommodate the tall, live palm trees felt by Janene to add a touch of class to the ultra-designed décor.

On Nicholas' infrequent visits, Sam called him "Nicky my boy," as in "Why don't you get some fresh desert air, Nicky my boy?" while Janene and Brooke fluttered between them, trying to keep things peaceful.

Nicholas hated it. All of it. He hated the very conversations that took place in the conversation-encouraging seating groups. He couldn't stand that this house represented *history* to his family. What were they *thinking*?

Meanwhile his family, and in particular Janene, enjoyed their lives in Palm Springs, where, only once in awhile, the various family members wondered just what it was that Nicholas – who, truth be told, they found a little ungrateful, and maybe even, well, effeminate, too – didn't like about their desert oasis, or their lifestyle as a whole, for that matter. After all, they had access to urban culture as well, when necessary, from their enormous house in an upscale L.A. suburb, with its own impeccably green lawn and a turquoise jewel of a pool (ditto, poolhouse).

Nicholas fancied himself to be a changeling. He'd been, since he was very, very young, different from his family. He'd been smarter, first of all. He'd been reading Schopenhauer at ten. By sixteen, he'd taught himself to speak both Russian and Danish because he'd wanted to read Tolstoy and Kierkegaard in their original languages. He'd dabbled in anorexia, various sorts of mortification of the body, and countless teen subcultures, from Goth to death metal, and by eighteen he'd decided that Kierkegaard was wrong: the choice to lead a refined yet hedonistic life, the aesthetic life, would for him not lead to misery and ennui as the philosopher predicted, but to continued pleasure.

He would take every precaution to ensure this outcome, for the other choices – ethical obligation or religious submission -- offered by this, the first philosopher who really spoke to him, looked like slavery to him. The first was slavery to his fellow man, the second, slavery to a distant, capricious god. Nicholas didn't believe in God anyway: believing in God was a way to comfort oneself in the face of existential angst. Like substance abuse, or nymphomania. Not that he hadn't indulged in some of his own self-comforting from time to time. Nicholas' fellow man didn't strike him as all that fabulous or deserving of a subject for self-abnegation either; and so he continued on his path, seeking the finer and more or less subtle gratifications, which gratifications made themselves readily available to this good-looking, cultured, multilingual, and well-to-do, rather twee young man. If he sometimes felt alone despite the many rewards, he tried to pleasure his alone-ness away. After all, what other choice was there for him?

In short, he was, both by nature and endeavor, alienated from his suburban, normal, pseudo (to him, at least)-happy family. To make himself feel better, to feel as if he was not so truly and totally alone in the midst of lots of others unlike him, he liked to tell himself he was much more aristocratic, really. Nicholas had been given no middle name. He knew he had some Icelandic blood from his father's side, and so he'd given himself a middle name, Olafur, after the Icelandic novelist, Olafur Sigurdsson. He felt connected to writers and philosophers through the ages, and to the old cities he'd traveled through in Europe and Russia, having spent his summers hitch-hiking and staying in hostels since he was first old enough to travel alone. California had no tradition, no old architecture...it had no history. The very air in California was new and uncharged. In California everybody was blonde, regardless of their natural hair color.

Nicholas had spent his life getting away from California. He had cultivated himself carefully and conscientiously until he was almost indistinguishable from someone who'd grown up in a castle, with nannies and private lessons in all sorts of arcane subjects and musical instruments, speaking a multitude of different languages to accommodate the veritable United Nations of houseguests welcomed by his family and their army of servants. Philippe Perez-Throgmorton had nothing on him.

Christia and Annie had both always loved the way he, Nicholas, dressed, but that might have been the only thing the two women had in common. He'd been attracted to Annie's purity, her freshness and innocence, which were all the more refreshing since she thought of herself as very worldly wise. Christia—it was hard to admit this even to himself—had touched a darker part of him. Annie had never even imagined just how torrid his little thing with Christia had been.

But that was all over now.

Now, there was something he hadn't thought of yet in all the tumult: some questions would be raised about his dissertation. Christia had applauded his unorthodox choice of subject matter, but others in the department might not be so supportive. His friend, Ibo, once Christia's star student and now, provisionally, an adjunct lecturer in the department, would be in trouble too. Who among the remaining faculty would support Ibo's study of a thirteenth-century B.C.E. Turkish priestess? And who would advise him, Nicholas, on the true beauty and metaphysical significance of worms? The answer to both questions was, probably, no one. Apart from Christia, the department was renowned mainly for its focus on epistemological religious philosophy.

His advisor was dead.

He'd have to find some way to convince one of the junior faculty members of the importance of his endeavor. It wouldn't be easy. He would have to come up with some very strong – ugg, how he hated to use this language – "selling points" for his research. For example, one thing he'd always liked about some worms was how hard they were to kill; one could cut them into pieces and each piece would become a new worm. Plenty of metaphysical arguments could be made regarding the death-defying regenerative properties of worms. Then again, that was probably not an appropriate observation to share at this particular time.

Nicholas wiped a few tiny tears of self-pity from his eyes. He assured himself he would find someone to oversee his work. He tried to erase any trace of fear from his face as he heard Annie fondly telling Pepita to take good care of Merlin, then, after shutting the door, begin to descend the stairway to the vestibule.

*

"Annie!" Nicholas greeted me as if I'd been hours not minutes and took my hand.

We left my building in something of a rush. I was curious to hear what people were saying about this crime in the hallowed and usually utterly uneventful ivory towers of our university. I was also more than a little concerned about the whereabouts of my note at the time of Christia's death, and wondering if word of a suspicious note had gotten around.

My neighborhood had a nice mix of students from Columbia and the University of New York, university faculty, and working class people, mostly Latino, who'd yet to be pushed out by gentrification. If you walked down my block, even at 3 a.m, you'd've heard at least three or four different languages being spoken before you reached Broadway. You could buy any sort of food, including some of the best bagels in New York City, as well as more spicy fare, such as several types of excellent kimchee, or a special kind of South Indian dosas, at any hour of the day. Central Park, Riverside Park, and Morningside Park were all just minutes away from my place. What you wouldn't find is chic stores; most notably, there were no shoe stores near my apartment, for which I and my wallet were very grateful. People in my neighborhood were friendly in a way that is rare in the city, and it wasn't unusual for me to run into people I knew in the local markets — and to wind up having a drink or cooking a meal together. Morningside Heights, as my neighborhood was called, was an international community that somehow managed to combine people from wildly disparate backgrounds into a bustling, relatively-harmonious whole.

Nicholas and I whizzed along through this eclectic scene, each with our own preoccupations. We passed the coffee shop where I'd written the note to "Kristi" – and where we'd first met and fallen in love – on our way to campus. We had so much history together and on the odd and upsetting occasion of the murder of someone we both knew fairly well I was glad of the comfort our long friendship afforded us both. I only wished I'd felt comfortable telling him about the note. I told myself I should be honest with him before we got to school but I just couldn't bring myself to do it. Wouldn't he think I was a real jackass? I certainly thought so myself.

As we passed through the imposing gates of the university I was struck as usual by the sheer masculinity of the campus. At my small women's college, the Gothic stone architecture was modeled after Princeton, on a more intimate scale. The idyllic, even pastoral beauty of that campus, replete with hidden, shady courtyards filled with the quietly mellifluous babblings of fountains, and leafy, winding pathways between buildings, inspired solitary musings and intense philosophical discussions. Admittedly, my undergraduate alma mater was hard to get into, but, once there, students were treated as if their least thoughts and ideas were worthwhile, and were encouraged to be creative and original in their studies.

The University of New York had a different atmosphere. If ever there were a school that embodied the traditional ideals of the patriarchal Judeo-Christian tradition, just by its very shape, this was it.

One felt as if the very architecture of the place was intended as a challenge: "Impress me," it seemed to say, with its imposing, boxy edifices. Its looming, intimidating-looking, ten-storied, greige stone campus center embodied the implied warning: "Don't dare to be too creative—just be RIGHT." Nicholas and I were on our way to this very campus center to get the dirt on Christia's death.

We noticed quite a few police officers around, even though we assumed the university was keeping Christia's death hush-hush. Bad things weren't supposed to happen there, and if they did they were not to be discussed—especially among the common people, graduate students and the like. People probably assumed the police presence was due to some visiting dignitary, maybe even the president, a not-infrequent campus guest.

Nicholas broke our silence: "D'you think they have a suspect? I mean, why else would they have so many cops here already?"

I shook my head, letting my hair fall in my face, avoiding his eyes. "I don't know," I responded, knowing full well that if they delved with any depth at all into Christia's recent correspondence I myself might be a suspect. "It's normal to have cops, in a death. At least I would think so, especially at a prestigious school where nothing untoward ever happens." We exchanged a skeptical look. "Everything is perfect here," I added in a singsong voice, eyes overly-wide.

The graduate student lounge was on the first floor of the campus center. It had huge windows, hung with floor-length crimson curtains, overlooking the main plaza of the university. It was elegantly furnished, which, in the context of graduate student life, often made for amusing incongruities. One often saw beleaguered graduate students asleep, even drooling, on one of several deep yellow velvet Edwardian sofas with books and papers piled precariously all about. Sometimes priceless side tables or antique Ming vases were used as props for used coffee cups, nibbled pencils, even not nearly commensurately–shod feet. This venerable setting was probably intended to placate us, conveying a sense of prestige and honor, when in fact we were remarkably ill-treated — economically *and* emotionally — by our dear alma mater.

In any case there was one clear advantage to be had therein: "tea." Every afternoon, the graduate student lounge staff laid out a spread of graham crackers, cookies, tea and lemon wedges that for most of us made for a meal that rivaled any others on a given day. My friends and I called it "lunch." We'd only nibbled at the food I'd prepared back home, and I for one had a rumbling stomach. I was hoping we'd be able to grab a snack before being enveloped in the whirlwind of gossip that was sure to surround the murder of one of the university's most visible faculty members.

People always noticed Nicholas and me. We looked a lot alike and were often told we could be brother and sister. It was a resemblance we cultivated to some extent, the titillation factor of which we enjoyed in our ways. We were both tall and very fair with blue eyes. On a good day, I can be quite presentable, clear-skinned and rosy-cheeked; on a bad day, I'm gray-complected and downright ugly: I'm one of those people whose state of mind is immediately apparent on her face. When I am feeling good, people are strongly attracted to me, and when I am depressed or angry, which was often enough in the days I am talking about, people tend to shy away. When I felt like being incognito, I wore my big old clear plastic-framed, way-out-of-style glasses, piled my hair on top of my head, slipped into an old hooded sweatshirt and walked the streets of my neighborhood completely unnoticed.

Nicholas was more of an all-around dandy. He always took the trouble to look good. I had been in old sweatpants when Nicholas showed up with his news, but I'd changed into a vintage green velvet dress and Granny boots to leave the house. Since most graduate students and faculty eschewed the undignified stylistic statements that spiced up the wild city outside the university gates, Nicholas and I stood out in a sea of blue and white striped cotton shirts, khakis and tweed. In this academic enclave in the wildest city on earth, I caught people staring at my tattoos on a fairly regular basis. Our group of friends, too, was, on average, more interesting-looking than the larger graduate student body, but then that wasn't saying much.

I surveyed the usual crowd of exhausted-looking pre-faculty drudges. "We might learn more if we keep our mouths shut. Should we maybe just sort of lurk around and see what we overhear?" I wondered aloud.

Nicholas shook his head. "Impossible," he said out of the side of his mouth, and took my arm. "I'd try to not look quite so inquisitive dear, that's all." We made our entrance and looked around for familiar faces.

My two best girlfriends from my department, Brandi Blumenthal and Gretel Shaffer, were at the afternoon tea, talking with Nicholas' friend Kirpal Anand Singh, and taking full advantage of the spread of no-name chocolate sandwich cookies that thirty thousand dollars a year bought those students unlucky enough to have gotten no university funding. Brandi was in the cohort one year ahead of mine. I'd met her in the feminist theory class I'd taken in my first semester at the university, where I'd had a crush on her because she was just so lush. She had huge brown eyes, and a big cupid's bow mouth that always looked just-bitten. She also had an outrageous figure, curvy and generous. With her wild curly black earth mother hair, in a tight black Ramones T-shirt with purple stretch bellbottoms and five-inch platform shoes, she was immediately recognizable on campus from any distance.

I'd confessed my crush to her months later, at some party. She'd been flattered, but by then we were close friends and with the sort of incest taboo friendship often, but not always of course, entails. Like me, Brandi sometimes felt like an oddity on our campus. The mixed crowd at Theadora Harmon's talk had probably comprised the entire flamboyant faction of the student body; graduate students who didn't look like characters from Talbots ads were much more rare than funky undergraduates.

Once, when I'd complimented Brandi on some colorful get-up, she'd said, "Thanks, but I feel like a drag queen whenever I'm here." I knew how she felt.

Gretel Miller, eminently less recognizable, was my first friend in my department. We'd bonded over Szechuan food at the get-to-know-each-other dinner gathering for our entering cohort at the university. The dinner was filled with the awkward silences as such things often are. Gretel, to my relief, loved to talk, and I loved to listen. I'd been drawn to her partly because I'd never met anyone so unabashedly and unselfconsciously interested in self-improvement. During our very first conversation, she'd admitted to having read assiduously – not perused by chance as most would claim – several guides to New York City over the summer. She'd been eager to see "the neat areas, you know, Soho and 'Green-wich' Village," as well as all the tourist attractions a lifetime in Wisconsin had never afforded her.

There was an openness to Gretel's round, pinkish face. Her eyes were a cool gray-green, and could seem calculating and translucent at the same time. She'd fixed those eyes on me and told me, within the space of a few minutes (as the rest of the table awkwardly tried to initiate conversations about New York City and Comparative Literature, and Comparative Literature in New York City), that her Hong Kong banker fiancé had refused to buy her an apartment in the city when they'd become engaged and thus, naturally, she'd called the whole thing off: "What was dating someone with money good for if he didn't, you know, want to spend it on you?"

"So now I want to have some fun," she'd concluded. She'd taken a large bite of greasy eggplant with garlic sauce. "And I think I'm in the right place!" With this, she'd actually winked.

46

After that, the fact that we both loved bargain shopping was grounds for instant best-friend status, at least in the context of the comp. lit. department. We spent the first few weeks of that fall prowling the streets of our new neighborhood looking for the best place to buy cheap toilet paper, fresh vegetables, bagels, magazines, etc., talking at great length about the current tangled states of our romantic lives and speculating about students and faculty in our department. After that, we were more and more inundated with work, and our time together became scarce; we spent our best quality time at the coffee shop ostensibly studying for exams, in reality endlessly discussing those same themes of love and school. In short, procrastinating as only procrastinators who've made it through some sixteen-odd years of school can procrastinate.

Gretel was a Mennonite from tiny, snowy Mundelein, Wisconsin. She was rugged and no-nonsense. Reliable. The type of gal who thought nothing of walking twenty blocks through a blizzard -- with pre-menstrual me -- to buy Haagen Dazs on sale at Fairway. When she first came to New York, she dressed in "tasteful" ensembles; I particularly remember a matching camel wool Bermuda shorts and jacket set worn with sheer stockings and pumps. Now in our second year together, Gretel had transformed herself into a New York hipster, partly through overtly copying Brandi and me, partly through her own observations. The funny thing was, no matter what she wore, one could tell she was from the Midwest. She was just too *nice*. She frequently said, "You betcha." Also, she still slipped sometimes and wore those flesh-colored stockings or pastel loafers with an otherwise more New York look.

While Gretel had questions about some of the more dogmatic elements of her religious background, she remained a staunch Mennonite who believed fiercely in adult baptism and in nonviolence. This made for interesting discussions with our friends from the religion department. Nicholas and I had introduced her to Kirpal, a Sikh from a large and close Canadian family, and the two often sparred over the idea of being born into a faith, not to mention their conflicts over the possibility of an honorable, noble warrior culture, for which Sikhism is known.

I had long sensed a possible element of flirtation underlying the tension between these two, and I hoped to encourage this fledgling romance. Both Gretel and Kirpal were family-oriented in a way that most ambitious young New Yorkers, including graduate students, aren't, and I thought they might make a good match. Both were rebelling in their own ways against the constrictions of their faiths, but there was something wholesome about each, too. Most of the people I knew had been raised believing in little more than television or money, whereas these two grappled daily with bigger questions.

As we watched, Brandi turned to Kirpal, and asked him something. His response seemed to fluster her even more. As she waved her long purple nails, in animated discussion with both Gretel and Kirpal now, I thought how easy it was to underestimate her. Make no mistake – Brandi was one of the sharpest people I'd ever known. On top of that she had one of the hugest hearts. She could be a little histrionic, true, but generally that quality worked in favor of her friends, for whom there was nothing she wouldn't do.

We joined our friends, who were talking about Christia, as we'd expected. They had little more information than Nicholas had shared with me, but had been speculating as to possible suspects. They did say they'd heard that it had been indisputably determined that she had not died of natural causes.

"What have you two been up to?" Kirpal asked with a good-natured smirk.

Our friends could not seem to get it through their heads that we were no longer lovers and occasionally resorted to innuendo. I knew

48

Nicholas had told him enough of our saga that Kirpal of all people had meant nothing by his question, but our relationship—or lack thereof—had become something of a stock joke among our group of friends.

"What do you think they're up to?" Gretel retorted. "Isn't it obvious that they've been doing exactly what we're doing, basically gossiping about who might have killed a poor dead woman?"

"Hey, Gretel, my middle name means peace. Anand: peace. OK?" Kirpal smiled at her. "You too, Brandi," he assured her as she glared at him, "I wasn't accusing you of being bitchy, just trying to say that we can't really suspect anyone yet, not on such absolutely minimal news. Christia. Dead. Eh?"

"I only stated that her husband probably did it, as anyone in their right mind would," Brandi retorted.

Nicholas looked nonplussed. "Wait a sec. Th-that's-that's…just not possible."

"Why, because you like him?" I was interested in what Nicholas' explanation would be, since it did seem a logical suspicion.

"I've spent a lot of time with Philippe and I just can't see him doing something so, let me think, so – strong. The man is so laid back he's almost falling over. I don't think he's ever worked a day in his life. He's nobility in the old sense of the word."

"Nobility in the old sense of the word meant warriors and princesses, my friend. Which is he?" I was joking, but I was fuming inside a little too. I had naturally noticed Philippe's appearance of softness and delicacy, but I often suspected such people of harboring all manner of latent violent fantasies, even more so than their more energetic brethren. Nor had Nicholas' adulation of a man I thought perhaps unworthy of it gone unremarked. Even Christia had once commented on it. I looked directly at Nicholas, whose face still swam with a mixture of emotions. "Anyway, why do you have such a thing about this guy?"

"Look, Philippe is just a very sensitive man," he responded, more thoughtfully than maybe I deserved, "I have a *thing* about him because I know what it's like to feel like the world is too much with you and like you're fit for a finer place, or a more refined, more cultured era. One without WrestleMania on TV, for instance."

"What, now he's too good fah TV? You are so full of yahself!" Even Brandi was beginning to take things personally, and it brought out her New Yawk accent.

At this point, we were all somewhat overwrought. Kirpal took a deep breath in the silence after Brandi's outburst, and, lucky for us, smiled again. It reminded me of why I liked him so much. He didn't take himself, or anyone else, too seriously. He was a good counterpoint to Nicholas, for whom everything had elaborate and complex potential philosophical implications, and for me, because I just plain tend toward an overabundance of self-righteousness.

Kirpal was a brilliant scholar of comparative religion, and a friend of Nicholas' from his cohort of graduate students in the religion department. He was prone to using the word, dude, as in, "Sikkhism isn't Yoga, dude." He was about 6'3" and of average build. He wore jeans and t-shirts with his turban and the other visible insignia of Sikh faith, the bangle and small symbolic sword. He loved obscure alternative (real alternative, not what passed for alternative in the mainstream press) bands, and would regale us with tales of being the only Sikh at some obscure venue. He was also extremely trustworthy, one of those rare souls whom one knows upon first interaction one can trust with one's deepest secrets. His smile was a balm.

"Let's keep it together, guys," said dear Kirpal.

"I feel bad, too," I agreed with Gretel, after thinking for a minute. "You hate to gossip about a murder, yet you can't help it," I said, as if murder was daily fare. "I guess I'm having a hard time feeling pity for her…even though she obviously didn't want to die.

Who does? But, you know what? I feel like Christia Thompson wasn't someone who'd've wanted our pity."

Nicholas agreed. "I knew her really well. Believe me, she's probably having a grand laugh over all this drama from wherever souls go—hey," he elbowed Kirpal, "let's not even get into where souls go right now! But I do want to know what happened. Here's someone who's murdered at the University of New York, *on campus*. Someone we all knew. A colorful figure, to say the least…I, for one, am really curious, I'm not ashamed to say."

Nicholas and I decided to go to the religion building and ask around, if the police would allow us into the department. Kirpal and Gretel said they would stay in the campus center since two people snooping around would be more subtle than four; and Brandi set off for yoga class downtown, saying she needed to clear her head.

If anything, the religion department was even more forbidding than the campus center. It was one of the oldest buildings on campus, squat and dark, with gargoyles peering at you from every possible nook in its façade. Inside, there was a strong musty smell, the distilled essence of decades of the study of defunct beliefs, and archaic rituals, and it was darker than one might expect a building devoted to the study of religion ought to be. Small windows were set high into the corridors, letting in very little light. The few light fixtures along the halls were art nouveau masterpieces, ornate and delicately filigreed, but they gave off merely a sort of sickly ochre glow.

The only police officers we saw were on their way out of the building. I love bats, black cats and Anne Rice novels, but even I always got a creepy feeling in that building and I imagined they did too. Nicholas made fun of my Religion Hall shivers, but he's about as sensitive to psychic phenomena as a brick. Maybe less so. In his mind, people who have non-rational experiences are a very interesting subject matter for study, but are essentially delusional. For a scholar of religion, Nicholas was remarkably positivistic and Kantian. He felt that the world could, and eventually would, be wholly described and delineated in a rational and scientific way. But then, maybe that made a kind of sense. Academia is full of literary theorists with no love for the beauty of language, painfully shy would-be future politicians in international studies programs, and so forth. Why not an atheist religion scholar?

As we neared the department's administrative offices, the home of its graduate student mailboxes and the locus for departmental gossip, the trickle of exiting officers ended. We found the departmental assistant alone in the main office, slouched at her desk, looking dejected and persecuted at once.

Brenda Fujiki was a small, androgynous-looking half-Japanese, half-Irish woman. She was a graduate student in the Department of Women's Studies on work-study. We got along very well, on my end because she reminded me of my undergraduate days when I spent a lot of time discussing gender issues. I once made my boyfriend at the time take down a Sade poster because I felt it objectified her -- and me, as a fellow woman. I'm not sure why she'd taken to me, but always attributed it to two things: first, we had similar tattoos, black ink celestial bodies – a five-pointed star for her, a waxing crescent moon for me, on our upper left arms; and, second, because I, unlike most of the people one encounters in academe, was not arrogant and condescending.

Brenda had straight, medium-brown hair that she wore scraped back into a wispy ponytail. She was short, and wore shapeless clothes -- baggy jeans and large sweaters -- so that she projected an image of bulk; but underneath, she was quite slight. She had very dry skin and she always looked somehow withered, although she couldn't have been much older than me. She might have been attractive, if not for the way she carried herself and treated herself. As it was, it was hard to even see her face, since she generally had it buried behind a book. Most of the time, book or no, she kept her shoulders hunched, her neck bowed and her gaze to the desk in front of her. Queries from department members were answered in a barely audible voice, without recourse to actual eye-contact. It was a wonder she ever engaged in interactions at all.

When she liked someone, though, she could be drawn out so that her true grit –which she clearly, and perhaps correctly, felt was threatened by the university system -- would come through. Brenda was an interesting case.

Once, at a religion department party, I'd seen her furtively wrapping her food in a napkin and slipping it into the garbage. Having, as a teen, like many women, struggled with mild eating disorders myself, I'd always suspected her of having one, more in the vein of St. Teresa of Avila or of a Bronte sister, than supermodel-style. She always looked hungry to me.

By chance I'd also been made privy to another of her secrets. Last spring, there'd been a party given in honor of Guru Rich, that department's biggest star, to which only a select few junior faculty had been invited. Typically, inclusion in these sorts of parties signaled acceptance in the department, and offered great opportunities for contact with important people. Brenda had "accidentally" also invited a struggling member of the department and, when pressed, had taken the blame herself, calling herself "scatterbrained." This sub-junior faculty member had told me himself of her deed, and of how she had finally admitted to wanting to help him.

In short, Brenda was neurotic but benevolent. That afternoon she looked more dejected than usual. She raised her serious eyes to mine. "You're not going to believe this," she said.

"Oh, we already heard! Christia was killed, right?" I said. Realizing I'd sounded almost casual, I tried to restore the appropriate tone of respect-for-the-dead to my demeanor. "Terrible, isn't it?"

"No, I mean how it happened," She dropped her voice to a whisper. "I heard she was throttled with her own stockings. Garter belt stockings. With seams. Talk about misogyny. What – are women supposed to be androgynous or – or –" she began to cry, "or they get killed?? "

I pulled a handful of tissues from the box on her desk, wondering how often people had cried in that office. Never, I guessed. I'm sure plenty of crying went on, but faculty in the religion department at the University of New York would never show such unseemly emotions in public. I handed Brenda the tissues and patted her back, making small comforting sounds.

"Brenda, are you OK?" I motioned for Nicholas to leave us alone.

The poor woman made a visible effort to control herself. At length, she responded. "I know Christia was not everyone's favorite person, but she was my favorite person, actually. I know she had things going on with a lot of people. Including Nicholas." She looked at me to gauge my response, which consisted of a nod of acknowledgement, and continued, "And she could be pretty – rude, I guess…and pompous! But she was really special to me. She treated me like a person, unlike most of the people around here, who see me like a secretary. Even students, like Nicholas, act like that. Sometimes I just want to yell, 'I am getting a Ph.D. too! I am just as smart as you.' I feel so inadequate. God, how did I get on this? Oh, yeah, Christia brought life into this department. I've seen her be snobby. A real bitch, actually -- but just with other faculty, not with *people*."

"I'm sorry -- Nicholas can be snobby, but it's just insecurity," I noted. "You were talking about Christia, though. I'm sorry about that, er, too. I didn't know you guys had a relationship."

"You wouldn't really call it that. It was more like I looked up to her. A lot."

Nicholas was raising his eyebrows significantly over by the mailboxes. I rolled my eyes. Nonetheless, he sauntered back to us.

He ignored poor Brenda and turned to me. "What should we do?"

"*You* should see if Ibo's in his office, maybe he knows something about what's going on. I'll wait here." Ibo, pronounced "Ee-boh," was short for Ibrahim, a big name which must've never fit the petite, ingenuous fellow we counted among our closest friends. He was also the aforementioned teacher included by Brenda in Guru Rich's party invitations. He had been grudgingly granted a small cubbyhole-like office next to the bathroom. We often joked that it had been a closet before conversion to a small, window-free room with just enough room for a desk. Ibo could be found there, or at his carrel in the library, just about 24 hours a day.

Brenda, who'd returned to her shell, as it were, emerged again when Nicholas left for the second time. We were just about to resume our conversation when several faculty members wandered in. They did not seem to notice the two of us, but one could never be sure. I decided to go find Nicholas, instead of waiting around in uncomfortable silence while the faculty took their time doing whatever it was they'd come to do.

"Alright, Brenda, the snob is waiting for me," I whispered. "See you later." She cautiously took her gaze toward the others to be sure they weren't paying any attention to us, as usual, and then confided, *sotto voce*, "Cyrus is on a tear. This is bad for the department, you know. Friggin' ghosts."

Cyrus Wilson was the chair of the religion department, a stentorian sixty-something African-American who was loved and feared in equal measure. In the classroom and out, his wit was withering and he did not suffer fools gladly. On the other hand, he was a tireless advocate for much-needed – and scarce -- funding for students he deemed promising, and, as a self-professed "survivor of the bayou," a legendary champion of the underdog. Hence, the very female Christia's appointment, and hence the overall diversity of the department. He had been one of the few people I'd never heard Christia disparage.

My impending departure provoked a long outburst from Brenda: "Anyway, I've been questioned by the police. Everybody in the department was, which Cyrus was really psyched about. But they didn't find out anything conclusive from the faculty. After that they noticed me sitting here. Meanwhile, who do they think patched their calls through to the departmental chair, the 'Director of Religion,' as one of them said? Damn straight. After they noticed that I *existed*." I winced. I imagined she did sometimes fade into the background. "It seems they thought I might know something, and I do. Well, not a lot. I just told them who I'd seen go into her office yesterday, and when. They were excited to have that information, you can be sure. Teach 'em to ignore the person who runs things around here," she concluded with a shake of her head.

I waited.

She looked at me expectantly. "I thought you had to go."

"Oh, Brenda, come on. You can't have just told me all that and then not tell me who you saw."

Her face crumpled. "You know what, oh man, I am so sorry, Annie, I just can't. They told me not to talk to anybody and here I am. Shit. Please don't put me in that position. I know, I know, I put myself in this position. Ugh." With that, she started to cry again.

Her thin shoulders were shaking under the gigantic fisherman's sweater she'd worn that day, and I couldn't help but pity the woman. "Jeez Brenda, what do you think. I'm not Chri -- ugh." I'd been about to defend myself by saying I wasn't her favorite (dead) person in the whole world. "Here, take this tissue. And -- this is my number." I scribbled it on a post-it by her wool-encased forearm, and tapped it to

56

try to get her attention. "Call me if you need to talk. I mean it. I won't badger you. You seem like you could use someone to talk to."

With that, I went to knock on Ibo's door.

I waited a minute for a response, and, hearing none, looked up and down the hallway for Nicholas. Once more, I knocked, and the door swung open just as Nicholas' voice became audible to me.

I only heard a snatch of what he said, "… trying to help you…," before they both noticed the slowly swinging door and me standing in the opening. I couldn't read their faces.

"Oh – hey, Annie," Ibo said quickly, his face flat. I noticed he had shuffled the papers on his desk and slipped the ones he'd been holding under a pile.

"Hi, Ibo." I tried to disguise my curiosity about their interaction by indulging an actual interest in how Ibo managed to fit the trappings of professorial life in so small a space. The solution seemed to be: stacks. Towering, tilting stacks, since there was scarcely room for an actual bookshelf.

I adopted an innocent expression. "Guys? How can it be possible that this is considered an office?"

"I'm not exactly a revered faculty member, Annie. Just provisional. Lower than adjunct." Ibo looked uncharacteristically bitter. "Anyway, I've gotta go. I have to, *uh*, meet someone at the coffee shop." He glared at us, as if challenging us to push him to reveal the cause of his snit.

He gathered up some of his papers, including the reshuffled pile, and pushed past us into the hallway. To be fair, there wasn't much room to get by, but still it was unlike him. He had always appeared, without fail until now, a creature of old-fashioned, "European-ish," as I liked to say – fondly -- manners. "Just close the door behind you," he barked as he left.

57

We did so, reluctant to linger where we were (or at least *I* was), for some unknown reason, unwelcome.

"Darling, *dear* Nicholas. I have this little problem lately," I began, once we were alone in the hallway. He ignored me, lost in his own head. I decided to be blunt, and raised my voice. "Listen, you are always interrupting me during really important moments and I'd really like it if you'd stop! Like that time I was talking to Guru Rich at Caffé Taci. That's nothing to you, but to me it's a big deal to talk to him. I was hoping to get him on my dream dissertation committee! And just now with Brenda. She was about to tell me something."

That got his attention. "What?"

"What, what?" I can be obtuse, too.

"What does she know. You mean you think she knows something about Christia, right?"

"No, I know she knows something about Christia. What I don't know, partly thanks to you, is *what* she knows."

We were saved from our own conversation by the appearance of Nicholas' close friend, Abdus. Abdus Syed, an admittedly gorgeous scion of Pakistani royalty, and another of Christia's favorites, was the person I liked least among our group of friends. He had a simultaneously paternalistic and flirtatious attitude toward Nicholas. Also, I found him possessive of Nicholas in a way that made me uncomfortable. On his end, my being Nicholas' significant other at the time we first met probably did not earn me any points.

Aside from the fact that he hadn't taken to me either, and was not terribly subtle about it, I didn't like the fact that he was always borrowing money from Nicholas, who refused all but the bare minimum from his nouveau riche family in California and worked in the library part-time to augment his fellowship. Abdus was supported in lavish style by his father, Nawaz, a Professor in Pakistan, and his older brother Ishaq, who'd taken over the family holdings when he'd finished his

Wharton M.B.A. I'd met both of them at a recent dinner Abdus had thrown at Le Cirque for forty of his closest friends. I'd sensed an undercurrent of annoyance on his family's part that Abdus was in his seventh year at university and showed no signs of beginning his dissertation research. Nawaz Syed had asked me how long it could possibly take a committee to approve a dissertation proposal. I'd answered, truthfully, that I did not know. I suspect I wasn't the only one thinking to myself that four years after completing coursework was probably longer than usual.

Every month, like clockwork, Abdus managed to run through his extremely generous allowance by the third week or so. He'd then try to borrow money from anyone who'd lend it to him, even me. Once he'd said, "I know we're not the best of friends," -- he was, at least, honest – "But you're a bleeding heart sort. Take pity on an old broke chap?" I didn't have any money to lend him, so I hadn't "taken pity," but Nicholas lived abstemiously in certain ways and always had an extra few hundred dollars. Abdus always paid him back first thing the next month, but still it grated on me.

This being early in the month, I thought we were pretty safe, moneywise. Abdus had a different sort of bomb to drop on us.

After we'd exchanged pleasantries, some of which were more naturally pleasant than others, Abdus became more serious. "Brenda told the cops that Ibo was alone with Christia in her office yesterday, and I'm really worried. He's been acting kind of odd lately."

Odd was right, but I wasn't about to add to Abdus' apparent suspicions. Despite his earlier demeanor, Ibo was one of the nicest people I knew.

"Where did you hear that?" I asked.

He looked at Nicholas, and then back at me. "I shouldn't say."

I felt exasperated. Why give partial information and then not follow through? It was the second time I'd been frustrated for this reason within less than an hour.

"I don't really have time for this. Let's go, Nicholas." I realized I was acting like Abdus. I sighed. "Or would you rather stay? Look, I'm just freaked out over Christia's murder, and I have to get home." I practically spun on my heels, and began to walk away, *à la* Ibo, moments earlier.

"Annie, wait, I need to talk to Abdus for a minute," Nicholas called after me.

"I'll be in the foyer," I called back. I wondered if I'd been overly rude to Abdus, and then decided we'd been no less civil than usual. When I thought about it, Abdus reminded me a lot of Christia: they were both power hungry and manipulative, and not particularly nice. Most telling, they both used their sex appeal to get what they wanted from members of either sex. In fact, Abdus was rumored to have been one of Christia's lovers – and to my mind he'd always had designs on Nicholas as well. Abdus might have been casting aspersions on Ibo, but I wondered just how much interest and involvement he himself might have had in Christia's murder.

I sat fuming in the foyer, waiting, trying not to crave a cigarette. After a few minutes Nicholas and Abdus sauntered out together. Nicholas took a detour to the loo while Abdus continued on to join me, sitting down beside me on the top stair. I was surprised he'd risk getting dust on his ironed, perfectly-creased jeans. I really liked Nicholas' other two best friends, Ibo and Kirpal, but Abdus I could do without.

"Annie," he practically simpered, batting his long eyelashes for effect, "I'm having a little get together *chez moi* this weekend. I'd love you to come."

What did he have in mind? My suspicion must have crossed my face, for he added, "Tommy will be there. Kalinka talked to him yesterday."

Kalinka was Abdus' long-suffering girlfriend. My aforementioned crush, Tomás Bautista ("Tommy"), was a student in the religion department. He was in his late twenties, and was in his first year at the university. Like most of my friends in that department, he was in Christia's circle. He was a tall, quiet man, the type one could invest with all sorts of qualities because of his mysterious air. To me, he seemed deep, brooding, gentle. He was not so much handsome as compelling-looking: his face had an endearing cragginess, and a look of having seen a lot, and his body was strong and lean. I was nursing a growing infatuation with him that had begun to emerge soon after things with Nicholas began to deteriorate. I believed, with reason, that my feelings were returned.

It only took me a moment to realize that Abdus was encouraging my crush for Tomás in order to get me out of the way of *his* crush on Nicholas. That depressed me, just in principle.

"Isn't it kind of a strange time for a party, Abdus? Let us know if you actually decide to have it, given the circumstances, OK?"

Religion Hall's murky atmosphere and Abdus' cheekiness together were too much. I got up and walked outside into the darkening afternoon. I headed back to the campus center. Nicholas would know where to find me.

On the walk home, we stopped off for a cup of coffee at the coffee shop. It was an in-between time of day and most people had left for dinner, while the dessert crowd had yet to arrive. Only a few solitary people sat huddled at two-top tables, their almost-but-never-entirely-empty cups declaring their right to stay on indefinitely. We had our choice of seats.

We decided on a table outside – it was still just barely warm enough to enjoy what fresh air is available to New Yorkers – and sat in companionable silence while we waited for our order. I was almost too drained to talk anyway. Little by little, the place was beginning to fill up again, with couples and groups of friends chatting and drinking, as well as people sharing tables with piles of books. We both felt much better after our caffeine consumption but decided we ought to wait to discuss current events until we had more privacy. Instead, we talked about alternative relationships in more general terms. It seemed clear to us that Christia's polymorphous perversity must have had some connection to her murder.

"Isn't it interesting," I ventured, sitting back in my chair and crossing my arms, "that polygyny is so much more common than polyandry? I bet we wouldn't even be thinking about this if Christia were one of these typical philandering males. It's an accepted form of power for men, really." I paused. Nicholas was listening, his expression unreadable. "And class, too: Only rich men can have more than one wife, under Muslim law anyway. That's because you have to be able to treat them all equally, and that takes a lot of dough, I guess. I don't know about Mormons, but I think they may be taking over the world anyway, so they probably have a certain degree of affluence.

"It's the alpha males who marry more than one woman in the cultures that allow it. You won't find some lame-o lording it over more than one wife. Or an untouchable-type, no siree…Just he-men with big clubs…Anyway…" I trailed off.

"That's what you want, isn't it." It wasn't a question. "You want someone who treats you badly and dominates you."

I saw that he'd been thinking about us during my tirade. "Nicholas, it's so much more complicated than that. I love you more than anything. You're the only person I've felt truly close to since I moved to the city. But, yeah, something chemical just doesn't work for me. I feel like, for you, reality is slippery. You can argue any side of an argument, maybe because you're so smart? But it makes me feel like you're lost. I feel lost, too, sometimes -- but I pretend even to myself that I'm super-solid. that I know what's right and wrong. good and bad. I'm able to keep it together in a way that makes sense for me. That is a kind of strength, right? So, I guess it is power-related a little bit."

I thought for a minute and sipped my coffee. "I've always had to be so strong." I reached out to hold his hand across the table. "And when we were together I felt like I had to be strong for you too. I'm sorry. I've said this all before."

He laughed dryly. "So you're an alpha female. You have--had," he cleared his throat, "*have* more in common with Christia than you might've thought, huh? Maybe you'd be happier if we tried a non-exclusive relationship? But then you'd probably decide I was not man enough to satisfy you or to demand monogamy."

"Not person enough," I corrected him gently. "And that's really not it. I don't need a lot of people fawning over me to feel worthy or to stay interested. It's you and me that's the issue. And can we drop it?"

"OK, madame, but I just happen to know that it's the same thing usually with polyandry, where it occurs. Only the alpha females will have more than one husband. Brothers sometimes. You find it only in matrilineal cultures, which are obviously quite rare. Malabar coastal India. Parts of Tibet. Poor areas, where there's a shortage of women or other 'resources,' unlike here."

"Right. Look at our culture. Too much, all the time. 'The Patriarchy of Plenty,' to coin a phrase," I was amused by my own wit -- more so than my audience. "Although Christia was an alpha female, to be sure," I added thoughtfully. "And she certainly got around."

"These terms don't exactly correlate with promiscuity. They actually refer to marriage, strictly speaking. Heterosexual marriage. Oh. Also Inuits."

"Inuits -- ?"

"Have all different kinds of marriage."

"Oh. My concern would be, if we live in a culture that doesn't support men having more than one female partner, never mind the opposite, how would you think the husband of the person under discussion -- the cuckold, in the eyes of his fellow men – would tend to respond, even if they did have an agreement?"

"Well if I were in that situation, I'd be ethically bound to keep to my word."

"You see?" I said, exasperated. "This is exactly what I was talking about: Everything is abstract to you! What if you found you'd agreed to something untenable?"

He gaped at me. "I see where you've been leading! Would I kill you? No!"

He focused on my eyes, hard. "Dammit, no."

We stared at each other across the table, both a little flushed. Stale coffee and baking sugar smells filled the quiet air. I watched a tiny tear flow down his right cheek.

Nicholas broke the silence. "I saw Philippe cry."

I was immediately alert, spat forgotten. I leaned forward, excited. "When? Why didn't you tell me?"

"At the dinner for Harmon. When Christia was telling her May Day story. I saw tears in his eyes. And I didn't tell you because I knew you'd take it the wrong way. What I saw in his eyes was love, not anger."

"Oh, riiiight. He just loooooves to have his wife discuss her escapades in public. Tears of humiliation is what I'd say."

"Forget I said it. But I'm telling you I'm right."

"We'll see." I was eager to deflect suspicion from myself, not, I'll admit, the noblest of motivations; I also knew most murders are committed by someone known by the victim – and who knew Christia better than Philippe?

My stomach was rumbling, and, since stale pastries were not what I had in mind for sustenance, we agreed to have dinner together at my place.

After walking Pepita and calling to have food delivered from our favorite Ethiopian restaurant, Nicholas and I settled in to dissect the eventful day. I took the couch and he took the chaise and we looked at each other expectantly. All of a sudden, the brief lull felt awkward, as sometimes happened between us since our relationship became more ambiguous.

I jumped up and walked over to the stereo. "Arvo Pärt or Billie Holiday?"

"Both?" He smiled. "No. Pärt would be good. Something for voices."

I poured us both large glasses of honey wine to go with the food we'd ordered.

"So. Who d'you really think did it?" Nicholas finally asked.

"Well, there's the obvious choice," I suggested.

"I really, truly believe he is innocent. Both as a person, and as a murderer. Wait – don't take that literally. He is *not* a murderer," Nicholas insisted, again.

The buzzer rang – our food. We spent a few minutes spreading out our feast. We always ordered the "vegetarian combo" for two, which included daily specials as well as several staple dishes. The main dishes usually had a stewlike consistency and were meant to be eaten with large rounds of a crepe-like kind of ancient-grain bread called *injera*. As is traditional, instead of using utensils, we tore off pieces of bread to use as ladles for the delicious, spicy vegetable dishes.

I scooped up a mound of steaming lentils with a piece of the spongy bread and popped it into my mouth. "What gets me is, her life seemed so perfect," I said through my mouthful of food. I swallowed. "Not that she seemed happy, exactly, but clearly her life was – orderly…Successful. Satisfying in its way, or, I should say, on her terms." I took another large mouthful. "Polished? Yes, I think that's it."

"What elegance of table manners," Nicholas said affectionately. "I agree about her life, though."

"Look at your hands," I retorted. Nicholas looked up from a large scoop of the dish we just called "chunks," made with some sort of indefinable but extremely toothsome Ethiopian style meat substitute in a savory sauce. He was capable of being completely unaware of his own manners when not in a more impressive social situation, and just then he had food all over his fingers.

Nicholas wiped his fingers on his cloth napkin. "Alright," he said. "You've made your point about Philippe. Now give me another valid, reasonable suspect."

I took a sip of honey wine between bites, the sweet wine perfectly complementing the spicy food. By nature, I am incurably curious. I am also gullible and trusting to a fault of the people with whom I am close. I could think of plenty of people who might have issues with Christia, but it was hard to imagine any of them strangling her with a stocking. It was also a uniquely unpleasant mental picture, one I knew I'd spend a long time trying to purge from my mind.

I busied myself with tearing up some *injera* for Pepita and feeding it to her at the table. "I'd say Ibo, only he's one of the nicest people I know," I admitted after a while."Maybe he's just –"

"No," Nicholas interrupted, "It's not him." He shifted on the chaise and sighed, "Whew, I'm full."

I wiped my hands clean with a napkin and put the takeout remains on the floor for Pepita, who had been shaking with starvation after the unforgivably small bread handout.

"All I'm saying is, Ibo isn't usually given to fits. And he was there, and he was pretty close to Christia…His work relied on her…At the very least, he was not himself today. Wouldn't you agree?"

Nicholas' body language had grown much less receptive over the course of my musings. He ignored my question. He got up and washed his hands at the kitchen sink.

He called from across the room, "Listen to that harmony, Annie, isn't it so different from the usual Western European choral sound? It almost seems to resonate in the viscera. It's so gorgeous, yet it makes me nauseous, a little." I looked at him suspiciously. "It really does," he protested. "You know how sensitive I am to music."

I pounded a fist on the table. "Wait, we're not done with this. How did Abdus know that Ibo was in Christia's office? Maybe he was there too!"

Nicholas looked closely at me. "Hey, Nancy Drew, why so obsessed?"

I looked sheepish, professionally sheepish, and shook my head. "You were obsessed too — until I started to come up with suspects you didn't like." He looked hurt, so I backed off. "No, I think it's just -- I feel bad for Ibo. He's going to get some flak until they figure out the truth…"

"Well, Ibo is a big boy. He can take care of himself. We *all* feel bad about Christia. She was a brilliant scholar who had a lot more to say, I'm sure…Which reminds me, I know it's earlier than usual, but I have to get some work done. I-I had some ideas." This was a first – usually I had to not-so-subtly drive him out before bed.

"I love you, Annie. I'm sorry you think we aren't getting along. Maybe you're right." With that, Nicholas got his stuff together and left, leaving me, as usual, with a mess to clean up. Emotionally, too, I felt a mess; and I was glad to have the dinner remnants to busy myself with.

I'd told Nicholas the truth at the coffee shop: he had been the only person I'd connected to on a deep level in New York City. Since we'd separated I often felt very lonely, and never more so than I had since finding out that someone I knew had been murdered. It brought up a host of questions, abstract as well as personal, about human nature. Chances were I'd passed the murderer on the street, maybe even spoken with him or her. Chances were the murderer seemed like a perfectly decent person.

This last thought sent tears coursing down my face. What would drive someone to murder? Rage, of course, but also pain, betrayal, greed…There seemed to be countless reasons, now that I thought of it, though I'd read in many detective novels that it always comes down to love or money. My throat felt choked with the thoughts I was having. I kept cleaning even after the kitchen was spotless, with Pärt's haunting music on repeat.

Much later, therapeutic cleanup and crying done, I tucked my legs underneath me on the soft sofa and let out a sigh of contentment. Finally I was alone, not just feeling lonely in a sea of people. It had been a terribly long day. When the phone rang, I let the machine pick it up. After the announcement, which featured Halloween-y music and a mock-scary "Leave a message, boo-hoo-hahahaaaa," I heard a short, tight laugh and then Philippe Perez-Throgmorton's dulcet voice: "Wonderful choice, Shostakovich. Very of-the-season. Annie, I wonder if you'd have a moment tomorrow to stop by. I'd like to have a word with you and Nicholas. I don't have his new number. Tomorrow, say ten-ish? I'll make tea, or, em, coffee for you coffee-types. Call if not. Ciao."

Coffee. It was only then that I realized Ibo had not been at the coffee shop.

I called Nicholas and left him a message to meet me at Philippe's place, which I was still thinking of as Christia-and-Philippe's. I wondered where he was at midnight on a weeknight and was surprised to find myself feeling abandoned when it was me after all who'd called things off between us.

I pressed play on my own outgoing message just to hear a voice in my empty place. Come to think of it, the music on my answering machine just about summed up the day. Every Halloween season, I put the second movement of Shostakovich's fifth symphony on my answering machine. It is so spooky, at once sweeping and jumpy and dark, and it brings to my mind little ghouls and goblins cavorting wickedly at an infernal dance.

Chapter Three – The Power of a Free Woman

The Witch sees things as they truly are, not as they are colored by social structures – and so, often, she is angry. She is also deeply wise.

The Slut experiences her desire as valid and compelling. She is a free female, and as such is a locus of anger.

"Her kind," as Anne Sexton would have called these women, have power that is immanent to, and inextricable from, their selfhood. It is this very power that kindles the patriarchal rage and engenders the animosity of *hoi polloi*.

What separates the average woman from being a Witch and a Slut? A thin veneer – a modest hem, a downcast eye — if anything at all. This dreaded power, *our* power, is waiting to burst forth at the merest opportunity, much to the consternation of the hegemonic oppressor.

We are dangerous, but they have a head start of two thousand years. Fortunately, we have magical, protective powers available to us. We have only to seek them out and cultivate them; and we begin by trusting in our instincts toward empowerment and our visions of freedom.

Christia Thompson, *Sluts and Witches: Mysticism, Patriarchy and the Power of the Free Woman*

Philippe Perez-Throgmorton sat alone in the apartment he'd shared with his wife for many years. The seconds ticked by on the mantel clock and he tried, unsuccessfully, to stop counting the ticks. Whenever he was under pressure, his obsessive compulsive disorder flared up. He knew that counting to 49 over and over to the relentless beat of the second hand would not keep him safe, would not keep him happy, but he counted nonetheless. Seven times seven. His lucky number, multiplied by itself.

If he counted it every time, without a second's pause between countings, for the rest of the year, Christia would still be dead -- and he might still be the prime suspect.

He held his heavy head in his hands. He knew they would come for him soon enough and he tried to compose himself in such a way as to not appear as angry and scared as he actually felt. His blood rose at the thought of his wife. She had not been a cozy or loving wife, but she had been challenging and exciting. Often too exciting.

His mind rested on Annie and Nicholas, her latest conquests. Both were like naive, awkward children next to his and Christia's dark sophistication. He and Christia had always presented themselves in austere, even avant-garde looks, whereas one never quite knew even which era, or eras, Annie and Nicholas would show up wearing.

Somehow their mismatched attire only served to underscore how attractive each was, and how free-spirited.

Their innocence, lurking just below the blasé veneers they'd adopted, was what had attracted Christia most. "They think I don't know exactly what goes on between them," she'd muse, "but their ambivalence and confusion makes them all the more vulnerable." Philippe was expected to endure these speculations, even to be excited by them—well, he was—but in truth he himself was ambivalent about his open marriage.

In his Oxford days, he had been the prettiest boy on campus, and had enjoyed liaisons with straight and gay men alike. Women had found him less attractive. He wasn't sure why. In fact, Christia had been the first woman he'd ever fallen in love with—and the first to pursue him with the mad intensity he required in order to feel wanted, in order to trust.

Before Christia, his one great love had been his tutor in the Classics department. He'd stretched out his doctoral studies in order to be near him longer, and when he was offered a position in the department, he'd been overjoyed. Raphael Kavitaris, University Fellow in Greek Classics, and long in the closet, hadn't been pleased. There had been a restrained and dignified falling out, after which Philippe had fallen apart and Raphael had returned to his books.

After several months of a life that consisted of the bare minimum of food and sleep needed to survive, teaching his classes and counting, counting, counting, the dull, quiet agony of his own life became apparent to Philippe. He'd decided it was time to transform himself. For some time he was at a loss as he'd grown so far from his fellow human beings. By chance, he'd fallen onto the path that had brought Christia to him.

Emerging one day from the Ashmolean Museum of Art and Archeology, full to bursting with ancient ideas about magical transmutation, Philippe had felt ready to transform himself. Taking his inspiration from Oxford's ancient, yellowed buildings around him, and the alchemical traditions of the Rennaissance still pulsing within him, he'd decided on a sort of scientist-warlock persona for himself. He'd grown a devilishly pointed beard so as to appear more butch, bought some tailored black clothing, and had taken to attending the meetings of a local coven with a female friend.

A year or so later, Philippe had formally met Christia during her studies abroad. They'd first met at the Beltane fires, though Christia did not know it. He'd watched her, and wondered at her silence. She'd participated willingly in the circle dance, but shared none of the conviviality that followed. She'd simply remained an observer, responding only if directly addressed, a little coldly it seemed to him. Philippe, vaguely attracted to her, as he was to several other participants, had left to wander in the forest surrounding the fire. From there, he could watch unobserved the goings on around the fire and in the firelight-dappled forest at the edge of the glade.

When he'd seen Christia leave the fire and come toward him in the wood, in her cautious pace a wariness that was betrayed by the glow in her green eyes, he'd looked at her fully for the first time and recognized her on some primal level. What was true in him reached out to what was true in her. He'd asked himself how he knew her, seeing as he was quite sure they'd never actually met; somehow he'd felt as if he'd always known her. Once he'd touched her cool, pearly skin, inhaled the clean fragrance of her soft hair, he'd been sure of it. He'd been suffused with wonder.

They parted without ever having spoken.

Having never before loved a woman to fulfillment on any level, Philippe determined to have the ice-cold, fiery woman he'd met at the Beltane fire as his bride. From there it was a simple matter to be introduced at an end-of-the-year party thrown by one of the neo-Pagans,

Ruby, an old friend of Philippe's and the one who'd introduced him to the whole gang.

Philippe had sensed that Christia – he'd found out her name from another friend, Mary – would not be inclined to reunite with her Beltane partner and so had shaved his beard and asked Mary and Ruby not to comment on the change in front of Christia.

"Why, Mr. Confirmed Bachelor, I believe you are smitten," Ruby, a voluptuous, horsey blonde, had teased him.

Philippe cleared his throat. "I've got honorable intentions," he muttered.

Over Pimm's Cups, Philippe had introduced himself to Christia. She'd said she was sure they'd met before, but Philippe insisted they hadn't. "However," he suggested, "Perhaps we ought to meet again nonetheless." He felt proud of his boldness. Her fervent "Absolutely!" had confirmed his intent.

The two soon found themselves spending more than a little time together. She'd been the first woman to awaken a sustainable heterosexual passion in him. He was the first true aristocrat she'd ever met. They'd quickly progressed to a depth of seriousness neither had ever before experienced; each had something indispensable to offer the other. They'd never again experienced the magical, passionate connection Philippe knew they were capable of creating together, but their love was, for Philippe, strong. For Christia, safe. She'd never mentioned "The Bear" in front of him until that night at Caffé Taci.

They'd mutually decided to marry by mid-August, a few weeks before Christia was scheduled to leave for the U.S. to begin as a junior faculty member at an almost-adequately renowned Midwestern university. She hadn't planned to be there long – she had big dreams and a book in the works – but she certainly didn't want to be there alone. To Philippe, the American midwest had an obscure allure, and he was happy to accompany his bride.

The wedding ceremony was small and informal – a few neo-pagans, a few faculty, and the newlyweds gathered in a chapel and then strolled the cobblestone street to a nearby pub.

Raphael had died of seemingly natural causes around that time. Now Christia, too, was dead.

Philippe had to admit, he was unlucky in love.

*

Waking up, I found myself all tangled up in humid sheets and the smell of dog. I had not slept well, but it was time to begin my day. As if sensing my fragile state, Pepita did some yoga-style morning stretches, a few upward and downward facing dog poses, keeping her eye on me to make sure I was noticing the cuteness. Feeling a little better, and sure that someone loved me, at least, I threw off my sheets and opened the window to the unseasonably warm day. My plants on the windowsill were still thriving, but they would need to come in once the warm spell ended.

What a beautiful day, I thought, wishing I wouldn't have to spend it on my own little murder investigation.

It was nine-thirty. I had only twenty minutes to walk Pepita, shower and eat. Classes had been cancelled in honor of Christia, so I planned to spend the day finding out what I could about her death, starting with tea at Philippe's apartment. Not for the first time, I resorted to washing down a vitamin with chocolate as I, the consummate junk food vegetarian, rushed around the apartment getting ready to go. I dragged on a pair of faded purple corduroys and a black peasant blouse, and ran a brush through my tangled hair, which I then pulled into a loose bun. I checked my reflection in the mirror and saw that I looked strung out, and so I took just a moment to compose my face and deepen my breath so as to pass for someone who wasn't afraid of being accused of murder.

I met Nicholas on the street at ten on the dot. He was carrying a paper bag with coffee in it and had dark circles under his eyes.

He brushed my cheek with a brief kiss. "I had the ringer off on my phone last night," he said, before I'd even opened my mouth. "I went to sleep early and just slept very soundly through the night."

"You don't need to explain yourself to me," I replied, wondering why he'd been so keen to explain himself in the first place. It was easy enough to tell that Nicholas hadn't done a great deal of sleeping.

We rang the bell and were buzzed in immediately. Unlike student housing, faculty buildings tend to have elevators, but Christia and Philippe had a second floor apartment and so we walked up. I remember I was feeling a heightened awareness of the possibility for deception as we mounted the staircase. If Nicholas would deceive me about his doings the night before, whatever his reason, why shouldn't anyone else do so? Thus, I was thinking about the questions I might ask Philippe about Christia, but I also was thinking about how I might discern truth from lies in his responses. I hadn't forgotten my own little deception, either.

Philippe opened the door and the immediate impression I had was of a man bereft beyond imagining. Already thin, he seemed to have become even more skeletal over the course of the less-than-48 hours since Christia had died.

I braced myself to not immediately collapse with compassion. Chances were he'd been the murderer, after all.

"I'm so sorry, Philippe," I murmured, as I leaned toward him to give him a hug, and felt him trembling. I felt his bones through his summer-weight wool suit, but also a surprising wiriness. He was probably much stronger than one would assume from his habitual manner of fey diffidence, I observed to myself.

He drew back, holding me at arms length and leaning to accept a pat on the shoulder from a tongue-tied Nicholas, who never knew what to say in emotional situations. "Darlings," he said in his still-velvety, cultivated voice. "What can I offer you? Please, sit down."

We walked through the curved entrance hallway, past several closed doors and a gallery of what looked to be ancestral oil paintings. I'd always assumed they were of Philippe's family. The hallway opened up into a vast living room with a balcony. A large, hand-hooked pearl gray Tibetan rug covered the central area of the black-stained, wide-planked floor. A low bleached pine table sat in front of a black leather and aluminum sofa. There were a few coffee table-type books, art and architecture mostly, stacked neatly on the table, next to one of those Frank Lloyd Wright glass vases from Tiffany's. The deep purple calla lilies in the vase, angled at a stylish 45-degree angle, were beginning to droop. The only other furniture was one plastic Eero Saarinen wineglass chair that was set at the far end of the table. The sofa faced a fireplace that was too clean to have been used recently. The mantel was bare, but for a gray-faced clock that was framed in black granite. Floor to ceiling bookshelves covered every wall. The overall effect was one of cutting-edge style, but a distinct lack of warmth.

Philippe went past the living room into the industrial aluminum kitchen. I remembered an arresting Nan Goldin print of a ravaged-looking person of indeterminate gender that hung over the sink in the kitchen. It was one of the few things in their house which to me seemed to speak of personal choice, rather than impeccable taste. We heard some muffled sobbing and the opening and closing of cabinets.

We milled about, trying to figure out where to sit. I perched on the edge of the stiff leather sofa and Nicholas did the same, at the other end. I don't have a skinny butt, but I could feel my sit-bones cutting into the hard seat. I looked around, trying to discern something I liked about their taste, and I finally settled on the spaciousness of the room, and its lack of clutter. It was a room in which, if one could get comfortable – and that was a big "if" -- one could really concentrate on one's reading, or whatever was at hand. But where was all their *stuff?* I knew there were two bedrooms, one of which they used as an office, but from what I'd glimpsed of them, they were as spare as the living room.

The minutes ticked by in silence. I was not about to offer Nicholas more opportunities to lie to me by asking him anything.

"It's a little early, but how about a drinky-poo?" Philippe came out with a tray laden precariously with the makings for coffee and tea, a bottle of scotch and several tumblers. To my surprise, I opted for the single malt along with the the men. I am sure it was a fine vintage, but it burned my hardly-awake throat and only very subtly calmed the humming of my newly-suspicious mind.

Philippe downed two tumblers of the scotch, neat, in quick succession and took a deep breath. "I know there are scads of rumors flying about. Doubtless you've heard the one about being strangled with her own garter belt." It wasn't really a question, and I was startled by his frankness. "Garter? Untrue. Strangled, yes. Someone, someone probably male and about my size from the looks of it, strangled Christia with their bare hands. Her stocking was found next to her, yes. And her shoes, too, for that matter."

Philippe spoke calmly, but I'd been watching his skin become whiter and whiter. Now, he smiled at us – a hollow, flat-eyed smile. "Poor cold feet."

He sighed. "I am going to be accused of Christia's murder. It seems only a matter of time. I have no alibi. I was doing exactly what I do every afternoon: attempting to work on my long-awaited scholarly research, which research I lost interest in years ago; in short, I was doing nothing. I might've been writing a new haiku had it been a good day, but it wasn't."

There was a silence and then Nicholas said, valiantly, "But Philippe, no one saw you there. There's no evidence."

"Thank you, Nicholas, for your loyalty. I've no idea how I earned it, I'm sure. However, I haven't asked you here to defend myself. I wanted to see your fresh faces. You are the only two people I wouldn't suspect of killing Christia. That's why I invited you."

He must have seen the surprise in our faces. "I don't expect to see too many more fresh faces," he explained. "Even if they don't convict me, people will be looking at me as if I did it forevermore."

Philippe was trembling again, this time with indignation. He'd probably had at least four drinks by now, probably on an empty stomach.

"They are going to rip me to shreds – useless, pathetic, cuckolded fag, and they're right. Bloody right! *Mea Culpa. Mea Maxima Culpa*," he snarled. I'd never seen Philippe so angry, or so bitter.

As I watched, he gathered his composure. I saw the anger drain from his face, and I wondered if the anger was draining into some place deep inside him. His voice was calm again as he continued. "I just never realized what a perfect target I'd make until my wife -- who, believe it or not, I loved -- got herself killed. Oh, and by the way, add mentally disturbed to the mix. Yes, Philippe Perez-Throgmorton has been in psychotherapy for obsessive compulsive disorder and phobic behaviors for years. Please don't tell anyone, natch." He folded his hands together and leaned back in the Saarinen chair. He sighed, rather dramatically, and then, having resigned himself I suppose, concluded, "Oh, why bother? There's no hope for me. No hope atall."

"What if they find out who actually did it?" I countered. "If they convict someone else…I've heard plenty of aspersions cast on other people, not that I want to think any of them – or you, for that matter -- strangled someone."

79

Nicholas had a thoughtful expression on his face. "You must know more than we do. What aren't you telling us?"

Philippe paused for a moment. He'd added some ice to his latest drink and it tinkled as he casually tipped the glass back and forth. His focus on the gentle sloshing seemed almost theatrically intense, as if what he was about to say was purely incidental to this chummy moment among friends.

Finally he began to speak: "Well, my friends, Christia was somewhat well-to-do – her penultimate book was a publishing sensation. Have you read it?" I nodded eagerly, but stopped as I saw Nicholas shake his head. I resolved to let Philippe talk about whatever he wanted to talk about, without adding to much commentary, thereby perhaps forcing him to reveal some important clue. "*Sluts and Witches* was one of these postmodern, post-feminist books which, to my mind, doesn't really have a point. More of a rant, you know, 'Feminists are wrong, sexists are wrong; Nietzsche was right,' that lot. It was a longtime *New York Times* bestseller and we made a lot of money, well, she did. As well, through the speaking engagements that came with it."

"Oh yes, come to think of it, she spoke at my college. I noticed it in the alumnae bulletin. There was a nice picture of her in there too." I broke in, re-resolving immediately after Nicholas' quick frown to work on my listening skills.

"She attracted a lot of attention, a lot of, one might even say, animosity, over the success of that book and everything that came with it. I don't think it even mattered to anyone that her book on de la Motte Guyon barely registered in academia, never mind the book world. Well, it mattered to her, of course, because that was serious work. She'd spent years researching the woman and was quite taken with her, identified with her, even. But I digress.

"The point is, she was expected to begin work on another more commercial book." At our surprised faces - commercial, mass market aspirations were typically looked down upon in the hallowed halls of the university - he amended his statement. "Yes, insightful and brilliant…but, more importantly - though it might not be said in so many words - attention-grabbing. Famous - famous! - is what they wanted. There was a lot riding on it. We had bills, yes, but it was more the department and the publishing company who had a lot at stake. She'd been hired here on the strength of *Sluts*, and it's been a few years now. She had no intention of returning to the so-called heartland.

"It seems successful writers are allowed the odd vanity project, but are essentially required to produce books that sell well relatively frequently – and Christia's editor and publisher were beginning to put pressure on her. And Cyrus, too" he said after a thoughtful pause, "Not in an overt way, you understand. Departments are political players. They need names to stay strategically relevant. Christia was their big name. Her only rival was Rich Redmund." He tapped the table rhythmically with his knuckles as he uttered the latter name.

I suppressed a gasp of surprise. What was he insinuating about Guru Rich? Philippe, too caught up in his own musings, didn't notice.

"Every once in awhile," he continued in his genteel British drawl, "I would ask her how it was going, but she never seemed to have anything cooking, as it were. Until last week, when she began hinting about some discovery she'd made.

"I'm not an aggressive man, and with Christia it simply doesn't -- rather, wouldn't have done -- to force things. So I didn't bring it up again myself…Her discovery. I'd made that mistake once. I think you experienced a taste of the aftermath? After Theadora's dinner at Taci?" I nodded. "Mind you, it was something that piqued my interest, you may be quite sure." He sighed, less self-consciously this time, seeming far off for a moment. "In any event, in the last few days she'd seemed manic. Oh, I don't expect you to believe me." He'd noticed the incredulous look on my face, which I quickly replaced with what I hoped was an attentive expression. "I'm not even trying to convince you of my innocence. As I said. You're good people. Surely not murderers. I've no one else to talk to. No one I trust. That whole department was riding on the funding and popularity that came out of Christia's fame. My guess is that someone wanted what she discovered for their own purposes. I'd like you to keep your ears open."

Throughout his speech, Philippe had kept glancing at the clock. After greeting us shakily and his unseen crying in the kitchen, he'd seemed almost without affect. Apart from this one nervous tick, he was remarkably composed. True, he'd become angry at the thought of slander, but he'd spoken *so* calmly of the manner of his wife's death. The contrast was notable, reeking as it did of my day's nemesis, deception. I found it hard to fathom how a relatively normal person could evince the entire gamut of emotions, but only at intervals. It was as if Philippe's powerful emotions were a (calculated?) seasoning to the bland, cold exterior he displayed most of the time. Perhaps he was in shock, but his behavior seemed premeditated to me.

Another thing that bothered me about this turn of events was how unclear Philippe's motivation was. That is, did he want to catch his wife's killer – or merely the thief of her "discovery?" I wondered if his behavior was another clue in my mental case against him, or, to be fair, another sign of shock.

I excused myself and walked back through the hallway to the bathroom. The two men continued to talk, but I was not listening. I was looking for clues, if not to the identity of the killer, then at least to the quality of Christia and Philippe's home life. So far, I hadn't gleaned anything new from this visit. And I still felt like loading up a wheelbarrow with soft pillows and throws and kitschy knickknacks from putative loved ones and plenty of home-cooked, potentially messy food and wheeling it into their too-pristine, stylized lair for a redecorating spree.

In the bathroom, a small Aubusson rug in muted colors padded the floor next to the six-foot long marble tub. How did they bathe without ruining the exquisite rug? Guiltily, I opened up the linen closet and peered in. Carefully rolled up on a middle shelf was a thick, thirsty bathmat, still slightly damp.

I suppose I was uniquely qualified as an observer of the endless varieties and levels of status that we engage with in our everyday lives. I grew up with divorced parents. My mother, though highly-educated, was, economically-speaking, lower middle class, while my father became more and more fabulously rich post-divorce. I lived in two different worlds and as a result I was comfortable in almost any social milieu. If necessary, I can convincingly outsnob the snobbiest of social strivers while living on rice and beans and attired in salvation army finery.

I've noticed that people who have money for any length of time – generations – usually tend toward understatement, while people new to money, and people with less money – less than their neighbors, less than they want – tend to make more of a show out of their possession of "taste," in whichever of its manifold forms.

Philippe and Christia's home was so stark, so tasteful, that it felt antiseptic. The accoutrements of affluence and chic were somehow not mixed quite correctly, maybe because there was nothing non-chic in the entire place. I'd never known human beings to live that way outside of design magazines.

After I'd finished in the bathroom, sacrificing integrity and respect to the higher cause of truth, or so I reasoned, I snuck into Christia and Philippe's gray, black and tan bedroom. An open book on Christia's bedside table was essentially the only object in the room besides the minimalist furniture. A built in goose-necked halogen light shone on a heavily underlined passage from Carolyn G. Heilbrun's *Writing a Woman's Life*. I just caught a glimpse before my conscience and nerves caught up with me. Before I fled, I read, "…hidden lives of accomplished women who were educated enough to have had a choice and brave enough to have made one."

Because I was wondering what those lines meant to Christia, I was distracted for the last few minutes we spent with Philippe. Nicholas and Philippe reminisced about Christia a little bit. Then Nicholas and I talked desultorily about department politics and the annoyances thereof while Philippe looked mournful. We all tired of making small talk pretty quickly and Nicholas and I left not long after my sojourn to the bathroom.

I had to get some work done, so I went to the main library on campus. I didn't run into anyone I knew, and thus heard no more rumors. I spent several hours with Jack Hawley's translations of *Songs of the Saints of India* and then with that dear old nudist Long island boy Walt Whitman. By the time I emerged from my carrel, ravenous and with that mild disorientation that always follows being swallowed up in a really good book, it was after three. I headed home to fix myself a tofu dog and walk Pepita. Around four, my curiosity got the better of me and I dragged myself off the couch to go outside.

Back on campus, very few people were about because of cancellations. Most people were probably glad of the free time to catch up on work or sleep. From a mutual acquaintance, I heard that Nicholas was at the local bookstore, The Philosopher's Tome, and I sought him out. I found him in a corner, curled up under a reading lamp in a deep, faded chintz armchair. He was drinking a fluffy, delicious-looking coffee drink and reading Bulgakov.

"Let me guess. It's tragic writers month. Last week you were reading *A Confederacy of Dunces*."

"Close," he responded dryly, "But it's actually, if we must develop a theme, Misery Loves Company. You do understand that I am still in love with you. You do get that. How can you not?" He looked at his lap and muttered something that sounded like "*Ich bin heiB, auch,*" but I couldn't be sure. He shook his head, then he lifted his pale blue eyes to mine, where they lingered, registering my love and ambivalence and confusion. "Oh well. We great writers are always spurred on by our lame lives. We live in the mind. Thereby, we can avoid our actual lives or the lack thereof."

He straightened up and placed his palms down on the table with his fingers spread out over the draft of his manuscript on the symbolism of microscopic creatures, especially microscopic worms, in 17th-century metaphysical religious imagery and texts.

"At least, I'm not going to be like Philippe," he shrugged. "I'm getting my book done. Then, haha, when someone gets killed, I'll say, 'Why, officer, sir, I was finishing my book that day. Why don't you read it?' I could tell the officer about how Leibniz' monads predate the ideas of quantum physics by centuries, and that by either measure you cannot accurately prove that someone actually is or was or will be anywhere in particular." Nicholas loved theories that evinced the uncertainty of reality.

"Or I could explain how he can either measure where I was *or* how fast I was moving away from the scene of the crime…" he trailed off.

"Poor taste," I commented, adding, "You are delirious. Plus, writing isn't an alibi. Or really living." I thought about that for a minute. "On the other hand, what about this whole idea of living in the present? We are supposed to be right here in the moment. OK. But what if where we *are* is in our imagination, imagining a story we're writing, or the future…If we're enjoying that, then why isn't that moment as valid as, I don't know, living in the present moment of watching TV?

"'Be here now.' 'Love the one you're with.' This is maybe where people got the idea of open marriages. When Christia was cheating on Philippe…And, I mean, she *was* cheating, according to the internationally accepted parameters of what marriage means…She might have argued that she was just being present to the moment that presented itself." I wagged a finger at Nicholas. "I think that's just plain wrong. No one forces us to get married in this day and age!"

I realized I was getting all riled up. I wasn't against having multiple partners, just skeptical about doing so in the marriage context. "Hey, have an open, long-term relationship. But don't call it marriage," I concluded, somewhat breathlessly, as Nicholas sank deeper into his chair, shoulders hunched.

"What about same sex marriage, does your marriage theory exclude same sex marriage?" he asked from his safe distance.

"Absolutely not! Who am I to decide who can and can't get married? Who am I to deny any person happiness, if getting married will make them happy?"

Nicholas had a small smirk on his face. "Maybe getting it on with so many people made Christia happy."

"Always with the logic! And I don't think so…Did it make Philippe happy that she did that? I think not." I got up and ordered a mint tea from the Philosopher's Tome's makeshift drinks counter. While I waited, I looked around at the shelves and shelves of new and used books, interspersed with more or less rickety chairs and sofas meant to encourage browsing. Most of the books were on philosophy and religion, but there were sections on literature and poetry as well, and even some science and reference books. Under other circumstances, The Philosopher's Tome was a wonderful place to while away an afternoon. I took my tea and stirred in a tablespoon of honey. Blowing on the steaming surface, I made my way back to Nicholas' corner.

In a more conciliatory tone, Nicholas said, "I'm not saying I disagree with you. I simply don't feel good about analyzing Christia and Nicholas right now." He removed his metal-framed glasses and

86

rubbed his eyes. "By the by, regarding our conversation last night, I did some research on animals and polygamy in the reference section." He fixed me with a stare. "As we know, when males are with more than one female the species is called polygynous, females with more than one male are polyandrous species; but did you know that when both are with more than one opposite-sex partner it's called promiscuity? That's the scientific term. Very official. Isn't that funny? Well, with animals it's funny…"

"What about everybody with everybody? I guess that's called New York City," I joked.

He took me seriously. "But it's more liberating than that! If one isn't a total dupe who lets our sick society do all of the thinking, one can see that there are models in nature for every type of relationship imaginable, from black widow spiders, to monogamous swans, to meiosis. What that makes me conclude is that we are on our own on this one.

"Without relying on custom, or specific and limited examples from nature, every relationship, every sexual relationship included, can be logically negotiated on its own terms. Our so-called family values are merely a degradation of property laws and corrupted Christianity.

"Because you know Jesus was a freak –"

"Totally!!" I interjected, nodding rapidly in agreement.

"-- He was the type of person who'd be begging in Tompkins Square Park if he were alive today. Not judging people and criticizing them." With a defiant set to his chin, Nicholas folded his arms across his chest. "Like you are right now?"

"Huh?" I sputtered. Even though he was in his late twenties, I think Nicholas was still reacting against his bourgeois family's values. Nevertheless, he was making a strong point about something to which I'd given a great deal of thought. I agreed with him in that most of our social strictures come out of struggles over property and power, religious and otherwise. Even so, after our free-love-anarchist teen years, my friends and I had talked and thought a lot about why we have romantic relationships and the potential value of forming one's own family by engaging in a long-term, committed relationship.

We seemed to be arguing even when we agreed. It made me sad that we seemed to spar so frequently, when we'd once been so madly in love. "Let me clarify. Here's how I feel," I told him gently. "I'm pro-monogamy, once you've found someone who's a decent prospect. Not for old-fashioned values or something -- Goddess knows I'm no virginal spring chicken -- but because it's all about what you can learn about yourself and the other person, and extrapolating that to the larger world. It's a practice, like yoga. Wanting to leave, wanting to cheat, but sticking with it. Letting it become deeper and change and grow."

"It must be nice to have everything figured out," Nicholas said. I felt his tone was somewhat venomous, maybe rightly so. "Too bad I wasn't a decent enough prospect. Nonetheless, you've got it all figured out. All right, then. Go to it. Don't let me stop you."

"No. I really don't have anything figured out! You know that," I implored him. "All I know is, I'm trying to be good, and that often feels rather pathetic around here, with everybody debating the abstract value of just about everything all the time, as if life itself were a set of experiments and other people automatons on whom we are meant to experiment, without repercussions. I think that sticking by someone's side when it isn't easy must teach us how to be good or patient or compassionate.

"I wish we could've stayed together, Nicholas." Something hurt in the pit of my stomach, close by my heart. I tried to bring the conversation back to a more general level. "Philippe thinks we are good, unlike, I guess, everyone else he knows. I wonder why? This probably sounds simplistic but why *can't* people just be good?" Nicholas raised his eyebrows at me, incredulous. I thought about my own question for a minute. "I don't find I'm half as good as I try to be," I acknowledged. "Alright, I'm beginning to get it: being good is damned hard. Half the time you can't figure out what the good thing to do is, and the other half the practice of being good is just really difficult, and involves self-abnegation or going against one's instincts for greed, lust, what-have-you."

My tea had grown cold and I drank it down quickly. "Well," I concluded, "Thanks for listening to me. I'm all worked up and I don't know why." Really, I did know why: something terrible had happened to someone I knew. I was simultaneously afraid the authorities might find out I'd written the note -- or that someone I knew more or less well was a cold-blooded murderer. The latter being, obviously, more frightful.

I shivered. I smelled Nicholas' familiar, slightly musky scent as he wrapped his cardigan around my shoulders. "Thank you," I said, and bit my lip. There was so much more roiling inside me than I could express. We got up to go, and I impulsively grabbed Nicholas and gave him a big hug. As I had that morning, I sensed his distance, despite his earlier declaration of continued love for me.

'I'm meeting Abdus for dinner," Nicholas told me. "We were together the afternoon Christia died and we wanted to go over what we were doing, in case we were questioned."

"Why on earth would you want to do that?"

"You know, when they question you, there's the good cop and the bad cop and they get you confused and you end up contradicting yourself even if you have nothing whatsoever to hide."

"I guess I hadn't thought of that," I admitted. "But why would they interrogate you in the first place?"

"Didn't you know I was one of the last people to see her?"

"Oh god, no. Brenda didn't tell me. *You* didn't tell me! Was she, uh, alive?"

"Duh."

"Please, be serious."

"I am being serious." After a moment's pause, he added, "I have nothing to hide."

Later, after cooking an early dinner by myself, I needed some fresh air. The Upper West Side is the best place in the city to live if you crave trees and grass. That night I went to my secret spot, a small, overgrown rose garden on the grounds of the Cathedral of St. John the Divine. This time of year, the rose bushes were almost bare, but the thorny branches formed tangled archways under which I walked with Pepita by my side. I sat toward the back of the little enclosure on a stone bench, alone with my thoughts in my quiet green haven. As night fell, a lone spotlight shed just enough light to penetrate the branches without being glaring.

The familiar refrain of discontent with my lot in academia blocked out, for a time, my very real fears. I thought about how I'd hoped for so much as I began graduate school. I'd expected passion and brilliance and found little enough of that in my own department. Well, at least it wasn't sociology, I thought to myself with a little giggle. The sociology department at the University of New York was famously dull and outmoded. Different departments had different characters depending on the school, something I'd learned too late. The butt of jokes at one school might be another school's badge of distinction. My comparative literature department was neither; it was just – fine. My spirits lifted a little as I realized I had found some of that dreamed-of vibrancy in my few friends in the department, Gretel and Brandi, if not in the faculty.

The religion department was a whole different story. Granted there were plenty of dull theorists, but there was passion there as well, and inspiration. Guru Rich, Christia, even Nicholas, Ibo, Kirpal, and

Abdus had all piqued my interest at some point -- and they all certainly seemed full of ideas and enthusiasm for their subjects.

There was perhaps perverse anger there, too. What scholarly secret in that department could be important enough to kill someone? If there was a fortune at stake, I supposed, killing someone might be worth it to a sick, desperate person. Someone for whom the real world was no more real than the written word? Someone for whom killing might be no more difficult or depraved than turning a page? No less abstract than a logical equation?

It dawned on me that if such a person existed, he or she was still extant. For the first time since I'd moved to New York City, I felt unsafe. Still, I refused to give in to my feeling of vulnerability. I forced myself to stay calm and reminded myself how strong I was. I'd been doing a lot of running and a lot of strenuous yoga since I'd started graduate school.

There was a soft breeze whispering through the few remaining rose leaves. Encircled by brambles, I sat and enjoyed the evening. A few plump drops of rain were beginning to fall. I watched the rain's passage through the circle of light over the garden and listened to the rattling of the rose leaves under each droplet. I inhaled the fresh smell of new rain.

Pepita was under the bench, looking apprehensively at the falling water.

"C'mon," I said. "It's not gonna hurt you. C'mon, sugar booger." I wasn't going to admit to being a little afraid, even to my faithful dog; but I *was* exhausted, and Pepita would want to get home before it started raining in earnest.

We passed the coffee shop on the way home and through the fogged window I could make out the bleary images of Gretel and Kirpal sitting together, both buried in their books. There were the two people *I'd* never suspect in a million years, two truly "fresh faces." Good people. I noted to myself that I hadn't included Nicholas on my list of categorical non-suspects, but I quickly shook off the troubling thought. It was yet another fear I wasn't ready to admit to that night.

I was tempted to join Kirpal and Gretel, but dogs weren't allowed indoors in places that served food. Also, their study session might potentially be an intimate one. Taking one last longing look at the dry interior scene, I saw that Tomás was sitting near my other friends, his dark hair falling over his forehead as he read. The table in front of him looked empty, and I assumed he'd just arrived. I felt a small frisson in anticipation of Abdus' party; that is, if it really was going to happen, and if Tomás really was going to attend...

I hoped things with Tomás would develop into something more, but I was also content being alone. It was so much safer that way, emotionally speaking. People are complicated, and I often misunderstand their motives, being prone to imputing better motives to people than are actually in play. But I was learning, fast. For instance, I didn't know why Abdus wanted me at his party if not to demonstrate to Nicholas that I was interested in someone else. Yet I would have to tread carefully so as to not hurt Nicholas' feelings, while at the same time showing some receptivity to Tomás.

I might've spent my first few decades being too naïve, but I was beginning to engage in interactions that were teaching me plenty about subtlety and artifice. Christia had seemed calculating, but had probably made a misstep that had cost her her life. Perhaps she'd misunderstood her killer's motives, or trusted someone she never should've let in. I didn't want to make the same mistake.

Sometimes it seemed to me as if a life lived on the written page might be best after all. I was still aching inside from the dissolution of my relationship with Nicholas. Until recently, I'd felt that, in the balance, my solitary life was simpler and, thus, happier...if a bit lonely. Lately, the excitement in my life had been over books and friends and music; my moans of pleasure had been mostly related to food. This was all well and good, but with Christia's murder and Nicholas' strange behavior, my single state was beginning to feel too vulnerable. I was ambivalent about dating another religion student, but my strong attraction to Tomás felt almost chemical, irresistable -- all the more so because of my growing loneliness. A questionable motive, if ever I'd had one.

As the rain became more constant, I stopped on the way home to stand under the awning to a doorman building around the corner from my block. I kneeled to hug Pepita, who was indignant at the injustice of the rain, and cold. I looked up as I felt a presence in front of me in the rain, but at first it appeared as if there was nothing there. I squinted my eyes, trying to focus further out in the dark, rainy night. It was there, just at the edges of my vision, that I noticed a slight blurring of the raindrops in front of me. I blinked my eyes and the blurred shape, about the size and height of a human being, was gone. I closed my eyes and took a deep breath. Inside my head, the image of a body-shaped space in the rain was seared on my eyelids. Outside, nothing remained of the presence but a shivering puddle, no different from all the rest, where it had stood.

I hugged Pepita tighter and tried to dismiss what I'd seen. I told myself that my imagination was running away with me, as it was wont to do. When I next looked up, Gretel, Kirpal, and Tomás had just swished by me through the rain.

"…Kirpal and I …," Gretel's happy-sounding voice drifted back to me.

They hadn't seen me and all I saw of them was the backs of their three umbrellas, three flapping coats, and their feet, tapping out a fast tattoo on the wet pavement.

A large Indian family rushed along, several of the five children arguing over who was holding which umbrella incorrectly and how they should've taken a cab instead of the subway. The mother was wearing a dime-store clear plastic raincoat over a deep orange sari, wet at the hem but still splendid. The children and father were in western attire. I looked especially at one little girl of five or so as she passed. Her little face was wet with rain as she looked up at her mother, laughing and tasting the rain on her tongue. She was holding her parent's hands, and swinging her little arms to and fro, and chatting merrily as she skipped along.

They stopped under the awning I'd chosen for my shelter, shaking out their umbrellas and wet clothes. "My feet are still dry," the little one said, triumphantly. One of her big sisters gazed at her indulgently, "Nah," the older girl said, "You were the one who wanted to wear ballet slippers. Lucky for you I knew that was silly, sillypuss..." I missed the rest of their conversation as they entered their building.

Such love. Such trust. I wanted a family. I wanted to laugh and play and argue with people who trusted me completely and with whom I shared perfect trust and boundless love.

If a traveler from another time were dropped into my place at that very moment, I mused, they'd've marveled at the glow of electric street lights and neon shop signs, cars rushing by, horns and music blaring. There is so much in the world now that would've been unimaginable just as recently as the end of the nineteenth-century. But anyone, from any era, would've recognized the love between the members of that family. Throughout time, the search for and perpetuation of that love has been a major, if not *the* major, force driving humanity. That, and, not to put too fine a point on it, lust. Many examples of the latter quickly sprung to mind, but it was harder to conjure an example of lasting, conjugal-style love in my life.

I searched around in my mind for examples of plain old love in my social circle. Odd to think I couldn't really come up with any

94

conventional ones. Nicholas and I loved each other but weren't together. Abdus – who had a live-in girlfriend -- wanted Nicholas, but I doubt he loved him. Philippe claimed he loved Christia, who was dead…Were we all too self-absorbed to love, or did people in love tend to drift off into some finer realm, away from the fray?

There were a few potential love stories: It seemed to me that Gretel and Kirpal might finally be having a rapprochement, one which I suspected might lead to some romance between them. For myself, I had high hopes for Tomás and me. I was strongly drawn to him, but he also fascinated me as a scholar and as a person. I resolved to be frank with him, if the opportunity arose. I'd had enough of intrigue in the last days to last a lifetime. What I needed just then was simple comfort and bed. I stuck my hand out from under the awning and judged the rain had thinned a little. We walked the last block home quickly.

I changed out of my wet clothes into an old peach colored silk nightgown from the 1930's. It was a little the worse for wear, which enabled me to actually wear it without being too precious about it. I always felt glamorous in the soft, beautifully bias-cut floor-length gown, even with no one to see me in it.

I sat down on the edge of my futon and opened the small cabinet in my bedside table and took out the handmade red velvet purse I used to store my tarot cards. I unwrapped the cards from their covering scarf and held them gently between my hands for a moment, quietly centering myself. As I often do, I asked only that the cards tell me what I needed to know at that time. I shuffled the cards for a few minutes, continuing to focus, and then I drew one card from the center of the deck. The Lovers: passionate love, painful choices. Which one was being predicted for me? Both, I guessed.

A man and a woman were depicted naked, turned toward one another with a look that may be variously read as bliss or terror on their faces, representing the ambiguity of erotic love. Love binds us together, this card tells us, just as it shatters us, so that we may reach deeper and deeper levels of awareness. Or, if we are less lucky, The Lovers warn, love may lead us to darker and darker passions.

I felt that more and more familiar ache in my gut again. Given the emotional intensity of the day, I was glad to be in my home as I considered the implications of the tarot card I'd drawn. It had taken me years to achieve a stable domestic situation. My apartment was the first place I'd lived in for more than a year since I was a child. I hoped to live there for a long time. It was one of those rare spaces that seems imbued with positive energy. Corny, but true. I'd been struck by it the first time I ever walked in the door: One had only to walk into my apartment to feel at least some of the cares of the world outside begin to slip away. Furthermore, unlike other places I'd lived, it did not become atmospherically polluted by any conflict or depression I brought home.

I thought about the vision I'd had in the rain and it seemed, then, in my safe home, more intriguing than frightening. Whether ghost, energetic disturbance, or a problem with my eyesight, it could not disturb me there. The dear, wet family that had reminded me of my own hopes and dreams, though, seemed all the more real to me now that I was in my own space. I silently sent them a blessing, a wish that they'd never go through the sort of turmoil that those who'd been close to Christia, her academic "family" and Philippe, were experiencing that night.

Lying in bed with the window open a crack, I listened to the slap of the rain on the courtyard below. I let sweet peace wash over me.

I breathed in, I breathed out…in my next breath I was asleep.

I awoke at midnight from a disturbing dream. A crowd of people had assembled at my childhood home, an old white farmhouse with black shutters, perched on top of a hill in Greenwich, CT. I recognized no one, although I felt I was searching desperately for some particular person. Nicholas' face appeared in the crowd. He looked at me meaningfully, and then began to recede, still facing me, and floating away downhill. I turned to the person next to me and said, "He'll be back." To my surprise, the person standing by my side was Tomás, who said, "No. He'll never be back. And neither will I." I looked back toward Nicholas just as the speck he'd become disappeared. I turned back to Tomás and he was gone, too. I began to frantically look for them. Somehow, as one knows things in dreams, I knew they'd both gone to the same place. I never found them.

I woke up dripping in sweat and missing both men intensely, in Nicholas' case for what might have been, in the other I knew not why.

*

Unsent letter from Christia Thompson to Philippe Perez-Throgmorton, found by him in the pocket of one of her jackets, after her death:

October _____
Philippe, forgive me.

If you only knew what I know you would revise your assessment of me as a second-rate scholar and wife. My coldness [crossed out]

I have spent all my energy this last year working toward one goal. I am so close. The truth will make me free, and I want to tell you, my husband, what I know, and what I have discovered. Everything I understand I --

Oh, forget it. [handwriting becomes sloppy] I can't do this

Chapter Four – Roses and Roses

> Without the slimy, blind and writhing worms, there
> would be no flowers. Without the worms' worms, there'd be no
> worms; and so it goes, down to the quark, I suppose. So you see,
> my queen hornet, there's no beauty without ugliness.

> Personal correspondence, N. Iverssen to C. Thompson,
> undated

Early in the morning on a cold November day. Fair Annie in a
small, very isolated rose garden in flip flops and sweats, calmly reading
a book while her dog chases the last few falling leaves. The sun kissing
Annie's dark gold hair. The musty leafpile smell, the clean, chilly air.

Early morning bustle of the city. Garbage trucks. Mothers with
strollers. A few bedraggled students clutching coffee. Mothers with
gaggles of kids on their way to school. Joggers.

Unbeknownst to Annie, a few leaves have nestled in her hair
and in her collar at the nape of her neck. My hands – moving as if to
brush them away with a caress. Oh, I am a "heavy bear," like the poem

says, "A stupid clown of the spirit's motive." (Bet the poet -- Delmore Schwartz -- never did what I did.)

The last few late-blooming roses; the ones near me white, rotted brown at the edges.

Aching knees from crouching and hiding. Aching lungs from too many cigarettes. Is it too trite to say, simply, I ached? I ached. (Keeping up appearances, though, most of the time. Suave Bollo.) At the right moment, unseen, I straightened my legs, rubbed them, kneeled back down, continued my vigil.

Wondered: Are her feet cold?

Here is what else was running through my mind:

I hope I don't do it again.

After all, how can I know? I certainly did not expect to kill the first time. How can I know what to expect from myself? I might be crazy. Don't only crazy people kill? To wit: I'm sitting here, lurking, crooning to myself, "Come to me, my beloved," like some Old Testament loco. Surreptitiously watching Annie and her pup cavort among the skeletal rose bushes. Knowing where she will go next, guessing who she will see.

Vigilant, obsessive, jealous. If that's not crazy, what is?

And, maybe more than anything, flushed, heart pulsing, want: I want her. I'm not afraid of what will happen if I have her once, but what if I want her to myself, forever?

That's it. Those were the main thoughts I was thinking, sprinkled liberally with remorse. Sometimes.

I'd naturally been feeling unsettled since I killed Christia Thompson. I'd been alternating between general confusion, remorse, self-pity, and self-loathing. Highest concentration: the last.

Am I a monster? Signs point to yes.

Another question (bemused, baffled): Does a murderer ever deserve mercy?

A crushed white rose in my clenched fist.

*

In those days just after Christia's murder, we would all of us get random feelings of being spied upon, and feelings of generalized dread. Your basic free-floating anxiety...

Gretel called me the day after my rainy vision and kept me on the phone for so long talking about virtually nothing that I finally asked her if there was something on her mind besides, oh, whether we should share a subscription to *People* magazine, which was expensive, but would save us lots of money off the newsstand price, especially if we shared the subscription.

"I'm definitely into the *People* idea, sweety, and I'm not ashamed to say it, to you at least. But I'm getting the sense here that there's something else you want to discuss, eh?" I leaned back on the chaise lounge and propped my feet up. Merlin flounced by, tail curled in a question mark.

She giggled. "'Eh?' You sound Canadian."

"Um, that would be Kirpal who's Canadian, Miss Canada-on-my-mind."

"Guilty. But no, that's not what I want to talk about. It's all too mixed up in my head to even begin on that one. We had coffee last night and hardly argued at all. That's all I'm willing to say or even admit to myself.

"Basically, I just couldn't sleep. I felt like, this is someone we *know* who did this. What if, say, Nicholas knocks on my door late at night –" I began to interrupt, but she insisted, "No, let me finish. Hear me out on this. He knocks on my door and I let him in and it's *him*. The killer. Nicholas! And he *kills* me."

I sighed. "You're right. Absolutely. I'm looking at everyone differently now, too. There's a couple of people I would never, ever suspect. You. Kirpal. Brandi." I thought for a minute. "No one else. Three people out of everyone I know."

Gretel was quiet for a minute, and then she said, "Annie, you suspect Nicholas too?"

"That's not what I meant. I mean I can't *eliminate* him from the list of possibilities, which is, by the way, almost endless." I fumbled for my slippers and walked the few feet to my kitchen counter, stretching the phone cord to its maximum length. I was desperately in need of something to calm my stomach. I poured myself a bowl of Cheerios and returned to the living room.

"The other possibility," I continued, propping the phone between shoulder and ear as I ate and talked, as politely as possible, "is that it's a random killing. In which case there is virtually zero chance that we're in danger. To me, that seems less scary."

"To think there's a psychopath on the loose in Morningside Heights?"

"You prefer a psychopath who is our friend?" I could hardly keep the sarcasm out of my voice. Poor Gretel, with her "gee whiz" attitude, was sometimes a little slower than her East Coast counterparts.

"No," Gretel said very softly. "I prefer no psychopath at all. I prefer to sleep at night, thank you very much."

"Me too," I agreed, thinking of my own intermittently disturbed sleep. "This is no way to live. I, for one, can't wait till they figure out who killed her."

"Well," Gretel said, sounding tired, "I know you need to walk Pepita so I'll let you go. I'll see you later in the department, OK? I'm really OK."

I'd put down my empty cereal bowl, ready to hang up and give Pepita a good shoulder rub, when I remembered her earlier question: "Gretel! Do you really think Nicholas did it?"

I waited for what seemed like a long time. Finally, she said, "I always felt like there was more to his and Christia's relationship than we knew. Or even you knew." She was quiet again, thinking. "Also, the other thing is the way Nicholas is such a moral relativist. I feel like he's so smart he could convince himself of anything. Rationalize anything by a logical argument."

"But you're just doing the same thing yourself! He could have done it, logically,

Ergo, he did it?" I was upset, all the more because I saw her point and it made me more nervous than I cared to feel in the matter of my closest friend's innocence.

Gretel was flustered. "You asked me what I thought!"

This was the closest we'd ever come to an argument in over a year of friendship. "I'm sorry." I said. We needed each other's support to feel safe and here we were arguing over whether or not Nicholas had killed Christia. "Everybody's been a little nuts lately. Including me," I conceded. "The thought had crossed my mind about Nicholas too, but I do think he is just too gentle. No matter how much he dabbles in moral ambiguities, or pretends to be sort of a…" I paused, looking for the right expression, "…human scientific-philosophical test subject." It was a clunky but adequate choice of moniker.

"Let's hang out later. Tea-slash-lunch?" Gretel had finished discussing the subject of Nicholas' possible guilt with me.

"Yeah. See you at the campus center."

"You bet."

Moments after we rung off, the phone rang again.

"Annie?" It was Brandi.

"Yes, love. What's up?"

"I'm just gonna be up front here." She cleared her throat. "Someone told me that Nicholas is a suspect in Christia's murder."

I loved Brandi's frankness. She always spoke her mind. Just then, however, I was still waiting for my belly to register its food intake and was, to boot, un-showered, half-asleep, and grumpy from my conversation with Gretel. Not to mention generally jumpy from my social proximity to a murder. And I had a dog with a full bladder.

I tried to keep my voice level. However, anyone who knows me well knows that when I   get very quiet I may be about to explode. Perhaps this was hard for Brandi to discern over miles of phone lines.

"Please tell me. Now. Who told you that."

"What's your problem?"

"Goddamnit," I yelled, practically jumping up and down in frustration. "If somebody doesn't tell me *who*'s telling them *what* I'm going to lose it. Lose it!"

"Promise you won't tell."

I sat down, gathering myself. "I'll promise you that I will personally be nice from this moment forward, never losing my temper with you again, kissing your feet if you require it, if you just, friggin' right now, tell me."

"It was just Gretel –"

"Gretel? What the hell –" I exploded.

"You promised no more of this yelling shit, Annie. This is not my fault. Don't shoot the messenger." I could hear she was starting to get frustrated herself. I never fight with my girlfriends. Ever. Yet I'd managed to anger my two closest female friends within a very short time frame. That meant my attitude was probably to blame, not, by some strange coincidence of both suddenly becoming bad-natured, either of them.

I craved the peaceful solitude I'd been looking forward to only a few days earlier.

"Brandi, call me a beyotch, alright? But please explain, one, why you told me Nicholas was 'a suspect,'" and got me all freaked out when it was only Gretel saying so, and, two, why the hell everyone seems to think Nicholas killed Christia while, meanwhile, he's out there defending the real suspects all the time, and…and, three, why you and Gretel were talking behind Nicholas' and my back?" My angry act began to fail as I spoke. By the time I'd finished with my litany of questions, there was a sob in my voice, which sob turned into full-on tears as I concluded.

"Aw, honey, Annie, no one's blaming you." She waited for me to quiet down to a low sniffle. "O.K., baby," she continued in a soothing tone, "Let's see. One: Why I called Nick a suspect? I didn't mean to put it wrong, or shock you. Suspect was too strong a word. Two. What was two? Oh yeah. People suspect Nicholas because he's too perfect. Too smart. Cold. Like there's gotta be something very imperfect or bad underneath it all. You know what I mean?"

I nodded, then, realizing she couldn't see my tear-splotched face, admitted, "Yes. Too perfect," I sniffed. "Needs a fatal flaw." Kind of like "Kristi."

"And we weren't, like, gossiping about you guys. Gretel couldn't sleep last night. She called me 'cause she knew I'd be up late, and we were just talking about how creeped-out we felt. Just talking, OK?"

I gave a grunt of assent.

"Personally," she continued, "I think it was that husband of hers, but being as it's none of my business I'm just going to keep my big mouth shut from now on. So: Did you do the semiotics reading?"

"Bo-ring," I faked a yawn. "I think if we just blow a lot of wind and talk in circles we should be able to get through class today. The idea is to talk a lot while saying nothing, right? Like the *Tao Te Ching*, but the opposite: 'Those who speak…*seem* to know.' What they know, it's impossible to understand. And that's the point."

We both dissolved in a fit of laughter. Getting a Ph.D., at least, was funny.

After I'd showered and dressed, the phone rang for a third time.

"Annie, it's Nicholas. I'm over at Philippe's and he's just asked me for some help this morning getting ready for the memorial service. What he's going to say in the eulogy. Picking a poem. But, um, he needs you to pick up a book? I'd get it but he shouldn't be alone right now."

In the background, I heard muted sobbing. It sounded like Philippe's shock had worn off and grief – or guilt? – had finally overcome him. I'd forgotten the memorial service that afternoon, what with all the morning phone calls. I went to the closet and reviewed my clothes for something appropriate, while Nicholas continued.

"I called The Philosopher's Tome and they have a copy of collected Auden, can you get that? I can't imagine it doesn't have 'Funeral Blues' in it. That's been in all kinds of movie funerals." The sobbing got louder. "*Because* it *is* so perfect." The sobbing subsided somewhat. "And then can you bring it by?"

"Alright. Of course. Let me just walk Pepita. I should be there in twenty minutes, tops."

I changed into a simple gray, v-necked rib-knit dress with darker gray wool stockings and pumps, walked Pepita, more briefly than I'd intended, then headed off to the bookstore to buy Philippe's book. As an afterthought, I'd worn my silver pentagram pendant, with bloodstones at the points and a moonstone in the center of the star. I thought I might need some witchy protection, for whatever it was worth.

As I walked the short distance to Philippe's apartment, I read the last line of Auden's memorial poem: "For nothing now can ever come to any good." I knew the poem, this stanza in particular, well. A few years ago I'd lost someone very dear to me, under tragic circumstances.

105

I'd considered this poem for part of her eulogy and something in me had reared up in reaction to the idea. I'd trusted my instincts at the time and only months later did I gain a deeper perspective on my negative gut reaction.

When someone close to you dies, you have a choice: give up, or go on. Give up on joy, connection, love…Or choose to live life with double the joy, for the sake of the lost loved one. It's never a conscious choice at the time, but a series of small choices like whether to smile in response to someone's tender-hearted attempt to cheer you up, whether to allow yourself to listen to a beloved piece of music, whether to ultimately decide that something, *someday*, will "come to any good."

Philippe's choosing this poem did not sit well with me, even though I knew plenty of loving, true people had done the same over the decades, in memory of their loved ones. Something about the combination of this poem with his mercurial demeanor was ringing warning bells with me. Either he was really losing his mind, as I myself had threatened to do earlier that very day, or he was terribly calculating. That poem was sure to make the whole crowd cry, especially if read by Philippe's appropriately quavering yet elegant voice. Might even make *me* cry, I thought with sarcasm tinged with sadness.

How horrible I would feel if he turned out to be innocent.

Full of the restless energy that a confused and guiltily accusative conscience had brought me, I tore up the stairs two at a time and, out of breath, rang the doorbell. Nicholas let me in and we walked the gauntlet of haughty ancestors to the living room where Philippe Perez-Throgmorton sat, or, rather, had collapsed, really, crumpled in a teary heap. His shoulders shook and even the back of his neck was somehow wet with tears. He did not seem to notice my entrance. I handed the book to Nicholas and turned around without a word. We walked back down the hallway. Nicholas asked me to wait a minute: he wasn't sure how to respond to Philippe, how to help him.

"Follow your instincts. Be natural. You're a good person, aren't you? Give him a pat on the shoulder, or, let's see, bring him some tissues?"

"I don't want to touch him. I'm afraid he'll get the wrong idea. And you know I don't know how to act natural. In Palm Springs natural is *fake*, if you get my drift. Plus, he hasn't said a coherent word since he called and asked me to drop by. Oh – except to ask for the Auden."

I gave him a hug. "You'll figure it out."

We were standing there, close together, and I was beginning to think about moving away from Nicholas' warm body, when Philippe suddenly stopped his sobbing and muttered, loud enough for both of us to hear, "The jig is up!"

I must've jumped a foot in the air to hear the text of my note to Christia repeated aloud. Naturally, Nicolas noticed. I made a split-second decision to table the issue of Philippe's guilt. Also, I very much wanted to distract Nicholas from my odd response to Philippe's seemingly-random, histrionic muttering. So, quickly, thinking I might be able to offer some consolation, I returned to the stark living room. I scanned the room for crying jag supplies, and then took a detour to get some tissues from the bathroom and a glass of water from the kitchen.

Philippe's aquiline nose was swollen and red. His usually beautiful face was puffy, and his hair looked oily. His expression was one of a man stricken – and bone-tired. I sat down next to him on the couch and waited for him to blow his nose and take a sip of water. After awhile I began to wonder if he'd even registered my presence, and so I said, tentatively, "Philippe…?"

"Yes Annie, I know you are there," he began. "Thank you for being so patient with this old sod. Also, yes, I know I ought to get myself in hand, though you'd never say it outright. Stiff upper lip and all that. I quite simply literally can't believe someone's killed my wife! Someone actually went into her office and wrapped his or her hands around her neck until she died. Suffocated. Did they watch her eyes as...Oh, bloody hell..." He started crying again, and through his tears he said, "It just-just – it did *not* sink in, didn't penetrate this thick skull of mine until this."

"Until what, Philippe?" Nicholas asked with a puzzled expression. I already knew and dreaded the answer to his question.

"They found a note. The Detective in charge of the case, a fellow by the name of Tomasino called me and told me this morning. Gruff chap. But decent. Salt of the earth." He paused, wide-eyed, seeming mildly surprised to find himself discussing the personal qualities of a police officer. "I thought I'd feel better to know they had a lead, and I suppose it does take much of the onus off me, in terms of guilt. Mr. Tomasino was on the whole much more civil with me this time, to say the least."

"What did the note say?" Nicholas spoke slowly, as if to an upset child.

"That's what it said, 'The jig is up.'" He replied, adding, "The murderer who wrote the note called her Kristi with a 'K'."

I was in total turmoil inside. It sounded like the note-writer was the cops' number-one suspect. That would be: me?! I have never been a good actor. I did my best to look as if I wasn't about to have a nervous breakdown. I shifted uncomfortably on the slippery-hard leather sofa cushion.

"Ummmmm...'Kristi" with a 'K'..." I parroted, avoiding Nicholas' eyes.

Nicholas gave me a very dubious look and then continued to question Philippe. "Do they have any ideas about who might have written this note? Or what it means, for that matter?"

"It was only a brief chat, to let me know they had this note and that they'd already compared it with a sample of my handwriting that Christia had in her office and that they'd eliminated me as the author of the note. That they have some suspicions about who might've written it…They told me that if in fact the note was related to my wife's untimely death, and they suspect it *is* related, I should likely be exonerated. Unless, *naturellement*, I have an accomplice."

Philippe stood up and began pacing up and down the length of the room. I followed him with my eyes, then pointedly looked out the large picture window, across the treeless inner courtyard to the apartments across the way. My father is a nervous pacer, so it makes me uncomfortable whenever anyone paces. I feel as if I am about to get in trouble. Grounded, for example. Philippe, however, was not concerned with me. He was pacing as an aid to his thought processes, puzzling out what was going on in his head. This became clear as he began to speak again, in more measured tones.

"Now that I think of it, Christia was acting suspicious lately. You'll remember I mentioned yesterday that she'd said she'd been working on some sort of discovery." He dug the slightly pointy toe of his undoubtedly handmade shoe into the lush wool of the rug, frowning thoughtfully, and then looked up. "Could it be that she was fabricating something and got found out?"

"Or maybe she stole someone else's research." Nicholas suggested. I looked at him sharply because of the intensity of his tone. His brow was furrowed. "You wouldn't think so, but in the field of religion new discoveries can be extremely valuable both in terms of prestige and in terms of financial rewards. If someone felt that she was, er, stealing their research or discovery or what-have-you they could've been very, very angry."

I hadn't said a word yet. "I agree," I chimed in. "But -- and it's a very big but -- would someone actually murder someone over such a thing?"

"Stranger things have happened." Nicholas looked distracted as he spoke. "Philippe, is there anything we can do for you? For the memorial - or...? I have some matters to attend to at school."

"No," Philippe answered. "You've been wonderful as it is. Thank you, both of you."

Nicholas walked me home, ostensibly to say hello to Pepita. Back at my place, he bent down and gave Pepita a quick pat, and then he stood up, hands on his hips, and leveled a look of mixed curiosity and anger at me.

"I want to know what you know, Annie. I understand you may not feel like it, but you owe me the courtesy of being honest, after all we've been through. Through my brilliant calculations, I get the sense that you know something about this note. I, like certain members of our police force apparently, have my suspicions, but I want to hear it from you first."

I decided to be honest, as the alternative was sure to be unconvincing.

"I did it for you," I said.

A moment passed, during which Nicholas' expression shifted from mild bewilderment to utter shock. "What???" He sputtered. "*You* wrote the note? My god, woman, are you joking? Dear lord...did you kill her?" He shivered, then shook his head. "No, of course not!" His eyes were wild, pleading. "Please, please tell me you're kidding."

"No." Now that he knew I'd written the note, I felt less ashamed. It would be good to have an ally in figuring out what had really happened before suspicion actually fell on me. "I was sick of the way she'd been treating you, like some slave or something, and I just wanted to, I guess you could say, humble her. It seems like a really bad

110

thing to do now that she's dead, obviously, but when I was sitting around fuming over the injustice of it all it seemed like a funny idea." I flashed him a repentant look, followed by a tentative smile. No response. More insecure now, I ventured a small, "OK?" I'd underestimated his anger.

"Annie. I just don't know what to say." His jaw was clenched and I could see he was trying to control himself. He wouldn't even look at me. "That was a really lousy, nosy thing to do. I wouldn't have thought it was you in a million years. Come to think of it, I should have, since 'the murderer' called her Kristi, but I think of you as a sweet girl, not a vituperative witch."

"I did it for you," I repeated lamely. I let the witch slur slide. "I'm sorry. I thought, in my defense, that the note was funny. In a radically different context, you know, normal life, it would've been. Can't you see that?" Another possibility dawned on me: "You don't truly think I killed her, do you?"

"Of course not. Even now that I know you wrote the note. What I *do* think is that somewhere, maybe deep down subconsciously, you must've been jealous of Christia. Or maybe I flatter myself. I don't know. You know I'm not so astute a judge of people's motives as I'd like to be." He was not the only one to be confused about peoples' motives of late. I tried to dig around in my deep down subconscious in search of jealousy and didn't find it; still, I let him think what he liked: these were trying times and a little self-flattery was the last thing I was concerned about.

"Truth be told," Nicholas continued, "I had another suspect. And no, I don't want to discuss that any further so you can just close your gaping mouth." His tone had become more jesting and I was relieved; of course, I was curious as well, but decided not to push my luck.

111

"My question now is what to do next." I endeavored to draw him in.

Now *he* began to pace. "I suppose we are going to have to wait and see. There must be some way of getting a sense of whom the killer might be. We can't just trust our guts, *à la*, 'I like so-and-so, thus, she is not the killer.' No, we have to be more sinister-minded; and more objective, you could say, too.

"A killer has to have a certain sort of super-natural ability," he mused. "That is, it is not-natural to kill other human beings. It's extraordinary. So does that mean that the killer would seem extraordinary? Hmm. Maybe it means that this certain quality that makes him capable of murder – and murderers are overwhelmingly male – makes him all the more prosaic, otherwise. Are we looking, then, for signs of guilt?...Or a lack thereof?"

"Dammit, I'm going to jail and you are getting all philosophical on me."

Nicholas gave a conciliatory smile. "You're right. Let's drop it." Despite myself, I noticed Nicholas' full lips as he spoke. He had the best smile of anyone I knew, big, wide and radiant. The way his incisors were revealed when he smiled gave him just a hint of wolfishness.

I dismissed that renegade spark of attraction to focus on the matter at hand. "Listen, I need your help. I'm scared." I felt vulnerable, and now that everything was out in the open I'd resolved to try to trust my closest friend, ambiguity be damned.

"Well, just let me know what I can do. I'm always up for a spot of sleuthing. On the other hand, just so you know, I'm in deep shit here over my dissertation. I've got no idea who'll take it on. Probably no one." He shrugged his shoulders. "Maybe it's for the best. Christia was probably the only person who'd've enjoyed reading it anyway." He looked sad.

I changed the subject. "What about you, Nicholas? Where were *you*?"

He blushed. Why? Weren't his whereabouts the night Christia died a matter of public knowledge? "Look, I really have to go," he said. "I was at Abdus' place. Like I said, dude."

Nicholas *never* said "dude."

For the second time in as many days, I doubted the truth of his words. Just as I'd finally resolved to trust Nicholas completely, he was starting to remind me of someone from Palm Springs, where, he'd once said, nobody is a native and everybody has something to hide. Where fake is natural. Yeah, and where golf is the local religion.

I had a class to attend before the afternoon memorial service. Since I had about an hour before class, I decided to see if I could discover anything new in Christia's murder investigation. Although I hadn't heard from Brenda Fujiki, and didn't want to press her any further, I thought just talking to her might be a good idea. Perhaps she would have some new, non-confidential information to share. As in how close they were to figuring out who'd written that threatening, dangerous, "vituperative" note.

Brenda was seated at her desk, face buried in a book with a lavender cover. She looked up as I entered and I could see she'd been crying. There were a remarkable number of red noses extant, given that Christia had never seemed a particularly lovable figure.

I tried to be sensitive to her grief, regardless of my opinions about its subject. I leaned forward slightly to catch her eye. "Hey, Brenda. I'm so sorry you're hurting." There is nothing adequately comforting to say when someone is grieving. "Can't they get someone to cover for you?" Oops, I hoped I hadn't offended her. "I don't mean to imply that you can't do a good job, but, you know, maybe you could get a little rest…"

Brenda hugged her big, nubbly sweater closer to her tiny frame. "We're closing early today anyway. For the memorial. Wilson is going to talk, and Guru Rich. Which I think is a bit hypocritical, since I always got the feeling he couldn't stand her. Her classes were more popular than his. 'Shocking! There must be some mistake.'" She said this in a booming, affectedly jovial voice, puffing out her scrawny chest in her best imitation of Professor Redmund. Then she shook herself, as if to rid herself of that persona, and continued in her own voice. "Well, whatever he actually thought of her, he's sure to make everyone get all emotional. He's a very good talker, and he's very into catharsis.

"Professor Wilson, though, he's the real deal. I'm glad he's going to speak. He and Christia were very close."

"Hopefully he can do her justice then," I responded.

"Mmm," she nodded. "So few people saw her good side. Redmund is going to damn her with faint praise. I just know it."

"I want to ask you a few questions about what's going on," I said, pulling up a chair in front of her desk. That she didn't look taken aback, merely resigned, I took as a good sign.

"So," I began awkwardly, "What has gone on with the cops so far?"

She hesitated. "I don't know much. I know they did the usual – vacuum for hairs or fibers, dust for fingerprints…As far as I know, they didn't find anything unusual. The detective in charge is kind of brusque and taciturn, which I'm sure is part of the job.

"It's not as if he notices me," she added softly. "Just as well," she murmured, even more quietly, "since I get to hear a thing or two that way!"

"Like, for instance?" I was practically frothing.

"They are really pissed, basically. They've questioned virtually everybody, and everybody has their theories, but they have no hard evidence of anything at all. Their biggest lead is what I told them, about

114

who I saw that afternoon; but I was back and forth to my department or, you know, the bathroom, et cetera. I could have missed any number of murderers." She laughed weakly at her own attempt at humor. "None of the fingerprints matches anything they've got on file. There was a threatening note. That's about it."

I felt a tremor of anxiety go through me. That note had been a major mistake. I covered my nervousness with animation. "Wild! Maybe something'll turn up with further testing. A hair match or something like that. Or…" I paused, wondering if my mind was overly gruesome, then decided to continue. "Can they get fingerprints from skin? Or—or—paper?"

Just then – perhaps it was my avid expression -- Brenda seemed to realize I was incommensurately involved with the investigation. She began to close into her habitual wilted demeanor. In a terse voice, she replied, "I can't believe you just asked me that. Someone I really, really admired is dead, Annie. I can't even think straight, never mind contemplate police procedure."

I didn't know what to say. This small, subdued woman was sticking up for someone most people thought was a terrible, cold snob – or worse. Moreover, Brenda had direct, personal experience of Chistia Thompson's kindness. She would not be moved from this more-rosy view of her heroine.

"Christia was really lucky to have you in her court," I said sincerely. I got up to leave, picking up my chair and carrying it back to the corner of the office. On my way out I passed Professor Redmund at the faculty mailboxes, but he did not recognize me.

Semiotics was a required course for the Doctorate of Philosophy in Comparative Literature. I'd taken a similar course as an undergraduate and gone around "reading" everything, from dietary preferences to family behavior, much to the amusement and annoyance of those close to me, for the better part of a year. I tried to make the best of it this, my second time around, but as the ideas weren't new to me I found the class less-than-thrilling.

Oh, I found ways to pass the time. My fellow students took the class quite seriously, and I enjoyed watching their faces as they digested some of the more radical ideas espoused in the field. I analyzed the teacher's outfits and proclamations, letting my imagination wander where it would.

Always, I kept my gaze rapt on Professor Svankmeyer -- who regularly wore socks with crazy patterns to signal his status as one of the department's few free-thinking types -- while I scribbled furiously in my notebook.

"Flux," he was saying, "Signifier-signified fluidity. As Perinbanayagam says, there are spaces and moments between, and I quote, 'an internal world and the external world in the first capacity, between the current cognition and the previous in the second...' So -- Memory: fluid!" He waved the book at us and tapped the side of his head simultaneously. This was what passed for a dynamic teacher in our department. "A space and a moment -- or moments, or spaces!" He continued excitedly, "'between the signs of thinking in the third, and the various cognitions of the fourth.'"

Say what?

I tore off a corner of notebook paper and slipped Brandi a note to that effect. I'd actually enjoyed the reading: the material had been interesting, if dense. Svankmeyer, like many University of New York professors – at least in my department, could make anything dull.

"Four loci for transformation between what seems and what is seemed, to coin a phrase." He smiled a little at his own wit. "Therefore, all is no longer all rigidity, all black and white, as Enlightenment thinkers thought. Think about it. There. Is. No. Truth."

He paused for effect. "Flux."

116

I looked down at my notebook. In the margins, I'd doodled several attenuated black cats, some wearing jewelry. At the top of the page I'd written the course title and date, then, "Perinbanayagamgamgamgam." The rest of my notes consisted of fragments of musings about Christia's murder. "Who left the room???" I'd written, and "Ibo: too nice, until now?"

Brandi passed me back the scrap of paper. She'd written on the back. Brandi had a wicked sense of humor, and I could tell I was already slightly hysterical, so I considered not reading her note. Curiosity won. "I am Doctor Svankmeyer," the note read. "Listen to me speak/No matter how I signify/I still remain a geek."

It wasn't actually up to her usual hilarity, but I was ready to explode with little provocation. Laughter is, after all, a way of releasing tension. The French have an expression, "*attraper un fou rire*," to catch (trap) a crazy laugh, which I've always thought was the best way to convey what happens when one cannot stop laughing under inappropriate circumstances; which is exactly what happened to me after reading that note. I faked the beginnings of a major coughing attack. Then I excused myself to go to the bathroom, to which I retired after dealing with the icy glares of seven proper graduate students, one slightly befuddled professor in yellow and green striped socks and one innocent-looking friend, who'd adopted a comically serious expression of studious attention.

When class let out, we hurried to the chapel for Christia's memorial. Brandi took a huge brown crocheted scarf with copious fringe and wrapped it around herself, covering the New York Dolls logo on her black t-shirt. She was wearing three-inch platforms instead of her usual six-inch heels in honor of the occasion.

"Good thing it's so cold," she said. "Otherwise I'd be at a funeral in a t-shirt," she laughed sheepishly. The day had never warmed up and I realized our lucky Indian Summer weather was probably over for good.

I tugged my faux fur coat tighter across my chest, shivering. "You don't think they're gonna have the actual body there, do you? I think that's what a funeral is. This is a memorial. Please, Goddess. I don't have a need to be in close proximity with that finality." I hesitated, then added, "I really don't get why it's supposed to be healing to see your dead loved ones."

"For closure."

"Yeah, I guess. Have you ever seen a dead body though? They're like plastic. Like a…map of a place, where, you know, the place is a person. And the person is, uh, gone."

"Shh!"

We'd reached the top of the chapel steps without my noticing – I'd been deep in thoughts about death and dead bodies along with my blathering. The University of New York ecumenical chapel is one of the few sweet and intimate places on campus. It was built when the school was founded, in the 19th century, when the university was intended to serve several hundred students, not several thousand. A much larger cathedral was constructed in the "one-nation-under-god" fifties, but the small Gothic chapel was retained for weddings, memorials and such, tucked into a quiet corner of campus next to the building housing the Women's Studies and Creative Writing departments.

The chapel's windows were a well-known example of the non-figurative stained glass design that was in vogue for a while in the mid-19th-century. From the outside they looked dark and muted; inside, the skilled design rendered the light shimmery, like a colorful underwater world. This light was one of the chapel's only real ornaments, as it was devoid of the usual religious furbelows. Rows of plain wooden pews, much like those in a Quaker meetinghouse, served as seating for clergy and congregation alike. The chapel's rare simplicity was, in itself, one

118

of the reasons the chapel's many admirers made sure it was not razed when the new one was erected. It was the sort of place where the mind can float in grace.

I caught a whiff of heavy air, subtly perfumed with incense and the faint tang of grief, as we crossed the threshold. I sensed duty and curiosity in the crowd, but also real mourning. I saw Brenda in the back row, her shoulders shaking. A few pews ahead, a gaggle of first-year graduate students who'd been in Christia's thrall were huddled together, whispering and looking around solemnly. Several looked genuinely bereft. Christia had become important to them so quickly; she must've been extraordinarily inspiring as a teacher. I was once again amazed by the different sides she'd shown people: had those students even sensed her icy coolness? Or had they in fact been drawn to it?

Tomás sat at one end of the first-years next to a pretty blonde woman with that long, straight shiny, hippie hairstyle that I'd wear if it didn't make me look like my face is two feet long. I felt an arrow of jealousy shoot through me, and it was more intense than I liked. I sternly told myself to get it together. We were here to mourn the surprisingly well-liked Christia Thompson.

"Let's sit with Brenda," Brandi murmured, respecting the hushed atmosphere. I slid in beside her and gave Brenda's shoulder a quick squeeze. Looking around, I saw Nicolas, Ibo, and Abdus sitting together toward the middle of the chapel. The religion department faculty were loosely clustered in that area as well and had, to a man, adopted the pious expression of false mourning. I could only see the back of Philippe's head. He was sitting, ramrod-straight, in the first pew, with Cyrus Wilson on one side and Richard Redmund on the other. They faced the altar, which was decorated with a giant mural depicting many world religions. Each faith was given equal focus, with an enameled painting of its most central symbol – a cross, a five-pointed star, a crescent moon with a star, a six-pointed star – lavishly

119

encircled in gold leaf. Above us all, the stained glass windows shone in the afternoon sun, dappling the assembled mourners in deep reds, purples and greens.

A group of women, maybe eight or ten by quick estimate, caught my eye. They were sitting together filling an entire row, and every single one of them was dressed in dark red. It was not a bright, flashy red. More one of congealed blood. I was intrigued, and craned my head to discern more about the group. From the back of the chapel, I could not see their faces. I could see that they were all different colors and sizes. I saw dreadlocks and braids and a rainbow of hair colors, most topped with a deep red hat. At the end of the row sat a red-garbed woman in a wheelchair. These old buildings were often not easily accessible for all, but something told me these women would find a way to gain access wherever necessary. They were all of them perfectly still, and quiet. How curious, I thought. Maybe a feminist sisterhood or a womens' group Christia had inspired or been a part of?

Although no one seemed to be overtly gossiping, the women in red were the only people in the chapel who were actually silent. Certainly no one else there was so strikingly reverent. There was an excited hum in the air, which hum only became evident in its sudden absence as the school chaplain ascended the podium and gazed benevolently at the assembled mourners.

He spoke: "We are here to honor a woman taken from us in the prime of her life. Christia Thompson was a renowned writer who reached many with her books; a popular teacher who was an inspiration and help to many students, and a wife and partner to her husband." Cyrus Wilson put a manly arm on the back of the pew behind Philippe, ready to give a consoling pat on the shoulder should the need arise. "On this day," the chaplain continued, "we would do well to remember both the cruelties and the mercies of life, for although they are irreconcilable they are part of the shape of our great universe - though we may rue the cruelties as we do today. Let us pray."

I bowed my head, trying not to be consumed by the matter of theodicy, and bringing my mind to the matter at hand. Chances were – or so I'd read – the murderer was in our midst, a seemingly innocuous party to the memorial rituals. Thus, I'd hoped while at the memorial to get some sort of feeling or hunch about who the killer might be. There were perhaps two hundred people in the chapel. Most of them I didn't even know by sight. For instance, I didn't know the lovely woman sitting next to Tomás just a few short rows directly in front of me, although I guessed she was a first-year student like the rest of the bunch. As the chaplain began to speak again, I lifted my head and I scanned the crowd, finding after a few minutes of this that no one looked particularly murderous. This was going to be hard.

I returned my attention to the chaplain just in time to hear him introduce Richard Redmund, distinguished blah blah, etc.

"We all loved Christia," Guru Rich began, his tone warm, inclusive, comforting. There was an audible groan from somewhere in the room, and then a few titters of surprise, then silence. He gave no sign of having noticed the interruption. "One never feels adequate in eulogizing anyone," he continued in a more self-deprecating mode, "and so, rather than nattering on, I am going to offer two readings today, in hopes that they will in some sense encapsulate the strong regard in which we held our Christia and the pain we feel at her loss." His audience was riveted. "But first, a few words about Christia Thompson…"

It was true: Redmund was a compelling speaker. To me, though, there was something of the performer in his eulogy. He'd said he was going to simply read two readings and yet he went on for some time extemporaneously, as if mesmerized by the sound of his own voice. I would never have noticed this but for Brenda's comments about his

121

jealousy of Christia. Now that I'd given it some thought, I could see how there might well be a grain of truth to her suspicions. After all, department administrators are privy to many of the most subtle of department machinations.

"…and now, without further ado, the readings. The first is from the *Tibetan Book of the Dead*: the bardo prayer which protects from fear. It begins, 'When the journey of my life has reached its end…'" I listened to his strong, compassionate-sounding voice caressing the noble sounds of the prayer and wished I could lose myself in the old invocation of compassion and wisdom, "bliss and luminosity." He finished the reading and cleared his throat. "This one I have learnt by heart. It is the request of Christia's husband, Philippe Perez-Throgmorton, that I recite W.H. Auden's 'Funeral Blues.'" He closed his eyes, and with just the right degree of plangency in his voice, began to speak. When he came to the line "I thought that love would last forever: I was wrong," even I, all my usual vulnerability almost entirely eclipsed by distrust, began to get choked up.

He was so good that I thought, feared, some of his audience might be moved to applaud as the performance drew to a close. There was not a dry eye in the house. I was sobbing and analyzing at once, a new experience for me. After conscientiously giving us a moment to compose ourselves, Redmund asked us to join him in a moment of silence, after which he gave a heartfelt "Thank you. Blessings," and slowly, gravely descended from the podium.

When Redmund finished, Cyrus Wilson began to speak. He spoke briefly of the honor Christia had brought the department and the field, and then of their friendship, which he called "unique on several levels." "We both came from the same place," he explained. "We both knew how hard it was to get here. We were both fighters. Were. Both. Now I have lost my friend, and, like all of you, I want to know why. And I want, nay, *demand*, justice."

Here was someone not so comforting, not so quick to bring everyone together for a nice, cathartic bawl. As a department head, Wilson was risking a lot by being overtly emotional, even confrontational, over the loss of his friend, grisly death notwithstanding. Clearly he was, rightfully, angry. Wise, too: realizing he'd gone far enough in that direction given the circumstances, he changed his tack. "We will remember Christia Thompson as someone who gave everything to her intellectual and emotional endeavors. And as someone," he could not resist concluding, "who was struck down before the fruition of many of these endeavors could come to pass."

For all his anger and studied self-control, Wilson's eulogy rang more true to me than Redmund's emotional sobfest. As he closed with a few more appropriately soft words, I noticed that his eyes flashed nonetheless, and then, as I watched, intrigued, he turned in my direction and sent his gaze toward the back of the room. To me, it seemed as if he was looking right through me to my soul.

"Rest in peace, friend," he concluded, without changing the direction of his focus one millimeter.

As people began to file out I remained seated, keeping alert for any possible clues - odd behavior and so forth. Also, I wanted to figure out who the blonde was. Tomás, however, stayed in his seat as well. He was listening as she talked, leaning in to hear her in the still-quiet chapel. Brandi had noticed my gaze and sighed, "Girl, you are in too *deep*." She gathered her shawl around her. "I can't do the reception. We've got that big deal paper due next week and I haven't even started it and there's a bunch of required parties this weekend, so I have got to get going!"

A moment later, Nicholas came up alongside me and dropped his overflowing attaché onto the bench next to me.

"Whew," he said into my ear. "Did you feel like Wilson knew who did it or what?"

"What do you mean? Heck, I thought he was looking at me like he thought *I* did it. And, the way he was looking at me…I felt like I did. That man has some sharp eyes alright. You going to the reception?"

"No. Can't deal with talking to faculty. There's only so much we can discuss Christia, and then it's 'So, Iverssen, any progress?'"

"Well?"

"And it's 'No, no progress. My advisor is, how you say, dead? And I'm a big mess. Alrighty, Professor so-and-so?'"

"Ooh, can't wait for that phase. Not. That's one thing to be grateful for while you're still in the coursework phase: no demands for progress reports on your dissertation. Although you get a lot of, 'So…Any ideas for your dissertation? Any plans?' Yeah, in my copious spare time I've written a 50-page outline. Why, this very afternoon I plan to engage in some preliminary research after I attend this here memorial reception. Ha."

"Are you actually going to the reception?" Nicholas looked incredulous.

"Yes."

"Whatever for? Are you *that* interested in hobnobbing with the various pseudo-mourners?"

"Not exactly." I shrugged. "I thought I should probably go in case anything comes up. I'm pretty sensitive. Maybe I'll get a psychic feeling."

Nicholas was actually laughing at me, in a chapel, after a memorial service. "Well, Madame Zarathustra, please let me know if you get any emanations. I'll be…Oh, wait! You'll be able to psychically figure out where I'll be, so I don't need to tell you, right?"

When he left, I realized that Brenda and I were practically the last people left in the chapel. I'd missed the exit of, among others, the mysterious group of women in red. Without all the bodies to muffle the sound, even our quietest utterances – "Are you going to the reception?" "Yes, you?" "Yes." – echoed eerily.

The gathering was held at the Faculty House, yet another imposing Greek revival building facing the campus green. We passed a few students hanging out on the lawn in front of Women's Studies/Creative Writing, looking like refugees from downtown. They feigned major disinterest in us as they smoked and talked, but I'll bet they wondered why so many people had been in the chapel on a weekday. As we walked, I pondered the few small bits of information I'd gleaned from the service. Brenda was characteristically subdued, giving me plenty of space to ruminate.

For one thing, Philippe hadn't been up to reading the poem. Why? Was it because he was afraid of being overcome by grief? Or was it because he was afraid somehow his performance, his demeanor, would arouse suspicion? As usual with him, I was torn. He'd seemed genuinely devastated that morning, yes, but he had seemed calculating and cold the day before.

For another thing, Cyrus had said he and Christia were from the same place. Did he mean literally? Despite Nicholas' and my ongoing joke about Kristi-Bob, it was hard to imagine Christia actually being from the deep south, the bayou, if memory served, like Professor Wilson. While he was certainly a cultivated and refined man, he was suffused with the warmth of his southern heritage. Along with this, there were hints of both sweetness and spiciness in his manner that spoke of a childhood of extended family and home cooking, Louisiana-style. Christia, in my experience, had nothing of the sort.

Many of the people who'd attended the memorial service had not come to the reception, so the crowd was much smaller. There were, however, several police officers present; they'd been polite enough to stay out of sight during the memorial, but were probably here to do just what I was doing, and surely doing a better job of it.

Upon arrival, Brenda was collared by a junior faculty member who wanted to discuss something red-tape-related. With neither Nicholas nor Brenda with whom to talk casually, I felt quite awkward. People were loosely grouped – first-years, again, junior faculty, tenured faculty…As I lingered just beyond the front doorway near the cold cuts, crudités, and sodas in bowls of ice, I saw Ibo and Abdus heading out a side exit, deep in conversation.

"Would you like a drink?" The voice sounded vaguely Latin and for a second I thought Tomás was offering me a drink, but it was one of the waiters.

"No, thanks." I replied, adding – as if he cared, "I think I'm going to go. I don't know anyone here, really."

"Aw," he said. "Well…Hey, you did your duty, now go find some friends." With a smile, he walked off with his tray.

Probably an undergraduate on work-study, I thought to myself, someone yet to be ruined by academic snobbism. I wanted to do some investigation, but I was never good at starting conversations with people I didn't know, never mind interrogating them. I decided, with a sense of failure, that I might as well leave. Because I am always trying to be good, I braced myself to approach Wilson, Redmund, and Philippe with my condolences. They barely noticed me. Philippe gave me a curt nod and I slunk away, only to see Tomás and hippie hair walking in together.

I could not avoid them without blatantly turning around mid-stride.

"Annie!" Tomás looked, if not happy, at least pleased to see me. That was enough for me to work with, given his strong, silent, brooding qualities. "This is my cousin, Solange."

Ah. I tried not to look ridiculously relieved. "Pleased to meet you," I said.

"How do you do?" She replied in a French accent. "I will go to get us some champagne," she announced, and wandered off.

"Were you on your way out?"

"Um, I was just leaving but I have a few minutes."

"I have to spend some time with my cousin – she's only here for a few days. Maybe we can get together soon?"

"I'd like that." A lot.

On my way home I analyzed those few sentences to death. Spending time with cousin instead of me: sort of bad. Getting together soon: good. No definite date: so-so.

All in all, I decided, a neutral-to-good interaction.

I put Pepita in her harness and tartan dog sweater and took her out for a long walk through Central Park. On the way home it began to sprinkle, so I picked up Pepita and took refuge in West Side Super Market amid acres of gleaming bright fruits and vegetables and the bustle of after-work shoppers. Toward the back of the store there was a gigantic Nutella display that I tried unsuccessfully to bypass. Lines were long that time of day and while I waited, economy-sized jar of Nutella in hand, I noticed that Abdus was in the line in front of me.

"Can't they go a little faster?" He sneered, to no one in particular. "Can it possibly be that hard to handle a cash register?"

"Sorry, sir," the checkout person, a nice-looking middle-aged woman, responded. "We're really busy right now, as you can see."

"Then you should have more people working here." It was Abdus' turn and he put his groceries down on the counter in front of the cashier. He still hadn't noticed me. After ringing up his purchases, she told him the total and held out her hand to take his money. With a disdainful look, he dropped his money on the counter, taking great pains to avoid any contact with her, and then grabbed his bag and stalked out, not even waiting for his three-cents change.

It was hard to look at the checkout person's face. Abdus had wounded her, though she tried to cover it with a calm, impassive dignity. "What a jerk," I commented. She nodded and gave me a small smile. I was sure he wasn't the day's first unpleasant customer, but he was the close friend of my close friend and I felt ashamed. I've always thought there should be a mandatory national service program in which everyone would be required to work as a cashier or waitperson for six months.

I didn't want Abdus to see me so I faded over toward the fruits and vegetables, turning my back to him and scrutinizing the exotic fruit section with intense interest. The Asian pears looked deliciously just-ripe, so I returned to checkout and bought some of those to dip in my Nutella. I put Pepita back down once we left the grocery store, and we strolled toward the little, semi-wild rose garden behind St. John the Divine.

On the way, I called Nicholas.

"Abdus did it!"

"Huh? Annie, don't you have any work to do or something, er, worthwhile to think about?"

"No! I mean, yes, but hear me out on this: I was just at West Side Super Market and he was so, so incredibly rude to the checkout person that I realized – he's evil. A sociopath, essentially."

"Abdus didn't do it."

"What, like Philippe?" I didn't wait for a response. "I believe you should act the same way with everyone, not be on your best behavior only with important people and then be a total chump to everyone else. Don't you?" I waited, listening to the crackle of the phone. Only the faint sound of an aria, too faint to identify, came from Nicholas' end of the line. "Oh, you're such a snob, forget that line of reasoning. Let's take it philosophically, then, if you will: You should always behave as if those who matter to you are watching, or God."

Nicholas chuckled. "What about sex? 'Hello Mummy, just having a spot of the old in-out —'"

I cut him off. "Oh for God's sake, you know I don't mean that. Spirit of the law! Obviously you give my theory no credence. I understand. But mark my words, there's something *off* here."

"You can't base a murder case on treatment of clerks." He probably had more to say but my battery was low. I hung up and continued down the street, turning in at the St. John rectory and following the narrow path all the way back to my secret garden. Dusk was beginning to fall, but I could still see better than the night before. The air felt soft and wet on my cheeks. The quiet little garden, as usual empty but for Pepita and me, was a welcome haven far from the events of the day. I enjoyed the solitude, much preferring it to the feeling of being alone in a large crowd I'd experienced at the reception.

Here and there, I saw a late rose blooming – lavender, yellow, white. On the ground lay a blurry white cabbage rose, pulpy in places, and wilted to brown at the edges of its petals. I listened to the season's last crickets, enjoying the gentle shush of cars going by the wet road beyond the garden walls, the thicket of rose bushes all around us. I munched contentedly on my fruit and scratched behind Pepita's ear with the other hand. For the first time in days I felt, as my grandmother Lorene would say, "Real peaceable."

Chapter Five – Starving

I will arise and go now, and go to Innisfree
And a small cabin build there, of clay and wattles made;
Nine bean rows will I have there, a hive for the honey-bee,
    And live alone in the bee-loud glade

The Lake Isle of Innisfree, by William Butler Yeats

Brenda Fujiki lived in Greenpoint, Brooklyn on the edge of artsy Williamsburg. Her apartment was over a Polish restaurant that served pierogis and borscht and stuffed cabbage to a steady stream of hearty Poles and the occasional pioneer from another ethnicity. Her place was small, just one room, and very tidy. A desk and chair, small table and twin bed were the only furniture. A small pearl-gray Tibetan rug cushioned the floor beside her bed. One large window looked over the sidewalk below, where the local residents could be seen going about their business. It was a working-class, family neighborhood, very safe. People knew each other and looked out for one another and everybody knew everybody's business. Since Brenda didn't really have any business – her social interactions were limited to school – she was known, to those who noticed her at all, as a quiet, good girl.

Once – they'd run into each other on the subway -- Brenda had visited Brandi Blumenthal, who lived in Williamsburg proper. Brandi's apartment was filled with faux fur and chinoiserie. Leopard-print throw pillows rested on plush, fuzzy purple beanbag chairs and lava lamps competed for attention with many-limbed candelabras. Three white Persian cats had lounged, sullen and beautiful with their bright green eyes, on Brandi's furniture, fur on fur, leaving poufs of hair to float about whenever one moved.

Brandi's music collection was so diverse that she had been overwhelmed by the obvious comparative inadequacy of her own more-limited musical tastes. Brenda liked opera and chamber music. She listened to Simon and Garfunkel for spice. Oh, and every recording Joni Mitchell ever made, including the Mingus collaboration, which was sort of edgy, she guessed. But Brenda didn't even recognize any of the bands Brandi listened to. They all had names like "The Damned" and "The Cramps." "Pulp." Angry-sounding stuff. Brandi had never seemed angry to Brenda. Brandi was exuberant!

Where Brenda's apartment was functional, even dull (if tidy), Brandi's was celebratory and exuded kitschy chic. Embarrassed by her own lack of style, she'd never returned Brandi's invitation. Instead, she had continued to lead her solitary life, deferring in matters of style only to her idol, Christia Thompson.

She herself had a large gray male cat named Chester, shorthaired and oft-brushed, who'd been handed down to her by one of her older sisters en route to a month-long heritage-discovery trip to Japan. She'd become attached to the cat, although he was quite grumpy by nature, and in any case her sister had stayed on in Japan, and so they passed the days agreeably together. She grew wheatgrass for him in low tubs around the room, so as to save her many houseplants from his ravages;

131

and she fed him tidbits almost constantly, so that he really was almost obese. It was her pleasure to keep him sated and happy.

Brenda sat by her window with her feet on the floor and her hands in her lap. It was almost time to start working, and she was very disciplined. She had three minutes left to relax. Chubby, pre-weight-loss Maria Callas had three minutes to finish her aria from *La Traviata*. Brenda watched her own bony fingers with pride. She felt strong and delicate at once, for today she had managed to stick to her diet: exactly four-hundred calories, distributed however she liked. Yesterday there had been an incident with some pickled ginger that had caused her to suffer hours of shame. Today was a new day, filled with satisfaction, she thought to herself. Although, she realized, Christia's autopsy was today. What would they discover? Would their findings point them toward the right person? It was all too horrible to think about.

Two minutes of relaxation left.

She took a set of measuring spoons on a metal ring and selected the quarter-teaspoon. An amber jar of honey sat in front of her on the table. She unscrewed the lid and brought her nose to the golden liquid. With a sigh she breathed in the honey's scent, and then she put the jar back down. Carefully she dipped the tiny measuring spoon in, filling it just so. The taste of honey filled her mouth, flooding her brain with a buzzing sweetness. Twenty-five exquisite calories. Too soon, the taste was gone. She had a fleeting feeling of guilt: the honey that had clung to the outside of the spoon should have been wiped off. Too late now, though later she would suffer for her lapse. Her own mind would make sure of it.

She looked out of the window again. How lonely the city can be, she thought. Rows upon rows of tall buildings, full of people I might be friends with; instead I sit alone, and the rows of buildings might as well be fields of corn. She closed her eyes.

Christia's body being opened up flashed before her eyes.

In general, she didn't like to let her mind run away with her. That was another reason she planned everything so compulsively. She'd had enough confusion growing up in small-town Ohio amid people she could never relate to. The local schools were mostly white, with a sizable minority of black students. In her town, there was one Chinese family. They ran the Chinese restaurant and so had some renown, such as it was. Her father Netsuke Fujiki, was the only Japanese person in town. "Ned" had tried to fit in, but there was in him always something of his namesake, those small, carved-ivory figurines, inward-folded by virtue of the scarcity of the precious material they were carved out of. Although he'd been handsome and virile when he'd married his wife, his life showed on his face. There was something small about Ned Fujiki, something rounded, defeated, even, about his posture. Still, he'd kept going, spending his time working double shifts at the knife factory and drinking heavily with his co-workers several nights a week.

Her mother, the (now) very prim Mary, nee Eakins and a debutante to boot, had been disowned by her family when she married Ned. Like her husband somewhat beaten down by life's vicissitudes, she spent what time wasn't consumed in raising her three daughters and keeping house lost in books. She raised her girls to be readers and they all did very well in school -- especially Brenda, who was always the strange one, who never fit in no matter how hard she tried.

It wasn't just being half-Asian that set Brenda apart – after all, her sisters were both well-assimilated cheerleaders. Her history of confusion and alienation was multifaceted. Part of it had to do with always trying to achieve perfection in her studies. That took up a lot of time and energy and was not exactly endearing at Nathan Hale High, football champs of the county. Part of it had to do with confusion over her sexual orientation. If she'd been even just a little less confused she might've been able to glom onto the small but close gay crowd; however her confusion was such that she ultimately decided she was a

133

non-sexual entity. In any case, she certainly didn't encounter any others like herself in her hometown high school.

Mary tried to help. One quiet day she'd said to her youngest daughter, then a teenager, "I know things are hard for you, Brenda. Lonely." She'd wrung her hands, trying to proceed with the utmost tact and empathy – for wasn't she lonely, too? "Would you like to know my private solution?" Her daughter nodded. "Well, First you must know that in life there are very few true friends. Maybe one or two for each person. We must do everything in our power to protect the sanctity of that relationship once we have found it, as I did with your father.

"But I digress. I mean to convey that your loneliness –" She took a quick look to make sure this blatant recognition of her daughter's state had not wounded her unduly, and then continued. "This being lonely is in truth quite normal, especially for special people like you. One day you will find someone who…completes you…But you must not count on that. Instead you must cultivate your own inner peace."

Brenda had never heard so many words come out of her mother, except when she'd read aloud to her family when her children were younger. She basked in the attention, closing her eyes and letting her mother's voice wash over her like a balm.

"Many years ago I figured out the way to be the most powerful person in the world: accept and welcome everything that comes your way as if you had planned it yourself. Then you will be powerful and serene." Mary folded her hands in her lap.

Brenda, disappointed, glared at the insides of her eyelids and then opened her eyes. "Ma." She stopped. She'd been about to tell her mother that she found her neither powerful nor serene; rather, her mother was of a delicacy that was a source of pride and anguish at once to Brenda. Why cause this fragile woman pain? Her mother had been trying to help her, and besides, there was some truth to what she said: perhaps pretending nothing bothered her, that everything was just as

134

she'd expected, nay, planned would make her powerful. After all, she could not be less powerful than she already was, a misfit among any group she encountered.

Her mother and father, who loved her in their way, but found themselves unable to help her be happy (and so felt inadequate as parents), were perceptibly relieved when she told them she'd received a scholarship from the state to attend Barnard. From there, she'd headed a few blocks away to graduate school at the University of New York. Once in the big city, she'd found that there were all sorts of people, and that she was not so strange after all. But city life and university life were still rough on sensitive souls. She'd tended to form strong attachments to one single individual at a time, and to devote her emotional energies to that person, whether or not the recipient was aware of her affections. She would do small things to express her feelings, like leaving little gifts in their mailboxes, or sending emails from "a secret admirer." Sometimes she got angry at how thankless people were, and then she had to discipline herself. After all, she was an anonymous lover.

She'd loved Christia because, for one thing, Christia was a good person, as demonstrated by her treatment of Brenda. For another, she knew how to play the game, as demonstrated by her comportment around the higher ups. Brenda had aspired to be just like Christia someday and worked hard to cultivate the intellectual and emotional rigor the transformation required, preparing herself and biding her time, unseen, unnoticed, unrecognized.

Brenda sighed to herself. Three minutes were up and it was time to do her work. Callas' brave, sad song about a woman who is *sempre libera*, always free – yeah, sure -- had ended. Maybe a courtesan could flit from pleasure to pleasure, but not Brenda Fujiki. She, like Kierkegaard, knew that the only worthy life was one of intense, constant commitment to duty. The ethical choice.

Brenda prepared herself to perform that afternoon's obligations. She moved her chair back in front of her desk and turned on the computer. She took the top book from the neat stack to her left and began to read, marking relevant passages with a pencil. From time to time she fed Chester a morsel of meat from a bowl beside the books. After an hour she gave a stretch, got up, and used the toilet, washing her hands carefully afterwards in the tiny sink. As she did all this, her mind started to race. She quickly returned to bury herself in her work, a study of the ninth-century Byzantine nun, Kassia, only to begin crying involuntarily as her thoughts continued to crowd her brain. Christia had thought Brenda's work might be very important, and had even offered to help. Now she was on her own. Until she found a Women's Studies faculty cheerleader who could find merit in her chosen subject, the ascetic Byzantine poetess-nun. she would have to manifest her own inner Christia. Christia got Kassia…Christia got *Brenda*. Who else might? Brenda hugged herself tightly and rocked back and forth. She couldn't stop thinking about the autopsy. Her stomach rumbled.

*

Early the next morning, while walking Pepita along Morningside Park, I ran into Cyrus Wilson walking his St. Bernard. Pepita was never inclined toward members of her own species. When I'd take her to a dog run she'd sit down next to me and adopt a disdainful air. I always imagined she would say, if only able to do so, "Um, those are *dogs*? Please have them removed." She made the rare exception, however, for extremely large dogs, and Wilson's dog was firmly in this latter category. While our dogs sniffed one anothers' privates, with Pepita deigning, ultimately, to allow the other dog to engage her in some canine tomfoolery, we humans stood side by side, overlooking the last bits of post-dawn mist in the hollow of the park. It was a beautiful park to look at, but a notorious location for drug deals and prostitution because of the way its central cavity was surrounded by

136

hills and full of trees. There was no way to see what went on in there from above; one only saw the tops of trees and cliffs – and most of the invading academic community preferred things to remain that way. Out of sight, out of mind.

In his big overcoat and fedora, the 6'3", 60-ish Wilson cut a handsome and remarkably chipper figure, given the hour. His choice of pet suited him: like his dog, he was large and affable, someone you'd want by your side in an emergency. Something told me he would be a formidable enemy, too, if forced to defend what was important to him.

"Ms. Campbell. As Philonous would say, 'I did not expect to find you abroad so early.' Berkeley." He pronounced it "Barkly," with a wink. I was only vaguely familiar with the empiricists and so chose to keep my mouth shut, hoping to convey an air of amused wisdom and deference at once. Wilson's next comment showed me just how unsuccessful my ingenuous façade was: "You're quite involved with religion for someone only connected to the department by the most fleshly means, if you don't mind my saying so." He turned to face me directly. "What did you think of the memorial service yesterday?"

For a moment, I didn't know what to say, then I decided to be frank. "I appreciated what you said, and was grateful for it. As for the rest – the chaplain had clearly never met Christia, but I guess that's normal in this non-churchgoing day and age; and Redmund…" I chose my words carefully. "He's a star, isn't he?" I waited to see how he would respond.

He laughed a little. Bitterly, I thought. "It was thought it would do her honor to have our most distinguished faculty member eulogize her." His drawl was more pronounced this early in the morning. "Do you disagree?"

"It's not my place –"

"Oh, no. It certainly is your place, from what I've observed. It is obvious to me, if to no one else, that you're in this up to your eyebrows

137

and I aim to find out why." He fixed those soul-boring eyes on me once again and nodded. "Good morning, Ms. Campbell." He called to his dog, "Baruch! Come!" and then – before I had a chance to respond…or ask where he and Christia were from -- walked away, seemingly lost in thought. I heard him muttering to himself: "Non-churchgoing…hmm…Yes…"

He didn't seem angry with me, *per se*, yet he did suspect me of being involved in some capacity. I wondered if he'd told the police about his ambiguous suspicions. I kept walking.

Back on my corner, mind cleared from the long walk, I passed a homeless man who had made the corner his headquarters. For months I'd been giving him my spare change and then one late night we'd had a sort of argument. I'd been coming home from a club, somewhat tipsy, and noticed a bright red beaded dress draped over the lip of the garbage can. When I'd taken it out to look at, he'd shouted, "Hey! You! That's mine. Ten dollars." I couldn't believe he was trying to sell me garbage. Speechless, I re-draped the dress on the garbage can. "You can have it!" I said as I walked off. Now I was always agonizing over whether he recognized me, whether he resented me, whether I should still give him change or even should have "bought" the dress from him, though I hadn't had any money left at the time…New York City was full of such conundrums.

I was friendly with the roast-nuts guy on the other side of the street and today I decided to discuss this important matter with him. He was all bundled up for the morning cold and just beginning to set up his pans as he listened. "It's like this," he said thoughtfully: "You got your peanuts, you got your almonds, you got your mixed nuts. Kinda like people in New Yawk City. He don't care if you need the dress, you don't got ten bucks to give him. OK? OK. That's that. Over." How elegant in its simplicity was that solution? "Thanks," I smiled. I bought a package of yesterday's sweet roasted coconut for his time and waved goodbye. I fed most of it to Pepita once we were far enough down the block. All that stuff smells better than it tastes anyway.

Once home, I was inclined to expend yet more energy on saving my butt by figuring out who'd killed Christia -- especially since I'd been inspired by the nut vendor to come up with a pat solution to this admittedly larger problem, pronto. However, I forced myself to sit down at my desk and concentrate. My own work had been sadly neglected of late. I spent the rest of the morning organizing things in order to regain my academic bearings. I caught up on the reading for the class I was assistant teaching and began Paule Marshall's *The Chosen Place, The Timeless People* for my Colonial Fiction class. Marshall's spare, compassionate narration of a story of generations of hard-living, strong-loving island people drew me in and lunchtime passed without my noticing.

I had a rendezvous with Nicholas at his place before tea and so at 2:30 or so I pushed away from my desk and stood up. I splashed some cold water on my face to get rid of that otherworldly feeling one gets from extended reading of a good book. I had violet circles under my eyes. Clearly, I'd been thinking too much and sleeping and eating too little. Then again, that was the status quo for me; the problem was that I was afraid, both of being accused of murder and – irrationally, I knew – of being murdered myself.

Nicholas' place was further downtown than mine, in a still-ungentrified area of the west nineties. He'd found it on short notice when we'd broken up, and, though it was practically subhuman in size, he'd stayed on past the original one-month lease. The explanation he generally proffered, to the select few he invited over, was that it was exceptionally cheap. Most people, by his choice, didn't know about his background – and I think he enjoyed playing the role of the starving philosopher. But he also had a naturally abstemious streak, one which I knew was at odds with his more immediately evident decadent side. His belongings, from the pile of clothes covering the floor of the room, to his almost-empty refrigerator shelf in the communal kitchen (typically stocked only with a white Alba truffle floating in brine and Gerolsteiner water) reflected this mixture. He'd taken the pictures of me down. A black and white proof of the graduate students of the religion department, taken at the fall mixer, was hung above his desk. His Hasselblad camera, with which he'd taken the shot, was neatly placed atop the desk, alongside several thick library books.

He led me back out into the hall with the phone tucked under his ear. "Just a sec," he said, and then closed the door. Shamelessly, I put my ear to the door, but I couldn't hear a thing. I waited in the dirty hallway, feeling grateful for my university-subsidized housing. After three minutes or so, Nicholas came out, shutting the door behind him. He was wearing a silvery cashmere turtleneck under his black, wide-waled corduroy jacket. He looked rumpled, as if he'd gotten dressed in a rush and forgotten to comb his hair.

After giving him a peck hello, I fell silent. I didn't bother to ask him how he was doing, or what he'd been up to, given that I had no real way of knowing if he was telling me the truth these days. I was beginning to wonder why we even bothered to keep up what was beginning to seem like a charade of friendship. Perhaps, like many ex-lovers, we no longer had anything to offer one another. The week before I would've said we were best friends. How quickly things change.

Nicholas was clearly preoccupied. He tucked a forelock of his pale, silky hair behind his ear and looked at me closely for the first time. I adopted an inscrutable expression, hiding my hurt as best I could. Probably sensing my distrust, he adopted a tone of jovial camaraderie. "Lots of good stuff coming up." He looked over to gauge my reaction. I mustered a wan smile. "Abdus' party this Saturday. Our trip to visit Gram."

I'd forgotten, in the melee, that we'd planned to drive down to North Carolina over Thanksgiving. I gave a fervent prayer that Christia's murder would be resolved in the next week and a half or so before vacation, adding a wish for resolution and trust between Nicholas and me. I'd little desire to drive ten hours each way with someone whose every word I questioned.

"Yup," I nodded, my mind wandering to thoughts of seeing Tomás at the party, "Lots of good stuff."

Every month or so, there was a special tea for some occasion or another. The usual graham crackers and weak tea were replaced by all sorts of more or less exotic delicacies for Latino Culture Awareness Day, Friends of Uzbekistan, East Africa Mixer, or the Italian Club Get-to-Know-Each-Other…That day, it was sponsored by the International Students' Association and there was a veritable cornucopia of free food. I was immediately drawn to the voluminous cheese tray, piling heaping servings of ricotta salat, gruyere, manchego and fine English stilton next to a few slivers of pear and a half-dozen digestive biscuits.

Nicholas picked up a piece of oozing brie on a toothpick and examined it minutely. An amateur student of microbiology and aficionado of worms, he often had issues with food -- most particularly with foodstuffs owing their very nature to mold, such as cheese. Finally, he took a small bite, chewed thoughtfully, and then said, "I've been thinking. I have a crazy theory about Christia's death."

"Ye-e-es?"

"Well, who would you really suspect of killing Christia?"

"Her husband."

"Maybe he did it, then." I looked at him in surprise. "Don't be shocked. I'm allowed to change my mind. You see, in the world in which we live, that is, academe, the obvious becomes the too-obvious, and is thus discounted. I understand this is circular logic, but bear with me. This too-obvious obviousness was the main reason why, among other more subjective lines of reasoning, I ruled Philippe out as a suspect. However, given the juxtaposition of his behavior in the last few days with his admission of Christia's wealth and so forth…Also, his not eulogizing his own wife."

"Actually," I interrupted, "Plenty of people don't eulogize their best-beloveds. It's a matter of choice: if they think they can handle it and want to do it they do; otherwise, someone less intimate does it. A friend rather than the wife, or whatever."

Nicholas shrugged. "I passed Philippe on the street today and he barely acknowledged my presence. Clearly, he is afraid we've found him out."

I said nothing.

With a dramatic flourish of his cheese-on-a-toothpick, Nicholas exclaimed, "*C'est evident*! -- He revealed too much!"

"Ah," I said dryly. "You're pissed that your idol, who is probably just beginning to come out of shock, which is when the grief really starts to ache, didn't greet you pleasantly and warmly from the depths of his own personal hell."

He didn't answer immediately. When he spoke, he looked sheepish. "Maybe you're right. God, how shallow of me. And to think I've been tortured over this." Nicholas was nothing if not willing to analyze his own behavior in the strictest of terms.

"Yes," he continued, fastidiously nibbling on a graham cracker, perhaps the most relatively worm-free food available, "Come to think of it, I believe I was being self-indulgent, both as regards Philippe and in my circular logic. Clever, but not wise." With that, he gave a crooked grin and stuffed the rest of the graham cracker into his mouth.

"Mini-quiche?" It was Ibo, his mood a whole lot more cheerful today. He held out his plate to me.

142

Blechh, I thought, replying, more tactfully, "No thanks. I only eat eggs when I have a major hangover. But thanks."

I waited for the inevitable real men/quiche joke, but Nicholas just looked at the quiche in horror.

"Fine. So much for pleasantries…How are you, Annie?" Ibo raised an eyebrow, a sincere questioning look in his dark eyes. It struck me, not for the first time, how good-looking he was, with his raven-black hair, and velvety olive skin. He wasn't dashing like Nicholas or Philippe or Tomás, but he had his own kind of understated flare. Only, he was about four inches shorter than me. Since, at 5'8", I sometimes feel like a big galoot, I've always been drawn to tall guys. Maybe that was for the best in this case, I concluded. Our generally solid friendship was something for which to be grateful.

"Well, Ibo, I am *fine*, despite everyone around me acting like they're headed for the loony bin." I cast a significant glance at him and Nicholas, including them both in the aforementioned "everyone." "Not that there's anything wrong with being crazy. Around here, it's barely newsworthy. Any news in your job search?"

"Soon, soon," he replied, "I have my hopes reasonably high these days."

"Oh? Any particular reason?"

Nicholas was apparently not enjoying the direction our discussion was taking. Because no one had asked him about himself in an eternity? The fleeting thought crossed my mind, and I immediately squelched it, deeming it mean. In any case, before Ibo could respond, Nicholas said, quickly: "Like the rest of us, Ibo has been working like a demon to get some recognition." He poked me with a celery stick. "Annie, how is your work going, by the way? Are you still planning to write your semiotics paper on medieval illuminated manuscripts?"

He'd deftly changed the subject to one of my favorite topics. I didn't want to bore them, but I was very interested in reading these beautiful old texts and illustrations through the lens of contemporary linguistics. I noted that Ibo seemed interested, and so decided to let myself hold forth just a tiny bit. "I just logged on to the website of the Getty museum. In L.A.?"

"Yes, I know where it is, being, much to my chagrin, *from* L.A." Nicholas interjected.

"Well, maybe Ibo doesn't," I continued, "And, anyway, they have an extensive collection of illuminated choral manuscripts from the Middle Ages, including some that are attributed to some women who were in cahoots with Hildegard Von Bingen. Can you imagine? I mean, nuns were almost the only educated women in that era, but even nuns weren't generally meant to have alchemical knowledge, you know, how to make gold leaf, or certain of the colors used in these texts…It's just mind-blowing.

"I am almost – I say almost – tempted to change my thesis topic!"

"Didn't you want to work with Redmund if your department will back you?" Ibo asked.

"Yes, although I am wondering lately."

Before I could explain why, we were joined by several other students from the religion department, Kirpal and Tomás, cousin in tow, among them. They'd all just come from, speak of the devil, Rich Redmund's Tibetan Buddhism seminar.

Christia's death was still the order of discussion.

"I heard she was killed for a rare codex she'd discovered. That she had notes on it, but not the thing itself, on her desk when she died. The killer took the fragment, but forgot to eradicate any trace thereof. Duh." This, from Mahmoud, a portly, exceptionally nice friend of Nicholas and Abdus' from Lebanon who was in his third year in the religion department.

"I heard the note was traced," a vaguely familiar-looking fellow with horn-rimmed glasses and a pocket protector, shared with the crowd. There were murmurs of curiosity all around.

To catch my breath after the note-revelation (which could only amount to pure speculation, I reassured myself), I went back to the food table. I took my time selecting petite portions of three desserts – chocolate mousse, rice pudding with cardamom, and baklava: very international! -- although I'd lost my appetite. Solange was hovering over the fruit tray, a miniscule slice of guava and three champagne grapes on her plate. On second impression, her long, shiny blonde hair looked like it was very, very expensive, rather than an aspect of hippie-casual style. Her embroidered peasant top and flared brown velvet pants, too, looked much too fine and clean to be '60s relics. And she probably ate this lightly all the time. She was thin as a rail.

"Hi," I greeted her, trying not to compare thighs.

"Hi. Annie, right?" She pronounced it "Ah-nnie."

"Yes, and you're Solange. What a beautiful name." I tried to think of something else to say. "So. Um. Tomás tells me you're just here for a short while?"

"Yes, my aunt and uncle are here from Miami, so I popped over."

"I speak French." I said, à propos of nothing. Why did I want to impress her – so she could tell Tomás how sophisticated I was? Yes. "I spent a my junior year in Paris and fell in love with *un Francais* and all that, so I didn't end up hanging out only with Americans like most students do. I mean, your English is great, but if you ever want to help me practice my French…" I concluded, somewhat embarrassed.

She was obviously used to making people feel comfortable. Noblesse oblige. "I'd like that quite well." Her eyes were warm. "And now I must find my cousin. Ciao." She waved her graceful fingers at me. She took a few steps and then turned back to face me. As she moved, her hair swung to cover half her face, a heavy, perfect curtain. I was struck by how translucent her skin was. For a moment she looked searchingly into my eyes. She seemed to be carefully choosing her words. Finally, she said, still looking me straight in the eyes, "I love my cousin a lot. *Attention à ton coeur*." She returned to Tomás' side, putting herself in the narrow space between him and a woman I didn't recognize. He certainly had plenty of women around him, that Tomás.

He had his back half-turned to me and looked like he was listening attentively to the discussion. Suddenly, he glanced towards me. I averted my eyes, blushing at being caught mooning over him. I had a lot to figure out before I'd be a healthy candidate for any sort of relationship, never mind true love. I felt there might be enough potential between us to want to avoid beginning what could well be a rebound relationship with him.

Solange's inscrutable comment had me concerned, too: "*Attention à ton coeur*"…Had she meant I should pay attention to what my heart was telling me, maybe not agonize so much over the rebound thing?…Or that I should watch out? These were two very different courses of action. Unfortunately, I admitted to myself, the stricter translation would indicate the latter. And then there was the additional consideration of Nicholas and his good standing among the students in the religion department. A lot of the other students looked up to him, and knew of his affection for me. I sensed that Tomás was a gentleman, and that he'd give polite consideration to the Nicholas situation. I didn't know for sure, but I'd heard that Cubanismo was sometimes worse than garden-variety machismo, in which case Tomás might decide it was more honorable to leave me alone. I wondered what Tomás thought of Nicholas, who had, as one might say from a male-dog perspective, already peed all over me. I cringed at my own metaphor, then quickly glanced around to make sure no one had observed my self-induced discomfort. It was time to exit that festive yet fraught environment. I hoped that I would not feel as uncomfortable at Abdus' party.

I grabbed a pomegranate for the road from a decorative display, and made my way through the entrance hall outdoors to the campus green. The icy fresh air seared my lungs and I relished the distraction. When I'd become more acclimatized, I found myself thinking about Tomás again. This crush was getting serious.

I told myself to concentrate on more important things, like my possible arrest for murder, to rack my increasingly pathetic brain for clues. If the note had in fact been traced, I had to find a way to exonerate myself!

First, I had to calm down. For the second time in as many days I found myself in a church. This time I went seeking peace, and although my mind was too restless for what I sought, the great beauty of the Cathedral of St. John the Divine was nourishing in other ways.

I entered the great cathedral through the front doors, along with several tour groups. Behind us was the great rose window facing Amsterdam Avenue, with golds and reds in the center of the blossom and in the rays, and bright blues at the edges. I turned to gaze up at it, silently offering my thanks for the lovely sight. Above a smaller rose window in blues, above the stories-high pipes of the organ, high above all the gothic curlicues of the dark wood walls and giant carved wooden doors, the immense, justly-famous rose window shone on, impervious to all our mortal goings-on.

Everyone was chattering away in awe at the huge space as tour leaders waved flags and generally tried to restore order and get organized for the suggested donation. I slipped through the groups, nodding at the fellow at the donation box, and walked along the right side of the church toward the altar to escape the crowds. I stopped about three-quarters of the way down at an open door. Across a small courtyard, in another church building, the children's choir was

147

,practicing, their high clear voices ringing pure in the cold air. They were singing "Lo, how a rose e'er blooming," in preparation for St. John's annual solstice celebration, I guessed. Like the non-denominational chapel used for Christia's memorial, St. John's honored all faiths. This great cathedral took its catholic religious stance one step further, being a powerful force for social change and justice.

I listened to the carol for awhile, feeling mingled pain and pleasure: pain, at how lonely I felt, and at how long it had been since I'd been a child, with the open heart of a child; pleasure at the sheer, timeless beauty of the children's voices. I felt such nostalgia for an innocent past, and even a yearning to create that kind of environment for my own children some day. I knew I wasn't ready to have a family. I thought of the family I'd seen the other night and was unable to imagine myself, the frazzled graduate student, having any success in that mother's deft child-wrangling role, but I did feel an emptiness in my life. At least I had Pepita and Merlin and my friends.

I laughed to myself as the memory of Pepita at the Feast of St. Francis earlier that fall. Every fall, St. John's brings in various clergy, speakers and exotic animals for a parade and ceremony, followed by a blessing of the beasts in honor of the animal-loving saint. Pepita had been perfectly well behaved until her turn came to be blessed by an amiable Friar Tuck type in a rope-belted brown robe. Something about the robe had set her off and she wouldn't go near the man. Humiliated, I'd carted my growling Boston Terrier off to join the slack-jawed bunch of kids surrounding a ruminating camel who had a garland of flowers around her neck for the occasion. Pepita loves kids, and any animal she can look up to.

Feeling a little better, I walked outside and down the wide cathedral steps to Amsterdam Avenue. I crossed the street and veered left toward the Hungarian Pastry Shop, where I peered through the window to see if anyone I knew was there. I was surprised to see

Philippe. I'd never before seen him at the tatty coffee shop. I watched him for a moment before he saw me. He was acting noticeably compulsive: he had a napkin in his hand and was swiping at the table in a circular motion – I counted seven counterclockwise circles without a break, a pause, and then seven again – even though the table looked perfectly clean. In any case, if one is looking for super-sanitary, the Hungarian is probably not the place to go.

Philippe continued to "clean" as I walked toward him. He looked out of place in the rickety chair – he should've been reclining in a Morris chair in front of a fire, with a creamy silk cravat at his throat and several lanky dogs lounging about, shedding. Philippe belonged in an upper crust establishment; the Hungarian Pastry Shop, beloved as it was, was just plain crusty. I caught his eye and he dropped the napkin, as if burned. He looked ashamed.

I joined him at his table. "I won't stay long," I assured him. He had a passel of books and papers in front of him, with a small, cleared space for napkin-circles. Both of our eyes went to the crumpled napkin at the same time.

"Sometimes I just can't stop myself," he explained.

"Oh?"

"O.C.D. Obsessive-Compulsive. I feel like if I do something enough times, that is, the perfect *number* of times, in the perfect *way*, something will happen the way I want it to…" He slumped a little lower in his chair. "Actually, truth be told, it's usually to prevent something perfectly awful from happening." He looked terribly dejected. "But then that's already happened, hasn't it?" he observed, almost as an afterthought. He cocked an eyebrow at me. "What brings you here, Annie?"

"I saw you in here. I wanted to see if –" Philippe was so formal, so cultivated. One often felt like a blundering oaf around him. To wit,

I'd been about to ask him if he had any new clues. "Well, how are you, Philippe?"

"About as well as might be expected." He said simply.

"Have there been any, er, developments?" Oaf, oaf, oaf.

"If cutting Christia's body open and taking her insides out and declaring she died of strangulation is a 'development,' then, yes, there have been developments. Some bloke" – this last, inelegant turn of phrase I noted as I tried to recover from the grisly image he'd evoked, in a voice dripping simultaneously with elegance and contempt – "from the police department was gracious enough to inform me of the positive determination this afternoon. Otherwise, no." He looked around. "Does it seem to you that people are staring at me?"

"If they are, I'm sure it's because of your compulsive behavior, not because they know who you are. Also," I added, after further considering his question, "Most people in here are not wearing Savile Row suits."

"Hmm. I'm not sure. I suppose it's possible I'm being overheard as well."

I nodded, mouth shut tight.

"Annie, do you have any ideas?" He leaned toward me, a plaintive note in his voice. I shook my head. He waited for a moment and, resolving that I was not going to be forthcoming, he continued. "I suspect very little, and know even less." He held up a finger. "One, I am the prime suspect, soon to be brought in for questioning, despite a telling total lack of witnesses. Despite a vicious note I did not write." Had the note been vicious, really? No. It had been foolhardy, very vaguely threatening, but not vicious. Philippe held up a thumb and index finger. "Two, I know that Brenda is the so-called main source of information for the police. That girl is bats. Positively bats."

"What makes you say so?"

"For one, she was obsessed with Christia. And I know whereof I speak when it comes to obsession…Why aren't they considering *her* as a suspect?"

"They must have some good reason, I would think." I changed the subject. "And what do you suspect?"

"Oh, just vague apprehensions…hunches, you might say. Nothing concrete enough to give voice to. You?"

"The same."

"Then it appears that we are both of us full of hot air." He softened his words with a half-smile, but continued in a more mocking, even angry, tone: "Here we are, 'Leaning together / Headpiece filled with straw' and all that."

His reference to Eliot surprised me: earlier, in the church, I'd asked myself why I felt so hollow, and I'd thought of Eliot's hollow men. I'd decided I felt empty, rather than hollow, a fine distinction, but one that to me made the difference between being whole but lonely — and being a person who was missing some essential human quality.

Philippe was leaning away from me, now, and even under the suit I could see how tautly muscled he was, sitting there with his whole body tensed. His diffident, fey persona was no longer in evidence. He'd failed to get anything out of me, therefore I was not useful. Or, in a more kind light, he was no longer able to keep up his usual slightly insipid façade, which was, under the circumstances, understandable.

It came to me that he probably sensed, and was put off by, my interest in his wife's murder as a sort of "case." To him, it was all too real - if anything was real to his shifting personae — as was being a suspect in said case. I gave him a tight smile, one as sweet and as sincere as I could muster, bid him goodbye, and left.

I was very hungry. On my way home, I picked up dense, crusty peasant bread, olives, and sheep's milk cheese at the West Side Super Market. Back at my place, I put Debussy's Sonata for violin and piano

151

on the stereo and lay down with my spread of food on my stomach, otter-like, enjoying the romantic duet, marveling at my own ravenous appetite, and musing over the leads I had in Christia's death. I don't share the ambitions of most for wealth, power, or other forms of worldly success, but I do have a passion for the truth. Whilst the rest of us went around variously afraid and nervous and angry, Christia's killer went on with his or her life. That seemed unfair to me, especially as plenty of innocent people were getting dragged down in his or her wake. And no matter what I tried to do, I remained one of those unfortunate people.

I must have dozed off for awhile because I awoke to the last strains of Debussy as the sonata ended. The room was very quiet and my head was briefly, happily, empty. Then I remembered who and where I was, and that I had plans to meet friends downtown for drinks that night. I felt almost too shaken by recent events to enjoy a night out.

Just then, the cd player changed over to the next disc. The strong, righteous sounds of Patti Smith filled my apartment with just the energy I needed to continue my day. I left my place at nightfall and caught the downtown 1 train to West Houston. I walked over to Mulberry and down to Spring Street to the Shark Bar. Through the windows overlooking both sides of the corner, I saw the reassuring sight of people talking animatedly together in the warm, smoky light.

Brandi was sitting with a bunch of guys from a band we both liked and knew well enough to drink with, wearing a black spandex halter top over a patchwork suede micro-mini; for shoes, she'd chosen black suede platform boots with pink faux fur trim.

"Bubbe!" She jumped out of her chair and gave me a big hug. "I got these for you." She handed me a pair of red velvet hot pants. I whistled. "Thanks, mama!" I waved hello to the guys and sat down.

"We're drinking whiskey shots and beer chasers. Here –" she picked up one of several full shot glasses on the table. "Chin chin!"

152

I managed to down the whole shot before my rational mind could object, and followed it with a few gulps of her lite beer. Brandi lit a menthol cigarette, and then motioned for me to move closer to her seat.

"I did you a favor, too," she said, straining to be audible over the Johnny Cash song that was playing on the jukebox.

"Yeah?"

"I invited Tomás here."

"Oh, God, no! I'm already tipsy." I looked down at my jean-clad legs, my Doc Marten's boots. "What am I *wearing*? He can't see me like this." I made a face. "I'm like – a buffoon! I needed to *primp*."

"Yeah, that would've been useful. Three hours preening and getting nervous. But anyway, he couldn't come. He mentioned he was going to call you."

"Ooh. I better check my answering machine."

"C'mon, just have some fun. Let's dance."

We danced by the jukebox for a few songs, but I couldn't shake the feeling of wanting to leave. Sometimes a night out can be blown just like that. I apologized to Brandi and, promising her a wild time next time, gave her a big hug and skedaddled. I knew she'd have fun no matter what, so I didn't feel too bad.

A part of me definitely wanted to get my messages and to deal with the subsequent feelings of elation or disappointment all alone, but I also had a hunch I should be near campus. I took the train back uptown and stopped in at my local bar on Amsterdam and 110th Street, reasoning that I might run into someone from the religion department with lips loosened by alcohol. It was still fairly early, nine or so – too early to go to bed in my current state of mind. To my surprise, Brenda Fujiki was sitting at the bar looking glum, nursing a glass of something clear. Probably water.

153

She was remarkably happy to see me. "Hey! I was waiting for someone and they never showed up. I was just about to leave! What'll you have? I'm having vodka, if you like vodka you could share mine, we could get you a glass, or, I don't care, share my glass." She was tripping over her words. Here was someone lonelier than I. Taking pity on her, I sat down next to her and took a hearty sip, almost choking as I set the glass back down.

"Do you know where Cyrus Wilson is from?" I asked, casually.

"I think Louisiana. Why?" She looked befuddled, from drink and from my random-seeming question.

"Because he said he and Christia were 'from the same place.'"

"Oh." She paused. I could tell she was puzzled, maybe upset that I'd brought the subject of Christia up. "I don't know, exactly. I could ask him."

"Thanks," I said. Searching for something non-Christia-related to discuss, I fell upon school as a good conversational topic.

"Brenda, what are you working on these days, anyway? I can't believe I've never asked you that!"

"Hardly anyone does," she said in a resigned tone. "But since you asked, I'm doing a study of a ninth-century Byzantine Greek nun. She was a beautiful, smart aristocratic woman who was rejected as a bride by the emperor at the time for being too friggin' smart." She hiccoughed. "She wrote this hymn about Mary Magdalene called 'The Fallen Woman.' I'm taking that as a starting point for a feminist analysis of her life and work. My original angle is the analysis of her texts themselves for subtexts since there's already been plenty of feminist analysis of her life."

"What are the texts like?"

"Some of them are pretty standard hymns, so there's not a lot to go on."

"Sounds hard," I said sympathetically. "Original thesis work is a rough standard to meet in this day and age. I'm already nervous and I have, like, two years and comps to get through."

Brenda looked at me sympathetically. "Comprehensive exams are just memorization. Memorize and spew, is my advice. For me, it's motivating myself and coming up with ideas day in, day out that's difficult."

"I'll bet." I agreed completely. "When it's all depending on you, it's got to be terrifying sometimes. Looking at what you've got so far and asking yourself, 'So, *me*, what do I do next?' Ugg." I took another tiny sip of vodka.

"Especially since Christia was my key advisor on it." She looked about to cry. I handed her the vodka, which she drank without flinching. "No one in my department will even touch it. And it's completely worthwhile! Take 'The Fallen Woman:' first off, who wrote about Mary Magdalene in those days? No one, that's who – except Kassia. And this song," her face shone with enthusiasm, "is honoring her, and showing things from her viewpoint. However humble," she concluded. She'd leaned in close to me in her enthusiasm. Her breath smelled of alcohol, and of something less-than fresh.

I couldn't think of anything else to say, imbued as I was with the torpor of post-beer, post long-day exhaustion.

Brenda examined my face for a minute. "Are you scared?" She seemed embarrassed immediately after asking the question.

"Yes," I answered.

"Because murderers usually just kill one person, you know. They kill the person they believe needs to die and then they are done. In most cases. So chances are we don't have anything to worry about."

"Unless the killer was a serial killer of academics who" – I got carried away with my own idea – "is after, um, women in academia at the University of New York."

"How likely is that, really? I mean, I'm the first person to admit to being phobic, but it's just not warranted here."

There was another lengthy silence. I was just about to excuse myself when Brenda said, "There is something I am afraid of. Dark buildings."

I was confused. She continued, an odd mixture of furtiveness and pride crossing her face. "Would you come to Religion Hall with me? I need to check out some stuff in Christia's office."

I was speechless. Finally I managed to sputter, "You-you mean you...want to go there *now*?" The thought of breaking into the religion department at night was not an enticing one.

"Yes," she said with a strength in her eyes and a strong set to her chin that told me she'd been sitting there alone getting up the guts to do this all night.

"*If* we were gonna do this, how would we get in?" I was too shocked to make a decision.

"I have keys, dummy," she giggled, her eyes a little glazed.

I could not resist the opportunity "Alright." My body was thrumming with adrenaline, and I was instantly completely sober.

Religion Hall felt even more haunted at night, as if the lack of human comings and goings left more psychic space for the creepy energy that inhabited the gloomy building. Without any of the office and classroom light that usually spilled out into the hallways, it was almost too dark to see. The elaborate iron sconces shed only small circles of dark yellow light. We walked through silent hallways where, in the murkiness, shadows seemed to shift slightly as if underwater. We skittered quickly from light-pool to light pool, moving oh-so quietly. Brenda knew that a night watch person patrolled the hallways, but didn't know the schedule of rounds.

We went first to the department office to get the complete set of keys from Brenda's desk. A dog-eared copy of *Sluts and Witches* lay in

156

the small drawer that held the keys. She slid the drawer closed quickly, unaware that I'd already noted the contents. As we walked toward Christia's office, I reviewed what I remembered of it so as to be more competent at looking around – whatever it was we were looking for – in the dark. As I recalled, her office was one of the larger faculty offices I'd seen, with two large windows overlooking the northeast corner of campus. Predictably, bookshelves covered most of the wall space, but she'd also had a few matted and framed black and white photographs. Several looked like Mary Ellen Mark's prints of children, if memory served. Her desk faced the door, with the windows behind her. There was a small closet to the left of the door, a sofa along that same wall, and a few hard-backed wooden chairs for student conferences. I remembered that her own chair was of the same type, and that it looked uncomfortable. This latter came to mind because I'd wondered, when I'd been in her office (accompanying Nicholas on some errand or other), why she would sit not only facing away from such a prestigious, precious view but in such a lowly chair. It didn't seem in character with the power-hungry, style-conscious Christia I knew.

Brenda unlocked the door, while I carefully held the yellow police tape out of her way (with the end of my scarf covering my fingers – have I mentioned I read mysteries?) and we entered Christia's office. She quickly swung the door closed behind us. It was pitch dark. Neither of us had thought to bring a flashlight and, without light, we were both afraid to move in case we might disturb some important piece of evidence. I was further suffused with terror at being on the site of a death, a *murder*. It was so still in that room. A faint perfume lingered in the air. Although I'd never given it a thought while she was living, I recognized it, posthumously, as the smell of Christia. After that unsavory realization, I managed to hold my breath, without consciously meaning to, for so long that I almost passed out. My mind was racing and my legs were itching to run away, as fast as I could, but I forced myself to stay. I had come this far, after all.

After breathing until the subtle scent of Christia no longer registered, I had an idea: "Let's try to open the blinds. Maybe we can get some light that way," I whispered.

I felt along the wall to my left, turning the corner and making my way toward the window. The spines of Christia's books felt dry and dusty to my nervous fingers, as if already moldering from disuse. With my fingers, I discerned that the window was covered by an old-fashioned treated-canvas shade with a round pull. As I gave a tentative yank, the shade snapped loudly and rolled all the way up into itself. I jumped back about three feet, banging my right buttock on the corner of the desk. We both screamed and instantly thereafter, chagrined, covered our mouths at the same time. I was shaking, completely spookled.

As our eyes adjusted, we could see fairly well inside the office, but, it turned out, there was virtually nothing to see. Her desk had been cleared off, as had anything in the room deemed of possible relevance to the police in their investigation. Of Christia, only her books and scent remained. I tried to read the book titles, but it was too dark.

Brenda sighed. "This is what they've done to her. Let's go."

I was more than happy to leave that place. Once in the hallway, I realized there was one other place where I wanted to trespass, while we were at it. "Wait a sec. Would you mind checking out Ibo's office with me? It's just…He's my friend and I'm pretty sure he's under suspicion. Along with everybody else, of course."

"Sure. I guess so." She searched through her keys, frowning. "I think this is it," she said, holding up a nondescript key. She was right, and we entered Ibo's dinky office without a hitch. We were free to turn the lights on in his windowless closet, mindful only of footfalls in the hallway. On Ibo's desk was a sheaf of papers. The top page held the title, "Things truly new to behold: On the long-lost codex of the maid of Queen Puduhepa."

That seemed mildly suspicious, given the rumors about Christia's discovery, but I didn't want Brenda to notice my concern. "I'm not sure what I'm looking for," I said casually. "Lemme just look around, you know, see what strikes me..."

Brenda sat nervously on the side of Ibo's desk. In a small voice, she said slowly, "I really like Ibo, too, but I think this" – she indicated the aforementioned paper – "is the same thing they found on Christia's desk. Something about a maid. I recognized it because we were just studying the Hittites in my one of my classes – Women, Before the Common Era, it's called. I think this Puduhepa was a really big deal. A powerful woman. A priestess of Ishtar, depending on who you talk to."

"What do you mean?" I continued rummaging around.

"Most historians said for a long time that she was merely the daughter of a priest of Ishtar. As if a Goddess worshipping people would have just male priests! So her handmaiden might have been a priestess too. That's why this paper could be really important. It would essentially prove that the feminist scholarship in this field isn't nuts."

Her expression grew troubled. "But why would he have it? If Ibo has some sort of information he stole from Christia, that might be a motive... Maybe we should take it? If they find it here, he'll definitely be in trouble."

"Why should he be?"

"You know he was one of the last people in her office, right?"

"How would I? No one tells me anything. Plus, you wouldn't tell me who those people were, remember?"

"I was trying to protect you from being upset." The vodka had made her more forthright. "Do you really want to know?"

I thought about it. Her revelation might well unleash yet more suspicious thoughts in my head. On the other hand, it might reveal

159

something important, as revelations are intended to do. "Yes," I said, bracing myself.

"Your two other favorite people. Nicholas and Tomás."

That *was* scary. I gathered myself together. "There must have been plenty of other people in and out of her office that day. Doesn't she have office hours?"

"Yes, but earlier in the day."

"And don't you go to the bathroom? Or get lost in your reading? I've seen you lost in a book many times. I can recognize it because it happens to me. Sometimes you aren't busy and you're just sitting there reading, huddled into your book…"

"Well yes, I did go to the bathroom, and my memory isn't perfect. Everything you said is quite possible," she said thoughtfully, tapping her fingers on Ibo's scratched desktop, "It's all they've got to go on, though. I'm sorry I told you. It's not really Tomás or Ibo that would upset you, right? Nicholas is your best friend. I mean, Ibo is your friend, and Tomás is – maybe your'e a little bit into him, at least from what little I've seen…but it's not like a long-term thing yet…" She trailed off.

"What impresses me," she said after a minute, "is how you and Nicholas were so in love and now you've been able to turn that love into a Platonic friendship. It's inspiring."

I was impressed: Brenda had seen a lot from her quiet post. I stood still, thinking about what she had said. Nicholas, Tomás, and Ibo. Hmm. "I guess you're right, this is a potentially significant piece of news. But I'm not *too* surprised. All of those guys worked with Christia anyway, right? No big shock here." I gave her a reassuring smile, while my insides roiled.

Pondering how she'd discerned so much, I took another sweeping look around the room, but nothing caught my eye. It didn't take long to look around Ibo's office, since it was about one-tenth the size of Christia's palatial space. Except for a few miscellaneous piles toward the back of the space, I'd already examined everything. "Just give me another minute here and we'll get going, alright?"

She was looking increasingly nervous, but she nodded bravely. I headed toward the aforementioned piles, thinking of the last people who'd been to see Christia, and especially of Tomás. My back was to Brenda and I was leafing through a stack of papers and books in a corner when I heard a choked sound, as if Brenda was struggling to breathe.

"Annie." her voice held grave fear.

"What?" I was desperately quiet, afraid to the bone. If Brenda had told me she sensed or saw a ghost I wouldn't have been a mite surprised.

"I have a really bad feeling. Let's get out of here."

Between the atmosphere in the building and our own risky behavior, I was a bundle of nerves. She didn't have to convince me.

We ran, in our haste leaving the Puduhepa paper on Ibo's desk, the light on, and the door closed but unlocked. We rushed out of the building, practically bumping into each other in our fear of being too far away from another human being at that moment. My heart was pounding so hard I had no sensible thoughts in my head. Since we'd left the bar, in fact, I'd been so caught up in the excitement of our mission that I hadn't been particularly rational. I'd neglected to question Brenda's motives.

Once we reached the lawn, however, and my heart had modulated, I found that a lot more questions were arising in me about Brenda's role in all of this. Why was she so interested? Of course, she might well ask the same of me, since we were now both equally implicated in the evening's sleuthing. But was there a reason other than the obvious prurient one for her inquisitive behavior? And why wasn't

she being questioned, as Philippe had suggested she should be? Or --
was she in fact a suspect?

Away from the dim light of the bar and Religion Hall, under the
floodlights of the square, she was a sight. The rims of her eyes were
raw, and her hair was stringy and uncombed. I hadn't noticed earlier,
but she held a small book clenched tightly in her left hand. Her breath
was the worst part. Every time I'd gotten close enough to share the air
she breathed, as when we'd fled Religion Hall together, I'd caught a
whiff of something powerfully rancid. From deep within her, the smell
of old and rotting flesh emanated, as if she was eating herself – too
slowly, too slowly -- from the inside out.

I looked pointedly at the book. "Where did you get that?" I
wasn't ready to talk about the feeling she'd had in the building, because
I suspected it was similar to what I'd experienced in the rain a few days
earlier and I was too out of breath to talk about that.

For an instant, Brenda looked like a deer in headlights. Deciding
on honesty, she admitted that she had taken it from Christia's office, "as
a memento. It's a first-edition printing of an old book on Byzantine
women." She looked at me defiantly. "I didn't take it to sell it. She
would have wanted me to have it. It will help me with my work and to
remember her, too."

At a loss over what to say, I emitted a neutral sound, which
Brenda chose to interpret as agreement. I walked her to the subway, still
wondering what had happened in Religion Hall to scare her so much.

"There was something in there," she said, unprompted, as we
walked. "There was a shimmer in the air over by you, where the quality
of light changed. I don't know how else to explain it. I could still see
you, but there was something between us."

"I think I know what you mean." I didn't elaborate.

"You know it was once normal to have visions. Woman mystics
had them all the time. In her book, Christia said you should trust those

162

visions. I'm going to think about this. I think it means something. Maybe that Ibo is guilty? I don't know."

"I don't know either. That's the one thing I know for sure. I'm going to bed. Have a safe trip home." We'd reached the downtown 1 station.

I walked home as fast as I could. I was glad not to have a long subway ride in front of me. I thought of poor, strung-out, seemingly-anorexic Brenda with compassion mixed with a little suspicion. Really, though, I was too tired and -- having not eaten since my afternoon snack, unless beer and a little cheap vodka count as food – too hungry to think clearly. I'd forgotten to wonder if Tomás had called and would not remember to check once home and digging into some late-night refrigerator scraps.

On my block, a few buildings away from mine, I stopped under a scraggly tree and looked up at the lacing of the last few leaves in the never-dark New York City sky. For a few breaths I was stuck in a kind of exhausted hypnosis, mesmerized by the shifting of black silhouettes in the faint breeze, then I shook myself and walked on.

Chapter Six – Luxe

For I am full of matter, the spirit within me constraineth
me.
Behold, my belly is as wine which hath no vent; it is
ready to burst like new bottles.

Job 32:18

On the day that Christia Thompson died, she'd had office hours
and met with many of her students. At three p.m., when her office hours
were over, she organized certain papers in preparation for the revelation
she was prepared to make very soon.

Then she leaned back in her chair, closing her eyes to better
focus on the music she'd chosen earlier for her office hours: Hildegard
von Bingen, "the Sibyl of the Rhine." Von Bingen, she remembered,
was often ill and always afraid of being ridiculed (a *woman* composer?
Remember, this was the twelfth-century!).

She took forty years to gather the courage to compose, Christia
reminded herself. I still have time.

Diabolus, the devil, was calling enticingly to von Bingen's protaganist, Anima: *"Ego autem dico, qui voluerit me et voluntatem meam sequi, dabo illa omnia"*-- "I will give you *everything*," he promises -- and she, penetrated by his "burning sweetness," really almost *does* follow.

Christia took note of the trembling in Anima's voice. How close Diabolus comes to winning Anima to his side, she admitted to herself with a sigh. There is always the temptation to succumb to that world, where women's intellects and power are cast off for something easier, dumber, more-accommodating.

Her tasks done, she'd taken a snifter of cognac over to her window to admire the view of the campus. After awhile, she'd meandered over to her desk and taken her hairbrush out of the bottom drawer. Idly, she'd brushed her ebony hair and then coiled it into a small, perfect chignon, setting the brush back in its place. Then she'd walked back to the window, lost in her thoughts.

Her mind wandered, as it often had of late, to the field of bluebells she'd glimpsed that long-ago Mayday in Oxfordshire. Just for the briefest last moment of sunlight, the grassy meadow had remained illuminated. Under the deep blue-black sky the luminous field had been a slash of pale silvery green, carpeted with vivid, nodding bluebells as far as the eye could see. Then, the darkening sky had caught up with the field and the flowers had disappeared into the dark. Yet for Christia the stunning sight was seared on her psyche, so that the flowers had continued to bloom and glow even when she closed her eyes; and where a passerby might have seen a plain, featureless expanse Christia saw bright hope, and joy.

In the countryside that night, Christia had been so moved by the beauty and magic of her surroundings that she'd, perhaps involuntarily, and certainly to her own surprise, opened herself up just enough to remember how it felt to be purely peaceful.

In her office, Christia sat with her memories and wondered if she might someday soon recapture that fleeting feeling of innocent peace.

*

I spent Saturday on my studies, getting up early and taking brief breaks to rest my brain. I listened to Mozart's *Requiem* over and over until I knew some of the Latin by heart and then switched to the Velvet Underground and Nico's "Banana" album. I ate a lot of chocolate to keep myself going.

I had very little news from the outside world, huddled as I was with reproductions of, and articles about, illuminated choir books from the Middle Ages. I was too busy to be nervous or afraid. I had a call from Nicholas during which he told me a little more about the autopsy: that they'd determined that Christia died of suffocation, that she was strangled with the bare hands of a fairly large person, probably male; and that there were other traces of evidence that were being investigated apart from the body itself.

"That's not much news," I said, cradling the phone between ear and shoulder as I tickled Pepita behind the ear. I absentmindedly noted that my apartment was a mess.

Nicholas replied that he would keep me posted, and I thanked him.

I stood up, stretched, and began idly picking up the candy wrappers that covered the floor in an arc around the computer. Nicholas and I talked for a few more minutes and then he told me he had another call. "Detective Iverssen, signing off. Roger. A-O.K.," he said in a mockingly officious tone. I hung up the phone and sat back down in front of my computer. I turned my ringer off. I smiled to myself and acknowledged begrudgingly that I hoped he did call again, if only to leave a message on my voicemail, given that his call had been my sole instance of human contact so far that day.

That afternoon, after I found myself on the toilet where I'd been lost for a good ten minutes in a mental haze of Latin liturgy, I took a few hours off to go to the Frick. I took the M4 bus, catching it on the corner of Broadway and 110th, and riding east on 110th down the hill behind St. John the Divine. I passed Miss Mamie's Spoonbread Too and the C-Market supermarket, people-watching all the way. The bus went along the top of Central Park, where just a few trees retained scatterings of brown, papery leaves. The park's northern ice rink, artificially frozen, was already open for business. The sparse grass beyond the stone wall was covered with leaves, and park workers were using rakes and leaf-blowers to gather the leaves into piles amidst the rocky hills and boulders.

Along the east side of the park, the bus went down Fifth Avenue. Even in the low-hundreds, the buildings along Central Park were grand, with elaborate cornices and cavernous, well-lit entrance halls. A view overlooking Central Park has long been a precious, precious commodity. In the spring, summer and early fall I'd often seen weddings taking place in the park's Conservatory Garden, but by mid-November it was too cold and barren for such events. To my left, Museum Mile began to unfold, starting with the El Museo del Barrio on 104th Street.

I got off the bus at 73rd and walked south and east to the Frick. An old mansion, with several gardens within its bounds, the taupe stone building was solidly elegant. I'd been going there for so long that I thought of it as an integral feature of my life, somewhere I was sure to go at least once a year to take stock, and to recharge myself with the timeless beauty of its exhibits.

That year there was an exhibit of Victorian Fairy paintings in the basement. I had grown up believing firmly in fairies, despite much evidence to the contrary. As a child, I'd spend hours in the woods building houses out of leaves and twigs, with mushroom cushions and

167

carpets of pine needles -- palaces for fairies who, I was sure, would move in as soon as I left. As I wandered around the Frick that afternoon I was touched by the Victorians' love for these mythical, ethereal creatures. For them, I mused, fairies embodied all that was special about nature, her wildness, her mutability, her purity, while being, too, a safe expression of eroticism. I noted a dark undertone to many of the paintings, too, a Boschian quality that lent a frisson to the otherwise slightly twee exhibition. Pearly white and nearly-nude girlish fairies cavorted with angry red goblins and vulnerable looking robins with giant rust-colored breasts; sleeping humans snoozed in ignorance while their bedrooms and beds were explored by a mixture of sinister and benevolent sprites.

In the central courtyard of the museum, a fountain bubbled quietly, surrounded by leafy plants. Once again, I marveled at the fact that this sumptuous place, immense, and full of priceless art and furniture, had once been a home. I decided to take a quick look through the galleries, to greet my old favorites. In one, a late self-portrait, Rembrandt van Rijn gazed at me gravely, with a sadness so full of honor and honesty that he appeared completely devoid of self-pity. To me, his expression seemed to convey that the world is a sad place, but that is simply how things are. I always felt that the mere existence of that painting proved beyond the shadow of a doubt that Rembrandt believed life – hard and painful as it may be -- was worthwhile nonetheless. Broke and perhaps, as some have suggested, psychologically and emotionally broken at the time, he'd painted himself in rich raiments and gold, capturing his own nobility and perseverance in subtle brushstrokes. It was his gaze that was the richest aspect of all: to me he had always seemed, above all, kind.

Would anything I did endure so long? I had plenty of time left to figure out something to do, if that was what I wanted. Christia, though, her chance was over. Surely she had moved many people with her bestseller. Her work on de la Motte Guyon, along with the other more-obscure stuff, would be useful to scholars in the field. I wondered, however, what she'd been working on right before she died. I thought it was a pity that the world might never know.

That night, I ventured back out into the world around eight p.m., hours after nightfall. It was already getting dark so early, though there was still more than a month to go before the winter solstice. I'd taken a bath to cleanse the day of paper-writing munge off of my body and out of my mind. I was sick to death of illuminated manuscripts, facts about illuminated manuscripts and theories thereabout. I'd done my hair in pigtails so it would dry with a pre-Raphaelite wave. I was wearing my green velvet floor-length skirt with combat boots and a black jewel-necked cashmere sweater. My whole ensemble came from the Salvation Army on 96th Street. The skirt held a lot of memories for me: I'd worn it the first night I kissed Nicholas, having bought it earlier that same day. It struck me that those memories held a sort of validation of my recent psychic experiences.

Here is what happened: that dawn, I'd arisen from a deep sleep, scribbled something in my diary, and gone back to sleep. When I'd woken up again, I'd set off on a desperate pre-first-date shopping spree, culminating in the perfect find of a hand-sewn, deep-green velvet skirt, as soft as silk. When I'd returned, giddy, from the date that night, I'd opened up my diary to write about my evening, only to read, across the top of the page, what I'd written at six a.m.: "green velvet skirt." I remember being absolutely positive I hadn't been to the store in months, and that I had concluded that there was no other explanation for this incident but that there is more going on around us than we perceive in the realm of the five standard senses.

Thinking about this incident on my way to meet up with some friends at the bar on 110th and Amsterdam, I recalled once again

Christia's written advice to would-be powerful women. She'd advised them – us – to trust our visions and instincts. My instincts were clouded by emotion and stress, but I had definitely had a vision, as had Brenda. After another person had clearly shared my odd experience of some sort of, for want of a better word, manifestation, I felt comfortable trusting my vision. What I didn't know was what the vision actually meant.

Around nine, Gretel, Brandi, Mahmoud and I headed over to Abdus' apartment on Central Park West in the 80s. The apartment was in a pre-war building in which none of the grand old apartments had been subdivided. It was as gorgeous and ornate as the Dakota, but all the more desirable for the anonymity it afforded its wealthy residents. Its horseshoe shape, surrounding a paved central courtyard, was designed to offer a stunning view of the park, and especially its famed reservoir, to all apartments.

The doorman looked down his nose at us. Our shabby/tarty chic obviously did not appeal to him, or perhaps he was put off by the giant case of Budweiser Mahmoud was carrying in his ample arms. I decided to have a little fun.

"Mahmoud, Prince of Coleslawvia and the Princesses Helene, Justine and Routine. For the Syed residence," I announced in my most stentorian voice. Everyone tried to keep a straight face. Startled, and unsure of whether to believe us, he erred on the side of caution. He rang up and announced us – I had to repeat our names with all the haughty conviction I could muster, all the while repressing a major laughing fit - - and we proceeded to the elevator. Abdus' place was on the 20th floor.

"Darling," I said to Brandi in the elevator, "Are those platform shoes from Chanel or Gucci?"

"Oh, these old things?" She joined in, "Why I picked them up at a little boutique in Palm Beach last winter. Got them for a *song*. Under three-thousand bucks. Usually I wouldn't wear the same thing two seasons in a row but I just find these to be the *most*, don't you?" The elevator operator wasn't paying any attention to us, but the tastefully-attired couple sharing our ride shared identical expressions of utter shock.. Gretel and Mahmoud were giggling. We'd had a beer or two on the way over, and were acting like bratty children, but it felt like such a relief to let off steam over something not related to Christia.

Abdus himself opened the door in black velvet smoking with scarlet silk lapels. He was smoking a cigarette in an ebony and silver cigarette holder. He looked affected but gorgeous, and as he air-kissed me I smelled tobacco and bay rum and incense, a heady mix.

"I just had to greet the arriving royalty!" He smiled. "Everyone's here. I told you
this was a dinner, no?" We shook our heads. No. "Well," he continued, unashamed at his own lapse in politesse, "There's so much food left over. I'll just have Freddy make you each up a plate."

"Oh, you needn't bother. We'll help ourselves." I didn't want this Freddy to have to go to any further trouble, knowing that Abdus was likely not easy to work for.

"Suit yourselves. Here –" He gestured toward a wall of carved ebony shelves beside the entrance. It was half-filled with shoes on one side and pretty, pointy-toed pairs of Morrocan house-slippers on the other. "You can leave your shoes there, and then choose some slippers. Or just go barefoot, your majesties…not you, Mahmoud. Hope your pedicures are up to date," he joked, assuming that they would be up to date as a matter of course.

"Thank you Abdus." I was determined to be polite. "Thanks for inviting us to your party."

"Oh, I forgot." He ignored me. "There are party favors. Shawls for the ladies and cigars – Cuban, of course – for the gentlemen. Mahmoud, come with me. You can put your…" He looked at the case of Bud "…beer in the pantry."

171

We all spent a few minutes removing our shoes. I was in stocking feet, chipped toenails safely out of sight. Gretel slipped off her high heels to reveal – to my and Brandi's surprise -- bright green toenails through sheer hose.

We could hear some Brazilian music playing from the room at the end of the long hallway directly in front of us. Fragrant, tempting cooking odors streamed from the kitchen through a door on our left, through which Abdus had led Mahmoud. To the right was an open door to another hallway with doorways spanning its length. From previous visits, I knew there was a sitting room/den through the first door; I guessed the rest were probably bedrooms and bathroom(s).

"I guess we should just follow the noise," Gretel said after the men left. The center doorways at the end of the corridor were only partially ajar. We pushed them all the way open and beheld the most luxurious private residential room any of us had ever seen.

The room was the size of the graduate student lounge at the university. Huge windows overlooked the low expanse of Central Park, and across to the twinkling Upper East Side. Luscious Persian rugs in tones of red were practically piled atop one another. The floor was dotted with cushions made of intricate rug-pieces, and large enough to sink one's whole body into. A pile of jewel-toned shawls sat on a low, ivory-inlaid side table next to the doorway, next to several bright yellow cigar boxes. The gang was all there: Abdus' girlfriend Kalinka, Nicholas, Kirpal and Ibo. In addition, Abdus' brother, Ishaq, was there, along with a few dozen other guests I didn't recognize. Tomás had not yet arrived.

I knew Abdus' family home in Lahore was opulent. He'd told Nicholas it was on the Shahrah-e-Quaid-e-Azam, "the mall" near the Ravi river, and that it was one of the grandest homes in a very exclusive area. His family, he'd said, was nostalgic for the region's prominence in the Mughal era; he'd tried to recreate that sumptuous era in his

172

apartment. To my mind, he'd succeeded admirably. My head spun with wonder at the enchanting room. On the walls were paintings of the "orientalist" style, re-claimed by a descendent of their subjects, and filled with lush scenes of indolence much like the one in which I now found myself, though with better costumes. I thought of my sagging sofa and the museum-reproduction postcards on my walls; then I thought how proud I was of being a nice person and took succor in that.

Kalinka, Abdus' stunning German girlfriend came rushing over to me as soon as she saw me. "Oh, Annie," she gushed, "*Luff* your skirt. You've got to pick a shawl or two, to go with it! We've got these shahtooshes as favors for all the female guests. Do you know what they are?" I'd read something about them in a magazine – that they were illegal, I think, because they were made from the hair of an endangered species, by small children or some such. Ambivalent, I didn't respond, just looked at her attentively. Her eyes were set very far apart and her hairline was very high, giving her the look of an alien, or baby, albeit an exceptionally attractive alien/baby. Her auburn hair was parted in the middle and, stick-straight, hung down all the way to her waist. As she spoke, she caressed the deep maroon shawl she'd draped artfully over her slim creamy-fleshed arms. "They are literally the softest, warmest thing on earth and they are, like, very prestige, yes?" Her accent was strong, but she'd picked up some Americanisms. She took my arm and walked me back to the table near the room's entrance, while Gretel, Brandi and Mahmoud, back from his kitchen sojourn, joined the rest of the guests over by the windows.

As she walked, the bangles on her wrists and ankles jingled softly. "Do you like rugs? These all have a history, you know." Kalinka had been a Masters student in U.S. History when she met Abdus, but she hadn't gone on to the Ph.D. She was probably convinced Abdus would marry her and support her in perpetuity and saw no reason to be a university drudge. Personally, I had my doubts.

173

"Well, these rugs *are* among the most beautiful I've ever seen."

"Look at this one." We looked down at the deep reds and golds swirling beneath our feet. "It is called an Amritzar. It's from the 19th-century. The linked geometric flower designs were meant to inspire the viewer to think of lofty things." The latter came out "loafty sings." "Abdus' family commissioned that rug over a century ago, and used it for prayer as well as decoration. Or this one here." She led me to a darker-toned rug, with a more abstract, paisley-like design. "This one is a Sultanabad rug, from Central Persia. It was a housewarming gift to Abdus from the Pakistani Ambassador to the States."

My rugless house flashed through my mind once more. Again I cautioned myself against envy. I was here for a party and I wanted to enjoy myself. Why should it bother me any more than, say, the Frick had -- that is, not at all? Perhaps part of it was Abdus' barely-concealed rancor towards me, and his closeness with Nicholas, who had long been, after all, my dearest friend in New York City.

It occurred to me, as we walked back toward the pile of shawls, that Kalinka was being more chummy with me than usual. Although her wide-set eyes gave her a look of childlike innocence I knew she had to be whip smart to keep Abdus in rein. He was wont to flirt with anyone, male or female, he found attractive. I'd met her several times before at social gatherings and, until then, she'd never been more than politely friendly.

Kalinka sorted the shahtooshes into two piles and gathered the smaller one into her arms. "These are the ones I think might go with your green velvet. Let's go try them on in my bedroom."

We left the great room and took the long hallway I'd spotted on arrival. Some ten doors gave onto the corridor, all closed. I wondered, but didn't want to ask – too gauche – why they had separate bedrooms. I decided that there was so much space in the apartment they might as well have two bedrooms each. After I told her I was only familiar with

174

the den, Kalinka briefly opened each door, giving me a quick tour of the maid's quarters, now offices for them to write and do research in, and the luxuriously-appointed guest rooms, used by Abdus' siblings when they came to visit. She told me that Abdus' parents had their own pied-a-terre just down the street. Judging from Abdus' place, the maids' quarters of these apartments were bigger than most city apartments.

Her bedroom was done all in white, with curtains and bed-hangings made of the palest pink sari cloth. The only jolt of color was that of a worn, very finely made rug of a rose-colored floral pattern. Very old, I guessed – and priceless. Relative to the rest of the house, the room was very understated. "I have more simple tastes," she explained. "If I had my way the room would be almost-empty. Much in the way of Christia Thompson." She cringed, unsure of how I would react to her bringing up a dead woman in reference to interior decorating. She motioned to the bed and we both sat down, shawls momentarily forgotten. "It is all so sad. All of you are regarding the other as guilty. Many of you are scared. She was a hard woman, but she has left much sadness."

Kalinka's English was good, but I was confused by what she meant. "Do you mean hard as in cold, unemotional or as in complex."

"O-oh – complex, to be sure. This woman was a funny case."

We were interrupted by a couple looking for a private place to be together. The romantic atmosphere of the apartment had obviously gotten to them. They excused themselves, and Kalinka tactfully said, "If you two would like a place to talk, there is the guest room two doors down on the left." The woman blushed. "You can lock it from the inside," she added. The couple left.

We'd lost the thread of our conversation. Kalinka was sorting through the scarves, holding them up in front of me one at a time. Each was about five feet square, but they folded as thin and light as pocket squares. "These really are super-luxe," she exclaimed. She handed me a

175

royal blue scarf. "I think this one is so-so with the skirt, but it really goes with your coloring. It is the same shade as your eyes tonight."

My eyes get darker when I am troubled. I thanked her and took the scarf, rubbing it between my fingers. It was the softest thing I'd ever felt. After a moment, I found out why Kalinka was being so ingratiating.

"I know you and Abdus don't get along," she began. I steeled myself to remain polite, to not say anything critical about the man she loved. "I think he is jealous of you. You are so all-American. What do they say – W.A.S.P.? His family is a proud old family but some of them have been taken in by American culture. They try to be more American than the Americans. Same in England." She laughed a little. "Why, I do not know. We Germans certainly do not have this. Only guilt. But many other peoples have it when they should not. After all, their culture is the more ancient.

"For this and other reasons Abdus is insecure. I am asking you, Annie, to be tolerant of him. Also there are other things going on." Before I could ask her to explain what she meant by "other reasons" and "other things," she continued. "I ask you to see why Abdus is being so generous, with the meal, the gifts. It is that he wants people to like him. This is all he has to give, as he sees it. He is not the type to go about being so, you know, *süß*...so *sweet*, all the time."

I couldn't look at her. I focused on her shiny pinky-beige toes, curling and uncurling in the plush carpet. The tinkling of the tiny bells on her anklets was the only sound in the white room. She followed my gaze to her perfectly-groomed feet. "Abdus likes them like this. He likes pretty feet." She waved her feet in the air. "It's a good thing mine are so dainty."

It was kind of her to change the subject, but she deserved a response. "You're very loyal," I said, "Everybody should have someone like you in their corner."

"It's not just loyalty to him," she began, and then fell silent. I raised my eyes to her face and saw she was biting her lip. Frown lines had formed on her high forehead. She busied herself folding the shahtooshes in perfect rectangles.

I appreciated Kalinka's effort, but I didn't think she was getting to the root of the issue. Talking so frankly with someone she hardly knew, on behalf of her somewhat surly partner struck me as generous, brave -- and foolhardy. Sitting there in her bedroom, I reasoned that she was a decent, loyal person with sharp instincts and nerves of steel. That she'd fallen for Abdus demonstrated that he couldn't be all bad, although I had to admit he probably wasn't as good as she thought him to be either. Or that she was a gold-digger, which seemed unlikely to me.

We rejoined the festivities. Abdus and Nicholas were nowhere to be seen, and Tomás had still not arrived. A table underneath the windows held deep bowls of rice and several entrees, vegetables and one that I thought might be lamb. I took a plate from a stack of gold-leafed china and served myself a spoonful of rice, over which I ladled some of that delicious chickpea and green chili dish called Chana Ghotala, and a scrumptious-smelling, creamy veggie korma. An extensive array of chutneys and other condiments was spread out on one end of the table, along with fresh flatbreads enfolded individually in napkins to keep them warm and soft. I also helped myself to some red wine, and then I made small talk with various people. Deep down I was just marking time waiting for Tomás to arrive. I had butterflies in my stomach, and was trying to placate them with food, drink, and distracting conversation.

When Nicholas came back into the room, he made straight for me. I had been talking to Mahmoud and a pretty but fairly vapid woman with whom he seemed infatuated. I excused myself and took Nicholas aside. "Help," I whispered to him, "I've been trapped talking to bumbling-man and his clueless crush."

He laughed, showing his perfect teeth. "Looks like you found adequate sustenance, in any case."

"Ha! I've only just begun. This food is delish." He picked a chickpea off my plate with his fingers. I set my fork down and said, thoughtfully, "You know, Kalinka was strangely concerned about my feelings for Abdus. She took me into her private quarters and gave me a talking-to about Abdus' wounded psyche and how I should forgive him. I mean, it was nice of her. She loves him. But why me?"

Nicholas looked uncomfortable. Then he, too, launched into a defense of Abdus: "Listen, Anouschka, Abdus is not who you think he is. I know you find him rude, snobby, and misogynistic." He gave a grim half-smile. "Did I miss anything?" I shook my head, annoyed at having to sit through another paean to the fellow. "He's never been all that nice to you. But I care about him. You've got to see things from his perspective. Try to understand. Lahore was a cosmopolitan mecca when Abdus was growing up. The very rich lived on a different plane than everyone else. We can't begin to understand what it feels like to be, for all intents and purposes, royalty. In some sense, Abdus had to feel like others were below him, like animals. How else could he reconcile, as an innocent child, the horrors that were going on not so far away in other places in Pakistan like Karachi? So that's why he has a different attitude toward service people than we do.

"You know that his father, Nawaz Syed, is a distinguished poet and professor at the University of the Punjab. But what you don't know is that his uncles and practically everybody else in the family look on such intellectual pursuits as frippery. There was and is a lot of pressure on Abdus to further the family business with his brother and uncles. They think one academic in the family is enough, even if Abdus *were* really gifted at his studies, which he isn't. He doesn't apply himself."

178

"The heart bleeds," I said, with little sympathy. "You still haven't explained why he can't be just – a regular, polite person. He's always sneering."

"He's very family-oriented. I suppose you're just not part of what he thinks of as his family."

I decided that would have to do, explanation-wise. "I guess one can't pin a murder on someone for being bad-natured, anyway," I sighed.

I didn't know whether his long silence was intended to express agreement or to put distance between us. Finally he said, in a slightly disgusted tone, "You're still on that? For heaven's sake, Annie dear, give it a rest. Have some jollity." He raised his glass to me. His cognac snifter clinked with my wine glass with such force that I was surprised that neither glass broke. He walked off and left me standing alone overlooking the night-saturated park.

I felt a familiar stab of loneliness. Sure, I could make small talk with a glass of wine in my hand, but when it came down to it I didn't really fit in with any of the tightly-knit groups assembled around the room. The religion-department guys, the jet-set South Asians, the lovebirds Kirpal and Gretel, and Mahmoud and whatsername...Even Brandi was deep in conversation with a slight, poetic-looking man I recognized vaguely as a friend of Abdus' from the New York Philharmonic. A cellist, I thought. The cello was probably rock-and-roll enough for Brandi on a night like the one we found ourselves having. My girlfriends from Wisconsin and Queens were having a ball.

Unlike me. Maybe it was because I knew the host did not like me, no matter what Kalinka and Nicholas said; maybe it was because I didn't feel quite myself, hiding, as I was, a crucial piece of evidence; maybe it was because I am solitary by nature...I felt like an outsider and it hurt. Everyone I knew best at the university was there at Abdus'

179

party: from where I stood I could see Gretel, Brandi, Nicholas, Kirpal, and Ibo. Yet I had no one with whom to feel companionable.

Ibo must have noticed that I'd been standing alone for some time. He took pity on me, and made his way over to join me at the window. "There's a terrace through that door in the corner, wanna go have a smoke?"

Grateful, I nodded. "Let me just get this scarf wrapped all around me and I'll be more than happy to go outside."

The view over the park was even more breathtaking from the terrace, which ran all along the outside of the great room. Far below us, the city noise was a mere hum, and the air twenty stories up was cool and fresh. I accepted a cigarette from Ibo, although I was trying to quit. I've never been able to resist cloves, Ibo's cigarette of choice. I put my glass on a low table and sat down in a teak lawn chair, effectively denying myself sight of the fabulous view. Vertigo. Ibo sat down next to me. He looked preoccupied.

"What do you think of Abdus'place? "

"It's incredible." I savored my first drag, stifling the urge to cough once the strength of the clove-tobacco mix hit me. My eyes watered. I exhaled sweet and spicy smoke. "I'd only been into part of it, which would have been plenty!"

"I used to live like this in Istanbul." Ibo told me. He was quiet for a moment, and I could see the glow of the tip of his cigarette as he took a few puffs. "Better than this," he added softly. "My family was not a family of sultans, just hard-working. We were in import-export, especially Turkish Delight. You know, the candy?"

"Mmm," I murmured, face upturned to the sky, searching fruitlessly for stars. I knew that Ibo, full name Ibrahim Heyreddin, came from a rich family.

"We lived in one of these what're called '*yah*'s – these giant wooden mansions along the Bosporus. Ours was one of the biggest, and hundreds of years old. Sold to my grandfather by the descendents of the original pasha who'd built it. They were pissed." He was quiet. I'd been so enjoying the mental trip he was taking me on that I opened my eyes, startled at having been left stranded. A strange look crossed his face. He made a visible effort to compose himself, and then continued, in a less-dreamy voice. "We kept our yacht in Bebek Bay where we could see its sail lights twinkling at night. Assuring us, as we sat on the veranda eating delicacies, that the poor people in the hills above us had not yet sunk our ships. That the Muslim hard-liners hadn't taken our pleasures yet. God, we were smug. I mean, they were good people, my family, but they had such a sense of entitlement. Most of the people in our neighborhood were much worse. They looked down on people who had less than they did, which was almost everyone." His face was twisted into a scowl. "I hate smugness."

I thought of the two smuggest people I knew: Abdus and Christia. I wondered if Ibo hated those two, if they twisted his thoughts and his face as thoughts of his past did. I despise loose tongues, yet sometimes something will come out of my mouth, unbidden, that reeks indisputably of gossip. "The other day I saw Abdus be really mean to a grocery store worker and I just thought, 'How *dare* you?' It was the ultimate in smugness. That's why I was standing alone: everyone wants me to make nice-nice with him and I can't, not in good conscience." I waved a forkful of korma in the air. "I feel weird even eating his food."

I waited to see how Ibo would react, if he would judge me harshly for talking about his friend, as I judged myself. "Let me tell you a story," he said thoughtfully. Goody, I thought. I leaned back into my chair, plumping the pillow behind my head, and closed my eyes. "When I was little, my father used to tell me about a safari he went on in Africa with his father. On the way out into the bush, they'd seen a herd of elephants and my grandfather managed to shoot and kill one of them. The 'natives' who were basically slaves on the trip, had been forced,

181

over their objections, to chop off the elephant's head and carry it with the group on their hunt." He paused. "Horrifying, right?"

"Ugg," I concurred.

"But," he continued, "not all that remarkable in those days. So then on the way back my father, who was barely an adult – maybe sixteen, seventeen…and still sensitive, you know? -- saw the bones of the elephant. They'd been picked clean by vultures and other predators. But, and this is the part that kills me, the other elephants were still there. They were picking up the bones of the dead elephant. Caressing them. They didn't leave even when they saw my father's band of elephant-killers. They just stared from afar. And after awhile they parted to show a baby elephant, on its knees before what must have been its mother's bones, and crying. He said the sound was unmistakable: a baby crying for its mother. My father, at no small cost to his new-won manhood, begged the rest of the party to return the head, to reunite the corpse. They refused. However, when they got back to the base camp the elephant's head was gone. He knew the guides had done as he asked, of their own accord -- as they had wanted to do from the start.

"What came out of all this was that in our family we were taught, basically, that if elephants can be so sensitive then surely any human being can. Even though we were rich and we did not give all that filthy lucre away to the rest of the equally-deserving world, we did always try to be civil and fair at least. To everyone, no matter what. That's something I find very important." He paused. "So many people don't, though."

From the half-opened door, we could hear the sultry rhythms of Antonio Carlos Jobim. Ibo cupped his ear, listening closely for a moment. "He's singing about heartbreak. In Brazil, they have this concept called 'saudade.' It's like a bittersweet type of sadness that comes from nostalgia, and when the Brazilians sing about it - it's a also a music genre - we can all feel what they are feeling, you know? When you hear it you just feel, I don't know how to say this...As if it's all very sad and very sweet at the same time. Love. Lust. Loss.

"We have something like this in Turkish. It is called 'cile.' Like Chile, the country – 'chee-lay.'" He looked over at me and, as if sensing my need to stay quiet and listen, continued talking. " In Istanbul, any night, you can find this music being sung all over, from small cafes in the old neighborhoods to hip nightclubs in Taksim where the kids yearn for a little something to go with their electropop. Cile means sorrow, but also something more indefinable. Still, we all, young and old, know exactly what it means. Heartbreak. Lost innocence. It's a music of sweet pain.

"Hell," he concluded, "with all our earthquakes and other sorts of unrest we Turks have, even the muezzin are singing cile! Five times a day: cile."

We sat still and listened to the lilting Brazilian music, with its mournful, longing words set to exquisite melodies, and the wind blew around us. After awhile, Ibo lifted his glass in a toast. " Ah, I understand it," he said with a sad sigh. "Looks like you do too, Annie. Here's to we lonely souls!"

I raised my glass to him, a smile of comradeship on my lips. He shook his head, though, and did not return my smile. His mood had changed from wistful to irritated. "No. I should be realistic, for god's sake...it's not just us! We are all so alone in the end. And lonely. And, while some of us write songs or poems to cope, others can't be bothered to protect or comfort their fellow creatures in these ways.

"Obviously," he concluded indignantly, "it turns some of us bad."

My mind went immediately to Christia. Had her loneliness turned her bad? Had loneliness turned her killer bad? And, more pressing, what was Ibo referring to? I decided to be direct. "Do you mean, by any chance, Christia?"

He started. "What makes you think that?" Realizing he probably looked guilty, he looked me very earnestly in the eyes. "I just – you caught me off guard. Believe it or not I'd-I'd...forgotten about that!"

Nonplussed, I took a deep swallow of wine. "That's hard for me to believe, being as I've become totally obsessed, but maybe you're just a normal person." I spoke lightly, as I was trying to put him back on his ease. If he knew something, he'd never reveal it while feeling attacked. I marveled at my cunning: I was becoming a master of manipulation and I didn't like it. For reasons of expediency, however, I continued. "Weren't you working with Christia on some project?"

"She was helping me, yes."

He was not being particularly forthcoming. I tried another tack. "You specialize in before-common-era Turkey, right?" This was starting to feel like one of those stuffy interdepartmental mixers.

"Yes. Or the area now known as Turkey. Women in particular. My mother was one of the few feminists in Turkey when I was growing up, so I had a lot of schooling in that from early on. So, yes, I study B.C.E. 'Turkish' women. In religious context, obviously; but then in those millennia – well, until recently, actually – it was all about religion. Makes it a more inclusive field. Anthropology, archeology, religion – it's all pretty much the same when you go back that far. Just different angles."

"Um, how did Christia help you?"

He cleared his throat, looking uncomfortable. "She knew a lot about Queen Puduhepa, a Hittite Queen. You would be interested in her too, I'd bet. She was the wife of King Hattusili, but what modern scholars find most amazing is she was his *equal*, too. She was a chief priestess in the 13th century B.C.E. Some people call her 'the first feminist.' Christia had written an article about her, at least I think that's

184

how I made the connection…There's a link on the Women's Studies homepage that connects scholars who are interested in various historical figures… "

Ibo rather abruptly got up and excused himself to use the bathroom. I stayed on the terrace, sipping the remains of my wine and picking at my food. The breeze was increasing and I pulled my scarf around me. I was warm where it touched my skin. After five minutes or so, Ibo returned, with freshly-filled glasses of red wine for us both.

"I know I seem nervous, but I am innocent of any wrongdoing." A faint accent had crept into his voice from the stress. "I am going to tell you, Annie, in fact I've been going on and on trying to figure out how, precisely, to do so. Several strange things have happened. A possibly significant note was found next to Christia. And then, someone was in my office. My things were disturbed, door left open. I think the police are after me. Or, perhaps, the *killer* is after me, for it is not me." He looked at me imploringly.

To my shame, I was thinking of myself again, since he'd brought up the "significant" note, as well as intruders in his office. I hoped I hadn't left anything incriminating behind in his office, on top of having written said note. I returned his gaze with steady encouragement, willing him to continue, while inwardly seething with nerves.

He did. "Part of the note was about a ritual text from Hattusa, a prayer to the sun goddess of Arrina, attributed to Queen Puduhepa." What? That certainly wasn't my note! I felt the tension leave my body. I hadn't been aware of how stiffly I'd been holding myself. Listening more compassionately to Ibo now, I focused on the present conversation. Ibo explained that Puduhepa was a very powerful woman, who ruled in stead for her young son Tuthaliya IV after her husband's death. Puduhepa had served the protective goddess Ishtar, but had turned to the infernal goddess of the underworld, Lelvani, when she

185

desperately needed help due to her husband's ill health. When her husband was dead, she'd used her newfound power to build a temple to Lelvani, and to open it as a refuge for orphans and widows. "These people had no one," he said, eyes shining with pride over his long-dead subject, "but Puduhepa became their protector and mother figure.

"She was a good mother, too, from what we can tell. The seal of Tuthaliya IV is the only known royal seal to depict the names of both father and mother. Assuming she wasn't so domineering as to demand it, we think the son wanted her name on his seal.

"She was that rare thing: a woman both beloved – by her son, by her subjects, especially the temple women and children – and powerful."

"Amazing," I exclaimed. "Everybody always acts as if women had zero power once patriarchy came into vogue, like, once people discovered that sperm is one-half of the baby-makin' equation. It's great to hear another perspective. I've never been able to believe that all women were kept down for millennia until the suffragists. Not that sexism didn't exist, of course, but there have always been exceptions. Like Pu—uh..."

"Puduhepa. And that's not the only evidence," he said excitedly. "I might as well tell you that there is more from Puduhepa's court about to come into the light of day.I can't really talk about it, though." He changed the subject; managing to distract me with more talk of Christia: "Anyway, they asked me to look at a some notes that were found on Christia's desk, but that was a few days ago. Now I think, because I am involved with the subject matter, they suspect me. Rather than seeing me as an ally. My friend Brenda, an honest person, told them I was one of the people who saw Christia that day. She could not lie on my behalf, no matter how strong our friendship. I would not have had it otherwise. For all her forthrightness she's suspected now, too, or so I hear."

"I heard that too." I admitted. "Actually, I know Brenda, sort of. She was working with Christia too, right? On another foremother of feminism. Oh yeah, Kassia. Byzantine Empire?" He nodded. I pictured Brenda in my mind. No matter how hard I tried, I simply could not imagine her becoming violent, though I knew that might not mean much. "I don't think she would hurt a fly," I told Ibo. I kept my thoughts about quiet walkers carrying big sticks to myself.

"No, it is not her fault. But the religion department faculty. Maybe one of them could defend me?" His voice grew angry again. "They are the very definition of evil! These people do not have a kind word for anyone. They look out only for themselves. Professor Redmund actually told me I should talk to a lawyer, not to him. Not because he had no way to help me, mind you, but because he couldn't be bothered to do so." As he talked, Ibo was becoming more and more animated, almost manic. He waved his hands around wildly as he continued. "And the junior faculty! They act as if someone's got them on a leash! 'No, I can't stir things up;' 'I believe you, Ibrahim, but I have no voice here.' What is that? These people are heartless."

On many levels, I agreed with him, but I was feeling eased by the wine, and in an increasingly expansive mood. All I said was, "Academia is the wrong place to bring honor into the equation. I --"

With an indignant grunt, Ibo lifted his head from the chair, where he'd collapsed in exhaustion. "Yes, that's it! These people have no sense of honor. Please, continue." He settled back into his chair.

"Are they pompous? Definitely. But evil – I don't know."

"But that's just it. Evil isn't flashy. It's not extraordinary, it's passive. It's banal. Sins of omission far, far outnumber those of commission. That's what permeates this world we live in. You either actively are good or you're letting evil have its wily, quiet way."

And we'd both thought I'd needed some cheer. I felt tired.

"What's your stance?" he demanded. Once again, as he had that day in his tiny office, sweet, stable Ibo was acting somewhat belligerent

"I try to do good. But I often fail," I admitted. "Even tonight I did something I regret. I shouldn't've criticized Abdus to you and I am sorry."

"At least you care about how you behave. What I am seeing lately is people who believe in nothing at all, except maybe the gods of lust and money." There was great sadness in his voice, and something that sounded like regret. I shook my head in melancholy agreement.

The wind was getting strong on the balcony, picking up small bits of debris and swirling them around. My eyes were watering from the dust, as were Ibo's. Or maybe he was crying. His voice barely carried over the howling of the wind. "Doesn't anyone believe in truth anymore? Or is that just too old-fashioned?"

A merry jingling announced our pretty hostess. "You two must be freezing! Come inside and have some cocoa with Bailey's in it. Yum."

"Yum," I agreed, standing up and, with Ibo, following Kalinka inside. The warm air of the great room, scented with spices and rich chocolate, welcomed me back into the festive mood that reigned among the guests. I had been so engrossed in my conversation with Ibo that I'd forgotten I was eagerly awaiting Tomás' arrival. He'd shown up while I'd been outside, and had made his way all the way to the far end of the room, to, in fact, the corner I'd earlier been standing in all alone. Now, there were a half-dozen people standing there together and conversing over loud reggae.

Tomás was wearing a dark turtleneck with wool trousers. Brown wing tips peaked out from under the hem of his pants. Even from a distance – and that was a big room – he exuded confident masculinity. He was being quiet, as usual, but I felt, and I'm sure that many others did too, that were he to say something it was sure to be worthwhile. I felt my body humming, becoming more alive and attuned to everything around me in response to his presence.

By the door to the terrace, Kirpal and Gretel were having a heated discussion about adult baptism. I joined them as Kirpal was saying,"Knowing who you are is powerful. From early childhood, I knew who I was: I was a Sikh, like my father."

"Balony! How can you know who you are as a child? Religiously speaking, I mean. You could be raised a Moonie and think that's the only right way until, until, well, indefinitely, unless something comes along to change your mind."

"Well, I think –"

"Wait! I'm not done! While you were busy being a manly Sikh, like your father, where was your mother, huh?"

Kirpal yelped with indignation. "Men and women are considered equal in Sikhism!"

"In scripture, yes," Gretel retorted. "But in practice? Day-to-day life? I don't think so!"

Even-minded, calm Kirpal was getting flustered. "It's evident you know everything. Why even talk to anyone when you're on that level? If you're so exalted…Hey, Annie," he turned to me with relief, "We are just having a, ahem, good-natured argument about, basically, how I'm wrong about everything." He looked at Gretel with a crooked grin. To my surprise, she smiled back. This was looking more and more like true love.

Ibo and Kalinka had joined other conversations. I left Kirpal and Gretel to their own devices and returned to the food table. While it was strange to be the guest of someone who openly disliked me, and whom I disliked, there was something wonderful to me about being shoeless in such opulent surroundings with so many people. We were probably all sated by now, and yet the food table was still covered with a veritable

189

cornucopia of foodstuffs. How sensuous it all felt, and how beautiful. I was ready to talk to Tomás.

Someone had switched the disc and the room swirled and flowed with Sufi whirling dervish music - rhythmic drumming, reed flute dancing, plangent song. I heard snatches of conversation as I threaded my way through small, chatting knots of people, crossing the long room. From one group I heard just this fragment: "...thought it was Ibo who wrote the note..." As I didn't recognize any of the people in that conversation, I could only wonder which note they were talking about, though I thought I knew.

Two servants, a young, dark-eyed Latina I'd spoken to briefly when we first arrived, and the older white man, somewhat stooped, whom they called "Freddy," were passing trays of champagne for a toast. I overheard Kalinka saying, "Oh, Freddy lives in. He does the cleaning, shopping, etc.," and I noted to myself how different she sounded talking to someone else – in this case a bejeweled South Asian woman – how affected, really. Perhaps she was one of those type of people I was beginning to become aware of who change their demeanor entirely according to their audience. Like Abdus.

I couldn't shake the feeling that there must by rights be something sinister about someone who would behave in such a multiplicitous way. I thought about how most people, the people I thought of as more or less people of integrity, could be recognized as, in some essential way, *themselves* -- no matter where they were. A person without a central core might be capable of virtually anything. Self-destructive promiscuity, for instance. Lying. Murder.

As I passed nearby the entrance doorway, I decided on a quick detour to the loo to check if I had any spinach between my teeth. Partway down the hall, I heard a low, husky voice talking tenderly to my right. Without thinking, not expecting to actually see such an intimate scene, I turned my head to see the speaker. Through a doorway, the dim hall light revealed only Abdus; his companion was obscured by shadow. Somehow, I was frozen in place. I knew Kalinka was in the middle of a conversation, and yet Abdus' voice had sounded so seductive.

He was not pleased to see me. Our eyes locked. His flashed. "I'd watch out, Annie, if I were you. Little girls shouldn't mess with bad boys like *moi*." Putting his arm protectively around his companion, he turned back around to give me one last grin, but his eyes were hard and cold.

Sometimes I want to shut out the whole world. This was one of those moments. I went into one of the guest bathrooms. It was as big as my apartment, and filled with marble surfaces, gold fixtures and all the amenities – a giant bathtub with whirlpool, a separate glass shower enclosure, a bidet next to the toilet, which had its own separate room…There, I rested my head in my hands and thought. What could make somebody so mean? Was he mean enough to murder someone? Or was the guilty one more like Philippe Perez-Throgmorton, who, as with Brenda, seemed on the surface incapable of hurting a fly?

I seemed to be doing a lot of my thinking in bathrooms of late, though I hadn't come to any useful conclusions.

When I emerged, Tomás was waiting for me. He had a plate with little heaps of different foods and an opened bottle of *prosecco* in his hands. No forks, or glasses.

"There's a balcony off of the bedroom next door. Care to join me?" I could see he'd had a drink or two to embolden himself, but then so had I.

"But of course!" We took a turquoise mohair blanket off an ottoman and went out the door onto a small terrace. This one had topiary myrtle bushes all along the ledge, so that it seemed almost as if one was looking at the night sky over the horizon of a distant forest. We spread out the blanket and sat down. Tomás handed me the *prosecco* and I took a nice, long swallow. I tasted peaches and stars.

Tomás dropped a morsel of food in my mouth and, while I listened, he smoked and told me about growing up in Miami's Little Havana with his elegant and loving but somewhat distant parents Dahlia and Orlando. He told me about his grandparents' moldering away their lives in *Grey Gardens*-style decay, mourning their beloved son Tomás, Dahlia's brother, and endlessly discussing *nuestra Cuba Libre* – and doting on their only grandson. He talked for longer than I'd ever imagined he could, of burro rides at his birthday parties, of family ski trips to Switzerland with cousins from his father's side…

He told me how so many Cuban expatriates are like White Russians, yearning for a noble and illusive past: "So many *viejos* in *guayaberas*, solving the world's commie problems while puffing fat cigars. I don't miss that too much," he laughed. "But the smells! I miss the smells. *Café Cubano*. Fresh mangoes. *Arroz con coco. Con gandules.* That delicious rice that nobody else can make. I don't care what you put with it. Here, eat some more!"

"*Cariño*, I am *full*. Brrr." I huddled in a little closer to him. I thought maybe he would put his arm around me but he didn't.

"You're cold," he said, abruptly, "We'd better go inside."

Unsure if I'd offended him by not wanting more food, I arose and, after gathering up the almost-empty plate and empty wine bottle, we strode inside. The night had grown so much colder since my earlier conversation with Ibo. Despite the warmth of the wine, my face and hands were icy to the touch. Tomás felt around and turned on a lamp. The room was done all in shades of blue and orange, from the mohair blanket we'd borrowed for our terrace picnic, to the furniture, to the deep orange velvet curtains. Feeling dizzy from wine, company, surroundings, I sat down on a pale blue pouf at the foot of an overstuffed armchair upholstered in nubby saffron and aquamarine striped raw silk.

"Look at this." Tomás sounded a bit short of breath. Above us on the wall of the bedroom was a Turkish miniature painting, depicting a woman reclining on an ornate, mosaic-covered dais, her sex exposed like an offering to the turbaned man seated on the ground in front of her. I blushed, more at what was going through my own mind than at the subject matter of the lovely painting.

"Nice," I said finally.

He sat down on the armchair next to me and took my hands in his, warming them. His hands were rougher and much bigger than mine, and they were very warm. I saw kindness in his eyes, and a far-away pain. He seemed to be struggling with himself. Finally, he said, "Would you like to come over? I could make you a *Café Cubano* to fortify you."

I barely trusted my voice. "Sure," I said, casual-like.

In the vestibule, Abdus and Kalinka were seeing some of their guests out. Abdus turned to us with an accusing look. "You two missed the toast." He announced. "'To Christia: She knew how to live.'"

"I heard it," Tomás said through clenched teeth. There was a look of disgust on his face. "Now if you'll excuse me." He headed off to find the nearest bathroom.

Kirpal and Gretel were leaving together. Underneath the banter, there was a subtle yet palpable aura of attraction between the two. As I waited for Tomás, I watched while Gretel slipped her feet back into her stilettos. I laughed a little inwardly at how much our Wisconsin farm girl had changed – and how much she hadn't. With her stilettos and form-fitting black dress, she wore a sensible tan-colored trenchcoat and puffy nylon gloves. Kirpal didn't seem to mind: he was looking at her legs with his jaw hanging open. Only a woman – or a gay man -- could tell just how *off* her sartorial combination was; to any heterosexual man the stiletto heels would signal s-e-x. The rest of the outfit could've been a paper bag.

Brandi was on her way out, too. The cellist had turned out to be gay, hence, not a potential fling, but he was fun, and they were headed downtown to an underground club. She offered me a piece of bubblegum, one of those nasty bright-orange flavors. "Oh, gum! Thanks" I almost gagged at the thought of chasing Abdus and Kalinka's fine wine and food with a toxic-chemical sweet. I covered my mild disgust with effusive thanks. "Really. It's, um, my favorite thing to chew and not swallow!" I put it in my pocket. Brandi gave me a quizzical look. "Really! I'll save it for when I really *need* it!"

Tomás, already shod, had only to retrieve his coat and we were off. We hopped into a cab and headed uptown to his place. I don't remember what we talked about in the cab – nothing important I am sure. I suppose we were both aroused, possibly to the exclusion of rational thought. At Tomás' apartment, however, his answering machine showed 15 messages. I tactfully placed myself as far away from the machine as possible, sitting down at the upright piano in the far corner of the room and drinking in every aspect of my surroundings as subtly as I could. The place was larger than most graduate students' apartments, but white and boxy, without softening touches. Tomás, perhaps inundated as most first-years were by schoolwork, had yet to finish moving in, and there were still several unpacked boxes on the floor. The place did not feel lived in. I leafed through the scores on the music stand: Chopin, Schubert, Bach. Sure, his place was nothing special, but he must really play the piano, I observed to myself with a shiver of pleasure.

After listening to the first, a nervous message from his parents who were apparently visiting the city and wanted very much to see him, immediately if not sooner, he turned the machine off and told me he'd better deal with his messages, that he'd have to take a raincheck. There was something flat in his voice, and his eyes, so open mere moments before, appeared physically open but emotionally shuttered.

He apologized, I left.

I decided to walk the ten or so blocks back to my place. I had a lot to think about. Lately, truth was becoming more and more elusive. My love with Nicholas had seemed permanent, but it was not. He'd not even said goodbye to me before leaving Abdus' party, never mind getting jealous of Tomás. He'd hardly even noticed me beyond his defense of Abdus. I knew something had changed. Before, something had sometimes flickered across his face, a shadow of the love we'd had. All that was over, I thought.

Now Tomás was acting odd, and I didn't know if it was something to do with me or with the 15 messages. His hot and cold behavior made him all the more mysterious, more compelling. Of course, I needed to be sure to distinguish between sexy-mysterious and asshole-mysterious. Tomás seemed a man at war with himself. Why? Did he have a girlfriend back in Miami? Had he gotten someone pregnant? Was he questioning his sexuality? Did he kind of like me and kind of...*not* like me? My mind was going in circles.

Oh well, I told myself sternly, it was too late to worry too much about the ways of men.

Almost home, just before dawn, the undisturbed air surrounded me with hope. I relished that one time of day when the city was quiet. I looked forward with pleasure to my dog's stinky, warm breath under the covers, and to the curl of my cat behind my knees. It would be luxurious to sleep as long as I desired.

Chapter Seven – Practice

"Inasmuch,then, as marriage has to deal with
such external trials, the thing to do, of course, is to make
them internal."

Soren Kierkegaard, *Either/Or*

The strains of *Andrea Chenier* filled the steamy bathroom where
Philippe was performing his morning ablutions. In 18th-century France,
in the fictionalized life of the great guillotined poet, a mother was dead.
Pity, that. Philippe's Mumsy had never inspired a great deal of filial
adoration in him, but then she hadn't been the motherly type, had she?
Roughly scrubbing his skin with a thick towel until it was dry and
glowing pink helped Philippe to wake up in the morning, especially
since he hadn't been sleeping well since his wife's death.

"*Ed è la morte che mi salva!*" he hummed along,
absentmindedly and almost-tunelessly. He had a lot to think about.
Detective Tomasino would be stopping by shortly and he had to make a
decision about what he would tell him. It all depended on how close
they were to charging him with his wife's murder.

Marriage was hard -- even in death.

Still humming a wordless tune, he cleared a circle in the mirror with a corner of his towel and looked himself squarely in the face. If he pulled back his cheek skin just so he could pass for a man in his late thirties. Not bad for an old coot, he told himself. He combed his hair carefully, and then mussed it up so there were no more comb-stripes of scalp showing through.

He wiped the glass again, making seven circles counterclockwise. With extraordinary intensity of focus, he gazed into his own eyes. You have to do this, he told himself. He couldn't go on being wishy-washy. Even the opera he was listening to warned him to act, to take a stand (but *which* stand, precisely?). Philippe shivered at what had happened to the aristocratic Chenier in his ambivalence over the Revolution! Of course, so many of the privileged had burned because of the mob *mentalité*. It wasn't really their fault that they were rich, any more than it was the fault of those in the mob that they were compelled to kill as a mob. And didn't Maddalena sound pretty singing about watching her mother burn?

He shook himself a little to clear his head, and then made his face completely blank. It was time to practice his "honest" look. He softened his jaw and kept his eyes wide-open, though not too wide. He stayed like that for a few minutes while running various conversational scenarios through his head. And then he winked.

*

Brandi Blumenthal woke up with cotton mouth. Eggs, she thought. With Tabasco. Then, a *lot* of water. Or, no, she thought through the fog that was her brain, I'll skip all that and have a Bloody Mary. Something to shut out the images of last night's depravities that were beginning a fast-forward dance in her head. She'd always believed you could be a really good, kind, compassionate person and still be kinky, but after last night she wasn't sure that held true in all cases.

From somewhere deep in her brain there came a tickling feeling. She'd forgotten something, something she needed to tell Annie. About Abdus. What was it? Untangling herself from her hot-pink plush bedspread and leopard-print satin sheets, Brandi turned on the light next to her bed. Her beaded red silk lampshade gave off a muted light that under other circumstances, would've seemed innocuous. Now, she squeezed her eyes shut in shock, waiting for her exhausted pupils to adjust, slowly. Her blinds were all down and very little light seeped into what she thought of as her "dungeon."

After slowly, carefully, stepping out of bed, she practiced walking in a straight line to the kitchen, where she drew herself a glass of lukewarm water from the tap and choked down two aspirin. She stood for a minute in front of the open refrigerator and then shut the door. She drew her kimono tighter over her pink babydoll negligee and shivered. No, she wasn't hungry.

After she'd been up for about ten minutes, had used the bathroom and collected herself to a reasonable extent, she called Annie. When they got off the phone, she opened a white lacquered cabinet, with glitter and sequins glued all over it in swirling waves and spirals – her "office," she called this piece of furniture, which also held her computer -- and extracted several books she needed for her semiotics paper. She didn't like her school interests displayed for just anyone to see.

A few hours into her reading, she remembered what she'd meant to tell Annie: at Abdus' party, she'd heard Abdus and his brother arguing. Ishaq was threatening to curtail Abdus' allowance. "You're good for nothing," he'd said, and, "You've never lifted a finger to help our family. Father and I have been supporting you your whole life, and for what? For this *indolence*?" His voice had dripped with scorn and rage. "This debauchery is not acceptable for a Syed. We are well-to-do, but we are hard-working too."

Abdus had been groveling, to Brandi's astonishment. Practically whimpering. He'd begged his brother to reconsider to no avail. Ishaq had concluded by saying, "We will give you one more month. One month ago, we said the same thing, but we have some mercy. Why don't you take this month to practice living within your means?" With that, he had left Abdus' giant palace of an apartment.

Crazy, thought Brandi, with a shrug. These rich people were really over the top.   Glancing toward her rococo "office" she read what she'd written in big cursive script with her trusty gold glitter pen across the midline of both bedazzled doors, her *credo*, from the Baroness Elsa von Freytag-Loringhoven: "Illstarred women like me are sexscience's tools to make men confront their illogic." Ain't it the truth, she thought to herself with a half-smile, ain't it just the truth.

*

In my neighborhood, the sounds of cooking and conversation began just after church on Sundays. Here and there, gentrification had completely replaced the old apartment complexes and businesses, but the Latino community was still the majority population. This was abundantly clear on temperate Sundays when multi-generational families could be seen promenading along streets lined with shops advertising all kinds of *pollo* and *"Comida China-Latina,"* shopping for groceries for the afternoon meal, and greeting neighbors with friendly, languorous *"Bueeeenas..."*

As the tempting smell of cooking wafted into my apartment from the apartment next door to mine, I dragged myself out of bed and into my kitchen. I inspected the absurd contents of my own cupboard. It was not, strictly speaking, bare, but what was available was certainly meager: a few dried out baby carrots, some lentil soup I'd intended to reheat days ago, half a packet of tofu dogs, congealed Ring Dings…THe leftovers of my leftovers.

The light on my answering machine was blinking rapidly. I pressed the "play" button. The first message was from my mother: "Hi Anne, it's your mother-figure." She adopted a mock-nagging tone, "No one loves you like your mother. No one worries like your mother. Haven't heard from you all week...You O.K.? Love you. Call your Grandmother." My best friend Lark had called from Connecticut to plan our annual winter solstice get-together. She was wondering if she could invite Nicholas too, since, "even though you guys broke up you're still friends and we love him and we had so much fun last year, playing in the snow, decorating the tree...He and Ted could talk about music together again, and we could bake." I felt myself tightening up. I didn't know where things stood, or where they were going, between Nicholas and me. "Of course we'll be happy if it's just you. More cookies for us," she added, concluding with a cheery, "Loving you." Nicholas had called to talk about Thanksgiving. Gretel had called, in the morning while I slept in – I'd reached home at 6:30 a.m., bed by 6:35 -- to talk over her walk home with Kirpal: "I think there's something between us." Duh. Otherwise, why argue some much? "I mean, nothing happened, but let's talk." The last message was from my mother too. She'd called around noon and was wondering if I was up yet.

I called her immediately, to ease her mind. She picked up after the first ring. "Ann? I've been having this feeling that something was going on with you."

"I'm just stressed-out, Ma. Graduate school."

"Are you sure? We're very connected, you know."

I sighed. "I know. Listen, you don't even want to know. There's been a murder at the University of New York and everyone is all up in arms."

"Well, I heard about *that*. It's big news out here." Mom lived in Connecticut, in one of the small towns near swanky Greenwich that house mere mortals, including less-financially-fortunate Greenwich

200

divorcées such as herself. "You didn't – *know* that woman, did you? Reading between the lines she sounded like…not the nicest person. You always wonder when investigators say they have 'many possible suspects.'" This last bit came with a small chuckle.

"They just don't know who did it, that's all."

"Now c'mon. How many suspects would they have if someone killed you? None. My perfect daughter." I could imagine the smile of satisfaction on her face.

I disagreed. "For one, Nicholas. Like, after I broke up with him he made me a tape with this song from the Radiohead album *OK Computer* and the chorus goes 'I hope that you choke.' Or --"

"Wait! You don't think Nicholas is going to kill you, do you?" she asked, in barely-concealed panic.

"Of course not. Ma! I'm just saying –"

"O.K., O.K. But that woman was in his department, right? So…you think he killed her? I think I even remember you two talking about her. You called her 'Kristi,' to make fun of her because she was snooty." Even my mother knew we called her Kristi. What if the note was made public?

"Ma, I've gotta go. No food in the house. Low blood sugar."

"Go, go. Why do you do this to yourself? Don't just eat junk, O.K.? If you eat a bagel, get some protein on it."

"I will."

"Hummus or cream cheese. Be safe."

I knew my mother would try not to think about my being in danger, but that it would torment her, however irrational her fear. From what I'd seen, that was the way of the mother. I reassured myself I'd done my best to assuage her worry, but after a few minutes I found myself calling her back.

"Mom?"

"Annie!" She was so happy to hear my voice, clearly relieved I'd not yet been attacked. "I was just thinking about you."

Maybe I could distract her from my being in potential danger. "I was just wondering if you had any ideas about who killed Christia?"

Pleased to be included in the drama, she told me she'd read that the police were looking closely at other members of the department, following a rumor about some "discovery" she'd made recently. Her money was, however, "on someone who killed her for love or passion. How could something academic be that important? Anyway, academics are all cold fish," she said confidently. "I should know. Two advanced degrees and where has it gotten me?"

"Oh Mom, you could've gotten a job in academia, you just didn't want it."

"You're right, love. Now go eat some food."

"Thanks. I love you."

The phone rang as soon as we hung up. Brandi had just awakened, and she was feeling the effects of her adventures. After we'd said hello, she told me her cellist friend had been "one crazy-ass classical-music-playin' alternative-lifestyle-livin' freak." They'd stayed out until 10 a.m., and she'd apparently seen sights that shocked even her jaded eyes.

"Whew, ecstasy hangover," she concluded. "What happened after we left?"

"We went back to his place and…" I paused, embarrassed for Tomás.

"C'mon, mami," she urged.

"He had a bunch of messages from his overprotective parents and so I had to go home."

"Quit lying."

"Strange but true."

"Omigod, that is like the worst thing I've ever heard. New shoes! Immediately! Run, don't walk." Her tone got more serious. "Honey, when are you gonna get with this guy? You really like him!"

"Soon." Smiling, I stretched out on my couch. "Oh, and I think he's Catholic. His apartment is really empty. He hasn't even unpacked yet and we're in – what, November? But he has this big crucifix above his bed. I saw it when I sneeked a peek, just through the door…"

"Catholics can be pretty kinky. All that guilt." From her voice, I could tell Brandi was smiling too.

Our talk turned to our semiotics papers, due that week. I had, fortunately, finished mine – and I never wanted to discuss illuminated manuscripts again -- but she was planning to pull an all-nighter.

I was starving. I found a few Wheat Thins in a high cabinet and shoved them down my gullet. Promising myself a real feast when I finally left the house, I dialed Lark's number. I needed to talk to someone I trusted who was not even remotely involved in Christia's murder. I asked her if I could have some of her time to spew out the whole story of my week.

"There's nothing I would enjoy more," she replied. She explained that they were just vegetating: watching the travel channel from their king-sized bed, known as "the marshmallow," and trying to muster the energy to go downstairs and make a late lunch. I explained to her that Christia had been killed, telling her about my note and about how practically everyone I knew was either a suspect or scared or both.

"Who do you think did it?" she asked, when I had finished.

"That's just it. I have no idea. Her husband is very strung out, maybe from her death, maybe from killing her. Nicholas' friend Abdus was close to her, and he strikes me as a bad person. Though a killer, I don't know…The guy I have a crush on was one of the last people to see her. Some of the faculty could have had various motives vis-à-vis this discovery she'd mentioned. My friend Ibo – he works in her department -- is very bitter, and he's been working on project with her or something. On this priestess from three thousand years ago."

"That sounds interesting."

"Oh yeah, I'll tell you all about her when we come. After her husband died she started this whole worship of this underworld goddess, and saved all these marginalized people by bringing them officially under the goddess's protection in the temple."

"What was she called?"

"Puduhepa."

"Never heard of her. I'll look her up online. Who else?"

"Well, there's always Nicholas."

Lark gasped. "You can't be serious," she managed to exclaim in a small voice.

"I wish I weren't. He's been acting really bizarre. Lying to me about his whereabouts and stuff like that. He was one of the last people to see her too."

"Wow. I'm sorry if I offended you about Nicholas, given the circumstances. Not that I think he could kill someone, but I'm surprised he's being such a jerk. He always worshipped you. Oh, I'm so sorry."

"No, it's just that I think we should wait until I figure out why he's being so weird. I'd love him to come if things work out. We're supposed to go to North Carolina next week, so I should know after that. Is that too late?"

"Of course not."

I pulled on some leggings and a big, cozy hooded sweatshirt. Grabbing Pepita's leash, I headed out the door. The bagel store down the block allowed dogs, department of health be damned. The phone rang once again, but I let the machine pick it up. It was Nicholas, sounding smug: "I just thought you ought to know. I heard there are two major new suspects. Guess who?" He waited for me to pick up the phone. "Oh well. You know you want to know. Professor Redmund and

204

– get this – Brenda Fujiki. I don't know why they're suspects, but suspects they are. So, that's the scuttlebutt…The *autre chose* I remembered was, Philippe said maybe she'd told her coven about her discovery. That's it. Toodles." I locked the door and went downstairs, wondering where he'd gathered all this information. It could have been from any number of sources, I concluded with a sigh of resignation. Academia really was a veritable snakepit of gossip.

On Broadway, Pepita pulled me along on the leash with her usual squirrel-hunting stubbornness. I passed lots of neighborhood families in their Sunday best. I felt partly envious, partly glad to be so free in my unmarried, childless state. One little boy of four or five asked if he could pet my dog and I told him he could.

"What's her name?"

"Pepita."

"*¡Mama, este perrito se llama Pepita!*" he cried, a look of surprised glee on his face. It made me feel so good to make someone happy, especially a child.

In the bagel shop, I ordered an everything bagel with cinnamon raisin cream cheese and a large fresh orange juice. I sat down with Pepita at my feet, enjoying the smell of freshly brewed coffee and the moist, bagel-y air. I had Colonial Fiction the next day, and I hadn't finished the assigned reading. I opened *The Chosen Place, the Timeless People*, and read, "…she brought her gaze to rest on Merle, kneeling in the dust beside Vere, her entire self given over to her grief…"

*

The doorbell rang, five minutes early. The doorman had let Detective Tomasino in without announcing him. Somehow, that made Philippe feel a little ill. He'd always had a decent relationship with the building staff, or so he thought.

Detective Tomasino was a redheaded, burly man, with a good helping of Irish from his Irish-Italian mother's side. He was a decent, no-nonsense type, who didn't as a rule care for men who were too…pretty. Philippe's hairdo bothered Detective Tomasino. It was too perfectly mussed, and Philippe was prone to running his index finger under the curl of his cowlick, which habit Detective Tomasino found immensely irritating. Nonetheless, Tomasino was an honest and fair man, and, in his gut, he didn't think Philippe was guilty. The trouble was, Philippe had no alibi. There was no real evidence against him, either, but in the absence of an alibi, well, most murders *were* committed by the spouse. What could he do? Without a firm alibi he was practically convicted pre-trial. Unbeknownst to Philippe, Andy Tomasino, bastion of blue-collar prejudice, possessor of human decency, was there to drag one out of him.

The two men shook hands. The detective noticed that Philippe was trembling a little. He wanted Philippe to feel at ease. "This is just routine Mr., ah, Throgmorton. I'll ask you a few questions and you answer to the best of your ability."

"Please, sit down." Philippe motioned towards the sleek leather couch. "For the record," he said in a tired voice, "it's Perez-Throgmorton. Pronounced like 'Paris,' but Peh-ris." He cleared his throat. Try not to sound so pompous, he warned himself. "Sir, eh…Regarding your questions. I shall do as best I can."

"Thank you." Detective Tomasino lowered himself onto the sofa, thinking he was getting too old and heavy for this kind of footwork. Especially on weekends, when he could be home with Marj and the kids. But then, working long hours had gotten him where he was. Not everyone made Detective before they turned forty. So why did he feel old?

He returned his attention to the matter at hand. "We have searched your wife's computer for evidence, but we don't have the password for her email. We've got our computer guys on it, but they're busy with other cases too. University authorities are putting a lot of heat on us to solve the case, but they're dithering over whether giving us her password is a privacy issue. Legal mumbo jumbo." Philippe knew Christia's password, he'd figured it out when she started hinting around about something extraordinary. Her discovery. He knew for a fact that her emails, at least from the last month, revealed nothing of interest to the case.

"Certainly," he murmured, "if you think it will be of help."

Detective Tomasino took out his notepad.

"It's 'Puduchris.' Philippe couldn't help but smile a little as he spelled the password aloud. "She chose it as a clever combination of an ancient queen's name and her own name. I believe there was also a pop-culture reference."

"Gotcha." To Philippe, Tomasino's expression was unreadable. "O.K. Next question. Do you have any idea what we should look for? I been hearing a lot of talk about some kind of ancient artifact. Like she'd discovered the holy grail, for crissakes. That doesn't fly with me, but who knows." Tomasino shifted his weight to the other buttock. "You know anything about this malarky?"

Philippe squirmed in the Eames chair, wondering what the detective was getting at. Why was he acting so chummy, rather like a stereotypical cop ("malarky"?) ? Why didn't he just come out and accuse him? And he had left that damnable aria from *Andrea Chenier* on repeat: *Son l'amore! Intorno è sangue e fango! Io son divino!* Love and blood and mud and divinity…Lordy, the waiting was agony.

Detective Tomasino waited for Philippe to respond. The man was pale and sweating. He knew something, but what? It was time to shake him up a little.

"I'm gonna lay my cards on the table, Mr. Throgmorton. Most people think it was

you who killed Christia Thompson." Philippe shuddered at the sound of his wife's name.

"There's a lot of people," Tomasino continued, his eyes steady on Philippe, "who want me to get this case tied up nice and neat and *quick*. Whatever you can tell me that will help me accomplish my goal here would be much appreciated. My guess is some kinda affair gone wrong, but what do I know. It could be something with the school thing, too, competition gone wrong, like some folks are saying. One or the other: affair or university. Gotta be. So my question is, are you gonna help me find your wife's killer or not?"

"Of course," Philippe said earnestly. "I *am* trying. If I may ask, what about the various notes and so forth that were found on her desk?"

"You mean like the stuff you wrote?"

"Eh…Whatever do you mean?"

"The…poetry?" Tomasino's voice held barely hidden contempt. Yeats could write poetry. Seamus Heaney. This guy? Not so much.

"Ah, yes. Er, I'm sure that doesn't indicate any guilt on my part."

You're guilty of writing bad poetry, thought Tomasino, but last he'd heard that wasn't a crime. "As far as I'm concerned, no, there's nothing whatsoever that indicates guilt on your part, Mr. Perez-Throgmorton."

Philippe flipped his hair out of his eyes and looked Detective Tomasino directly
in the face, incredulous. "You mean to say you believe I am innocent?"

Detective Tomasino allowed himself to allow Philippe to wait for just a few seconds before he replied. "I need your cooperation to prove it. I need an alibi."

Philippe was faced with an impossible choice. Helpless to stop his own racing mind, he flashed upon himself leaving Oxford. He saw himself torn between feeling bereft at his erstwhile lover's death and full of excitement for his new life in the states. Boarding the plane, he'd known he'd never set foot in Oxford again. There was just too much of a mess surrounding Raphael Kavitaris' death, for one thing. At first, the authorities had thought he'd died naturally, but the inquest had revealed he'd been poisoned. There was speculation that he'd committed suicide, but most people thought he'd been murdered.

Raphael's – secret, as usual -- lover at time of his death had been Philippe's dear friend Paul. Philippe and Paul had been chums since their undergraduate days at All Souls College. Each sensing in the other a kindred sensitive spirit, they'd gravitated toward one another from the outset. Paul was a dazzling beauty and filthy rich, but dressed in threadbare suits under his robes; Philippe's shabby gentility was more out of necessity than he cared to admit; but the two shared an aesthetic and a frailty that each tried to protect in the other. Philippe had heard later, through the grapevine, that they'd been called "the *castrati*" by the other students in their college. The nickname hadn't surprised him one bit, though he'd been glad he hadn't known about it at the time. His delicate sensibilities would've been wounded.

Although Philippe had felt betrayed – nay, devastated -- when he'd found out his ex- and his best friend were having an affair, he'd stood behind Paul once he came under suspicion for Raphael's murder. The vice-chancellor had questioned Philippe twice: once in regard to Paul, once as to his own whereabouts at the time of Raphael Kavitaris' death. He had been only too happy to explain that he'd spent the day in question with his dearest friend, Paul Terwilliger. He'd reiterated his statement, twice, to the Oxford constabulary.

Unfortunately, it had been determined that physical proximity was not an essential factor in Kavitaris' death, since he'd consumed his poison (a hard-to-detect, rarely used, yet widely available component of antifreeze, ethylene glycol) via his afternoon tea, the teabags in his cupboard having been at some point previously imbued with enough of the poison to kill forty Classics Fellows – or anybody else for that

209

matter. Naturally, the surplus of poison had called the suicide hypothesis into question. Also, the evidence found splattering his entire home of the diarrhea- and vomit-filled last hours of Kavitaris' life had seemed to indicate he hadn't quite known what was happening to him.

It might've been sticky for Philippe, this whole bit about the poison, but for the disappearance of Paul Terwilliger. His friend, bereft at his lover's death, and terrified of unjust imprisonment, had fled as soon as he'd realized he was about to be charged. As the Americans were wont to say, he'd "gone on the lam." Paul, with his numbered Swiss bank accounts and innocent, boyish face, had never been found.

The flood of memories was not all painful. He remembered running to meet his lover, thrumming with the fiery sap of youth, through Christ Church's enormous Tom Quad. He thought wistfully of the yellowed stone walls and the heavenward-tilting spires of the ultra-Gothic All Souls College, and of the way moss grew between the stones on the cobbled walkways, as if the people who walked on these stones were especially light…He recalled long days in the 17th-century Bodleian Library, perusing biblical codices and nipping from his silver pocket flask. There were wonderful nights in Carfax, the center of the old walled medieval town, nights where he'd toasted the four quarters of the world from what had felt like its intellectual and historical center. In certain pubs, dons and students drank together -- and more, as the nights wore on.

He and Paul Terwilliger had lived through those halcyon days together…Until, shortly before Philippe's marriage and emigration, his dear friend had fled.

On the afternoon of the day of Christia's death, Philippe had been mentoring Paul at his and Christia's home. Paul had been a fugitive since Raphael's death. He'd been crucified in the media at the time, and the mysterious death of an honored Classics Fellow was still fodder for the news vultures from time to time as the decade rolled on.

Paul had contacted Philippe a few weeks before Christia's death because he wanted to get his life back. He was determined to prove his innocence and, in his words, "sally forth anew." Paul was, however, a wreck, and nowhere near his goals. Old beyond his years, and struck with a tremor that had surely developed from many years in hiding, Paul would not serve as a good alibi for Philippe. Nor would exposure serve poor Paul.

Philippe resigned himself to his fate. "Detective Tomasino, I have told you all I can."

Andy Tomasino's eyes grew very, very cold. His frustration flooded his plump limbs with the zing of adrenaline, but he stayed completely still. And waited.

Philippe's inner turmoil had him veering from one course of action to another. He could tell the truth, thereby exposing his old friend. But Detective Tomasino might not even believe him once he'd met Paul! That was the kicker: he might go to all the trouble of establishing an alibi, only to find his alibi was not credible because the man who provided it was a longtime fugitive. Shifty-eyed Paul looked like a criminal, too, albeit perhaps a prosperous one.

Had Tomasino pressed him, Philippe would've never succumbed. It was the waiting that did him in; that, and the sound of his own thoughts careening around like banshees. Philippe was not entirely spineless, but he had never been good at waiting.

"Did you see these beautiful oil portraits?" Philippe gestured toward the hallway. Detective Tomasino gave an inward cheer of triumph. He wasn't sure how his witness would get there – or what this tangent had to do with anything he could think of – but his gut told him that Philippe was on his way to revealing everything he knew.

"At school I had a friend. He was the real thing. A true aristo. We, the Perez-Throgmortons, were the usual impoverished aristocrats with the rotting country estate, run to weed and sheep. We had the

211

education, the breeding...the *dogs*. We had those paintings. But almost no income left. His family still had money. Heaps and heaps of it. We became friends." Philippe hesitated. He looked confused, as if he wondered how he'd come to be talking about a long-ago friendship with a cop.

"You became friends," Tomasino prompted. "And?" He knew not to rush Philippe, but the man obviously needed guidance.

"And, ten plus years ago, he was drawn and quartered by the British Press for a murder he did not commit." Philippe realized his story was sounding increasingly suspicious, almost as if he, Philippe had committed this other murder. Oopsy. One-two-three-four-five-six-seven. Keep calm, he warned himself.

"This chap, a Paul Terwilliger, late of Liechtenstein, then Brazil, where he lived as Paul Rose, was here with me." There, he'd said it now. "The entire day," he added.

Tomasino thought for a moment. "Lemme get this straight. You're telling me that your friend, a fugitive murder suspect who managed to buy his freedom for over ten years on the lam, was here with you. And that proves your innocence."

"Yes."

Tomasino was incredulous. "This, I gotta tell the guys." He stood up with a little groan. "And I thought you actually knew something about Christia's death. Not that you killed her, just – knew something."

Philippe was still shaking. "Don't you want his whereabouts?"

"Not now. This'll do you more harm than good." He watched as Philippe, clearly suffused with expansive relief, straightened up in his seat. "Wait, you may as well give me his name and number." He scribbled the information in his almost-blank notepad. Standing, Tomasino towered over Philippe, who had sunk back into his chair looking deflated. "By the way, did you kill this other guy, the Greek professor?"

Philippe gasped. "No! I-I loved him."

"Hmm. Welp, don't take any trips. I'll be in touch." Tomasino painstakingly brushed an imaginary crumb off his trouser leg and then lumbered down the hallway and out the door without saying goodbye.

Paul would understand that I had to do it, Philippe consoled himself. He went to the kitchen and poured himself a tumbler of Scots whiskey to further his self-consolation. Bottoms up, he thought, as he poured the drink down his throat.

He stood looking around his kitchen. Christia hadn't been a cook, but she'd chosen singularly elegant appliances – the subzero refrigerator, the restaurant-style range...Quickly, his hand no longer shaking, he filled his glass again. Another drinky-poo would block out the image of Christia being buried. Her private interment had taken place that morning and he'd managed to stave off remembrance until his eyes had fallen upon her perfectly-sharpened set of Schrade knives. They'd always reminded Philippe of Christia: beautiful, sharp, useful.

His phone rang and he reached for the extension mounted on the kitchen wall.

"Yes?"

"It's Annie."

"Yes?" Philippe repeated, still in too much of a daze for politesse.

"Um, Nicholas told me you said something about a coven."

"Oh yes," Philippe scratched his elegant head, then let his index finger rest under the whorl of his cowlick. "That's all I know, really. Christia met with them once a month or so."

"Do you know what they were called, at least? Or where they met? I'm thinking maybe of tracking them down."

"Why?" Really, why *was* Annie Campbell so interested in his tragedy? Even to himself, Philippe's voice sounded very detached.

"Oh, I don't know, maybe to figure out who killed Christia."

How dare she be sarcastic with the bereaved? Philippe's voice, and his heart, dripped with venom. "She's dead. Cold in the grave. What business of yours is it who did the deed?"

"God, Philippe, how can you be so aloof?" There was rage in Annie's voice, but, if Philippe was not mistaken, fear had a hand there, too.

Well, why not tell her? Reminding himself that his venom should be directed at Christia's killer, not Annie, Philippe let out the breath he'd been holding. He felt his shoulders sag away from his ears, his back round. "They call themselves 'Puduhepa's Sisters.' Theodora Harmon is one of them. That's all I know. I assure you."

With a sigh, without another word, Philippe replaced the telephone in its receiver. He felt terribly old.

*

Sunday night, I called Theadora Harmon, but her service said she was out of town until after Thanksgiving.

Monday morning, before Colonial Fiction, I spent an hour or so in the graduate students' lounge intermittently talking and studying. I hadn't slept well, and a few people said, with concern, that I looked tired. I *was* tired, and I'd become even more exhausted after listening to Brenda Fujiki first thing in the morning. I'd popped into the religion department office to check on her and the poor woman had been practically delirious. Her usually baggy clothes looked further stretched out, possibly slept-in, and her hair was lank and greasy. Seeing me, she'd jumped up and dragged me into the women's bathroom, darting suspicious glances around us the whole way there.

Once we were ensconced in the handicapped stall, she had gone on at length to me about how she was sure Professor Redmund was guilty. According to her reasoning, he was both jealous of Christia's popularity and power-hungry. Since Christia's classes and books did so well, the balance of power in the department had shifted, and his male ego found that unbearable. So, he had strangled Christia Thompson. As proof, she offered the fact that she'd called his home number, pretending to be a police secretary, and told him he had to come in to give a statement because he was under suspicion. "He was scared shitless, Annie," she'd said, her hands fluttering about, "And I just *know* he did it! Otherwise, why be scared, right? These men, they act all pompous, but when it comes down to it they are complete chickens."

"No offense, but I'd be scared too, Brenda."

She clutched my arms in a surprisingly strong grip. Her face was grim. "Oh, but you'd be scared *in a different way*. Believe me, I can sense these things."

I gave her skinny hand a squeeze. "Sweety, are you sure you're O.K.? Seeing that ghost-thingy can't've been all that easy for you. Did you sleep last night?"

"Yes!" Brenda drew herself up to her full height, and in a righteous tone said, "I slept like a baby."

Right, I thought. "Let's keep our eyes open with Redmund. I have to go study."

Brenda had let her arms fall by her sides. "Alright. But don't say I didn't warn you. He's a dangerous man. Like so many of them," she added sadly. "One more thing, they'll have those hairs and stuff they collected analyzed really soon and dollars to donuts it'll be a big surprise."

Dollars to donuts? "O.K. Let's talk about what we know for sure." I was trying to bring Brenda back to earth. "You said you saw Ibo, Tomás and Nicholas. Was it in that order?"

"Yes." She thought for a minute. "I think so. Yes."

"You didn't see Philippe or Professor Redmund, right?"

"True, but that doesn't mean anything." She grabbed my arm again.Her fingers felt like claws. "Good will triumph over evil. It has to! Christia was too good for these criminals, and they could not bear that she was alive!"

So far, I'd been winning my internal struggle not to say anything bad about the sainted Christia, largely because I was beginning to gather that Christia had been, in essence, the opposite of Abdus: she'd been on her best behavior with the least of the universe's creatures – and on her worst behavior with those of us who were more privileged. This last statement of Brenda's, however, was something with which I could not in good conscience agree.

"Brenda! Christia was – just a person. No, don't interrupt me." I gave her a reassuring look, but continued apace. "Like the rest of us, she was imperfect. Good to some, bad to others. She didn't deserve to die. I agree with you there. And I'm with you – we need to find out whodunit. But right now I have to go." I hoped Brenda wasn't going to collapse right in front of me in the bathroom stall. I made her look me in the eye and told her to please try and keep it together.

After that ordeal, I was happy to see Abdus, Kirpal, Gretel, and Nicholas come in a quarter of an hour after I arrived in the lounge. Seeing me, Abdus glanced accusingly at Nicholas, turned on his heels and left. I decided to let Abdus's snub be my "let-it-go *du jour*."

"Hi guys," I said, moving my heavy book bag off of the scuffed yellow velvet sofa.

"Greetings, Detective Campbell. I have news for you in the matter of Christia Thompson's death." Nicholas wiggled an invisible cigar, raised one eyebrow at me and sat down on the sofa by my side.

"Do you think maybe we could talk about something else?" Gretel had her hands on her hips. She sounded about as annoyed as a Mennonite from the Midwest is capable of sounding in polite company, and her blue eyes looked harder than usual.

"What else is there to talk about?" Gretel looked shocked; and even I was surprised by Nicholas' cavalier attitude. He turned to Gretel, instantly sheepish. "I apologize. I just have a few things to tell Annie. If you'd prefer we go somewhere else I understand."

"No, that's O.K." Gretel said, resigned. She and Kirpal sat down across from us in adjoining armchairs, their arms almost touching..

"Alrighty," Nicholas resumed. "I talked with a few other little birds last night and, as it happens, Brenda Fujiki had a major crush on Christia. They found love notes from her in Christia's office; apparently they were all about her being a 'magical inspiration,' and 'beautiful goddess.' Those are direct quotes."

Poor, loony little Brenda. I tried to defend her. "Brenda is researching this 9th-century Byzantine nun, Kassia, in the women's studies department. Christia was helping her with the religion angle and she was really grateful. Maybe she went a step or two beyond grateful. But she's no killer. She really cared. I've talked to her about it!"

"I forgot to mention that she was somehow implicated in the whole Puduhepa question as well." To my chagrin, Nicholas seemed almost to be enjoying Brenda's being under suspicion. If, as often seemed the case with Nicholas, everything is abstract, I mused, then murder is just another logical puzzle. A game to enjoy. A look of smug satisfaction, detectible only to someone who knew him well, glimmered under his look of concern as he asked, "You know, how they found all those notes about Puduhepa that they were questioning Ibo about? I'm not quite sure how, but I heard it's all related…"

I had no response to that. It occurred to me that his satisfaction might be more due to pulling one over on me, than to finding reasons to implicate an almost-surely innocent woman. I hoped so. In light of her being a suspect, though, I felt somewhat guilty about our evening escapades. In the interest of being thorough, I also admitted to myself that seeing Brenda angry but unafraid was a little odd. I'd've expected the opposite from the shy, cowering woman I knew. Could be she's not scared because she knows who did it…or did it herself, I thought – but I did not say it aloud. Brenda had been increasingly unstable lately, but in my heart I believed her to be innocent, and completely incapable of violence.

I changed the subject slightly. "Where are you getting all this information, anyway? From Philippe?"

"Partly, and from Cyrus Wilson by way of Philippe. That's the main…channel, you might say."

He needed to be taken down a notch, for sure. "That's all well and good," I said slyly, "but you don't seem to quite be getting the fact that you are the major suspect. The last one known to have seen her."

Gretel blinked , and said, too quickly, "Heavens! Nobody would ever suspect you, Nicholas!"

Nicholas' gaze never moved from my face. "Annie, if you think I am capable of murder, you don't know me very well. I'd have to assume you never did."

"You're right," I agreed, forgetting our company, "Maybe I never did. But if you want to know, no, I don't think you killed Christia, I'm just wondering how you intend to prove it."

"So you're…concerned about me?"

"Yes."

"Oh. Hmm." He did not look entirely convinced. "Well, from what I've heard, they've determined that she died – was killed – some time after my visit to her office, when I was miles away."

"Have the police questioned you?" This was Kirpal, a look of worry on his face despite Nicholas' explanation. Kirpal was the only one of us who looked well-rested.

"As a matter of fact they have, briefly. They've questioned almost *everybody*. Now, shall we discuss something more palatable?"

It was time for class, so I gathered my books into my bag and bid everyone adieu. Nicholas followed me partway out, into the vestibule. He gave me a hug and then, with his hands still resting on my shoulders, said, "Here's something you can do with some of your surely-voluminous free time: figure out who actually did it and save both of our butts." I gave a little salute and went on my way. All this bickering with Nicholas was starting to get to me. I resolved to have more self-discipline: to stop snapping at him, and to take his jabs with serenity, as the signs of broken-heartedness they surely were.

I always feel better after a good inner talking-to. I noticed the pretty late-fall campus around me for the first time that day, and I smiled at the jaunty undergraduates with their bulging backpacks casually slung over one shoulder.

On my way home from class, I passed the chapel where Christia's memorial service had been held. I sent a prayer to the powers that be for the spirit of this confusing woman, dead before I'd even begun to figure her out.

That afternoon, I took the subway downtown, changing at Times Square to get across town toward the central Village. I met up with Brandi in the entrance lounge of the Ishwara Yoga Center on the Bowery. Brandi was already changed into her purple velvet hotpants and spaghetti-strap tank. She had her purple yoga mat on the bench next to her, and was examining the small Krishna decal she'd put in one corner, just under the border of red sequins she'd sewn around the edges of her mat.

The Ishwara boutique, where one could buy all sorts of enlightenment accessories -- at a hefty price -- was right across from where she sat. Several well-known people were milling about, perusing posters, t-shirts, clocks, nightlights emblazoned with brightly-colored Hindu deities, and $100 and up Ishwara-brand yoga togs.

"Hey," she waved. After I had my class card class scanned and was assured there was room for me in the class I'd signed up for – sometimes classes sold out, and it was rumored that preference was given to certain Ishwara students over others -- I went to sit with my Brandi in the lounge. We exchanged hugs, and then sat quietly for a minute, people-watching.

I was riveted by the sparkling abundance of the boutique, and wishing I could fool myself into thinking that if I just bought the right Ishwara-brand yoga outfit I was sure to achieve enlightenment more quickly, when Brandi leaned toward me and said, "Look at Dagger with all those models, SO ever the top!"

My mind must have been really distracted, because usually I find the sight of slightly over-the-hill rock stars strutting and preening for an audience of Hindu-wannabes quite amusing. That day I was in a more serious mood. "Wonder where his wife is?"

"Oops," Brandi joked, "'Honey, I was just at the yoga center, practicing my mantra, and these, these *models*, they just *attacked* me!'" That got me laughing, at least.

Even though the Ishwara yoga center was glitzy and pretentious, the teachers were inspiring; some even seemed like really decent people. Classes there were a good workout, too. On the way to the big, lotus-festooned classroom we passed our teacher, Daphne, chopping figs and walnuts in the kitchen for the evening *satsang*. Several nights a week, people came to Ishwara for chanting and meditation, led by the teachers at the center.

"Hi Daphne," I gave her a shy smile.

"Hey, Annie. Hey, Brandi. Om Shantih." Daphne was one of the newer teachers at the center and not too proud to learn her students' names, but she was heavy into the whole Indian culture thing.

"What does Om Shantih mean, exactly?" Brandi asked as we unrolled our mats and sat down on folded blankets.

"I think it means something like 'the universal vibration of peace.' Pretty nice, I guess…"

Daphne came in and the forty or fifty students in the room became quiet. She cued her music mix on the stereo and placed a bottle of scented oil on the shelf, then she sat down at the front of the room.

"Take a good, comfortable seat," she said, 'Lifting up along the whole spine all the way up through the crown of the head, the *Sahasrara Chakra*, the thousand-petalled lotus." She looked sternly around the room. "Close the eyes and take the inner gaze to the *Ajna Chakra*, the third-eye. Now, take a deep inhalation –"

As the whole room inhaled simultaneously, the door opened with a loud bang and Dagger and his entourage clattered into the room. Astonished by this breach in yoga etiquette, we all opened our eyes, and then most of us closed them again quickly, not wanting to be caught staring at a celebrity. Celebrities were old-hat at Ishwara.

Daphne ignored them all: as she reached the top of her inhalation, she began to chant, "Oooooooom…"

I did my best in the class, but what little peaceful energy I had mustered had dissipated with Dagger's grand entrance. My self-assessment was that I was a lame-ass, but with some justification. My yoga teachers were always saying that we should try to take the external aches and pains and challenges and draw them in with the breath so that they could be released through the internal combustion of yogic breathing. Likewise the scattered thoughts of the brain should be flooded with breath, so that the mind learns to become more still. Neither was happening for me that day. I was accustomed to concentrating pretty intensely in yoga class, and it felt disorienting to be in class with such a wandering mind. My balance was off. I kept getting lost in the sequence of poses and doing the wrong side at the wrong time.

It reminded me of practicing pirouettes as a young ballet student. As I crossed the floor in a line with the other little girls, I would get dizzier and dizzier; and as I got dizzier, I would be flooded with shame, afraid that I would be the one to break the perfect formation. Sometimes, I did mess up – and sometimes other little girls were overcome by their dizziness. Sometimes we all made it across the floor. It was awful, but thrilling, too.

After my third or fourth mixed-up posture, I was really mad. I guess, I thought, trying to soothe myself a little, this is what it is to be human: clumsy, imperfect, scattered…

At the end of class, there was a five-minute silent meditation. I still couldn't concentrate, but I directed my thoughts to something both productive and appropriate: "quietism." Jeanne Marie Bouvier de la Motte Guyon, the subject of study for several of Christia's last years of life, was a great proponent of meditation, or contemplation, which was known in the 17th-century as quietism. All I could recall of the synopsis I'd read of her life in a review of Thompson's last book was that de la Motte Guyon struggled at length over whether, while meditating, one should be filled with God, filled with awe toward God, or at one with God, or something like that. I reminded myself to pick up the biography and to ask Philippe if Christia ever meditated. She'd never seemed like the type.

After class, a cute teacher dropped something on my head in the coatroom. I looked up into his velvet brown eyes and felt an involuntary surge of attraction. The few male teachers at Ishwara were a precious commodity and were known for having better sex lives than their celebrity students. I was not going to get sucked in, despite the teacher's exceptionally long lashes.

After he left, trailed by several lithe, nattily-dressed women, Brandi elbowed me. "Didn't you notice he was flirting?"

"Listen, he's married. Plus, he's a smooth operator." Still, I ran back into the women's bathroom and checked in the mirror to assure myself I still had rosy post-yoga cheeks. When that hunky teacher had asked me if my head was hurt, I'd found his voice at once soothing and exciting. Like Tomás' voice.

We took the subway back uptown together. When I got home, I invited a few people over for an informal dinner. After Brandi spent an hour in the library, she came over to my place with a six-pack of fruity beer and we began to chop vegetables for a Moroccan tagine. While we cooked, we listened to Frank Sinatra and did our own versions of swing dances with spoons and squashes as partners. The inviting scent of spices – cinnamon and turmeric and cloves – simmering with olives, apricots and vegetables wafted through the air. Just before eight I changed the music to opera, turned off all except my Christmas lights, and lit candles all over the house.

Nicholas brought pink and orange gerbera daisies. He'd told Ibo over the phone that he was bringing flowers. When the two had met up at the Hungarian Pastry Shop before coming over, he'd been surprised to see a giant, live fuchsia orchid on the table in front of Ibo. That orchid, Ibo brought to me as thanks for dinner. It smelled strongly sweet and somehow gave the impression of being more sentient than other flowers. Kirpal and Gretel showed up with two bottles of champagne, "to toast to getting along," Gretel admitted to me later.

Nicholas and Brandi had always had a certain degree of tension between them. Brandi felt that Nicholas had run away from his cheesy roots - hurting people in the process - while she'd embraced hers; Nicholas felt that Brandi was tacky. They made an effort to get along, though, for my sake, even turning their differences into a joke. They managed to have a civil conversation for a few minutes before Brandi turned away in disgust.

"What? What did I do now?" Nicholas held out his hands in a gesture of honest bewilderment.

"Nothin' baby, you just go on being you." Brandi retorted, in a sickly-sweet tone. Nicholas turned his back to her, ostensibly to light a cigarette.

"I'm from Queens and I don't know about that snobby shit," she said to me in a low voice, "but your ex- is one hifalutin' bastard."

I laughed. "He's just pompous. He spent so many years perfecting his aristocratic act that he doesn't remember how to be just folks, you know? Here, have a drink." I handed her a raspberry wheat beer.

"Jolly good, old chap," she raised the beer bottle in the air in a toast, a cigarette in her other hand. "Shall we break out the bubbly? I hope it's worthy of our prestigious soiree here in your enormous flat." Brandi's giggle was infectious.

"What are you guys laughing about?" Kirpal was amused by our good humor.

"The usual," I replied, setting the lid back on the pot I'd been stirring and taking a sip of beer. "Human foibles. Ourselves." I sprinkled some chopped cilantro into the tagine.

"Yep," he sighed. "Me, I'd like to be laughing a wee bit more lately. Hopefully this beer will help!" We clinked bottles and then Kirpal went to sit back down.

A few minutes later, Nicholas, Kirpal, and Ibo were engaged in a debate over whether Redmund or Wilson would be the most powerful figure in the religion department now that Christia was gone, while Gretel, Brandi, and I clustered in the kitchen, organizing the meal. After awhile, it occurred to me that we were perpetuating gender stereotypes in our own microcosm.

"Break it up boys," I said, half-serious. "We ladies are going to put our feet up and solve the world's problems right now, while you finish getting dinner ready. For you see, our time has come..." I pumped my fist in the air, "...to rule the world!!!"

"Yeah," Ibo retorted, "You can have my office for your base. It's just the right size to fit in the senior faculty's closets." We all laughed, and the guys – more or less reluctantly – stood up and went about the motions of helping us. We got dinner on the table and set to serving ourselves from the big bowl of steaming, fragrant stew.

Later, Nicholas pulled me aside to share yet more secret information with me. He took in my slapdash post-yoga outfit of a long, belted forest green mohair sweater over loose orange corduroy bellbottoms, accessorized with still-wet-from-the-shower hair.

"Fetching," he said with a wink, and took another bite of his tagine. He was still chewing a mouthful of food as he began to talk, his company-elegant manners forgotten in his excitement at what he was about to reveal. "They're going to question Redmund." He saw I was impressed by his constant stream of privileged information. "Who's your daddy now?"

"You've been listening to too much Kool Keith," I replied. "Anyway, the 'daddy' in question is a something of a...murder suspect." I looked down at the floor, ashamed of my own thoughts about my friend. And this was just after I'd resolved to internalize any critical urges. Yeah, right.

He must have read my mind. "You suspect me, don't you. Not a lot, no, of course not, but enough to not be able to say you 100% believe I am innocent." There was a confusing mixture of emotions in his tone. In retrospect I think he was more amused than anything else. Why not, if it's all a game? He did not wait for an answer, but rejoined the rest of my guests at table. We spent the rest of the evening in jovial camaraderie, helped along by a few joints and ample alcohol.

Night. After I cleaned up the mess from dinner, I sat down with a cup of chamomile tea to ease myself from social mode to sleep. When I'd finished my tea, I found my body more willing to rest, but my mind still aflutter. I washed my teacup and put it in the dish drainer, feeling small. Nicholas, my dearest friend, was a possible murder suspect. Almost everyone else I knew in the city was involved in the case in one way or another. Things seemed to be happening on a more subtle plane too. I got goosebumps just thinking about the presence Brenda and I had both seen.

I knew trying to sleep was out of the question. My left eye would not stop twitching. With my fingers, I squeezed my eyebrows together and rubbed my forehead. To avert the increasingly spooky course my thoughts were taking, I decided to compile a list. Something concrete to subvert the heebie-jeebies in my head. I got a piece of paper and sat down at my kitchen table, lighting the butt of a cigarette I found in the ashtray and then extinguishing it once I tasted the stale smoke. (When will I ever learn that lesson?)

I wrote down the names of all of the possible suspects. I marked an "X" next to the names of people who in my opinion had been acting strange lately, and placed an asterisk next to those I believed actually capable of having murdered Christia Thompson. Then, in parentheses, I added any conceivable motive for each name on the list. After a few minutes, I ended up with the following list:

Ibo X (work?)

Tomás X

Nicholas X (affair?)

Philippe X * (cheating?)

Redmund * (work/power competition)

Brenda X (obsession…affair?)

Abdus * (affair? jerk)

I perused my list for a minute, to see if anything else came to mind. Other faculty might share Redmund's motives, and even someone in her coven might have killed her, but I had no evidence in either of these cases. In the latter, I was actually hoping someone from the coven might have some insight to share with me – if I could find them. After some hesitation, I added one more person to my list of suspects:

Me (X? Probably.) ("motive:" note)

Then I took out *Cremalgo's Compendium of Ghosts, Night Terrors, and Haints*, and began to do a little research on "invisible air-disturbances," the closest entry to what Brenda and I had seen. Apparently, such phenomena were associated with anger and grave danger. Maybe the book was a little out-of-date — merely a century or so — but that made sense to me. Reassuring, it was not. I felt no closer to sleep.

As a last resort, I looked out my window, hoping to find the street empty and to be inspired by the knowledge that my neighbors were cozy in their beds. Alas, no luck there: New York City was still awake.

Exhausted, I turned off my lights and flopped down on my bed. Pepita gave a loud snore in sleepy greeting. My doorbell rang just a few minutes later. I had to my surprise been just barely asleep. I groped for my glasses, while Pepita growled and yipped, but when I got to my buzzer no one was there. I walked toward the bathroom, stopping short in the doorway. There it was again, in the faint blue glow of my Holy Mother nightlight from the Dollar Store: a human-sized presence in the air, not shimmering but – *disturbing* the air, there's no better way to explain it.

In the clarity of that liminal state between waking and sleeping, somehow I knew it was her. Christia Thompson. This at last was my instinct emerging, the very thing we witchy women were told by Christia to trust. Was she haunting me? I took a step back. Pepita had whimpered once and then flattened herself to the floor. I had chills up my spine. From my first shocked intake of breath, Merlin was glued to the side of my leg, her pupils huge and her tail puffed up. The hair on the back of my neck was standing up, I could feel it, itchy and electric. Having recoiled once, I was now frozen in place. Time, too, seemed to stand still. In my peripheral vision, in the vague blue light, the shadow cast by the orchid on the kitchen table looked menacing, and, yes, sentient -- like that of some oversized, carnivorous insect, or a small, very patient and still monster.

Christia's ghost – for once the realization came to me I knew it must be true – hovered in front of me, there and not there, as it had in the rain the first time I'd seen her. This time, I could hear a high keening sound at the edges of my audible register. The horrible sound stopped abruptly when she disappeared.

Maybe five minutes after the apparition had faded my breath remained shallow, rapid. Those five minutes, in contrast to the stretched-out seconds of my paranormal vision, passed in what felt like an instant. I steeled myself to go into my dinky bathroom. She was gone. People always talk about being afraid of monsters and that sort of thing. I'd always thought human beings were potentially the scariest creatures of all. Ghosts, I guess, are both human and monstrous; and now I was seeing one – regularly!

I faced my reflection and asked myself: am I crazy? (Was Brenda crazy, too? And Merlin? She was still by my side, but calm now, purring reassuringly.) My eye was still twitching. In the mirror, my face was chalky white, and haggard. I looked like a blancmange, really. The idea made me giggle a little and that, thank the Goddess, got me to bed and to sweet, unbroken sleep.

*

Obituary for Christia Thompson -- *The New York Times,* November, ---

> **THOMPSON—Christia.** The University of New York and her family honor the passing of this beloved scholar and wife. Renowned feminist scholar and full Professor of Religious Studies at the University of New York, she died last Monday. She is survived by her husband of over ten years, Philippe Perez-Throgmorton, and a brother, Motte DuPree Thompson, of Bayou Grosse Tête, Louisiana. Dr. Thompson received her B.A. from Tulane and her Ph.D. from Yale. She did post-doctoral work at Oxford University. Prior to being recruited by the University of New York, she taught at the Miami University of Ohio. Her specialty was 17th-century women mystics, composers, and metaphysicians. Her most well-known book, the *New York Times* bestseller *Sluts and Witches: Mysticism, Patriarchy, and the Power of the Free Woman* argued for female unity in the face of a woman-hating culture; but she wrote less-incendiary books as well. Her most recent publication, *Mystical, Quiet and Deep: The Life of an Extraordinary Seventeenth-Century French Woman*, limned the life of the rich widow-philosopher, Jeanne Marie Bouvier de la

Motte Guyon in subtle, perceptive style. She was thought to have been working on an important new discovery at the time of her death. Her wit, intelligence, and style will be missed. In lieu of flowers, contributions may be made to charitable organizations supporting equality and education for women. Services private.

What about me? I should be *central* in there.

*

One of my most vivid memories of the beginning of my second year at the University of New York was seeing a tall, raven-haired man arguing in Spanish with his fair, patrician parents. Even in argument, they were a stunning family, and I'd found the son most attractive of all.

When I'd first been introduced to Tomás at a religion department function, I'd remembered that scene, but hadn't mentioned it for the obvious reasons. There had been a heat between us from the start. That was why, when he called Tuesday morning to ask me to go out with him that very night, I agreed, my usual courting principles notwithstanding.

Tomás took me to dinner at Shun Lee Palace, where we ate delicious, succulent, haute Chinese food under the glowing red eyes of the carved monkeys on the walls; and then he took me to see Deborah Voigt sing at City Opera. Spinning with the romance of the evening, we began to walk back uptown through Riverside Park. After walking for a few minutes in a fog, I looked over at my companion. While I was inwardly floating, Tomás seemed subdued. He had his hands in the pockets of his overcoat, and he was clearly preoccupied.

"What's up, Tomás?"

"Nothing," he said firmly. "Hey, I just remembered I have an invite to a party downtown. Would you like to join me? It's a launch party for a new album. It's a band called Spiritualized. They're going on at midnight."

"Are you kidding? They are one of my absolute favorite bands! Let's go!"

We crossed West End Avenue, with its stately homes and quietly luxurious apartment buildings and caught a cab heading down Broadway. In the taxi, Tomás and I talked about what kind of music we liked. We had a lot in common, taste-wise. We'd also both grown up playing the piano, but he'd continued his studies much longer than I. Our conversation was comfortable, but sporadic. Something between us had changed. My strong, silent, tall-dark-handsome crush was turning out to be more on the dark and silent end of things than I'd anticipated. The air between us no longer felt charged, and I sensed that he was no longer holding up his end of the electrical equation. I tried not to panic.

Just before the band came on, they turned on a fog machine, so that the dance floor was suffused with mist. It was a startling feeling, as if we inside the building were all floating in a cloud. Spaceman, the singer, came out in a puff of smoke and brought his mouth to the mic. "Ladies and gentlemen, we are floating in space," he began. For almost an hour, we listened and watched in awed silence, transported by the surreal soundscape.

When the concert ended, Tomás still seemed uncomfortable. He helped me on with my coat and we left.

"Let me get you a taxi," he offered. "I'm going to take the subway. I have to get to midtown. My parents –"

"I understand." I certainly did not, but I was in no mood to be rejected any further.

I wanted to scream, I wanted to grab him and shake him, I wanted to cry; but I did none of these things. I took it all inside – not to repress it, but to transform my drama and his mercurial behavior into compassion and inner-strength, like a yoga practice.

Haha.

Anyway, I stood there holding myself with my arms crossed on my chest and my hands in the opposite sleeves of my coat. The skin on my forearms felt cold and dessicated.

I gave him a dry peck on the cheek and began to walk away. Over my shoulder I called, "I'll get myself a cab. Goodnight Tomás. Thanks so much for a wonderful evening." I'm not even sure he heard my thanks, but I heard the next thing he said, and carried it with me for days like a little lit coal to warm my shivering heart.

"Next time I'll take you salsa dancing," he'd said to my rapidly retreating back.

What a mixed-up world.

Chapter Eight – Gratitude

> Most extraordinary lives go through many
> phases, some of which seem full, others, more empty. In
> her autobiography, *Vie de Madame Guyon*, Jeanne Marie
> Bouvier de la Motte Guyon describes her life as a series
> of alternating phases of agony and grace, culminating in
> an "apostolic state." This book will focus on this last
> period of her life, in which de la Motte Guyon
> experienced not only her greatest joy but her fiercest
> trials.
>
> Christia Thompson, *Mystical, Quiet and Deep:*
> *The Life of an Extraordinary Seventeenth-*
> *Century French Woman* (20--: vi)

Oh, I was there when he came in. Go in the closet, she said.
Take the drinks. Hurry!

He told her she should acknowledge others' work, not take all the credit. Called her ungrateful. He was angry and they fought. After he left, no one else came for a long time.

Later, I left. Now, I wonder who found her? Did they scream? This clinical detachment is new to me.

Of course they screamed. Anyone would have. (Not me, though. A scream denotes not just horror but surprise.)

*

Cyrus Wilson, Departmental Chair of the Department of Religion, Professor of the History of Religion, cleared his throat. He waited a moment for the last speaker to cease his chatter, and when he did not, said, quietly, "Redmund, when you are ready?"

Professor Redmund, holder of an equally prestigious endowed professorship, turned in a leisurely fashion to face his putative boss. "My bad, Cyrus."

Wilson's face reddened at Redmund's cockiness. He scanned the dozen or so faces assembled at the table. Few, if any, looked attentive enough to have noticed the little drama going on between the department's two alpha males. He sighed. He looked down at his notes as if something written there would help him in the coming task, and then began to speak: "I've called this last-minute meeting to discuss what will happen with Christia's classes and her graduate student advisees." The faces of his faculty were carefully blank. No one wanted to take on more work, especially the junior faculty – who were the only ones sufficiently cowed as to attend the meeting out of fear rather than curiosity. At the same time, nobody wanted to be seen shirking, either.

"As it happens," he continued, "I've already assigned her classes to Ibrahim Heyreddin." Now he saw a unanimous expression of shock cross their faces. "He's been underutilized in this department so far, and he's really the only one with any time. Furthermore, he and Christia were working closely together."

An uncomfortable silence filled the room. Wilson decided to try to dispel it. "Any questions?"

There were a few awkward attempts at beginning to explain from the junior faculty along the lines of "Isn't he...um..." before the room fell silent again.

Redmund gave a lazy smile. "I imagine I'm speaking for many of us here when I say I am surprised by your choice."

"Why?"

"For one thing, he is a murder suspect."

Wilson was very still. "And from whence comes this information, Professor Redmund?"

"With all due respect Professor Wilson," Redmund responded with a subtly exaggerated deference, "It is something that is, quite simply, known. By everyone."

"Well, it seems to me that until he is accused openly of said crime, he should be given the benefit of the doubt."

"Of course. I meant merely to suggest that he was perhaps not the optimum choice to replace Christia. Those classes are very popular, you know."

"I am aware of that fact. Anything else?"

Redmund leaned back in his chair and folded his hands together. Afterwards, the rumor spread among the faculty that he'd been seen twiddling his thumbs behind the screen formed by his knees.

If the junior faculty had been uncomfortable before, they were now rendered much more at ease by the spectacle before them. In other circles, Redmund and Wilson's dialogue might've been taken for a polite conversation. Here it was perceived for what it truly was: a searing duel of wits.

"One question, if I may." Wilson's jaw dropped to hear the voice of a painfully shy, recently-hired teacher, a skinny, weasel-y young bookworm – and, incidentally, a remarkably brilliant scholar of

235

19th-century alternative religious movements -- named Daniel Fleishacker.

"Yes, Fleishacker?"

The young professor blinked twice, swallowed, then asked, "Why, um, isn't he here?"

Good question. Probably afraid of you all, Wilson thought, and did not answer. "Next order of discussion: Who would be willing to take on Christia's graduate student advisees?" The faculty had returned, en masse, to their previous carefully blank expressions. "She had an unusually large number of dissertations on which she was the main advisor. These thirteen students must be looked after. I recognize some of you have little in the way of shared interests with them, but we must all pull together on this. Anyone?" The silence loomed longer and longer.

"I'm going to speak for everyone once again," Redmund – sheepishly, chummily -- began. Wilson shot him a millisecond-long deadly glance. "There are some concerns about the, ah, quality of some of her students and the...direction, shall we say, some of their work was going in...These questions around legitimacy may be tempering the eagerness of the non-tenured elements among us," he looked around, "— and I think that's everybody but you and me – to volunteer their services for something which might well not reflect favorably on them. Am I getting this right?"

There were small nods of affirmation all around.

"I see," Wilson said. "Obviously, such considerations would be taken into account. Now. Any volunteers?" One by one, four of the eleven other faculty members present volunteered to take on a student. After waiting another minute or so, pointedly staring out the window, Wilson slowly turned his head back to the his papers, noting as he did the thick dust on the heavy velvet drapes. Usually, full faculty meetings were held three times a year, and student reviews once; the faculty lounge was probably cleaned once a year, if that. Every time he sat in his chair at the head of the long table, he noticed the fustiness of the room and it bothered him.

He was being forced to resort to a more authoritarian strategy: time to channel his irritation. Without looking up, he began writing in his notebook. He tore out the page, folded it several times and then unfolded it and tore along the folds. "I have here the names of all of the students in question. Those of you who volunteered may have your pick, and the rest of you will pick names out of a hat. Let's see here, you, Fleishacker--" he nodded at the young man, "and you, Ashante-Amani, you two are on leave next semester. So that leaves nine." He scratched his chin in thought. "Alright, Heyreddin will get the other four. It will do him good to have some responsibility. Help him move up in the ranks," he concluded with a discerning glance that took in every individual in the room.

Ten minutes later, the meeting adjourned, and Wilson strode off to his office. Moments later, through his partially closed door, he overheard a male voice mutter, "This certainly is all working to Ibo's favor, wouldn't you say?" He shook his head. So some of the resentment of the other professors — who'd thought Christia was tenured because she was a woman (or for her sex appeal, or her "trashy" books) — would now be transferred to Heyreddin? The fellow would simply have to learn how to play the game. Such were the slings and arrows of departmental politics. Wilson was not surprised to hear the scurrilous speculation outside his door. In response he'd heard only a dry chuckle. Redmund's snide laugh – he was almost sure of it.

*

When I unlocked my door and walked inside, the gerbera daisies seemed to greet me like little, bright smiling faces. *Cremalgo's Compendium* was open on my dining room table and the orchid was bent over it, as if reading, emitting its enticing, almost sickly-sweet smell. I leaned over the table to see what chance page the book had fallen open to and read:

> And what of those who are killed by those they love? For they are the most torn of all. These tormented spirits are most justifiably known as "haints," for they are neither truly dead nor, perforce, alive, and neither entirely angry nor entirely at peace. 'Tis an unlucky spiritualist who comes across such a spirit in his travails, for he shall be sorely tried and find himself afflicted by confusions of the most bitter sort. These undead spirits have been known to linger for centuries. They can find no succor. Relief is impossible for them. Killed by love, even _for_ love, these spirits will haunt anyone they perceive as an avenger. Yet, voiceless, they cannot achieve their desire, vengeance. A desperate and never-ending circle of hell is their lot.

On the facing page, a dark-haired woman, scantily dressed, writhed in agony, her heart encircled by a thorny ring of briar. She looked like Christia! My stomach curdled. I felt faint, but could not take my eyes from the illustration. Pepita barked sharply to get my attention. I pivoted at the sound and, with relieved gratitude for the change in focus, put Pepita's harness on and went back outside to take a walk.

As chance would have it, Cyrus Wilson was also taking a walk with his dog at dusk. I hadn't heard from Brenda regarding my questions about what he'd said at Christia's memorial service, and so I decided to find out for myself.

After exchanging pleasantries, Wilson seemed about to move on, so I asked, quickly, "Do you have a moment?"

"A moment, yes. But that's all – it has been quite a day." He looked exhausted and his medium brown skin had a greenish, waxy tinge. Our dogs sniffed around companionably, undisturbed by our discomforts.

"Professor Wilson," I took a deep breath. "This is what I think. Christia was rumored to have discovered some valuable information – maybe an important codex of some sort -- by accident. She told certain members of the faculty about her 'stunning discovery.' But there's also suspicion, from, ah, other quarters, that Christia was trying to claim Ibrahim Heyreddin -- Ibo's -- translation and insights as her own. So what I was wondering-" it was hard to dissemble under his powerful gaze, "is, is Ibo a suspect? I was told he was."

"Ibo is one of many people who were associated with Christia Thompson on the day she died," Wilson corrected me.

"Alright, but I know Ibo pretty well and it galls me that he's a suspect. Isn't there some way they could show he didn't –"

"Didn't what?" Wilson interrupted, "Didn't threaten her? Or didn't write the notes she left on her desk?"

I didn't want the conversation going in that direction! "Sorry. May I ask one other question?"

He nodded, but still looked miffed. I'd meant to ask about his and Christia's shared background, but something else was troubling me – and something told me Wilson was a good person to ask. Before I could think too much about it, I blurted out my question: "Professor Wilson, do you believe in ghosts?" Hey, he wasn't in *my* department.

He scratched his chin. "Where I come from we used to call them 'haints.' What – have you seen one?"

"Yes and-and –" I squared my shoulders and continued, bravely or foolishly, depending on perspective, "I think it was Christia."

He rubbed his eyes wearily. "Oh," he said sadly, shaking his head. "I should have thought she'd show up. Was she…Well, how did you know it was her?"

Incredulous at his total acceptance of my experience, and very relieved, I told him the whole story of both times I had seen "her." I left out Brenda's sighting for the obvious reasons. I finished by asking him how he came about his belief in ghosts, and thereby chanced upon the answer to the very question I'd meant to ask.

"Where I come from ghosts are an everyday thing. They live with us like pesky relatives. In Louisiana, particularly in the bayous, chère, they're as common as the boggy mists and always being mistaken one for the other – 'Thought I saw Aunt Jolie out in the mists today, turned out it was just a curl of fog lookin' like it had a face,' and so on.." He looked at me to be sure I was paying attention. I was rapt. "Christia Thompson would've grown up the same. We both came from the hardscrabble life on the bayou. Didn't talk about it too much, but we both knew." A wistful expression flitted across his face. "Spicy food, fresh-caught meat and seafood, pickin' on guitars and fiddles. Food and music. And family, always family. Seems like everyone's related down there…And I mean that in a good way," he deadpanned. His gaze grew far away again. "But violence and feuds and poverty were a big part of our growing up too. Some down there'd kill you for chump change. And there's always some tension between Cajuns and Creoles, even though we're all mixed up and your pasty-lookin' Momma could be my dark-skinned Daddy's second cousin, and probably is – even if I look Black and you look White. Or Indian. Or Melungeon." He was quiet for a minute, but I was happy to see some of the color had come back to his cheeks. Not wanting to stare, I looked over at Baruch and Pepita. Pepita had the huge dog wiggling on his back and grinning, with his giant tongue lolling out of the side of his mouth.

"About your friend, Ms. Campbell." I looked up, surprised. "I shouldn't think he'll be a suspect much longer. The truth is, I have my suspicions that the real killer will snap soon enough." He added that up until now Ibo had been passed over for a job because he wasn't doing important work. "Now I'm giving him the opportunity to teach Christia's classes, and we'll see what he makes of it."

I told him I had some more ideas, but he'd explained that he really had to get going. He had quoted John Locke, "'Complex ideas are made by the mind out of simple ones.' Make sure your simple ones are sound." This last was added for my particular benefit.

I had dinner with Nicholas at The Mill, a local Korean restaurant. We had a quiet, cordial dinner, during which we discussed nothing more serious than Nicholas' affinity for obscure German techno bands. For once, I was able to restrain myself from eating my Bi Bim Bop too quickly, so that a golden crust had formed on my stone bowl rice by the time I'd made my way through the accompanying side dishes, vegetables, and tofu. I broke off a portion of the highly-coveted rice for my dining companion and then greedily ate the rest in a few bites. I took sip of acid green limeade and patted my stomach contentedly.

"Oh, I almost forgot to ask. Nicholas, I have this nutty idea. I don't want to get too excited prematurely, so let me ask you this first: Do you have any classes next week?"

His handsome brow furrowed. "Come to think of it, no. Cancelled, pre-Thanksgiving. Why do you ask?"

"We-ell, looks like we have a whole week: What do you say we go to New Orleans? I've been meaning to get down there one of these years. We could leave Friday morning. Track down Christia's brother. It said he lives down there still in her obituary."

A big smile spread across his face. "I'll call Philippe and get his number. How's that for stellar detective work?"

"Bravo," I smiled back.

We made plans to spend the next day packing and tying up loose ends, then we went home to our respective beds. I still had a few late papers to grade, he had to pick up his car, a red '72 Alfa Romeo Spider, at the auto repair place. We would leave the day after next.

I called Gretel and asked her to watch my "kids" for a few extra days.

"You bet," she said, her sleepy voice full of sweet helpfulness.

To ease myself into sleep, I used a familiar bedtime ritual, lighting a fat beeswax candle, and enjoying its honeyed smell and soft glow. I concentrated on the steady flame and mentally listed all of the things I was grateful for that day. The first thing that came to mind was Cyrus Wilson's listening to me. He was a kindly man, but a very busy one, and he'd taken a chunk of time out of his day to respond to my ravings. I was thankful that a day had passed sans any supernatural events. Also, I hadn't fought with Nicholas -- great. I was grateful for my animal companions and my good, soft futon. I blew out the candle and sunk into my bed.

We left before dawn on Friday, aiming to drive straight and get into New Orleans Saturday morning. We both shared the sort of temperament that prefers to get things, in this case a long drive, done in one fell swoop. Also, Nicholas, who'd be doing most of the driving, was known for his ability to go without sleep for long stretches without adverse effect.

It was an easy drive: 95 down to Richmond, Virginia and then 85 to Mobile, Alabama. From there, we took 65 going southwest all the way to New Orleans. As soon as the air was tinged with warmth, we took the top down. The route, taking interstate highways, didn't have a whole lot of character 'til we reached the deep South below Virginia and the Carolinas. Still, 'round about Richmond, the roadsides began to be lined with red dirt peeking from under the grass, and McDonalds hamburger restaurants to give way to Waffle Houses. Birches and maples became willows, sweet gums, and crepe myrtles.

As had become my policy, I refrained from mentioning my amateur sleuthing efforts as we drove along, but it was Nicholas who brought the matter up. We'd put the convertible top back up against the chill in the air after the sun had set. I'd slumbered for awhile in the dark car, in and out of dreams and snatches of songs from the radio. It was around the witching hour, three a.m., when he said, without looking at me, "Do you remember when I told you how Philippe and I don't know how to act?"

"Yeah," I responded, half-asleep.

"I just wanted to clarify. What I meant was not that Philippe doesn't know how to act *socially*. Of course he's socially adept. With that plummy Oxford voice he could convince anyone of his social acuity." He peered at me, making sure I was awake. This was clearly something he'd been mulling over for awhile. "I meant emotionally. He doesn't know how to express his feelings." I gave him a quizzical look and he pondered for a minute, his eyes on the road. "No, that's not right. He doesn't know what he's feeling, and then consequently doesn't know what, exactly, he should express."

"Well, there you have it. The very definition of a sociopath."

"By your definition, I'm a sociopath too."

"It's not *my* definition," I retorted. He woke me up for this? For the next few minutes, I sulked. I fiddled with the car radio. As we'd neared the Gulf of Mexico all I could get in tune were Christian rock stations and Tejano music. I gave up, frustrated, and turned the radio off. I dangled my forearm out of the window, playing games using my hand as a sail. Finally I gave in to my craving, even though it was criminally early in the morning. I grabbed Nicholas' crumpled pouch of tobacco from the glove compartment and rolled myself a tiny pinner. I rolled a thicker cigarette for Nicholas and passed it to him.

"Peace? Don't mind hitching a ride and a smoke from a sociopath?" he queried.

"Sugar booger, we ah in the South now, where everything is eeeeaaasy. I mean to remain thataway mahself." He let out a throaty laugh. I looked at him sharply. "But don't y'all push it now, hear?"

He seemed relieved. Some of the tension had gone out of his grip on the steering wheel of the Spider. I, however, was wide awake, trying to conceptualize an interior life so abstract as to preclude obvious emotions. Just before the sun rose, we stopped off at a rest stop to use the bathroom. I made it back to the car first and sat there, listening to the hum of travel, as I waited for Nicholas to return. I wondered where all those people, truck drivers and others, were going at such an early hour; and I wondered whether, like me, they sometimes felt lonely and confused. Like us, they could've been headed anywhere, fortified by the American dream of the wide-open road.

Dawn on a road trip is the most magical hour. Moving through the luminous air, passing by the sleeping world of people cozy in their homes under the new light, made me dizzy with bliss. We took the top back down and watched the stain of pale pink creep forward on the endless horizon to our left. I finally fell asleep after the sun had officially risen, and only woke up several hours later as we crossed the Mississippi, driving low over the wide river, on our way into New Orleans.

Nicholas had made – and paid for -- reservations at the famed Hotel Ste. Cocotte in the "revitalized" French Quarter, and we had plans to meet Christia's brother for dinner that Saturday night. This early in the day, Bourbon Street was quiet and relatively clean. We turned off on Toulouse Street and barely took the time to admire the cake-like cream and pale blue façade of our hotel, with its gorgeous wrought-iron balconies and tall, shuttered windows, before turning in to sweet sleep again, as we'd planned. I noticed only the crimson, flocked-velvet fleur-de-lys wallpaper – which figured, vaguely, in my dreams -- before extinguishing all light sources for a good long nap.

We awoke at dusk to the strong, luscious smell of jasmine and the fainter underwhiff of magnolias. I jumped out of bed and practically skipped to the french windows to open the shutters. We'd been given a room with a private terrace -- a "gallery," they'd called it when we checked in -- overlooking the inner courtyard of the hotel. My eyes feasted on tropical abundance; my ears thrilled to the sunset calls of songbirds. White, waxy – almost flesh-like – magnolia blossoms peeked from underneath dark green leaves. Vines overflowed giant cement urns, climbing statuary and crumbling stucco walls. The subtle odors of pretty ginger lilies and gardenias mingled with the sweet air. Giant palmettos waved gently in the soft breeze. Mossy stone fountains bubbled, sculpted nymphs cavorted.

Happily, I turned to Nicholas: "Yup, it's pretty much as I expected. Very lush, very Old World." Our room, too, was luxurious and done in high French style. The two Queen-sized beds were four-posters with gold-tasseled blue velvet drapes, and velvet-trimmed paisley duvets. The delicate Louis XVI bedside tables had ormolu detailing, as did the carved ceiling moldings, above the flower-covered walls. A faraway sound of jazz floated in on the evening air. I'd always wanted to go to New Orleans and that moment seemed to encapsulate what I'd imagined the place would be like: full of secret hidden places and fabulous nightlife, decay and splendor, so much history. And magic.

I rested my chin in my hands and gazed over the courtyard with a satisfied smile. "Hey! There's a pool, too. Though I guess it's too cold?"

Nicholas had folded his sheet down just below his armpits and was lying in his bed staring at me. I lowered my gaze to avoid meeting his eyes. His shoulders, slender but broad, were momentarily enticing. I turned back to the now-open french doors and walked out on our balcony. I breathed deeply of the damp early night air. Thick wisps of fog were beginning to weave their tendrils among the plants and fountains. It was still warm out, though. I would relish leaving my heavy winter coat at the hotel.

The bathroom was filled almost entirely by a pink faux-marble whirlpool tub. I ran myself a bath, lavishly laced with the hotel's jasmine-scented bubble bath. I poured myself a glass of red wine from the bottle thoughtfully supplied by the hotel, and padded into the bathroom with a guide to New Orleans in-hand. I sank gratefully into the bath, letting tension and travel dust both slide off me, and rested my head on the edge of the tub. I closed my eyes. Once I felt rested, I opened my guidebook and began to read. I occasionally called out bits of information – "Hey, wait a sec', Anne Rice lives in the garden district, not here!" – but Nicholas did not respond.

He was still in bed. Who knows what he was up to? At one point I did hear him talking in a very low voice. I hadn't heard the telephone ring, so I assumed he'd made the call.

I slathered myself in lotion and dressed in my favorite warm-weather dress, a slinky black chiffon, and drew a vintage beaded cardigan over my shoulders. A swipe of translucent red gloss and I was ready to go. Nicholas had finally gotten out of bed and dressed. He still looked somewhat puffy around the eyes.

"Have a drink," I suggested. "Cure what ails ya. Washing your face with cold water might help, too."

"Thanks for the tip. It's so nice to be informed when you look awful." He went into the bathroom and I heard him splashing around. "Maybe I *will* have a drink," he called. "Could you see if there's some diet Dr. Pepper in the mini bar?" Nicholas often attributed his superior powers of concentration to diet Dr. Pepper.

I laughed. "Minibar? What are you, kidding? First of all, there's, like, a bottle of excellent red wine on the, I think it's called, *Directoire* table and then, in the 'fridge, Veuve Clicquot…" I bent down lower to get a better look.

"Maybe in the back? Just look around," he said sternly. "They make Dr. Pepper down here."

Sure enough, there was a can of diet Dr. Pepper behind the finer drinks. I brought it to him in the bathroom. He was examining his blemish-free cheek for some minute imperfection. "Did you get a chance to finish the guidebook?"

"Nah. Too relaxed. Wine, bubblebath…Anyway, I just want to walk around and get a sense of how people live down here. It's like the opposite of New York City."

"I'm very interested in the aboveground cemeteries here. I've heard they're *divine*."

"Yup. Found those – they're just on the edge of this neighborhood."

The fog had drawn in close to our balcony, lending a feeling both claustrophobic and cloistered to our abode. I thought ahead to our planned dinner with Motte DuPree Thompson. Nicholas had told me his name was pronounced as "Moat Dah-Pree," but that he'd said most people knew him as "Mo." I didn't think this Mo posed any danger to us – as far as I knew he hadn't seen his sister in years – but the fog was filling me with a sense of the darker side of New Orleans. I said a little spell of protection and added my pentagram amulet to the evening's ensemble.

Just off our quiet block, the lurid tourist carnival of Bourbon Street pulsed and flared, to the tune of clashing accordions and saxophones. We ventured Uptown, to Franky & Johnny's on Arabella street. There, we found Motte DuPree Thompson, a devilishly handsome man in his early forties, wearing a leather biker jacket and a few full days' worth of stubble on his angular jaw. He looked like an older, more care-worn Christia; though in point of fact we knew he was younger. They had the same green eyes. His were bloodshot.

He looked me up and down. "Welcome to N'Awlins, Lose-iana, Annie." He gave me a warm, sexy smile. He turned his body slightly, and nodded curtly. "Nick."

Nicholas turned bright red. I could tell he was furious, all out of proportion to the situation. Obviously, something about Motte rubbed him the wrong way. For one thing, he hated being called "Nick" – it reminded him of Sam and Janene and Palm Springs. He gestured toward the door of the restaurant, curled his lip, and said, dismissively, "Yes, *N'Awlins*. Of 'show us your tits' fame. Also known for its fake magic tourist traps and aging jazz performers. It's superior government and municipal efficiency." He dropped his hand and crossed his arms in front of himself. " Zydeco!" he exclaimed in a voice dripping with disdain. I nudged him.

Motte Thompson was remarkably composed. He gave the most subtly sly of smiles and said, mildly, "Well, don't come down for Mardi Gras, then, chèr. And, by the way," he looked me dead in the eye, "there is real magic here too, 'specially in the Vieux Carré." That was what locals called the French Quarter. He held out his hand to me, never letting his eyes drop from mine, and murmured, "*Enchanté*. So pleased to meet you." My breathing was a little shallow. Lately, every dark-eyed, semi-suave guy was reminding me of Tomás. Or something.

"Mr. Thompson, I am so sorry about your sister," I began.

For a moment, his face became very hard, very closed. "Thank you," he said curtly. "Now let's talk of other things, shall we?"

He turned to Nicholas and again extended his hand. Nicholas took it, reluctantly. "Please," he said with a winning smile, "Call me Motte."

"And I prefer, frankly, to be called Nicholas," Nicholas divulged.

"Of course. My apologies. And you, Annie, do you have some other preferred form of address?"

Our eyes locked. He was an extraordinarily attractive man, but there was something of the roué about him, even something a little rotten beneath all his gorgeousness. He reminded me of the city we found ourselves in. "Nope. Annie is fine." I decided to capitalize on his edgy image. "Motte, you seem like the kind of man who'd know where to find the legendary vampires of New Orleans!"

"Well, ah just might," he said easily. Nicholas was clearly disgusted, and I made a face at him behind Motte's back. "But then again maybe ah might not. Depending." Beneath his easygoing manner, there was a dangerous glint in his eye.

We sat down at a table and read the menu, posted on a large blackboard. There was checkered oilcloth on the tables and beer came in big Mason jars. Several bottles of different hot pepper sauces were placed in the middle of the table.

Motte settled in his chair and tucked a checkered napkin into his collar. He ordered beer for the table. He tapped his fingers on the table while we waited for our drinks. I studied the menu, concerned about finding decent vegetarian food, and Nicholas tore up a sugar wrapper with elaborately casual precision.

The waitress, a bleached blonde with a bouffant and half-inch red nails, set our beers down at the table and, with her hand on her hip, smiled coquettishly at Motte. "Y'all ready to order?"

He raised an eyebrow at us. "I need a minute more," I said. She pursed her lips at me and flounced off.

Motte shrugged, with a lopsided grin. "Angelique knew me since I was a baby," he explained. His expression grew more serious. "What ah was sayin' before, about the vampires and all. Well, a lot goes unsaid in this town. There's the tourist stuff and then there's what really goes on in the mists and the swamps and the old houses, in the old families. We DuPrees -- that is, Maman was a DuPree -- are Catholics. All Cajuns are Catholics. Our Christie was raised a good Catholic girl." I shivered to hear her called by our old nickname. I took a sip of beer to cover my reaction and almost spit it back out.

"What is this?" I held out my glass.

"It's malt liquor, girl. Ain't you evah had the malt liquor?" He took a deep swallow and raised his glass to Nicholas with a smile. He had exceptional dimples. "Anyway, here's to good Cajun Catholic girls!" Good, he was becoming more loose-tongued. "Christie was the epitome of that. Heck, Christiane is a feminized form of 'Christ,' *n'est-ce pas?*"

"Was she really devout?" The question hid my emerging surprise over how little Motte seemed to be mourning his sister.

"Until she fell in love, yes. Mind you, ah haven't seen my sister in almost thirty years. She left here. Twice. Second time she never turned back. I always thought--" he paused. His eyes might've been a little wet, I wasn't sure. He looked down at the checkered table. "I expected to get up there and see her, but she had no reason to come down here besides me, and plenty of reasons not to come.

"But yes, to answer your question, she was a devout girl in the way that the women of our family have been."

"What about Voodoo and tarot and African Powers candles all that? Aren't those things a big part of life here, not just a tourist thing?" I was on the edge of my seat.

"Well now, that's what I was about to speak to. Catholics down here, depending on who you talk to, might have a looser interpretation of doctrine than you might expect. Lotta Creole influence, African influence. *Gris-gris*. That," he turned to Nicholas, "means a Voodoo charm. And then there's a lotta worship of the Holy Mother, much in the way you might find in Mexico. Not the kinda thing the old men in tall hats in Rome would cotton to. More complicated and mixed up and, far as ah'm concerned, more glorious."

"Is that what you mean when you say Christia was devout in the way of the women of your family?" This was Nicholas' first contribution to the conversation, and an important question.

"You could say that." He looked slightly taken aback by Nicholas' prying. "But I wouldn't say much more about it. See, we don't mess too much with other folks' business on the bayou. You might see us as xenophobic but that's not it…The DuPrees around here, well, I guess you could just say we keep to ourselves." It sounded like he said "us elves," which, looking at him, I didn't find hard to believe. He was long and lean, and his features were slightly attenuated. His bearing was solid yet he seemed light on his feet. Yes, he looked like he ran with a rough crowd. At the same time, there was something shimmering just below his biker surface. I kept catching glimpses of refinement beneath his rough exterior. How many super-tough guys were not only courtly but occasionally erudite? I realized there must be more to him than his appearance suggested. After all, he was Christia's brother.

The restaurant's atmosphere was thick with smoke, and redolent of deep fat frying. The patrons were decidedly blue-collar, with a sprinkling of tourists and drunk jocks. Oddly enough, there was something oddly appetizing about the combination.

"Do you have any vegetables not cooked with animal fat?" The waitress, Angelique, looked at me like I was crazy. "OK. Um, I'll just take two sides – macaroni and cheese and the cornbread, but, you know, enough for a meal."

"Sweet pea, one side here is enough to fill up a toothpick like you." I'd never been called a toothpick. A medium-sized stick, maybe. From the tone of her voice I guessed she'd actually meant it as an insult.

Nicholas, unlike me, ate seafood. He turned to me. "Alligator: Seafood or not?"

This was a question we'd never expected to encounter and in the end he, like me, went with the macaroni and cheese.

Motte had the shrimp pie and the crawfish pie, "Since you're payin'" with a wink at Nicholas.

I spent the next few minutes figuring out how to word the query I wanted to pose to Motte. The malt liquor did not aid my mental process. At length, I simply said what I thought: "Motte?"

"Hmm?" He looked up from his plate, mouth full.

"You're from a small bayou town, right?"

He nodded and swallowed his bite. "Grosse Tête. Murky, swampy place. Wild. Right on the bayou proper. Why?"

"And now you spend a lot of time here in the city, right?"

"Aunt Marie-Rose has a house in the quarter, yes. Real magical neighborhood. Haunted. By the old Lalaurie place on Royal Street. Where all the chained-up slaves burnt to death?" He looked steadily at Nicholas, who smiled uncomfortably. "Anyhoo," he resumed with a wink at me, "I stay there when I have meat and skin to sell here. Alligator."

"O.K. So if you are an alligator seller from a small, isolated town, why do you use words like 'xenophobic,' or "feminized,' if you don't mind my asking?" I was betting he'd understand the incongruity.

He didn't seem offended. I got the feeling he was debating how much to tell me. "I suppose," he finally began, "that mostly it's 'cuz Daddy put on airs. Heck, why d'you think I'm readin' the New York Times when I find out about Christie? You think people in Grosse Tête read the New York Times as a matter of course?"

He'd found out about his sister's death from a newspaper. How devastatingly inappropriate. "Didn't Philippe call you?" I asked, aghast.

Our food arrived and Motte busied himself assessing his pies, sprinkling each liberally with dots of three different hot sauces, before answering, carefully. "Ah have never met the man. He told me, and I am inclined to believe him, that in his grief he plum forgot to call me. But he did send you my way, did he not?"

Mollified, I took a few bites of my deliciously rich macaroni and cheese. I nodded thoughtfully to myself, and then said, "I guess that makes sense. That is, Philippe and Christia didn't seem to have friends or family outside of their academic milieu. That's what it was all about for them."

Nicholas nodded in agreement. I was glad to see him exhibiting compassion for poor Motte.

"Did you two talk much recently?" I had to ask, tactful or not.

"No more than usual. Maybe once a month? At most." He looked bewildered. "Why? Are you tryin' to figure out what happened to her?" The odd nature of our errand had finally occurred to him. "I dunno why I didn't ask when you called, why you wanted to see me…"

"We are trying to figure this all out, but you're not a suspect or anything," I reassured him. He glared at me. "Not that you were thinking that we were suspecting you, uh…" I trailed off. "I just thought you might shed some light on Christia. You know, her background and stuff."

After a few minutes of silence, Motte said, in a considerably less jovial tone that brooked no mumbo-jumbo, "You said very little on the phone, just, you wanted to talk to me. What I wanna know is why are you two really here? Are you police?"

I took a deep breath, looking at Nicholas questioningly; he nodded. "No, we were – friends of hers. You see, Motte, there's a lot of weird confusion over who killed your sister." And we are both more or less potential suspects, I thought, grimly. "I'll be completely up front," I continued, wishing I had something other than malt liquor to refresh my

253

dry mouth, "We have no idea who killed Christia. We don't even share the same suspicions." I waited for his reaction.

"Mm," he said finally. "And you just wanna pick my brain? That's it?"

"Yes," I said with relief.

"I s'pose I can oblige my new Yankee friends." We both laughed.

Nicholas, slightly disgusted at my groveling, got up to use the bathroom. There was real sadness in Motte's eyes, behind the dissipation, and I decided to speak to that. "You know, about Christia. She was the most popular professor in her department. Students were completely entranced by her." I saw pride in his big sister swell in him. "She was really, um, cool, compared to other faculty. And really smart, you know?" And a bitch, too, some would argue, though not me – or at least not just then.

"She come a long, long way, our Christie." He swiped at his eyes. "Lawd." He shook his head a little, eyes closed. When he opened his eyes, there was more vulnerability than before. "Miss Annie, would you like to come to luncheon tomorrow with me chez Aunt Marie-Rose? That's my mother's sister's place. She's away on the continent as is her wont in the winter, but Snowy, the maid, will cook us a fine meal. And chaperone."

Nicholas wouldn't be happy, but I would excuse myself by saying it was "for the cause." "I'd love to, Motte."

"Uh oh!" he suddenly exclaimed. I started at the panic in his voice. "Tomorrow's Sunday. I got church. Absolutely gotta go to church." He leaned toward me with a boozy, flirtatious grin. "Ah'd still like to see you again. Monday just as good for you?"

I smiled. "Yes sir. I'm just here to talk to you." I hoped he'd stay more sober on Monday.

Franky and Johnny's was getting more and more noisy, and we left as soon as Nicholas returned and paid our bill. In the parking lot, I gave Motte our number at the hotel and we made arrangements to speak after church on Sunday. Motte admired Nicholas' car, thereby restoring some of Nicholas' threatened machismo and then drove off in a mid-seventies Mercury Cougar, burnt orange.

Back at the Ste. Cocotte, I didn't feel like sleeping. I went into the courtyard and watched the mists drift to and fro over the swimming pool. It was relatively early, maybe nine o'clock, and still warm. I sat down on the edge of a fountain, curling my fingers around the cool slate of my seat. Seeing Christia's brother had touched me more deeply than had her husband's grief. Motte's bravado seemed to hide a more authentic loss than Philippe's histrionics, but that was just my opinion. Having seen Motte, I couldn't help but imagine the two of them as children: two little dark-haired urchins, with bright green eyes and sharp wits, playing near the bayou.

Motte and "Christie."

I felt terrible. Because of me, one of Christia's final acts had been to read a mocking note. I should have kept my silly idea for a prank to myself! A few other guests had come into the softly lit courtyard and I didn't want my solitary tears to make them uncomfortable, so I retired to our bedchamber. Nicholas was sitting in the dark, sleepily watching an opera on public television. I sniffled to announce my presence.

"Heeey…Weepy!"

"Hey, Creepy."

"Are you really crying? I thought it was just rain shining on your cheeks!" He saw that I was. "Whatever for?"

"I just can't believe I added to the misery of Christia's final moments. When I first found out she died I wasn't that upset because she just seemed so, I dunno, cold. So cruel. But the more I find out about her the less cut and dried it all is and I just feel awful. How could I have done that, Nicholas, how?" I dissolved into tears again.

He put an arm around my heaving shoulders and sat me down on the sofa. "First of all, above all, you had no idea she was about to be murdered. And Annie," he continued gently, patting my back, "Christia was a bitch most of the time. She had some really good moments though, where she could be almost –" Nicholas was crying now, too, "tender. Motherly." I looked at him in shock. "Well," he explained, "You know, moments of not being a power-sex-witch type, just a friend."

"I guess you knew her pretty well."

"I guess I did."

"If that's your cup of tea."

He back-tracked: "Well, not really;" then he was silent.

Since I was slightly miffed, I brought up Monday's lunch date.

"I don't know as I'd trust that guy to keep his hands off you, but I'm sure I'll be able to entertain myself," was all he said in response, before clicking off the TV, rolling over, and falling asleep.

Sunday dawned bright and temperate. We went to the Café du Monde, a major tourist trap overlooking the river, for café au lait and beignets. We sat under the giant awning, watching the ferry go back and forth across the Mississippi, and gorging ourselves. I couldn't help but squeeze the soft little pillows of fried dough, covering my fingers with warm oil and melting sugar, which I then licked off with delight. Then I stuffed the now-chewy beignets into my mouth. I must've eaten ten or twelve. Luckily, they were not too steeply overpriced.

New Orleans was quiet that Sunday, perhaps especially so in the Vieux Carré. Most locals were in church and with family; most tourists were sleeping off their novelty drinks from the night before. We spent most of the day walking around aimlessly, but with great enjoyment.

Despite the slightly ravaged air in the streets and buildings, I was reminded at every turn of Paris: the many street artists reminded me of Montmartre; and the aboveground cemeteries reminded me of Père Lachaise, where Jim Morrison was buried.

Near Jackson Square – "Where," Nicholas remarked, "all the local executions of yore took place!" -- and along the river there was an even higher concentration of artists and street vendors. One could have one's portrait painted or one's caricature drawn; one could buy a painting of some charming neighborhood scene; or have one's future told by card or palm or crystal ball.

French and Spanish settlers have been living in the French Quarter since the early 1700's and the it showed in the architecture. Brick buildings ranging from the darkest crimson to the palest rust color, adorned with black shutters and curlicued iron railings graced every street, interspersed with painted brick and stucco. Spiffed-up town houses alternated with crumbling old buildings. Many homes had private courtyards with lush tropical gardens that could be tantalizingly glimpsed through wide first-floor windows. Most windows, though, were shuttered well into the day, and we had to content ourselves with imagining the goings-on in houses humble and grand.

The quarter was eclectic, too. On one street, Marie LaVeau's Voodoo Bar pulsed with music and loud, drunken conversation, on the next, priceless French antiques sat delicately in lace-sashed storefront windows.

We walked and ate, ate and walked. We even took the sightseeing ferry from Jackson Square, but only once back and forth: the vegetable jambalaya mixed with red beans and dirty rice mixed with more beignets and strong, chicory-laced coffee in our stomachs made for a slightly nauseating boating experience.

As the hour grew late, warm yellow lights came on behind shutters and people started to gather in restaurants and homes for dinner. The sky turned a bright, saturated blue, and the moon rose over the city. For a while, we continued to walk, but my feet were getting achy. Full as can be, we took a table at the elegant Bayona, on a quiet stretch of Dauphine Street, for aperitifs. The restaurant was located in a sensitively-renovated 19th-century Creole cottage. The soft apricot light indoors was a relief after the many sights and sounds of the day. We drank *herbsaint*, Louisiana's version of anise liqueur, and admired the well-dressed crowd over our exuberant table-top flower arrangement. People at Bayona dressed like average New Yorkers, that is to say they wore sleek, mostly all black clothing -- unlike the tourists of both New Orleans and New York, who invariably wear T-shirts and khaki shorts, or windbreakers and khaki pants, depending on the weather. Nicholas had purchased a claret-colored velvet blazer at one of the local French tailors, and it looked dashing with his black silk shirt and trousers. The dark ensemble brought out the darker tones in his blue eyes, giving him a slightly mysterious air that suited our environment.

Only the mellow jazz music being played at low volume marred the mood.

Nicholas looked at me with a twinkle in his eye and put on his DJ voice: "Yes, ladies and gentlemen, we are playing for your delectation, here in the city of Nouvelle Orleans, the song stylings of smoooooooooth mediocrity."

I giggled. "Gimme a drag," I demanded. We finished our apéritifs in comfortable silence.

It wasn't far to our hotel, and although I still had a lot of questions I wanted to ask Nicholas – about his recent behavior, about his relationship with Christia – the tone of our conversation was for once simply too convivial to bring all that up. I called home to check up on Pepita and Merlin, and then decided I was too pooped to do anything else. We had well earned our rest that day, and after a half-hour of TV – neither of us had televisions back home, so it was a real treat to zone

258

out – we fell asleep. Every once in a while, with my sleep-numbed senses, I sensed a change in the weather. The intensifying breeze through the shutters, the heavy pings of rain on our metal balcony, and the splash-splash of water falling in the fountains and birdbaths in the courtyard seeped into my slumber.

The rain-washed sky was still dove gray when I woke up. Nicholas slumbered in the other bed, a ribbon of drool pooling next to him on the hand-embroidered silk paisley pillow sham. I pulled a thick, nubby cardigan over a long, wine-colored velvet dress and went down to the chintz- and flower-filled breakfast room. That cheerful room doubled as a solarium and overlooked the inner courtyard. The company and surroundings were much too dainty for my tastes at that hour, so I took a croissant, spread with sweet butter and strawberry preserves, and a large Mimosa out into the courtyard.

At that hour, I had the inner sanctum to myself. The air was so thick with moisture I felt like I was underwater. A faint drizzle tickled my scalp. The atmosphere was hushed, as if the very air were too sodden to carry sound. Only sounds of water, endlessly falling, could be discerned. Fat drops fell from palm fronds onto the clean stone walkways. Taller trees and vines seemed to sag under the weight of last night's storm. Water ran through minute, heretofore unnoticeable, crevices and cracks in the slowly decaying walls of the old hotel. The overall effect was spooky, and I shivered. I went back inside and traded my Mimosa for a hot cocoa with extra whipped cream, and grabbed two *pains au chocolat* for good measure, giving silent thanks for the local heritage of French baking.

The gray day felt like the right time to ask some hard questions. I waited (hours) for Nicholas to wake up, brush his teeth and have his first diet soda before I fell to it.

When he seemed fully awake, I sat down on my bed in front of him. He had a stricken look on his face. I took his hands in mine. "What's up?" I asked.

"I want to talk to you. I was worried all last night. I don't think you should go to lunch with Motte." I looked at him, incredulous. "Annie," he squeezed my arms in emphasis, "how do we know he's not the killer?"

It was not the first time that question had occurred to me. "For starters, he didn't even know she was dead." -- "That could be an act!" he interjected -- "And," I went on, "he seems to have genuinely loved his big sister. Not in a dramatic, maudlin way. In a for-real way."

"People kill people they love all the time," Nicholas argued. I gave him a withering glance. "O.K., Not *all* the time, but often enough to have inspired plenty of literature through the ages."

I rolled my eyes. "Motte promised we wouldn't be alone. He was being courtly, not defensive, but still…there's a servant who'll be there…" I trailed off, and then remembered my own concerns. "Anyway, *I* want to talk to *you*." I handed him one of the *pains au chocolat* as a bribe.

He looked nervous, but resigned.

"I feel like you've been acting really strange," I complained. "And I'd really like an explanation." When he just looked at me, I asked, "Does it all have something to do with Christia?"

He shrugged. "Annie, sweets. Isn't it a little…early for this line of questioning?"

"Mayhap, but then again, maybe I'll catch you unawares." I smiled and plunked down on my bed across from him again. "I'll start real simple-like. In brief but complete terms, please tell me about your relationship with Christia." He blushed, and I thought he was about to speak. I was wrong. A full minute passed.

Finally, Nicholas sighed. "Why are men and women so strange? Why not just have a cloacha, like chickens do, and be done with it?"

"Talk about strange. That word is a real pet peeve of mine. And as far as I know males don't have 'em, so it wouldn't make everything better. Roosters have, you know, cocks. Er, I think." I glared at him, daring him to argue, and then continued. "Back to the subject at hand. You and Christia. Please. Please?"

He lay back on the bed, plumping up three or four pillows under his neck and back. "There's not much to tell. My first year of grad. school, my mom came to visit during the department's fall party. She wore some kind of flowing caftan and expounded on the joys of the Kabbalah, her hobby at the time. As if the Kabbalah can be a hobby." He looked mortified. "Also, she wore her Chanel sunglasses -- you know, the big logo kind? – the whole time. Inside." He shuddered at the memory. "A few days later, I went to Christia's office to ask her to be my advisor and she suggested I might have a few Mommy issues with that mother of mine. Subtly, of course. But she intimated that I might benefit from a more, shall we say, *refined* female influence in my life."

I laughed, but quietly, thinking how malleable men can be.

"So," he continued, ignoring my interruption, "We made a lunch date for the next week –"

"Oh God, speaking of which, what time is it?" We both looked at the tinkly, gilt cherub-encrusted clock on the ornate carved table between our beds. "Eleven? I gotta take a shower and go!"

Nicholas looked extremely relieved. I wagged a finger at him. "I want to hear this. And I will! You never told me, even when we were together."

"Especially when we were together," he couldn't help retorting, his words adorned by a mouth full of chocolate.

On my way out I took an umbrella offered by the concierge. It had started to rain again, though not hard. Marie-Rose DuPree's house

261

was located on Ursuline Avenue, toward the river. The homes on her block were large, but moldering. It had clearly been a genteel neighborhood in the not-so-distant past, but had fallen on harder times. Marie-Rose's house, a four-story faded violet townhouse with white-painted windows and yellow shutters, was the best-repaired on the block, probably thanks to her nephew. Stone lions guarded the front door, with pots of ivy and roses on their broad backs. I mounted the crumbling steps and rang the brass doorbell. A few seconds later, Motte peered through the half-circle of windows at the top of the door and then threw the door open.

"Welcome," he said, with a big, generous smile and his arms thrown wide. "This is my home away from home."

"Beautiful," I gushed. It truly was. At the windows, faded yellow Toile de Jouy curtains lent a sunny cast to the weak, rainy-day light in the entrance foyer. The walls were painted the palest yellow, with moldings and ceilings of ivory white. Tall doorways led off to spacious, window-filled rooms on either side of the front door. A grand staircase with wide, polished mahogany steps and white wooden handrails mounted on carved white pillars stood directly across from the front door. Above the first landing, where the stairway split in two, a flock of delicate, slightly dusty-looking porcelain Meissen birds perched on the wall, with small tangles of equally fine porcelain roses here and there between them.

"Snowy wanted to make etouffée, but I told her you don't eat meat. She harrumphed a little but then she made a nice thick gumbo. As she said, gumbo filé -- that's the base, every family's got a secret receipt -- got nothin' to do with meat, she guessed. Mind you, we don't hear tell of too many vegetarians hereabouts." I stood there, stiffly, enduring the typical reaction people who don't live in major urban areas or college towns tend to have to my diet. "Cornbread, too, with crèpes for dessert. Oh, and a cherry tart. Sound alright to you?"

I was practically moaning.

A rotund woman came in, wiping her hands on her apron.

"Snowy, this is Annie. Annie, Snowy." I noticed he'd spoken to the older woman first, as a gesture of respect, and was impressed.

We shook hands. Her grip was strong. "How do you do," I said.

"Pleased to meet you, Annie." She turned to Motte. "I'll get back to the kitchen. The table is set and lunch will be ready in a few minutes."

"Thank you, Snowy."

Motte, sober in the light of day, was just as handsome as I'd remembered, but there was still a pallor about him, either of mourning or by nature. He offered me his arms and I took it. "This way, please," he gestured gracefully to the right with his free hand.

"If I might..use the…" My surroundings had me feigning the delicacy of a long-gone era. Motte saved me by pointing me toward the guest bathroom, saying, with a laugh, "We don't use that one much – hollar if there's no paper."

The small bathroom had the close air of a room that had been shut up for a long time. I sat on the toilet and gazed at the cabbage rose wallpaper. It took me awhile to feel relaxed enough to pee, and as I sat, the air became more and more foul and I began to have a hard time breathing. I made haste to get out of the claustrophobic, airless space.

Motte was waiting at a discreet distance in the hall. I gave him a weak smile and inwardly resolved to forget my experience in the bathroom. Enough was enough with this supernatural business.

The room he led me into was, like the hotel's breakfast room, a solarium. Big windows, with that slightly rippled aspect of old glass, surrounded us on all sides, and above. The walls below the window-topped wainscoting were a muted purple color. The ceiling, near the old-fashioned, many paned skylights, was lavender trimmed with cream. In one corner, a tiny canary the color of baby aspirin warbled tentatively in its cage.

A small round table had been set with a lace tablecloth over light yellow linen. Each place had a full setting of opulently decorated – peonies, poppies, ribbons, gold trim – dishes, and real, slightly tarnished, silverware, enough for a four-course meal. In the center of the table, on a hand-crocheted doily, two white roses sat in a silver bud vase. Two white wicker chairs, with plump, rose-imprinted cushions, awaited our lucky posteriors.

Motte stood by his chair. Wondering at the quirky, lovely room, I forgot mine, until he said, "Please, sit down, Miss Annie."

"What a sweet place. Special."

"Marie-Rose is delicate, like the other DuPree sisters all were."

"Were? Are they all deceased?" I shut my mouth quickly, realizing my casually-asked question included his mother.

He didn't seem affronted; just -- a little of that sadness I'd glimpsed returned to his eyes, faint but real. "DuPree ladies are unlucky in love. There were seven sisters and only one, Tante Marie-Rose, is alive today. And everyone knows it's cuz she never loved nary a man. The rest, they were all dead by forty!" He looked up through the skylights at the gloomy sky. "Two suicides." He ticked them off on his fingers. "Two gone batty and died in institutions. " He cleared his throat. "Eh, that includes my mother, Gwendolyn Pearl. Then, *voyons*: Emmanuelle died of a broken heart, well now, she furthered it along with pills in that very bathroom you used earlier," -- aha, that explained the air in there! Most Southerners sure seemed attached to their homes, why not Southern ghosts? – "and Cheri-Lynn of the pneumonia. From a broken heart. See, she got the pneumonia from her pain and wanderin' in the swamps…" Snowy set down a tureen of fragrant vegetables on a coaster and ladled some into each of our bowls. "Thank you, Snowy."

"Yes," I said with real gratitude, "Thank you. This smells delicious." She smiled, crinkling the corners of her eyes, and retreated to the kitchen.

"So it's a real southern gothic story we got here." Motte blew on his gumbo. "See, my mother was committed when Thompson, that's my Daddy, left. Christie was never gonna be like Maman! She wasn't gonna love no man, for starters. Least early on. We'd lost our parents by the time she was ten and I was seven."

"So who raised you two?"

"That was our Grandmère Luisah. She was not a DuPree. Married one. She was part Chickasaw, part Cajun Indian, I dunno what. Choctaw, Creole, mishmash, all that."

Snowy came back with a breadbasket full of warm cornbread and a bowl of herb butter molded into the shape of a rose. The butter knife was formed entirely of mother of pearl and gleamed like a large, flat opal in the dim glow from above.

Motte took a piece of bread and paused to eat a few bites plain. "Her and Marie-Rose, that's who raised us up," he explained. "But those two was opposites, lemme tell ya that. Grandmère was a hunter and a fisherman and a trapper. Grew up on the bayou and aimed to stay there. Strong woman. Knew her herbs and plants and could heal damn near everything. And cook? Whew! That woman di'n't need no Snowy!" He smiled, happy with his memories. "Alligator, crawfish, turtle, frogs, crabs, catfish, deer, squirrel. Fry it up with some onions, spices, pour on a little Sauce Piquant…Mmm, mmm!" He smacked his lips and grinned some more.

I returned the smile and encouraged him to continue, telling him quite honestly that I was enjoying his tales immensely. I even enjoyed the cadence of his voice; it was rich with the swamp and the city both, an intriguing mix that was evinced in his personality as well. Hmm, I'd speculated, what a captivating man. As I had no intention of moving to the bayou, and was, further, attempting to investigate a murder – on however amateur a level – I dropped that line of fantasy pronto.

Motte was crumbling cornbread into the thick stew. He looked up and winked at me. "So in the end, as you can see, I got more of Grandmère and I reckon Christie got more Marie-Rose -- and Daddy, too, come to think on't."

"You seem to be managing fine," I gestured to indicate our refined surroundings.

"Relatively speaking," he mused, "I suppose you're right. Even just being here in the big city is somethin'! People in Grosse Tête, they usually stay there. You can get a good job – in the sugar refineries, tin, oil, or hunt 'n trap like me – make a good livin'… The public schools are mostly black and struggling, so the whites send their kids to private school in Iberville Parish, heck, in most of the bayous. 'Course that means Catholic school, but then we're all Catholic, more or less. And then if your kid is inclined toward a higher education there's the big city, Baton Rouge, or here, if they're a real big-headed kid from Grosse Tête." He laughed at his own pun. "But most everybody comes home. Christie's one of the few who didn't."

"What do you mean, 'more or less' Catholic?"

Motte folded his arms, and leaned away from the table with his legs spread. "Voodoo Catholic," he said simply. "Same as I was tellin' you the other day. It's all mixed up around here. Go check out the shops around Jackson Square, even Bourbon Street, St. Ann Street…They're tacky and touristy, but they'll give you some idea. Some." He raised his eyebrows in emphasis. "Grandmère was a priestess, even though PawPaw DuPree was more of a devout Catholic type. Wasn't nobody tellin' Grandmère Louisah what to do or not do!"

"She sounds like an amazing woman."

"You know, she was. Actually, she used to say she was related to a famous French woman, Jeanne Motte-something, that's where I got my name. And then my Daddy -- from up North, Harvard-educated and whatnot, and slummin' in the bayous when he found him a wife -- Daddy Harrison Huntington Thompson liked the idea of a wife with illustrious ancestry, along with the Injun blood."

"Jeanne Motte-something—" I repeated thoughtfully. Then it hit me: "Motte! Do you mean Jeanne-Marie Bouvier de la Motte Guyon?"

"Yes, I think so." He looked very startled.

"That's who Christia wrote her last book on!" I exclaimed, before he had to ask the obvious.

"Oh," he looked guilty. "I never got to that. I do love to read, but more the classics. The name wasn't in the title, right?"

"No." I assured him. "Um, I didn't get to it yet, either." I planned to read the book as soon as I got back home, though. Harkening back to what he'd said a moment before, I pictured Motte and Christia's father – what was his name - Huntington Harrison Thompson? -- coming across the exotic DuPree sisters during his peregrinations. "Is your father still alive?"

"Nope, It's just me left, of the family line." He took in my crestfallen expression. More courses had been served, but I'd been distracted from the superb fare. "It's alright, Annie, I'm a happy enough guy. I got some kids here and there more than likely. I hadn't seen my Daddy in decades when he passed. And, as I think I mentioned earlier, Maman died at the home for the mentally infirm after Daddy left us. We called her death merciful."

I looked around quickly for a change in conversational focus. "These roses are beautiful." Obvious, very obvious. They were, though, stunning, almost candescent in the greenish light that seemed to permeate that day wherever I went.

He responded like a true gentleman. "Aunt Marie-Rose has a thing for her namesake." He looked at me thoughtfully. "You would like the bayou, I bet. Banana trees and magnolias and willows. Crickets and frogs singin', lightning bugs at night, all so busy findin' their loved ones that the air's humming."

"Sounds like heaven."

"Oh, I'd say so."

We sat in shared reverie for a few minutes, enjoying the cherry tart Snowy had brought out as a final course. My thoughts consisted largely of remembering the earlier courses of that stupendous meal: the gumbo and corn bread, the *vichyssoise*, the exquisite salad, the *crèpes à l'orange...*

I thought he was dreaming of the bayou, but he was thinking about his sister, and about helping me in my quest. He leaned toward me and said, sadly, "There was one other thing about Christie that was real significant in her life. After Daddy left and Maman died she came to rely on Grandmère Luisah as if she was her own mother." I nodded. That seemed natural. "But Grandmère Luisah was a woman, too. One day she up and left PawPaw for a handsome Black-Indian Creole man. Christie never got over it. Thought she was makin' the same damn mistake our mother Gwendolyn did. Followin' some foolish man for love." I raised an eyebrow. "Oh, yes, Maman followed Daddy to New York, but they came back down here soon enough. And then of course he left."

"Was Christie mad because Luisah went out with a Creole man?"

"Nah, she didn't care about that. I don't think she even would have cared that Grandmère was steppin' out with another man, so long as she didn't lose her head over it. That's what bothered her." He savored a bite of warm fruit, just touched with thick, fresh cream from Marie-Rose's silver pitcher. "And you can be sure she was mad as hell at *herself* when *she* fell in love. Oh yeah - you can be sure of that. Left the bayou for a man just like her foremothers. Came back pissed and bitter to get her stuff and left again. *Comme ça.* Never came back. Last I saw of her.

"As Grandmère always used to say, 'The Lord works in mysterious ways, his praises to behold.'"

So many questions! I started with one from the more-distant past."How did Luisah respond to Christie" — Kristi/Christie: my heart skipped a little as my mouth shaped the name — "when she got so mad at her for falling in love and leaving your PawPaw and you all?"

"I'm sure she was heartbroken, but she was a hard woman in some ways. Not like her sissy DuPree daughters at all. They all just exacerbated each other what with their fainting spells and ro-mance novels." He gave a wry smile. "Her granddaughter got some of her hardness, as I suspect you noticed." He thought for a moment. "Though I think she cultivated it," he added. "She was a tender, bright thing as a youngun'."

Motte busied himself with his fennel tea. "What I remember about the last day the three of us were together was, first, them fighting. Grandmère saying, 'Don't you cut your eyes at me, child.' And Christiane being shut up good. Grandmère meant business when she brought those words out. Then I remember the last thing she said, to both of us as she left. It was some of her what we called 'Voodoo advice:' 'Don't forget to protect yourselves from unwanted visitors with redbrick dust on your stoops.' She really said that with a warning tone, cuz I guess she knew something we didn't.'The two of you gonna need it!' Then - gone." A tear rolled down his cheek. "That was the first thing I thought of when I heard my sister was killed – 'Did she forget the redbrick dust?'" He wasn't ashamed to cry, that much I could tell. But it was hard for him to talk through his tears. I waited. "Then I said to myself, 'Of course she couldn't put dust on her doorstep, stupid. She was a bigwig in the big city.' Who would've thought she'd need it there?"

Above us, the clouds were roiling at their edges, as if about to drench us all again. Thunderheads, they looked like.

"I am so sorry about your sister," I said sincerely.

"Christiane?" He looked up. It almost seemed as if he was calling to her. "She got what she wanted: she got out of the bayou and into the history books with her writing." His expression saddened. "Well, and they'll recall her death, that's the grievous part."

Snowy had cleared the plates by now and just a small bowl of jasmine petal jelly with toast points remained. "A snack," she'd said, "in case you still have an appetite." Considering I'd just eaten the biggest meal of my life, it said something that I was nonetheless moved to try her jelly. It was excellent – subtle and somehow refreshing, the perfect ending to a perfect meal.

"I want to see this bird," I said, rising from my chair with some effort.

Motte got up too, and walked toward the cage – it was just one of those regular white metal ones from the pet store, on a white stand – calling, "Peacey, Peacey." He stopped next to me, quite close. "That's Peace," he said to me. "Boy or girl, we don't know."

The bird cocked its head and looked at us through its intelligent round eyes. Its pupils expanded and contracted several times and then it gave a questioning "Tweet?" It lifted a scaly little foot as if to wave hello.

"Aaw, you are so cute!" I exclaimed. To Motte, I said, "Is your Aunt a pacifist or something?"

"Or something. Peacey's named after a hybrid tea rose that same orangey color. Marie-Rose and her roses again, case you didn't notice."

I waved to Peacey and we walked to the entrance hall. Now that he'd told me, I could see the rose theme in the knickknacks and fabrics around me.

"I enjoyed making your acquaintance, Annie."

"It was nice meeting you, too. Thank you for lunch. Please give Snowy my compliments."

"Hey, I almost forgot these!" He went to a pretty Mahogany side table and picked up a wax paper bag tied with twine. "Snowy's pralines" – he pronounced it "prah-leens," with the accent on the second syllable – "for you to take on your trip. The best in town."

"Oh, thank you." I was genuinely excited. I'd heard a lot about this authentic New Orleans candy, made of brown sugar, butter and pecans.

"Well, I'd better be on my way." I held out my hand. "Thank you again--" Motte surprised me by drawing me into his embrace. "Oh," I managed to exclaim. I was startled but not unhappy to find myself in his arms. He smelled like roses and rain, and something earthy underneath.

He drew back first, and took a long look at me. Then, he gently kissed my forehead, led me to the front door and opened it. "I like you a lot. You're cheeky and you're smart. Easy on the eye. too. In a funny way, you remind me of my sister as a girl." Whoa, I thought, and tried not to think too much about it. "I'm headed back to Bayou Grosse Tête tomorrow, but otherwise I'd sure like to take you out…" I smiled shyly, transformed very briefly into a southern belle. I began to walk down the steps, noticing the redbrick dust under my feet for the first time. There was a gentle smudging of it out onto the banquette, and from there onto the sidewalk.

"Annie?" I didn't want to turn around. My face felt transparent and my emotions were a big mess of confusion: sadness, anger, loneliness, even longing. I turned and faced him, carefully composing my face into a politely receptive "Yes?"

"That guy's not the one for you," was all he said, and then he closed the door.

Tuesday, the weather turned temperate and sunny again. That night, our last in New Orleans, we went out to get one last taste of the French Quarter. I drank in the colorful sights, the Voodoo shops and tattoo parlors, the jazz bars and street musicians. I admired the old houses with their ubiquitous verandas. I drank in the deceptively delicate cast-iron latticework on every "gallery," the mysterious shuttered French doorways, the hidden gardens. All bespoke a more-civilized way of life than we isolated, apartment-dwelling New Yorkers endured. The combination of refinement and excess touched me more than I would have imagined.

I never got to see Anne Rice's house, but that night we did pass Mam'zelle Marie LaVeau's place, on St. Ann Street. She was a Voodoo high priestess for three generations and all the Voodoons in New Orleans venerate her. Her daughter, Marie II, threw legendary orgies, and many in New Orleans claim a drop of her blood. The old house looked as if it held many fascinating secrets. Nearby, a tall woman who looked like she carried the ancestry of all the races that make up the jambalaya of the Louisiana population called out to me. "You there! You need to pray to the big mother to protect you!"

Maybe I was feeling what folks down there call "tipsy," a little closer to the magical realm, a little more open, than usual, but I sat down in front of the small card table she had set up and covered with a red silk cloth.

She began to speak. "You're gonna wash a watermelon in wine. Pick a fine one, nice and heavy. With a sharp knife, cut out hole in the watermelon and put in a red candle. Then, listen, wash your mouth out with molasses mixed with water and lemon. That's for the sweet, the sour and the clean." She looked at me sharply. "You gettin' all this?" I nodded eagerly. "Now, you take that watermelon to the water under the moon and tell Yemaya." She sat down, spreading her skirts around her and closed her eyes.

272

"Thank you." My gratitude was sincere. She nodded in acknowledgement. I was about to walk away when it occurred to me: "What do I owe you, Ma'am?"

"Lagniappe," she said without opening her eyes. "A free gift to you from the spirits. Mother wit."

"But this is your living." I felt she should be compensated for her offering.

She opened her pale brown eyes – they had a striking navy-blue rim around the iris – and looked at me intently. "Just honor her." I did this. After extensive efforts to find all my ingredients in this unfamiliar place, I prepared my offering. I went to the Mississippi River and sat down on the stone ledge along the riverbank. I left my watermelon for Yemaya on the ledge, where I noticed (now that I had some idea of what to look for) other altered fruits and vegetables and everyday objects here and there along my path. There, I made my plea to the moonlit river on behalf of Christiane Eglantine Thompson, and all us other complicated women.

Chapter Nine – Trips: Thanksgivings, Intuitions

The relative poverty of Puduhepa's handmaiden did not preclude her self-expression. Clay *bullae* and her education were all she needed to, in a very real sense, survive the ages…There is strong evidence that Tavanaliya was prized by Puduhepa for her psychic powers, yet this researcher cannot help but wonder: could Tavanaliya even have imagined the world of today?

I. O. Heyreddin, *Things Truly New to Behold* (forthcoming)

In Annie's apartment, Pepita and Merlin snoozed while Gretel worked on a paper she was handing in late. The intermittent clang of Annie's radiator – so beloved of native New Yorkers – was making Gretel jumpy. She reached for the phone, but then let her hand fall back to her lap. Everyone she knew in the city was either away for the

Thanksgiving break or using the time off for catching up on work. With the undergraduate population gone, along with many graduate students and faculty, campus was deserted and the streets were quiet. Every once in a while these last few days, she'd felt a little lonely, even to the point of wishing Annie had a television – anything to fill the silences, make her feel as if she had company. With little to distract her but her work, she increasingly found her mind on Kirpal, who was in Canada visiting his family. Just thinking of him made her blush and feel simultaneously intensely warm and slightly discombobulated.

Annie's wall of overflowing bookshelves loomed large in her peripheral vision. Gretel had been daydreaming again. Fantasies about Kirpal, again. She sipped from her mug of weak, milky tea and, not for the first time, willed herself to focus on the quasi-Marxist implications of *Middlemarch*.

Hearing a mourning dove's call, she looked out the living room window for its source. The bird was sitting right outside, on the windowsill. She pursed her lips and imitated the sad cry: "Coo roooo cooo, coo coo." Keeping its beady eye on hers, the bird flew away the instant Gretel's call ended. She shivered, wondering if the bird's sudden flight was a bad omen.

Annie's place was so warm and cozy. It was private, too, which was the main reason she'd agreed to housesit: she shared her university-subsidized housing with three roommates of varying, though to a person relatively low, degrees of personal hygiene and friendliness. She was disappointed to sense her uneasiness returning in a place she'd heretofore considered a haven.

Since Christia Thompson's death, Gretel had been feeling nervous and paranoid. Despite the ingrained objectivity of her sensible upbringing, she'd been discerning omens and startled by shadows. She was not normally an intuitive woman, but of late her inner voice had been telling her, loud and clear, that Christia's killer was someone in her extended social circle. Someone Gretel knew. But who? All of the boys in the religion department seemed a little suspect to her, except, of course, for Kirpal. As far as she was concerned, the culprit might just as easily have been any of them. Or Christia's kooky English husband. Or that full-of-himself professor of Asian religions, Richard Redmund. Any one of these men might accost her alone on the street, "Just to say hello." What would she do? At least, unlike Christia, she had nothing to be ashamed of.

Gretel was of two minds about Christia Thompson. She knew it wasn't politically correct to think of promiscuity as "bad," and naturally nobody deserved to be brutally murdered. Nonetheless, Christia was an arrogant woman who'd used her sexuality and the affection of others to get ahead. She'd caused a lot of pain to a lot of people. Gretel couldn't help feeling that somehow the murdered woman had deserved to – if not *die, per se*, at least be forced to atone for her behavior. For if virtue was its own reward would not the converse also hold true? Chances were, Christia had been killed as a repercussion – albeit a very strong, possibly exaggerated repercussion – for her own actions. There it was: logical, not kind.

Nevertheless, who did the killer think he was, making himself the instrument of God's vengeance? Alone in Annie's eclectic living room, full of thrift-store treasures and books on every subject, a world of plenty and possibility, Gretel felt the injustice keenly, in her heart. Then her mind shifted again. On the other hand, she wondered, who will carry out God's will if not his most noble creation, the human being?

A small voice kept niggling at her through this line of internal discourse: You are a peaceful woman, it said, raised to honor pacifist ideals. Our God is not a vengeful one, it continued. For that, we have only ourselves to blame.

*

Ibrahim Heyreddin's eyes watered in the dry air as he read, for the thousandth time, the title page of his breakthrough manuscript. "Things truly new to behold: On the long-lost codex of the maid of Queen Puduhepa:" was this not a striking title? He hoped so. He gazed past the rather large person seated next to him to see the last traces of the setting sun. They'd just taken off from JFK -- nonstop to Paris, Charles de Gaulle.

That afternoon, he'd gone to Tom's Diner for the Thanksgiving platter. Not that he was celebrating the American holiday. He just liked the menu – and the special price for those pathetic few who were unable to be home-sweet-home for the meal. Maybe next year he'd be grateful, and then he'd celebrate.

Ibo was flying coach, something he'd been at great pains to hide from Tomás, who would also be in Paris. Tomás was visiting his cousins, and would be staying at the Hotel Plaza Athenée; while Ibo was visiting his brother and his brother's family, with whom he'd be staying. Tomás had flown the day before, on a flight Ibo had professed to be unable to catch due to a Wednesday-afternoon meeting scheduled long in advance. (A lie: as if anyone at the University of New York would work the day before Thanksgiving!)

The truth was, Ibo avoided meetings like the plague. Faculty meetings, committee meetings…They all bored him to tears. One only attended meetings to earn brownie points – and Ibo didn't work that way. Due to his nature or fate – whichever -- Ibo would never get ahead by traditional brown-nosing, committee-joining means, only by taking the next step of his plan. He wanted to be respected for the excellence of his work, no more, no less. But the meeting lie had served a purpose, allowing him to take a later flight, and an economy seat. So far, no one in his circle knew he was no longer the heir to a vast fortune.

So? Why should anyone know his family's business had been ruined by the descendants of the pasha whose house they'd taken over?

In Turkey, loyalties ran deep and complex over the centuries. Once they'd come of age, the impoverished pasha's heirs – who had seen their childhood home sold for a pittance by their desperate family -- had directed all of their considerable influence to systematically, bit by bit, destroy the Heyreddin's business. The Turkish people, Ibo thought with a sigh of resignation, had always had a special place in their collective heart for their historical authority figures, from the Byzantine to Ottoman Empires. Even Ataturk, that compulsive Westernizer, was venerated by many. Ergo, why should a pasha's descendants not be given special privileges in their quest for vengeance?

They had started small, tying up the processes of getting permits to operate the Heyreddin candy factory, so that production was delayed again and again; and inciting, through strategically placed moles, the factory workers to demand better pay and shorter hours. When Ibo reached his early twenties, the factories were barely scraping by. They'd closed when he was twenty-five and beginning his graduate studies. Their big, posh shop on Istanbul's bustling Taksim Square had empty shelves and, little by little, the customers began to go elsewhere for their *raahat Lokum*.

Raahat Lokum. His mouth watered and his heart grew tender at the thought of his favorite childhood treat. Turkish delight, they called it in the U.S., but in Turkey it was called the food of contentment; literally: *raahat lokum* meant "we have eaten contentment." How true, Ibo mused. He thought of his favorite flavors -- pistachio, of course, but then coconut, mmm, lemon…And rose petal! That was one he never found in the U.S.

After the factories closed, the Heyreddins had focused on their import-export business out of their shop facilities for the next few years, but that too needed permits and influence to keep things rolling smoothly. Dusted with cornstarch, and rolled in colored wax paper, Heyreddin's Turkish Delight stayed fresh for six months on its overseas journeys. Of course, one of the sons in the pasha's family had been an important cog in the port authority and had managed to hold up billions of Turkish *lira* in shipments for seven months. Their offices too, high above the candy shop, overlooking the minarets, domes and anonymous office towers of Istanbul, had ultimately been forced to close down.

The woman across the aisle was looking at him. He knew what she saw: pale olive skin,; dark eyes with ends that turned up like cat-eye eyeliner; kissable, bitable, rosy lips, or so his last lover had referred to them. His current admirer was reasonably attractive, but Ibo was not interested in a woman who would give a stranger the eye on a plane. Nor was he, in fact, interested in having any sort of intimate relationship until the whole mess of his family honor had been cleaned up. He had a two-step plan, and step one had already been executed.

The year after Ibo had finished graduate school, the Heyreddins had sold their house, the beloved old wooden *yah* on the Bosporus – at least the pasha's descendents hadn't gotten *that*! -- and dispersed to try their fortunes elsewhere. His father was working under someone else for the first time in his life; his mother, feminism notwithstanding, had been agog to find there were no jobs available to a woman with few skills and no work experience beyond raising a family. She had taken work mending her former friends' couture clothing. Now *that* was a melancholy story for a *cile* song.

Squeezing his eyes shut against the picture of his mother's once-delicate hands, now riddled with dry lines and pinpricks, Ibo slumped in his narrow seat. His seatmate let out an affronted "hmph," and nudged Ibo's arm off the tiny corner of the armrest it had commandeered. Ibo seethed with misplaced rage. He knew the man next to him had nothing to do with his family's misfortune. He forced himself to calm down, comforting himself with thoughts of the near future.

The present kept intruding. The Heyreddins' once vast family fortune was gone, the furniture and cars, the yacht, the vacation homes,

279

had all been sold (at a pittance, really – in that area he sympathized with his family's enemies). They'd kept only a few precious artifacts of their once-splendid lives.

Ibo had been struggling mightily with money over the last year, what with his pathetic pay from the university and his high-flying friends. Still, he'd somehow managed to keep his impoverishment a secret. Ah, for the days of eating contentment – the unquestioned abundance, the languid days. Now he was *poor*. It didn't bother him so much for his own sake, it was for his parents and sisters that his crusade had been undertaken.

Personally, he found that poverty made one find joy where one could, and to strive for distinction in ways a rich person could not imagine. Nonetheless, given his family's reputation, which so soon would be regained, it seemed very important to Ibo to keep up appearances. In Turkey, the Heyreddins were now trash; but in the United States they would rise again. They wouldn't be smug, God no, but proud they would be.

He told himself it was time to sleep. It was his custom to conform to the local time zone of his destination from the moment of his departure. It was past midnight in Paris. Thus, it was nighttime, and he would behave as if it were already so -- and, in the bargain, give his brain a small respite from thoughts of loss and honor.

It wouldn't be long now.

Ibo was a good son and brother, and Ibo, good old Ibo, was patient.

*

We had a hard time leaving New Orleans. For all our bickering and the ambiguity of our relationship, Nicholas and I still had a lot in common and, with her magic and her European flair, the beautiful old, debauched, devastated city suited us. We left early on Wednesday, to make it to Gram's in time for Thanksgiving.

After New Orleans, Greensboro, North Carolina was the land of the bland. It felt so relatively devoid of character: not intensely southern, yet not northern, either; not quite as devoid of *place-ness* as, say, Delaware, but close. What passed for winter there meant that the days were damp and cool, but not cold enough that one made sure to wear a warm coat, thus causing one to always feel vaguely underdressed and chilly. Magnolias, as common there as they were throughout the South, were long past flower, but here and there a tired bunch of chrysanthemums bloomed valiantly, a splash of color in the suburban landscape. Brick ranch houses and housing developments sprawled in all directions from the downtown.

Gram lived in one of those ubiquitous low brick houses. Hers was painted white with light green trim, and had a tiny weeping willow in the small front yard. Despite its contribution to the monotony of the surrounding architectural landscape, I loved it. With its size and character, her house seemed almost like a doll's house to me. Inside, the house was decorated country-style, with a red, white, and blue color scheme. There were Amish quilts on the beds, white, eyelet lace curtains tied with red bows, rag rugs: vintage adorable grandmother style. I knew she'd have something delicious and indulgent to eat waiting for us. It was worth coming to this bastion of middlebrow monotony to see my beloved grandmother, who was the last person one would ever call dull.

"Gram!" At 83, my grandmother, Lorene C. Miller, was still a stunning woman. Part Cherokee and the rest Scottish and Swedish, she was a tiny woman, with a trim figure, salt and pepper hair done in a bouffant, and cheekbones any model would've killed for. A fine mesh of wrinkles covered her face, serving only to enhance the kind of beauty that comes only from the combination of a big heart and a life well-lived. She'd grown up all over the South and was the epitome of a Southern lady: warm, kind and hospitable. I was so happy to see her.

Especially with all the upheavals and intrigues I'd been going through of late, it was good to see someone with whom I had a simple relationship. Gram and I just adored each other.

"Oh darlin's, I am so *glad* to see you. Come on in. I've got a cake in the icebox." My stomach rumbled at the thought of her cooking. That generation did not worry about butterfat. We grabbed our luggage and went up the steps to her front door. Her dogs, two rather rotund dachshunds, Sweet Pea and Maggie May, were yapping away. I knew they made her feel safe so I didn't say anything, just hoped the clamor wouldn't give me a headache.

"Pepita sends her love," I told them, "She couldn't stay at our hotel in New Orleans so we had to leave her in the city."

"Well now, you be sure to give her a hug for me when you get back!" I nodded. As we greeted the dogs, Gram noticed we were laden with luggage. "Let's see, kids. Nicholas," she directed, "You'll be in the Florida sun room on the fold-out bed, and Annie, I've got you in the room next to mine."

"Thanks, Gram." I gave her a big squeeze. "I'll be right back." I dumped my stuff in the guest room and freshened up in the bathroom before joining the two of them in the dining room. A generous slice of three-layered devil's food cake with vanilla buttercream frosting, served on Gram's Spode china, awaited me at my place. Gram and Nicholas were sipping from tall glasses of iced sweet tea.

After we ate, Nicholas and I offered to take the dogs for a walk. We wanted to stretch our legs after the drive. Gram came part of the way with us, and then we walked her home and walked in the other direction. A light drizzle was falling, dampening our cheeks slightly.

"I remember you told me your grandparents were really in love," Nicholas said, as we walked.

"Yeah, she misses him so much." I thought wistfully of my beloved grandfather. "I do too, but, I mean, he was her *husband*. They were married for over 50 years!"

Nicholas stopped and looked at me searchingly. "Do you think that kind of relationship is still possible in this day and age?"

I stopped too, pensive. In the yard next to us, the rain pattered on the glossy leaves of a tall magnolia tree. "You mean it might no longer be possible because there aren't the kind of social pressures that used to keep people together through hard times?" He didn't answer. I'd certainly left him as soon as things got rough, but I didn't think we'd have improved things by sticking it out longer. "Oh, or things that constrain them from getting it on with whoever they lusted after?" I winked and elbowed him in the ribs. "You know it was a whole different scene when everybody had peers, family, close-knit communities keeping an eye on everyone…" I added.

"Commitment and community. That pretty much says it all." Nicholas was nodding in agreement. His blonde hair had turned a darker shade in the rain. He earnestly tried to look me in the eye, but, unable to see clearly, he instead removed his glasses and wiped them smeary-dry on his undershirt.

I thought about my grandparents – the early years of their marriage spent traveling with the military, the years of struggle raising two kids on one teacher's salary; I remembered the way, until the day he died, my grandfather's eyes still lit up when his wife of 50+ years walked into a room. "All I can say is, for my Grams, it was worth it. I know for them there were very hard times. Pain, lean periods, sacrifices, but pleasure too - lots of fun. We -- I mean post-sixties youth, I guess -- tend to romanticize everything. We expect things to stay fiery and intense like they are at the beginning of a relationship. We want just the good side of things, you know, *le plus de plaisir possible*, as Stendahl said."

"Yes," Nicholas said quickly, and with conviction. "But Stendahl was talking about the *limited* nature of the romantic approach to things. That it works for a time only, a generation or two, and then the next thing comes along to romantically inflame the new culture being born. The old thing becomes, *ipso facto*, passé."

"Exactly!" I agreed. "That's like our romantic approach to romance today: this individual no longer tickles my fancy, so what's next?" I shivered. "Let's keep walking."

After that, we walked along more quietly, dragging the two fat dachshunds through the mushy brown leaves underfoot. So much remained unspoken. Above all, we skirted around the fact that our conversation might well be applied to we two – or to Christia Thompson's tragic life.

The next few days were a blur of hot cocoa and cinnamon toast, all the Thanksgiving fixin's, all the leftovers, trips to the Piggly Wiggly grocery store for entertainment…Everyone in the South minds their manners, but having to hear all those North Carolina-style "Thank *yeeewwws*" started to grate on me after awhile. Mostly we stayed home with the TV on, tuned to news and game shows, and our feet up, like a regular American family. Gram and I talked a lot about the past. I had such nourishing memories of childhood time spent with my grandparents.

I wondered if Christia's times with Grandmère Louisah had been a source of comfort to her. Certainly she had felt betrayed when her grandmother left, but what about before that? After all, as the old saying goes, there is no hate without love. Yet, I mused, how painful it must have been for young Christiane to see this bastion of womanly fortitude "brought low" by love.

Saturday night, there was a major fall thunderstorm. I lay in my bed watching flashes of lightning make patterns through the venetian blinds and thinking. Now that I had some distance from my currently tumultuous life in the city, I had to admit my suspicions were coalescing somewhat differently. I still felt that Nicholas had nothing to do with Christia's death. After all, we'd been together 24/7 for the whole week and he'd given no indication whatsoever of guilt or even more-than-usual odd behavior. But, my affection dimmed slightly by distance, I was beginning to wonder about some of the other men I cared about: Ibo, who'd been acting angry, for one; and, more particularly, Tomás -- whose behavior had lately been erratic and confusing. I did not then have any idea why either might have killed her, but I reasoned it must've had something to do with a love affair gone wrong or an academic slight – or some combination of the two. I finally overtly admitted to myself that, aside from Nicholas, Tomás had probably been the last person to see Christia alive. For the first time, alone and far from the scene of the crime, I felt scared not of anything supernatural but of real live people. People I knew and cared for.

It was only after the storm died down, and the flares of lightning were reduced to gentle pulses, that I finally fell asleep, only to find myself dreaming of Christia. At first, I did not realize I was dreaming. We were sitting, just the two of us, in my grandmother's sun room. She had a teacup and saucer delicately balanced on one knee. She was dressed smartly, in a matching rose-colored suit that was much more demure, more matronly, than the styles I had been accustomed to seeing her wear while living.

"I need to ask you to do me a favor," she said very politely, with a stronger Southern accent than she'd had when I knew her – before.

"Certainly," I said, echoing her Southern politesse.

"If you wouldn't mind, honey child," she began. At that moment, I started to realize, horrified, that I was conversing with a dead woman. Furthermore, I began to suspect I was experiencing some sort of psychic encounter, and not a dream. She, noticing my growing dismay, ceased speaking and waited patiently for me to acclimatize. She took a dainty sip of tea and then set her saucer down on the table, carefully placing the cup in its center. She intertwined her fingers and placed them in her lap. Her legs were crossed at the ankle. She looked at me, her expression very frank. "Annie, I only have a few more minutes here. Ask me what you like." She saw my eager expression. "Anything but...*that*."

"Well, in that case, um..." What does one do in these situations? I certainly did not know. "*Please* do hurry," she said. My heart was pounding and my brain felt completely fried. I settled on the only other question that came to mind: "How did you find me down here?" She laughed, and for that moment I saw a glimpse of the old, sardonic Christia; then she said, "I'm *dead*. I can do whatever I want!"

I sat in silence, unsure if she was messing with my head. At this point, I knew this was a dream visitation unlike any other I'd ever had. I got a little lost in my reverie on the nature of reality, until Christia grabbed my knee with her bony hand. "Look at me," she ordered. "I have come a long way to tell you this: Stop looking for my killer." I looked at her in utter shock. "I mean it." She had tears in her eyes. "This is all a big mistake." With that, she disappeared.

We left on Sunday morning for the twelve-hour drive back to New York City. Gram and I were both fighting back tears as Nicholas and I loaded up the Spider. Early Saturday mornings, most people are in their homes looking forward to the weekend. Sunday mornings are different. For some people, church is an onerous duty, for others, Monday's shadow looms large. In Greensboro, the sky was heavy and gray and the air was humid. The rows and rows of low brick houses looked no shinier after their storm-washing. My clothes felt saturated and cold on my skin, and my mood wasn't much warmer. Aside from leaving Gram's tender ministrations, I didn't mind heading North on that dismal day.

*

With a small smile on his face, Tomás Bautista listened to his cousins' musical voices for a moment before knocking on the door to their suite. They were such happy girls, and why not? Both were loose-limbed and beautiful: Solange with her long, sleek blonde hair and peaches and cream complexion, Ghislaine with her masses of black curls and enormous almost-black eyes. Both were smart, studying a year apart at Paris' most prestigious university, Sciences Politiques. And their parents were rich as hell. Plus, they were good people, loyal and loving cousins. Since they lived in the 5th arrondissement, the student- and school-filled Latin Quarter, across the Seine from Tomás' hotel, they'd taken a suite at the Plaza Athenée to be near their cousin during his visit. These were girls who'd attended Le Rosy for high school. They skied every winter in Gstaad. They bought ready-to-wear fashion when most of their peers were buying *aux puces* – at the flea markets. It was natural to them to take a thousand-dollar a night suite to save a twenty-minute taxi ride.

Tomás had grown up under similar circumstances, but was less sybaritically-inclined. He'd taken a single room overlooking the *cour jardin*, the Plaza Athenée's famed garden courtyard. He liked his room, which was decorated in 18th-century style, well enough. He even admired the fine gold-framed still-life over his bed. But most of all, he was grateful for the opportunity to be outside and alone at once: He had a small stone terrace off his room that was covered in rambling ivy. After arriving in Paris early Thursday morning, preferring to stay on New York time for the short trip, he'd gone straight to bed for a few hours. He'd enjoyed a late lunch with his cousins at the hotel and then gone back upstairs to write for a while. His life had been turbulent of late and he was behind on his schoolwork. While the day was still light, it had been warm enough to sit on his terrace, smoking and sipping from his favorite drink, that uniquely French combination of beer,

287

carbonated lemonade, and kirsch known as a Monaco. When he began
to feel a chill, around dusk, he grabbed the precious matelassé
bedspread from his King-sized bed, wrapped himself in it, and went
back outside to smoke, think and write.

Beneath him, the garden, lacking much of its summer splendor,
nonetheless offered a charming and peaceful vista for the weary
traveler. Bright red awnings surrounded the courtyard's central mosaic,
done in shades of navy and turquoise. In warmer weather, big red
canvas parasols placed around the periphery sheltered tables where
guests would sip cocktails and eat trumped-up Croques Monsieurs.
Dark green ivy, some of it just tinged with the reds and oranges of late
fall, climbed the hotel's interior walls and tumbled in glorious profusion
from the balconies overlooking the quiet, still courtyard.

Solange and Ghislaine had taken a suite on the top floor with a
clear view to the Eiffel tower. He'd come to see their rooms after they'd
lunched together on Thursday, and even he had been impressed. The
top floors were decorated in art-deco style, and their suite was done all
in white. In the sitting room, a tall vanity of ivory lacquer sat across
from a large picture window with a view across the rectangles of green
leading up to the Eiffel tower. Plump coral pillows, the room's only
dash of color, accented the upholstered benches at the foot of each
luxurious bed and nestled invitingly in the corners of creamy-white
sofas. Each bedroom had its own substantial balcony, with stunning
views of the Paris rooftops and the stately, prosperous, chestnut-lined,
Avenue Montaigne wending its way below. The girls took all this for
granted, he mused, just as, until recently, he had done himself.

Thursday night. Thanksgiving, he recalled with a pang.

He knocked and was let in.

The sisters had the stereo tuned to Radio Nova, Paris' coolest
station. The DJ announced an old song from MC Solaar, "Le Nouveau

Western." Squealing in delight, Ghislaine turned the volume up and Tomás' lovely cousins began to dance around.

Clothes now covered almost every available surface in the sumptuous rooms. Both girls wore Agnes B. for daytime, but their evening styles were very different. With her hippie-romantic style, Solange wore Gaultier and Lacroix, while Ghislaine tended toward the more hard-edged Mugler, and sophisticated Saint Laurent. It was almost 11 p.m., *vingt-trois heures* in the local vernacular, and Tomás was so hungry he felt hollowed-out inside. The three spoke together briefly, in a comfortable mix of French, Spanish and English. They shared a cigarette and the last few bites of a plum galette ordered earlier from room service before leaving the hotel to grab a bite at a local bistro.

After the meal, Tomás was ready to go to bed but the girls insisted he accompany them to Queen, a nearby discothèque on the Champs-Elysées. At that hour, the Avenue des Champs-Elysées was devoid of eager tourists. The Arc de Triomph, looming over the wide, almost-empty street, shone at their backs as they made their way from the hotel to the club. In the end, Queen was a disappointment and they didn't stay long. Although the giant nightclub was obviously popular – it was full of people, mostly men, dancing -- it was rather too brightly lit, and much too loud for conversation. They'd spent a half-hour or so with some friends of Ghislaine's in the VIP lounge overlooking the dance floor, but everyone was tired, and their luxurious beds beckoned from just steps away. As they left, Brigitte Bardot was singing, "*Je danse, donc je suis…*"

The three cousins had a much better time with Tomás' friend Ibo on Friday, drinking wine from baby bottles at a little fondu place in Montmartre and dancing like crazy, judging by the fact that none of them awoke before 11 a.m. the next day. Around noon, Tomás, Ghislaine, and Solange had tea in the Plaza Athenée's Galerie des Gobelins. The long, golden-illuminated hall was hung with crystal chandeliers. They lent a sparkle to the atmosphere as the sun shone on them through sheer silk curtains. Small tables, perfect for intimate conversations, were set along the edges of the hall. Giant topiary trees stood sentinal at each end of the room. The ambiance was of understated richness, sunny yet subtle.

They took their seats on soft, cream-colored velvet-upholstered chairs around a table intended for two. In the background, they could hear the sound of a harp being gently stroked. The atmosphere was a peaceful one, but the three whispering friends were not happy. On the way down in the elevator, the subject of family discord had come up. Despite Solange's determined efforts to change the subject, her more-fiery sister had refused to take a hint, and the conversation had degenerated. Solange and Tomás exchanged a look of distress as they sat down.

Ghislaine glowered from her perch at the edge of her downy seat cushion. "Why do you put your parents through this?" she hissed. She had a powerful, albeit black and white, sense of family loyalty and was affronted by what she saw as Tomás' breach of a tacit trust.

"Can't you see he is miserable?" Solange countered, with a glare at her sister, who ignored her.

"Why don't you act like an adult, admit your parents aren't perfect, *et puis voila, quoi.*" Ghislaine's pretty eyes snapped at Tomás, who rolled his in exasperation. "Maman says you've been treating Dahlia like you don't even know her." The girls' mother was an indomitable figure, full of the legendary Bautista integrity and passion, and her displeasure with a family member could have major repercussions. "And Maman's brother, your *father*, he is more stoic, but my sense is you are hurting him, too, from what she tells me. The way you've been acting towards them…*Ca ne se fait pas*, you know? It just is not done."

Solange stayed quiet, lips pressed tightly together. The sadness in her eyes was tinged with confusion and a little anger.

Tomás – he was a mess -- read her look as hostile. His insides were roiling, his blood hot. He felt feverish with rage. These, these *chippies* – they had no *idea* what he was going through. With enormous effort, he got ahold of his renegade temper. They had no idea of his pain, nor should they. Lucky, simple girls. He told himself he should be more giving, and – this, especially -- more forgiving. With a great effort to appear calm, he reached over and put his hand on top of Ghislaine's smooth white fingers. "I am sure this will all work out," he reassured her. "I will try to do better." He gave her fingers a squeeze and she melted a little, allowing him a small smile.

For just a moment, Tomás looked much older than his years, and very tired. His cousins were too happy at his apparent change of heart to notice.

Solange reached into her quilted pink tweed Chanel bag and pulled out a diamond-encrusted watch on a chain. "It's getting late," she announced after consulting her timepiece, "We'd better get going, if you want to meet Ibo on time later this afternoon, Gigi."

It was not a far walk to the Place Vendome, a large square surrounded by some of the most elegant real estate in Paris. Traffic was allowed only on the periphery, and the interior of the square was mercifully car- and moto-free. The square was peppered with the tall, three-pronged art-nouveau streetlights taken for granted by Parisians, and graced with a carved obelisk at its center. At the entrance to the Ritz, a chauffeured Bentley idled in front of the cypress trees in tubs. Faceted, round lanterns hung on wrought-iron loops, illuminating, day and night, the entrance to one of the world's most prestigious hotels. For intimacy and charm, the sisters preferred the Plaza Athenée – but for its spa, complete with *hammam* services, and Roman-style baths to boot, the Ritz was simply *le top*.

291

Tomás gave each of his cousins a big hug, assuring them that he would think about what they'd said earlier. He confirmed their plan to meet later that afternoon at the Café Marly in the Louvre, and then left Ghislaine and Solange, spa-ready, at the entrance to the Ritz and continued on his way.

*

Ibo walked down the stone steps to the Seine and let the sun warm his face. Lazily, he watched the play of light on the old cobblestone walkway alongside the river. After breakfast with his brother's family – honey, olives and homemade Turkish pastries -- he'd spent the morning at Shakespeare & Company, the Latin Quarter bookstore overlooking the Seine that served as a mecca for ex-pats of all-sorts. He'd passed several sweet hours watching women and leafing through overpriced English-language books (even the bargain books outside were beyond his means!) thinking idly and intermittently of what his next academic endeavor would be. He had no idea.

Ghislaine, Solange, and Tomás were probably still sleeping. He'd managed to avoid his friend and his friend's gorgeous French cousins until the night before – Friday night – a night they'd all spent carousing. Now he was nursing a slight hangover but he imagined the other three were contending with something slightly more serious, given that they'd mixed their alcohol with cocaine and the ubiquitous hashish, or "sheet," as Parisians called it.

A tour boat full of jaunty tourists puttered by, jolting him out of his reverie. Just across the river, the Cathedral of Notre Dame shone in the sunlight, her gargoyles and spires rendered cheery by all that light. Ibo squinted a little and then reached in his attaché for his sunglasses.

He'd enjoyed the restaurant where they'd eaten dinner. Le Refuge des Fondues was a tiny restaurant on the rue des Trois Frères, a steep and winding street near Butte Montmartre, the highest hill in Paris. The restaurant's storefront was painted a merry red, with a fat

292

clown stuffing his face decorating the window. Mopeds and Minis crowded the sidewalk in front of the entrance, and the festive sound of intoxicated revelers poured out from the restaurant's door every time it was opened. It was a destination for Parisians from all over town, but was also, tellingly, beloved by the bohemian local population.

Ibo had always loved the old artists' neighborhood of Montmartre, where the shabby old buildings housed all sorts of people – crusty old leftists, young, free-spirited Parisians, artists of all ages and talents. Just above the restaurant, the Sacré-Cœur cathedral, with her milky-white, nippled dome, sat overlooking all of Paris, affording all who came a panoramic view of Paris from her wide and welcoming steps. And just down the hill lay the neighborhood of Pigalle, with its erotic shows of every stripe, from the recently redone Bal du Moulin Rouge to the seedy bars where anything could be bought if only one had enough cash.

On his way up the rue des Trois Frères, Ibo had stopped to catch his breath and had heard someone playing the piano from an old and crooked house that looked as if its plaster walls were barely sticking together. Outside, it was dusk, and most people – if they were home – had turned their inside lights on. This house remained unlit, as if the pianist were blind to the end of the day, or illumined, perhaps, by some interior light. The windows were thrown open to the November chill as someone inside played a Satie song. The pretty, spare notes from the piano, so essentially expressive of Paris in the '20s, floated over the crumbling, idyllic neighborhood. Around the windows, ivy stirred gently in the evening air, Paris' ubiquitous plucky sparrows darting about in the tangled vines.

Up atop the twisting old street they'd had an uproariously good time from the moment their party had arrived. They'd been instructed to climb over one of the two long communal tables to get to the inside

293

bench. Ghislaine's short skirt had barely concealed her toned derriere as she hopped over the table giggling, assisted by a willing waiter. They'd drunk cheap red wine from baby bottles and agreed unanimously that cheap French wine outshone most American wines any day. They'd ordered the Fondue Savoyard, cheese fondue with chunks of baguette to dip. An old Romani woman had come in and sung an achingly beautiful rendition of Edith Piaf's *Vie en Rose*, accompanying herself on a small, hauntingly-played accordion. They'd tipped her generously and bought all the plastic roses she'd had to sell.

Tomás had been in excellent spirits, more cheerful and carefree than he'd been since Ibo'd met him in the early fall. Pink-cheeked Solange and dark-eyed Ghislaine had charmed him with their differences – they were like day and night – as well as with their shared Parisian wit. Weren't sisters the best, Tomás had asked him, and he'd felt he had to admit that, yes, they were.

Today, Ibo had a rendezvous at *quinze heures* – three o'clock -- with Ghislaine at the Jardin des Tuileries, and afterwards they would meet Solange and Tomás at the Marly Café for a whirlwind tour of the Louvre.

This plan had been agreed upon in the wee hours, long after their wonderful dinner. They'd closed out Paris' hippest nightclub, Les Bains Douches, an old municipal bathhouse in the basement of a building on the rue Bourg-L'Abbe. Les Bains was in the Marais, and Bourg-L'Abbe was a typical Marais street, narrow and winding like the medieval village street it once had been. Denizens of Paris's smashing nightlife often ended up at les Bains – it was open almost all night and located near the chic residential areas of the 3rd and 4th arrondissements.

Once there, they'd spent the hundreds of dollars it took to buy a bottle of liquor and, thus, secure one of the coveted tables surrounding the dance floor. Ibo was not much of a dancer, but the other three had

294

shaken their booties much of the night and were dripping with sweat by the time the four of them sat down all together for the first time since they'd arrived at the club. There had been some fracas with the doorman, who hadn't wanted to let the men in, but Tomás had slipped him some "*effectif*" as bribe money was known in some circles, and they'd been allowed to enter. The girls, *bien sur*, had gotten in for free.

Inside, the "*pipole*" of Paris, the rich, the hip, the famous, were gathered to drink, preen, flirt, and, above all, dance. The thick smoke made everyone look a little younger, a little more mysterious. It added to the air of possibility: wasn't that the supermodel X, over by the bar, bathed in the murky blue-green light reflected by the original bathhouse tiles on the wall and floor? And wasn't that Y, the extremely-married American starlet, who had slipped her hand into X's blouse? Probably, it was.

Sweaty, slim, beautiful people writhed in a slippery mass on the dance floor. Ibo watched and smoked, and smoked some more. He ran out of cigarettes and bought a pack of Gauloises Blondes Légères from one of the attractive girls in hot pants who went about with trays of candy, lollipops, matches, and cigarettes hanging from their comely shoulders. He noticed that Solange and Tomás seemed to be dancing rather close for cousins, and then he noticed that Solange and Ghislaine did the same thing. He thought he remembered that this was called "freaking," when two people danced very close, hip to hip, thigh touching thigh, undulating and so forth. He told himself it must be normal behavior in a place like this, a sophisticated, Western nightclub. Still, he couldn't decide if he was titillated or repulsed. He began to develop a headache.

At 5:30 a.m., when the club was about to close, Tomás told everyone it was time to plan for the next day. "After all," he said with a slight slur, "How else will we know what we *really* want to do once the wine wears off and our superegos take over?"

"We already have some plans, Tomás, *tu n' t' souviens pas*? We're doing the baths. Ibrahim," Solange said invitingly, turning to include him fully in their plans, "Tomorrow, we're going to the *hammam* at the Ritz. After, dinner at the hotel. Join us, Ibo?"

"You mean *hammam* like we have in Turkey?"

"Yes, but cleaner," Ghislaine laughed. Was there a touch of cruelty in her voice?

"Actually, there is a wonderful Turkish bath here in Paris, at the Grande Mosquée de Paris, in the 5th. In fact, I'm going there Sunday before I leave. Tuesdays and Sundays are men-only."

"Do they have a cold pool?"

"Yes – icy cold! It's a really stunning place. Like another world: there's the mosque itself, of course, very old-world, with mosaics and everything. Then there's the baths, and a *souk* -- a market, and a tea shop. There's a whole area where you can relax on rugs and drink mint tea after the baths…"

"But no one to wrap you up in the big, warmed, fluffy towel *après*, eh?" Ghislaine observed. She shrugged, with the perfect Parisian sneer on her perfect face. "*Chacun a son gout*, I suppose."

"Yes," Ibo muttered. "Of course." He was getting nowhere with these girls.

Or so he thought. While Tomás and Solange leaned back against the banquette, ostensibly gathering energy for the taxi back to the hotel, Ghislaine unwrapped a lollipop she'd bought from the cigarette girl and passed another to Solange. She began sucking pensively, her wet lips poppy-red and slick with some expensive high-gloss potion. Her eyes, too, were remarkably striking, fringed with outrageously long lashes, noted Ibo, his heartbeat quickening slightly.

"I like you, Ibrahim," Ghislaine stated, in a matter-of-fact tone. "You are just here for another day or two, why not have a little fun?"

Ibo wasn't sure what she meant. "Um, what did you have in mind?"

"I could be a sort of, *disons*, tour guide for you." Ibo's heart sank. He wondered if he was condemned to be a dork indefinitely, and he slumped a little lower in his seat.

"I will meet you *à quinze-heures* at the Tuileries garden," said Ghislaine.

He'd felt better the next morning, having slept well under his brother's roof. His brother, Ysan, had two young children and a wife in medical school, and was, understandably, not one for clubbing these days. Ysan's apartment, on the outskirts of the ethnically mixed 14th arrondissement, was comfortable, if cramped, and his family was sweet and noisy and affectionate. It was refreshing to be immersed in a wholesome family life after being in New York for so long and then, in Paris, being around these very sophisticated, louche types. After breakfast, though, he'd felt taken by a thirst for exploration, and wanted to revisit his beloved *quartiers*. He'd taken the metro to St. Michel, all along singing in his head, in his best Josephine Baker imitation, "*J'ai deux amours: mon pays et Paris.*" He'd grabbed a banana and Nutella crepe near the subway exit, and walked toward the Seine with a light step.

After a few minutes riverside, Ibo climbed the long flight of bridge-side stone steps back up to the Left Bank and the booksellers' stalls along the Quai de Montebello. A small engraving of the three arches and the rose window at the front entrance to Notre Dame caught his eye and he haggled with the bookseller until they reached a price agreeable to both of them. After his purchase, Ibo had only a few hundred euros left for the last two days of his trip. He crossed the street and sat down in a café across from Shakespeare and Company to resume his observations. All around him, people wrote, self-importantly and very seriously. He ordered himself a café au lait and gazed around, momentarily without a serious thought in his head.

At the table next to him, a grizzled old man sat across from a small yellow dog with a scarf around its neck. The dog had its own glass of wine. Only in Paris, Ibo thought, laughing. As he laughed, that part of his mind not occupied with laughter skittered around, avoiding the query to come at the end of his humorous moment: what next? Hell, why should he be bothered with such worries? He was on vacation, and he deserved a break from all that thinking. It was mostly self-torture, really, and he'd had enough of that for now. There must be more in me, he thought at one point, but, he concluded after a few less-tranquil minutes of mental searching, I'd better not push it right now!

Instead, he would spend the day walking around Paris, for there was nothing he liked better. He stopped at a *tabac* to fortify himself with cigarettes and a packet of Hollywood chewing gum. The first destination on his stroll would be the Marais, the hip, right-bank neighborhood just across the Seine. Part of that area was the old Jewish ghetto, and one could buy the most marvelous Kosher and Middle Eastern fare, including Europe's best (also, affordable) falafel, on the tiny, busy, charming Rue des Rosiers. Then he would walk over to Les Halles, the old marketplace that had been converted to shops catering to teens and young and/or fashionable Parisians and a small red light district. He would grab an espresso at the café facing the metro entrance, do some more major people-watching, and then revisit his favorite Nikki de Saint Phalle sculpture-fountain. If he had time, he'd check out the exhibits at the Centre Pompidou. He'd always enjoyed the architecture of that building, both because it had caused an international uproar, and because he secretly thought it looked like a cross between a radiator and a set of childrens' plastic building blocks.

In the Jardin des Tuileries, the starkly trimmed trees reached helplessly up, up – despite having been pruned to be perfectly flat on top, and all of a level. With their gnarled branches ending in knobs like woody fists, they reminded Ibo of the spooky trees in old black and white horror films. They'd look so much better in the spring, he thought, when tender buds, then leaves, would soften their spiky silhouettes.

Ibo and Ghislaine met near the giant, swamp-colored pool where children sailed toy boats and young lovers sat holding hands. Being neither, they were at a bit of a loss as to the proper activity, but they settled on a brisk walk around the pool, followed by sitting down at the water's edge and watching the rest of the crowd. Ibo watched, fascinated, as Ghislaine dipped the toes of her le coq sportif sneakers in the dirty water.

She noticed him watching and slapped her thighs with both hands, swinging her legs around to the sidewalk. "I guess we'd better go, eh?"

"O.K." Ibo hadn't even come close to making any romantic overtures with Tomás' cousin, and he deemed that just as well. Why chastise himself for sexual cowardice when his boldness of the not-so-distant past had gotten him nowhere?

They met up with Solange and Tomás at the Café Marly. The café was located in one of the wings of the Louvre, overlooking I.M. Pei's glass pyramid. Ghislaine mentioned that she'd been to see the fall shows under the pyramid that fall, and, predictably, Solange asked her if she'd noticed that other things went on at the Louvre as well. Meanwhile, on the Cour Napoleon, the vast courtyard of the erstwhile palace, tourists and Parisians mingled just yards from the greatest collection of art in the world. After their coffees, they went en masse to see the Venus de Milo, which they all agreed was so much more striking in the flesh, and then they made plans to meet up later at the Plaza Athenée.

Strolling back to his brother's house, Ibo stopped at a Belle Epoque style grocery, marveling at the care taken with even such a minor edifice. Well, after all, he thought, the French *do* love their food. He picked up a stem of translucent red, jewel-like fresh currants, and was cursed by the grocer for doing so. He'd forgotten one wasn't to touch the wares at these small, owner-run *alimentations*. He quickly offered to buy the berries, gesticulating to fill any gaps in his vocabulary, but the grocer dismissed him with a contemptuous wave. On the corner of Ysan's block, he stopped at a *boulangerie* for a baguette for his sister-in-law and tarts for the kids. They were short of money and he wanted to contribute what little he could. He wouldn't be eating dinner with them anyway, he had another rendezvous with the Bautista clan.

That night, the foursome ended up at Alain Ducasse's restaurant at the Plaza Athenée. The sisters were in their rooms freshening up at the appointed hour, so Tomás met Ibo alone, having agreed with his cousins to reassemble at the hotel bar. He brought Ibo past the long, illuminated glass bar counter, which contrasted with carved oak furniture and moldings, to the cozy back area, where dark-hued leather chairs encircled low ebony tables.

Tomás settled into his chair and lit a cigarette. He'd been chain-smoking black tobacco like an old Frenchman since he'd arrived in Paris, and had developed a bit of a rasp. "They have this incredible drink here. Let me get you one?"

"All right, thanks." Ibo wasn't about to refuse the offer of a drink after his long day of exploring Paris.

Tomás held up his hand to a waitress, who swerved, tray in hand, to come over to where they sat. "We'll have two Rouge Plaza Cocktails." He leaned toward Ibo. "That's champagne and geranium syrup," he informed his friend. "And, oh, whatever that is,"" he pointed to the drink on her tray, a bright blue concoction with a sugar-encrusted ring of dried pineapple as garnish, "We'll have two of those too!" He turned to Ibo. "Why not get a head start? Doesn't that look delicious?"

"Yeah," Ibo agreed, "and strange."

"Are you hot?" Tomás didn't wait for an answer, just shrugged off his gray wool pinstriped blazer, leaving a slightly rumpled white shirt worn with jeans and loafers. He tugged at the neck of his shirt, looking around. "It feels so hot in here." He took another drag of his cigarette and fell silent. They waited for their drinks. The girls came in, aflutter with an air of pleasant repartee that instantly changed the rather morose and masculine atmosphere at the table, and sat down. They ordered *Roses Royales*, champagne and raspberries, when the guys' drinks arrived. They spent a happy half-hour drinking and talking and then left in order to make their restaurant reservation on time.

When he saw the gilded ceiling and muted ivory and beige palette of the restaurant, Ibo knew the food would be way beyond his means. He should have known, he chided himself. Alain Ducasse was well-known, even in the United States. He started to panic, which he disguised by being very quiet until he trusted his voice to remain steady. Once seated, he glanced at the menu. Brittany lobster, flavored with spicy curry, sounded absolutely delicious. Ibo did a quick calculation in his head. Over $100 for an appetizer was out of the question: he had scarcely more than that for the whole meal. He settled on the duck *foie gras* appetizer, with roasted peaches. It was, at 60 euros, the cheapest item on the menu. By taking tiny bites and pushing the food around on the plate, he could manage to make the appetizer last through the whole meal. After making another calculation in his head, and remembering that his brother had offered to drive him back to Charles de Gaulle, he ordered a bottle of the house red to be convivial.

Solange and Ghislaine both chose the *"Menu Plaisirs du Table,"* a seemingly endless procession of elaborate courses. Ghislaine nibbled delicately at her food, while Solange ate with real gusto. Both seemed preoccupied, and neither thought to offer any of their food to Ibo, which, he decided, was just as well. Better that no one should notice him than that they should notice – and pity him.

Solange may have intuited that Ibo was particularly reticent that night, if not the reason why. She tried to draw him out, asking him about his work at the University of New York and his writing. In reply, he gave her a brief synopsis of his heretofore unremarkable university career, adding that he expected to be coming out with some more important work shortly.

As soon as he'd concluded, Ghislaine put down her fork. *"Alors,* what's the true story here with all the drama at your *université?"* She clearly loved the idea of intrigue, and had a look of greedy anticipation in her eyes.

"Oh, you know the story," Solange said dismissively. "A professor got killed. That's happened at *Sciences Po*, with little scandal, *tu sais."*

"That's different," Ghislaine protested. "Professors here aren't as involved with students. This woman had close relationships with many students."

"She certainly did." Ibo's voice bore a trace of bitterness, sensed by Tomás, if not his cousins.

He looked at Ibo in disbelief. "Did you sleep with her?"

"Yes." Ibo rarely lied. His honesty was a point of pride for him, especially given everything he'd lost. Also, he'd drunk lots of wine with nothing but a little fruit and duck liver in his gut. "Slept with her was about all I did. I pursued her aggressively and I think it intrigued her for a short while. Then she dropped me. My 'bold spiritedness' became 'a total turn-off.' Bam. She was like that. Complete

302

turnaround." He caught the fascinated looks of the girls. Encouraged, he continued. "Or maybe, like some men, she was a hunter who moves on to the next prey once the previous prey's been caught. Next I knew, I was 'stalking' her. Talk about a turn-off. That certainly made my interest in her wane!"

He took in Tomás' perplexed expression. "I think," he explained patiently, "Christia felt that, for a woman, total sexual freedom was a form of rebellion against patriarchal society. It was, in a sense, her duty. So she had a lot of what might be called inappropriate relationships with, as far as I know, mostly junior faculty – like me –" He scratched his head. "Her graduate students? Hell, I don't know who she slept with. A lot more people than I have, I know that much…" He took a big gulp of his wine, and looked around the table.

Solange had been listening intently. "But don't you think by doing so she was hurting herself?"

"She certainly hurt me. I don't know about her inner pain, or other emotions. She seemed at times to have none."

"So," Solange said quietly, "I think if I am understanding you, what you are saying is, she acted on principle. Her *idée* was to further the liberation of women. Hmm. I think I have heard this expressed before."

"It does totally make sense in the abstract," Ibo admitted. "But in reality, people have feelings. I imagine even she had feelings." He took a long drag of his cigarette. "But she came across as a real bitch."

"*Une saloppe?*" Ghislaine asked. Solange nodded. "That's wrong," Solange argued. "Why call her a *saloppe* because she didn't love you?"

"Hah! That's the least of it," Ibo retorted. "If that was the only problem half the school would've called her that."

"Is there anyone she didn't sleep with?" Ghislaine looked amused. "Total slut, *non?*" she smirked.

"*N'importe quoi, toi!*" Solange exclaimed. Ghislaine looked only slightly chastened. Both sisters lit cigarettes. "She'll just say anything," Solange, always thoughtful, translated for Ibo. The she turned to Tomás. "*Cousin*, are we embarrassing you? American women seem so funny about sex, that's all…Uptight, even with 'le Free love.' "

Tomás had been silent throughout this entire exchange. He shook his head, and then, bowing over his food, proceeded to ignore his dining companions. Sensing that the topic was a sensitive one, the girls dropped that conversational trajectory and began to chat about less-loaded subjects.

Ibo, lost in thought for a minute or two – recalling how Christia had called his lips "kissable" and "rosy," remembering the time she'd looked at him with a complete lack of warmth when she'd passed him in the religion department office mere hours after they'd made love – picked at his fatty foie gras and the cloyingly sweet peaches accompanying it. He was glad he'd only ordered the one dish: he'd lost his appetite.

As Ghislaine and Solange's penultimate course arrived, the waiter solicitously offered to bring Tomás and Ibo some dessert, along with the girls' final course. Fearful of the cost, Ibo rubbed his stomach and said, in halting French, that he'd had enough. Tomás ordered a slice of Vacherin cake, enrobed in wild strawberries with lemon and thyme. He offered Ibo a bite. "Won't you try this?" Ibo shook his head, and began his too-full-to-eat-another-bite routine.

Too late, Ibo realized the bill would probably simply be split four, or even two ways, in the civilized manner. He hoped his credit card wasn't completely maxed-out.

Tomás looked at him gravely. "Ibo, you don't have to hide anything from me."

"*Alo?*" Ghislaine interrupted. "Why are you two so serious *ce soir?*"

Ibo laughed uncomfortably, his face drained of blood. "Why don't you ask your cousin," he retorted, with forced joviality, "he's been acting funny all night."

*

Back home in the city, life resumed its workaday rhythms. After class on Monday I went downtown to take a yoga class. Subway reliability was extraordinary that day, and I arrived with a good forty-five minutes to spare. I decided to go to Enchantments, a store for neo-Pagan accouterments on East 9th street. I thought maybe someone there might be able to direct me toward Christia's coven, Puduhepa's Sisters, or at least tell me how to go about *finding* said coven. Theadora Harmon, my only lead, had yet to return my call -- and it wasn't as if covens were listed in the Yellow Pages.

The narrow store was filled with the scent of strong, musky incense. On my left as I walked in, a long wall of shelves held books on every magic-related subject, with a focus on Witchcraft, or Wicca. To my right, a waist-high glass counter displayed amulets and talismans – pentagrams, sickle moons, dragons, and fairies, all made of silver and semi-precious stones. A black-haired, tattooed white woman in her mid-forties sat at the register, leafing through one of the many decks of tarot arrayed behind and around her.

"Can I help you?" She asked. I noticed she was helpful only after she'd glimpsed my pentagram pendant. Even today, we Wiccans tend to be careful, and the wearing of jewelry or other insignia – tattoos, etc. -- to signal to others that one is of like mind is by no means a merely superficial thing.

I placed my hands, palm up, on the counter. "I don't know," I began. "I'm looking for this coven. A-a friend of mine was killed and I think they might know something." She looked at me, newly guarded. "You mean you think one of them did it?"

"No! Absolutely not. I just think that maybe one of them will have some idea of who might have done it. That's all." I tried a different approach. "Have you ever heard of Puduhepa's Sisters?"

She thought for a minute, making a noncommittal sound, and then shook her head. "I couldn't say, really." Frustrated, I started to walk away. She held up a heavily-ringed finger, indicating that I should wait. She shuffled her tarot deck and then laid three cards down in front of me, watching my face closely all the while. First she drew Judgement, then the Queen of Swords, and then the Prince of Swords. I drew back.   "Don't like it? She looked at the cards, considering. "I can sense how you'd feel that way. I see pain and misunderstanding, but I also see truth. So it can't be all bad." I thanked her and turned around to leave. "Wait!" She called. "Ask Pan back there about Puduhepa's Sisters," she nodded toward the back of the store. "He knows all the gossip in the community."

I thanked her and headed back toward the counter where essential oils and herbs are mixed to make spells to order. Among the colorful candles and potions, a short, hairy, decidedly goat-like man eyed me suspiciously.

I approached him with an open attitude, hoping he'd meet me with the same if given the chance. I was trying to formulate a good opening salvo when I noticed something about his face. "Hey, you have glitter all over the end of your nose."

"I do?" He laughed at himself. "Figures. I'm always getting elements of my spells stuck on me somewhere. Rose oil stains on my shirts, woodruff in my hair, that sort of thing…" he looked at me with a more friendly mien. "What can I do for you, my lady?"

I didn't have time to beat around the bush – I was due for my yoga class in a quarter hour. "I am looking for a coven. One of the members was killed and I think they can help me find the killer. I don't

306

think any of them did it," I added, preemptively, "and they're called Puduhepa's Sisters." I stopped to take a breath.

"Whew," said Pan, if that was in fact his name. "I'm gonna level with you. It hurts me to say this, but I don't know 'em that well personally."

My face fell. Barring an increasingly-unlikely return call from Professor Harmon, this was my only hope.

"But!" His tone was coy. I looked at him hopefully. "I *can* give you the address of a private consulting firm where they might be able to help you. It's called Intuitions. It's just around the block. They don't have a sign, so here's the particulars." He scribbled something on a piece of lavender parchment paper and handed it to me. "I'll call them and let them know you're coming."

"Oh, thank you so much!" I left with a new spring in my step, yoga class forgotten. As I passed the front counter, the black-haired woman smiled at me. "Blessed be." She had a beautiful snow white cat in her lap as she rang up someone's purchase.

"Blessed be." I replied with a grin.

Out on 9th street, I took a deep breath of fresh air. I sat on Enchantments' stoop, below the wooden crescent moon sign, in order to give Pan time to make his call. The street was alive with colorful characters. A couple of kids passed me, their allegiance to the newest generation of punk rock written all over their faces and plaid-ragged attire. Between the two hippie-mamas with their fringed coats and babies bundled in batik slings, the Japanese couple with bleached platinum hair and foot-high platform boots and the black-clad loner with a patch over one eye and a cowboy hat, no one blinked an eye at the baby punk rockers. Probably to their chagrin. Me, I loved that about the village: it's hard to shock anyone there, and so style becomes more about what one really likes, rather than a rebellious statement. Sidestepping a flashback to my days as an anarcho-feminist

Connecticut misfit, I quickly headed around the block to the address I'd been given.

There was, as he'd mentioned, no sign on the outside door. I was buzzed in and directed to the third floor, first apartment on the left. On that door, there was a small sign in silver scrollwork that read, simply, "Intuitions," and, in yet smaller print on the line below, "Consultations." Before I had a chance to knock, the door swung open to reveal three women sitting behind a long table. On the wall above the backs of their heads, the phases of the moon had been painted in metallic silver paint. Other than that, the room was completely bare, and there were no windows. Two of the women were Black: one was a middle-aged woman, plump and pretty but forbidding at the same time, one a younger woman, maybe in her mid-twenties, who looked like she might be related to the first. The third woman, thirty-something and of average build, looked Middle Eastern, with thick, lustrous dark reddish-brown hair and warm -- yet, here too, there was a forbidding aspect -- almond eyes. The tall, rail-thin man who'd opened the door bowed slightly to me, and more deeply toward the three women, before exiting soundlessly through a side door.

The oldest woman addressed me. "We understand you are looking for Puduhepa's Sisters?"

I stood in front of them, feeling completely exposed. "Yes," I replied. I judged it best to let these powerful women lead any discussion.

After glancing at each of her cronies, she turned back to me. "Usually we charge a fee, but these are special circumstances. We will contact the other members of the coven and we will get back to you, Annie Fay." I got the sense that she knew that my middle name meant "of the fairies."

But how had she known my middle name? After I'd spent much of the trip home fretting over how they would get in touch with me, I realized that not only had the woman who'd spoken known my full name, she'd referred to the "other" members of the coven. Puduhepa's Sisters! Perhaps they'd know how to contact me after all.

Chapter Ten – The Spies and the Women in Red

I must rise and go about the city,
the narrow streets and squares,
till I find my only love.
I sought him everywhere but I could not find him.

Song of Songs: 3:2

He stood close by her. Too close.

"Do you still like my smell?"

Her nostrils flared, like those of a prey animal, but she said, with a thin note of bravado in her voice, "A bit gamy today, aren't you?"

He laughed, a scratchy, humorless laugh. "As ever, Christia." His eyes pierced hers. He laughed to himself again, then added, "In any case, that's irrelevant at this point."

*

In Bay Ridge, a historically Italian neighborhood in Brooklyn, the Friday after Thanksgiving is the appointed day for putting up Christmas decorations -- the gaudier the better. Detective Tomasino and Andy Junior had been up on the roof since right after breakfast. Andrew the Senior had woken up with a groan at his leaden-feeling gut and visibly swollen stomach. He'd plaintively asked Marj to get him some Tums, but she'd rolled over with a snort: "Get it yah-self. I cooked fah tree days to feed you and yah family."

Tomasino's extended Italian-Irish family had decided to grace Marj with their presence on Thanksgiving for the fourth year in a row. Marjorie Tomasino, née Slivka, was in truth only half-Italian, but her mother had been an excellent cook and had schooled her daughter well. Subsequently, her husband's family (without ever overtly admitting to the superiority of Marj's culinary skills) spent more holidays than not at the Tomasino's. Almost every major holiday now, they'd come to eat, and eat, and eat -- the best food in the neighborhood -- at the Tomasino's side of the large two-family house they shared with Detective Tomasino's partner on the force and his family.

Down on the sidewalk, nine-year old Mary Nicole, her mom's red down parka hanging down to her knees, directed her father and big brother as to matters of precision in the placement of Santa's sleigh and eight lavishly illuminated reindeer, three glowing eight-foot plastic angels, and ten strings of flashing lights. Next door, the D'Addarios were all busy doing much the same thing, calling out encouragement to each other and good-natured ribbing to the Tomasinos.

Near the front door, Marjorie Tomasino struggled with the two giant plastic toy soldiers who guarded the front door every holiday season. When she'd finally gotten both soldiers upright on either side of the steps, she stepped back, her hands on her hips, to admire her handiwork. Then she gazed with satisfaction at the crèche scene she and Mary had set up outside, under the living room's picture window. Life-sized figures of Jesus, Mary and Joseph sat together in familial bliss. Above them, long strands of the red tinsel Marj had hung in the window waved gently behind the glass. The D'Addarios bay window was filled with a busy Santa's factory scene, which Marj found slightly tacky but the kids loved. Every year, Andy Junior requested Santaland, and Marj insisted that the Holy Family was more important and deserved that central spot.

Soon he'd be too old to care.

She looked up at her beloved son, her first child -- only ten years old and already a smaller version of his father: macho and reliable and smart. Steady. Her heart swelled at the sight of him. She longed to tousle his curly hair, to grab him and squeeze him and inhale the smell of him as she had when he was a baby, but she knew without even trying that he would pull out of her grasp with a disgusted, "Aaw, Ma, c'mon!" Oh, she knew he loved her, would do anything for her – but please, mom, none of that corny stuff.

Inside, the smell of Christmas cookies baking imbued the house with holiday cheer. It was never too early to start baking in preparation for the grueling rounds of holiday festivities one had to endure when one was part of a large Ukrainian-Italian-Irish family. Marj laughed good-naturedly to herself. Really, she only thought of these times as grueling in order to justify a month-long eating binge. She was a short woman, and only slightly rounded, but most of her rounding came from that one month of every year when she was powerless in the face of pumpkin pie, pecan pie, butter cookies, and the traditionally capacious Christmastime lasagna. With a wave to Mary -- she knew her daughter would soon run to her side to help her much-adored mother in the kitchen -- she went inside to begin mixing the batter for fruitcakes. After baking, they would need to sit and soak in plenty of rum.

During the week, Marj worked part-time as a paralegal at a local law firm. She got home shortly before the kids got home from school, just in time to fix them a snack. As a Detective, her husband had to be available at the drop of a dime, so she had to be there, every day, to make sure her kids had the stability that was the foundation of decent character. In some ways she wished Andy Senior hadn't won his gold

312

shield at such a young age, but it was in his nature to work hard. Getting dinner on the table was about all she could do most days, between the kids' activities and her husband's erratic schedule, so she knew she'd better get a head start on her baking while she had the chance.

She could hear her son and husband clomping around on the roof. She was glad Andy would get at least this day off. He'd told her about his latest case and it sounded like a doozy to her. She generally thought his theories were pretty sound, but this time she thought he was missing something.

"Hon," she'd said right before turning off the light on her side of the bed and going to sleep, "If it really was just a jealous teacher or a jealous boyfriend, I think yah would've caught 'em by now. I have a feeling about this in my gut." There was no response. The lights outside blinked on and off, pulsating with Christmas cheer. "Hon?"

A small, bubbling snore escaped from his lips. Andy Tomasino was asleep.

*

Twenty-four hours after my return, Pepita was still excited by my homecoming. She would run around the house, panting, with her tongue flapping, every time she noticed my presence. When I got back uptown after my interesting experience at Intuitions, she did her glee-routine. The smile was wiped off my face when I noticed, unharried enough for the first time to take stock of my place, the meaty stench of the orchid sitting on my kitchen table. Without water, its top parts had rotted, its lips folding into its throat, while the bottom of the stem had withered. I picked it up and marched right to my garbage can, depositing the entire plant, pot and all, therein. Standing over the garbage sadly, I apologized for my neglect to the (clearly long dead) plant. Pepita stopped for an instant and soothingly licked my fingertips.

On my answering machine, there was a message from Theadora Harmon: "Hello, I'm back from my trip. Let's get together and talk." Lark had called about my trip out to Connecticut for the Solstice, promising lots of snow, and Nicholas had left a message to call him when I "got back from that infernal gymnastics class." He'd never thought much of New York City yoga classes, with their emphasis on butt-firming.

I called Lark first. I assured her I was still planning to come out in two weeks or so, and that things looked promising in the bringing-Nicholas department. "We had a really good time down South," I told her. She made a suggestive sound. "No, no hanky-panky. I think that's really over, even if it is flattering to have him carry a torch for me. The torch is dimming, I think. But he didn't act weird and/or murderous."

"Well," Lark laughed. "That's something." I could hear her tapping away on her computer, looking busy at work while she talked to me. "There was something else: I went online about this Puduhepa character and I can't believe I'd never heard of her!"

"Yeah," I agreed, "But, you know, there's so much to know these days. You can find crap online about anything."

"I think you'll be interested in this, though: there's a whole lot of buzz about this article that's about to come out in some important academic journal. It's about Puduhepa...and it's by your friend Ibrahim Heyreddin." She seemed to think this was a major clue, but I had already seen the cover sheet to the article. What I hadn't known was that the work was of widespread interest. Perhaps Ibo had something to gain by Christia's death after all – besides taking over her classes. Maybe he was going to try to claim her discovery as his own. The thought sobered me. "I'd better go, love. I need to think about this."

"Hold on!" She begged. "Just tell me, briefly, what's going on in that tumultuous love life of yours." My romantic roller coasters were as endlessly interesting to her as Lark's stable marriage was to me.

"Nothing," I admitted. "I haven't even seen the guy I've fallen mildly in love with since the week before last."

Her tone became serious. "Annie, I *know* you know this:" She paused as she carefully chose her words. I squeezed Pepita, who had settled finally in my lap, awaiting her walk. "I guess all I'm gonna say is you have to *know* someone to love them," she cautioned with a sigh.

I knew she had to get back to work. "You're right. As always." My best friend had always been wise beyond her years. I was very much looking forward to seeing her for the holiday, which I told her with affection. "And hey," I added as she started to hang up, "that snow had better be 'deep and crisp and even'!"

It was true that I still hadn't seen or heard from Tomás, who'd spent the break in Paris with his family, but I was in a good holding pattern, neither increasingly obsessed with, nor entirely dismissive of, our mutual attraction.

What with my extended trip over break and my various investigations, my own work was beginning to suffer. On Tuesday I decided to put in an appearance in my department, to keep up the facade that I had a deep and abiding interest not only in comparative literature but in the movers and shakers in that field at the University of New York. Perhaps the hardest to bear aspect of the Department of Comparative Literature was that it was dull. None of the romance or beauty or tragedy of the books we read filtered through to daily departmental life. It was nothing like the religion department, with its intrigues and prestige; just mostly creaky, near-retirement white men and a smattering of self-proclaimed hip junior faculty. Adjuncts didn't even count. After a year at the University of New York, all this no longer surprised or even disappointed me too much. No one takes literature seriously anyway once they graduate from college. It's almost as bad as sociology.

Almost.

I sat (prominently facing the door to the hallway) in a hard, uncomfortable chair in the tiny student lounge the graduate students had lobbied for so assiduously a few years back. I sincerely tried to concentrate on an article about the geopolitics of the written word. There was little to distract me, since no one ever came into the lounge: after the initial enthusiasm had passed, it became clear that even a shared space was not enough to invigorate social connections between students in the comp.lit. department. Either you had bonded with some of the other students who came in with your cohort, or you were on your own. Gretel and Brandi were my saving graces; otherwise, I had no one in my department I felt close to.

I had chosen the wrong day to show my face, for there was virtually no one around. In any case, I wouldn't have been fooling anyone. I was something of a pariah in the department, due mostly to my inchoate inability to brownnose. My outsider status also had to do with my apparently wider-than-usual range of interests. I was always being chided for trying to include references in my work that weren't considered quite valid – like rock 'n' roll songs and websites.

It had taken me the better part of my first year in graduate school to find someone who appreciated a modicum of creativity. Professor Winifred MacGregor was a joint appointment with the French department, and as such had somewhat more freedom of thought than the average faculty member. She was married to the dashing, well-known political scientist Yaakov Segal, with whom she frequently was called to the scene of some event of international importance. She herself also had fabulous style, having spent a decade in France finishing up her dissertation and then, as she put it, "gadding about." She wore berets, deftly draped scarves, and pointy shoes with Louis XIV heels. Her features were sharp, but her warmth, along with her perpetually mussed, silver-blonde hair, softened her demeanor, so that

316

she seemed at once surprisingly pretty and very sophisticated. I thought she was really cool. To my delight, she seemed to like me too, and was always willing to hear me out regarding my latest intellectual interests – even if they didn't strictly fit the discipline as conceived of in our department.

I checked in my agenda and saw that she was having office hours. Her door was open and I knocked before walking in. She was sitting at her desk with her pen poised as if she was about to write, but her head was tilted thoughtfully to the side. She hadn't heard my knock and I felt slightly uncomfortable for disturbing her reverie. I backed away and knocked again, more loudly this time.

"Come in," she called.

I re-entered her office and sat down in the chair she indicated. I looked around, automatically comparing her office to Christia's. It was smaller, but more cheerful. The wall facing the door was taken up by two large windows with art posters around them, and the right-hand wall was occupied by her large, neat desk, which had a lovely view to campus. On her desk were a fountain pen and old-fashioned blotter. A vase of irises brought a hint of far-away spring into the room. I remembered she loved Van Gogh. But for the doorway, the other two walls were completely covered with bookshelves.

She shook her head. "Nostalgia doesn't do us any good, does it." It wasn't a question. She raised her eyes to mine and I saw a quickly-concealed flicker of raw pain. I looked away, to give her space to re-group, and also to hide my wonder at being addressed as a real human being by a member of the faculty. Unsure of how to respond, I simply sat and waited. When a few minutes had passed, I began to feel uneasy. Winifred MacGregor was staring out the window again. It seemed she'd forgotten I was there.

Finally, she spoke. "I'm due at a ghastly committee meeting – a search for a new junior faculty victim," I gasped, but only in my head;

outwardly, I smiled slightly, as if I was accustomed to having senior faculty members treat me like a pal. "However," she continued, "My mind is absolutely *stuffed* with some news I received today."

My mind rushed to find the right thing to say. "I just happened to be in the department and I was just dropping in to show my face. Maybe I could be a sort of…sounding board," I offered tentatively.

"You don't mind if I…vent a little?" She rolled her eyes self-mockingly. "No, of course you don't. You've just said as much." She hesitated, then began, in a rush: "This news is – confidential of course. I've, eh, heard from an old colleague of mine from my Paris days, who thinks he's under the microscope for murder."

"You don't mean…" I attempted to stay casual, feeling as if I were in some '50's spy movie. "…the murder of Christia Thompson, by any chance, do you?"

I knew immediately I'd guessed right, but something made her hesitate; maybe a desire to protect her friend, or to maintain our heretofore relatively traditional teacher-student relationship. Perhaps both. She looked away from the window, toward a large, matted and framed Mattisse print on the adjoining wall. She fiddled with her fingers, turning a ring around, checking her fingernails, buying time. "How did you guess?" She asked, at length.

"Oddly enough, I'm sort of involved in this case too." I felt her forthrightness deserved the same in return; also, I was rendered positively gaga by her apparent trust in me. So I told her what I knew – in condensed form, but including the part about how I'd written an incriminating note. I told her about how my ex-boyfriend was one of the main suspects and that the fellow with whom I hoped to begin a relationship was also under suspicion, along with the whole faculty of Christia's department, particularly my close friend, Ibo. Also, that Christia's husband of ten years was a possibility. I concluded by throwing my hands up in the air. "I have no idea what to think at this point!" I admitted.

"May I let you in on a little secret?" Her tone was conspiratorial. I nodded eagerly. She leaned back a little. "I'm not sure this is proper." She was fidgeting with her hands again, and had a worried expression on her face. "Oh, what the heck." She relaxed somewhat in her seat, returning to her usual ramrod-straight posture, but with a less stiff comportment. "To tell you the truth it's actually an old flame of mine who's concerned about his reputation. Perhaps you know him? Richard Redmund? I'm sure you've heard of him, at the very least. He was always very ambitious and has done well for himself."

I nodded, wondering what – and how deep -- the connection was between MacGregor and Redmund.

"As you might know, he worked with Professor Thompson. He wasn't specific about why he might be in trouble." She leaned toward me. "Have you met him?"

"Yes, I have." I pictured the two, young and in love, and it made for an incongruous picture. Winifred MacGregor was so refined, and Redmund so blustering. Maybe they hadn't always been as they appeared now. "I can't believe you two dated. I mean," Help. Foot-in-mouth. "He seems, so much more, um, flashy than you."

"I suppose that's one of the reasons for which he is an *ex*-beau." She smiled wryly. "Along with his being a major misogynist, who thought a woman's place was in the kitchen being servile rather than, say, parsing irregular French verbs for fun. It must have been unbearably galling to him that a female was outpacing him in his department!" She covered her mouth with her hand. "Annie, I can't believe I just said that. You must think I suspect him. I don't." She was quiet for a moment, thinking. "I do bear him some malice," she admitted frankly, wrinkling her aquiline nose in unconscious distaste, "but not that much. Once upon a time, when I was young and living in the most romantic city in the world, I was madly in love with him. There's still enough love there for me to believe him incapable of such a gruesome act. He's a pompous, self-centered boob. Maybe a *mild* narcissist. But, no," She gave a Gallic shrug, pursing her lips, "I don't see him as a killer. Though," she added, "I am fully aware that many people operate under just such assumptions about their murdering friends, relatives, and colleagues."

"He's just so jolly," I said. "That kind of bonhomie makes me nervous."

"Hmm." She replied. "There was a time when I'd've called him light-spirited. Jolly, as you put it." She wrinkled her forehead, looking distressed again.

"I won't say anything about this, in case you're worried," I informed her, earnestly. Possible obstruction of justice was a small price to pay for her respect.

She took off her reading glasses and squeezed the bridge of her nose. "No. I hope you won't." She laid her hands on her desk. "Was there anything else? Surely you didn't come here to talk about this!"

"Maybe, in a strange way, I did." I felt safe saying this, because, just as she'd spread out her hands on the blotter I'd noticed something I'd never seen before: Along with her wedding and engagement rings, Winifred MacGregor wore a wide band of silver on which was engraved a miniscule pentagram. Bringing this up would've been going too far, but I liked to think she knew that I knew. I thanked her for her time and she smiled.

"Thank *you*," she said. She pulled a black beret over her silvery hair. "I feel I have a real weight off my chest. It's not something I can discuss with Yaakov – he and Richie were terribly competitive. As for you, I expect someone – maybe you," she winked, "will solve this crime before the suspicion somehow falls on you for having written that note!

"Meantime," she looked at her watch, "I am late for the faculty search to-do." She saw me to the door, and I left, feeling grateful for the coincidences that had taken the conversation in its roundabout direction.

It was hard to gauge, so soon after, whether our conversation had paved the way for a more chummy relationship between us, or would make her wary of my company. My hope lay with the former. I had great need of an ally in the department, and a mentor who inspired me; MacGregor fit the bill on both counts. I would keep my word, and not say a thing to anyone about what she'd shared with me. I thought Winifred MacGregor was a true example of that rare anomaly, a real, live, *good* person in academia, and she'd invested extraordinary trust in me, a lowly graduate student. Perhaps I, too, shared the burden of being a good person in a field not exactly rife with goodness. However, none of that meant I couldn't speculate as to how far an ambitious, strongly misogynistic man might go to keep his top-dog position.

After I met with Winifred MacGregor, I decided to stop by and say hello to Brenda. Outside the comp.lit. building, a couple of students from Intro. Comp. Lit. stopped me and asked me about "the murder."

"Isn't your boyfriend in her department?" one of them, a cheeky gal with choppy, turquoise-streaked hair asked.

"He's not my boyfriend…Hey! How do you guys *know* these things???" They giggled. "I mean, not that you actually know anything," I continued jokingly, flustered despite my best attempts to maintain my professional dignity as a T.A., "But you certainly *think* you do…"

In the religion department's administrative office, a few holiday decorations were on display. A lopsided plastic and tinsel wreath that looked like it had been packed away for a lot longer than a year shared the abundant wall space with a gold-foil menorah banner and a picture of the Kwanzaa candle-lighting ceremony, the Mishumaa Saba. Last year, the room had positively sparkled with holiday cheer. This year, Brenda's heart clearly wasn't in it.

Brenda had lost weight. I wouldn't have imagined it possible for her to do so and still function, but there she was, looking like a skeleton with a membrane of skin tightly stretched over its bones. Her normally baggy clothes swam around her as if devoid of any substantial living matter. She looked up from her reading with a blank stare. Very little light seemed to reach the centers of her eyes. It's impossible to explain how the eyes convey so much, yet we humans can read a great deal from these windows to the soul. "Hey, Annie," was all she said, returning immediately to her reading.

I had fallen out of favor.

"Brenda," I began cautiously, "I –"

She made a moue of disgust. "Please, spare me. Obsequious doesn't work on you. Or me. Just go do your thing and let me get my job done." After a minute or so, during which I – gambling on waiting her out -- didn't move or speak, she put her book down with a bang and favored me with a brief moment of icy eye contact. "Look," she said impatiently, "I've had it with people. If I was gonna talk with someone it would be you, O.K.? But I spent several hours being questioned by the police over the matter of Christia's murder because of a *crush*." Her sallow cheeks flared with two bright spots of anger. "They even commented on my eating habits," she said indignantly. "As if being vegetarian and refusing to eat the dead flesh they offered me was, like, some admission of guilt."

"Oh, gawd," I had to genuinely sympathize. "I spent most of my childhood dealing with that hooey." I didn't mention that her physical condition was not a good inspiration for conversion to vegetarianism for any mentally healthy meat-eater. "It's torture. I don't know why people take it so personally, either."

In my sincerity, I had unwittingly fallen upon a way to make Brenda open up. She looked me in the eyes for the first time. "You're telling me! Sheesh." I heard a trace of a gee-whiz Ohio accent in her voice. A little bit of color had returned to her gaunt face.

I decided to be honest. "I know you're sick of talking about it, but I thought maybe you could give me just a minute or two. I assure you, this is not prurient interest on my part." I think she believed me. Still, she was exhausted, near starvation, emotionally fragile. I regretted pressing her as soon as the words were out of my mouth.

She, however, had pepped up some. "Well," she began, looking around to make sure no one was listening. The hallway appeared empty, and we were alone in the office. "After they finished their questioning of me, I heard someone tell the main detective – I think his name's Tomasino, but I'm not sure, he wasn't the one who questioned me – that the test results were in for the 'trace evidence,' and that the hair appeared to belong to Christia."

"I guess that makes sense."

"Maybe, but they were definitely surprised over it. I think they were saying it didn't really match her hair visually, or something. I couldn't quite catch what they were saying. Sorry."

"Please don't apologize. I don't know what to make of that, but it *is* an interesting piece of information." I had been about to say "tidbit." I thought of what Winifred MacGregor had told me. "Do you know if Redmund's more of a suspect these days? Or less of one?"

She brightened the slightest bit more. "No! But I was just thinking about finding a way to incriminate him." She looked sheepish. "I mean, a way to prove his guilt, not, like, plant fake evidence in his office…That jerk. Today he told me the coffee wasn't 'up to snuff.'" She squared her shoulders and muttered, under her breath, "So kiss my ass." Brenda was showing some spunk. That gave me hope for her survival.

323

"What an M.C.P.!" I exclaimed. After a moment of mutual disgust at the patriarchal regime, I asked, "Is Philippe still a suspect?"

"I don't know. I didn't hear anything else. I pretty much told them that I was either in the office, in the bathroom, or at my shrink that entire day. I have group on Monday nights, right after work." She tucked a few thin strands of hair behind her ears and shifted to face me directly. "Oh yeah, I have the report on Cyrus Wilson. I forgot to tell you because it's no big news. I asked him what he meant when he said he and Christia were from the same place, like you asked me to. He said they were both from the deepest area of the South and that also they both 'live by their own rules.' Or," she sniffed, "lived, I should say. Lived."

I tried to cheer her up, to stop the decline into the maudlin. "What is your favorite memory of Christia?" It was worth a try.

She thought for just a moment, eyes cast toward the light of the round, etched-glass ceiling fixture. "Right before Christia died," Brenda began, looking reverent, (Oh God, was my immediate reaction, did she mean right before she, Brenda, killed her? My tendency to be suspicious was becoming second-nature…) "…she was telling me about this hymn written by the Abess Hildegard of Bingen. Do you know her work?"

I nodded. "Some of it. I just wrote a paper in which I mentioned her. That incident where she got inspired by a vision of tongues of flame from heaven was a popular subject in medieval illuminated manuscripts. Tongues, right? I mean it's symbolic now, but back then it must've been an even more startling notion. She was famous." I was, I realized, babbling, practically heedless of my own words with all the buzzing in my head: Did Brenda *kill* her? Was I sitting in front of a murderess? Was I in danger? "Brenda?"

"Yes?" Her eyes were flat again, as if she sensed my suspicions. She let her stringy hair fall back in front of her face.

I was also wondering how much longer a woman this unbalanced, unhealthy, and disheveled would be able to function. Hadn't someone in either this or her own department noticed her condition? I stuck to the matter at hand. "When are you talking about? When did Christia tell you about von Bingen?"

Brenda was far away, lost in her recollection. Her voice came as if from a distance, "It was the morning of the day she died." Of course, I acknowledged to myself, she could well be lying. But I did feel better. Christia's murder had been determined to have taken place sometime in the late afternoon or early evening.

After a minute, she continued to speak. Her voice that day had a singsong quality that you rarely hear outside of movies in which female teenage mental patients figure prominently, or children are possessed by demons. "*O Clarissima Mater*. That was the name of the hymn. It's about Mary, star of the sea, mother of the Christ child, as she who redeemed womankind for Eve's folly. In her light, the darkness of women's sin is obliterated." It was almost as if she was speaking to herself, so deeply introverted had she become.

"Um, how did that come up?" I tried to draw her out.

"Well, Kassia – you know, the nun I'm writing about -- wrote an ode to Mary Magdalene, the other, 'fallen,' Mary. It's about how she kissed Christ's 'immaculate' – that's from the hymn -- feet and dried them from the wetness of her tears with her own hair. I was thinking about doing something with that, the whole virgin-slut angle, so I went to her. She was my inspiration." Suddenly, and to my great surprise, she began to yell: "Nobody else cares about this stuff! Nobody!" Gone was the singsong voice of an unbalanced little girl. "What the hell am I supposed to do now???" She keened, bereft. I looked around wildly to see if anyone from the religion department was witnessing this outburst. I saw no one, but that didn't mean no one was listening. Brenda pounded her desk in a violent rage. "What? What? What?" Her voice got louder and louder, ending in a wail. She was literally tearing her hair, too, and had messy strands of it in her bony fists when she, abruptly, became quiet. A sick smile came to her lips, but her eyes stayed frantic. For a moment, they rested on me, gleaming with malice. For that moment, I thought she was about to attack me. Then she rushed out of the room.

Well, I had learned something I hadn't known before: Brenda Fujiki was, to say the least, emotionally labile – and she had a temper. Whether she tended to take her anger out on herself or others was another question. I waited five minutes for her to return and was just about to give up when Detective Tomasino strolled in. I knew who he was because of his badge, though I could barely make out his name on the pin below it. I am so nearsighted, even with my lenses in.

Disingenuously, I sat back down.

"Do you know where Ms. Fujiki is?" He asked.

"No, I'm sorry I don't." That was true, for sure. "Can I help you with something?" What was I thinking? He would obviously think I was a member of the department and that was perjury or some such. I could always say I thought he needed help getting around campus.

"I am supposed to meet someone here, so I'll just wait."

"O.K." I would kindly allow him to do so.

"Sit down?" I gestured to one of the empty chairs near Brenda's desk.

"Don't mind if I do." He was a heavy man, with thick red hair. Even though I had the lifelong freak's natural distrust of any cop, I could tell Tomasino was one of the good guys. His face showed he'd been through some things no one should have to witness, but he'd maintained a certain sweetness around the mouth and eyes. He had deep laugh lines.

Next, in walked Philippe Perez-Throgmorton, in a gray flannel suit, worn with a pink shirt and yellow tie. I'm sure his outfits must've

326

been a big hit with the police force. Tomasino got up and they shook hands.

"Let's go," said the detective.

"Yes, let's get it over with," Christia's husband replied.

"Philippe?" He turned to face me, having not previously been aware of my presence.

"Annie." His face flooded with relief. "Can you, would you – help me?" He gave me a strained but winning look from under his floppy thatch of hair.

"Sure, Philippe. What's up?"

"We have to clean out Christia's office."

"Oh, I'm so sorry." The task sounded macabre, to say the least. Nonetheless, a widower was asking for my help. And maybe I would make a new discovery in what I'd come to think of as "my" investigation.

As we set up the packing boxes, it became clear to me that Philippe was no longer the main suspect. The detective was treating him as a grieving husband, no more, no less. Tomasino radiated tactful sympathy and admirable patience as Philippe went about, chattering nervously to fill the silence, aimlessly picking up objects around his wife's office and putting them back down. Tomasino didn't ask Philippe any questions, except to occasionally ask where a certain book or folder should go. "We've been through all of these," he told Philippe, "so now it's just up to you to organize them."

"Alrighty," Philippe said, gamely. "This will go here. That…" he looked at what he held in his hand, "there. Er, this will go in that pile…"

Where would all this stuff go? Where does the detritus of any life go? To family? Who did Christia consider her real family? I tuned out Philippe's patter and my mind flew away to the wide Mississippi river. I wondered what Motte DuPree Thompson was up to. I wondered if I'd been wrong about his innocence, but then I recalled his very real sadness at his long-gone sister's murder. I briefly considered asking Philippe why he hadn't called his wife's brother following her death, but kindness – or tact – got the upper hand. When Tomasino left the room for a drink, Philippe told me he'd given his alibi to the police. Briefly, he told me about his friend Paul Terwilliger, and how he'd wanted to protect him at great cost to himself. I was touched.

"What if they go after Paul?" worried Philippe. "I would blame myself."

"That would be awful," I agreed solemnly. " But I hope it won't come to that! They seem pretty busy as it is." Philippe laughed that super-dry, unfunny laugh of his. English humor, I thought. Dark.

He seemed receptive that day. I searched my brain for a good question as I piled a shelf-full of books into a box. "Did Christia ever seem, I don't know – *scared* to you?"

Philippe sat down with a soft "Ah." He looked at me and I thought I detected pride in his eyes. "My wife was not afraid of anything."

Tomasino came back, but Philippe continued his informative talk, all the while – it began to dawn on me -- grouping things in piles of seven. "You know Nicholas and Ibrahim were taken in for questioning, the police were bloody pissed that they had left on vacation in the midst of their investigation. They kept tabs on them while they were away!"

"When?"

"When did they question them or –"

"Yes, right," I interrupted him, impatient.

"This morning. They'd found both of their fingerprints on a binder on -- her desk." I guessed he couldn't bring himself to say her name aloud. "That's all I know."

If they fingerprinted me, they'd find my fingerprints on it as well, I feared.

"Annie, you do know that she and Nicholas had quite an *affair du coeur* awhile back." I glanced at Tomasino, but he seemed engaged in his task. He was checking off each item from Christia's desk on his clipboard, and then placing it in Philippe's to-sort pile.

"I'm not sure I would characterize it as such, but, yes, I knew there was something there." I searched his face for pain and saw none. "In the past," I added.

"You don't have to spare me." He said, to my surprise. "Those two were mad about each other."

After that, I kept my mouth shut, although my mind was racing. I had no idea why Nicholas had always underplayed his relationship with Christia. If Philippe was to be believed, there had been much more to their affair than the brief and tepid fling Nicholas had described to me.

I didn't find anything out of the ordinary in her office. After about twenty minutes of packing, Philippe said he needed a break. He'd found two copies of his poetry manuscript among the piles of papers in the office and seen that Christia had written "What should I TELL him?????" on the title page of the first. "I always knew she hated my poetry," he remarked. "I should've told her so." That it was too late now was left unsaid by all of us.

He told me I should go, since he didn't know when he'd be emotionally able to start working again. I watched him as he said this, and all I saw was the frail, fey man I'd known before Christia died. All the oomph had gone out of him, *pobrecito*. I wondered what a man like Tomasino, who was slightly out of shape, but obviously pretty darn tough, would think of Philippe. Probably not much.

I stopped off at the library on my way home to fortify myself with some department-approved texts for my next paper. I passed by

Ibo, who had nodded off in his carrel. He looked like a sleeping baby, his long dark lashes on his cheeks, his mouth soft in repose. I drank in the sight of my friend looking peaceful for the first time since Christia had died, and then I tore myself away. I didn't want him to wake up to someone, even if that someone was me, spying on him.

*

In his tiny cubbyhole of an apartment, Nicholas was arguing with Sam Green, his stepfather. "I'm coming out there," Sam shouted over 3,000 miles of phone lines. "I don't just do litigation despite what you might think and you might need a good defense lawyer!"

"That's all very nice of you to offer," Nicholas said, cordial but cool, "But I'm not really in any trouble. And you aren't licensed in New York."

"Yes I am! And your mother told me you were taken in for questioning today regarding the murder of your advisor? I think that's rather serious, my boy."

"Sam," Nicholas began, exasperated.

"Dad!" Sam insisted. "Call me Dad."

"All right, 'Dad,'" Nicholas continued, "Would you listen to me? I am not in any real trouble. As soon as they find out who did it, I'll be completely exonerated. I was just in the wrong place at the wrong time."

"Oh, like when you were a teenager?" Sam was angry now. "Now you listen to *me*. You think everybody who's convicted of a crime is guilty? You got another think coming. I'm coming out." He hung up.

Nicholas sighed. His time at the 28th Precinct had been sort of thrilling, actually. Very like the gritty cop shows he'd occasionally watched on TV when he had trouble sleeping back in California. He turned his mind to more serious matters. Annie was coming over and she would have questions. Revealing his alibi to her was going to involve certain distasteful admissions on his part.

*

"Come in."

I froze at the tone in his voice. He sounded both shaky and cold. Distant. He took my elbow and guided me into his tiny room.

"What?" I'd started to get agitated myself. I shook his hand off my elbow and twisted to get a better look in his eyes. "What is it?"

"Please, just sit down." He offered me the only chair in the room and stood in front of me. "There're a couple of things I need to tell you."

"Talk then! Jesus, Nicholas." I shook my head. "You're making me very uncomfortable."

He tented his hands and tapped his fingertips together. Insofar as it was possible in that space, Nicholas was pacing. The only sounds were those of his padding feet and the shush-shush of the silk of his pant legs rubbing together. We were both breathing carefully and quietly, as one does when one is afraid others can hear the pounding of one's heart.

"I was questioned by the police today." I nodded in acknowledgement. "What I told them is this: I visited Christia that day to show her what Ibo was working on and to tell her she had no right to claim his work as her own. He'd been idealistic enough to think he could show her a major discovery he'd made, a fragment of stone that had been in his family a long time. She immediately took it and ran with it. Began talking about some 'discovery' she'd made. He was losing his mind." My eyes widened. So this was what had been going on with Ibo and Christia. It figured. This news would surely put Ibo in an even more difficult position in the police inquiry.

As if he'd read my mind, Nicholas continued. "They asked me if I thought Ibo had, as they put it, 'done Christia in;' I told them that he'd told me he'd tried to discuss all that with Christia earlier that very afternoon. But he hadn't even had the guts to confront her about stealing his work! How would he have gone so far as to have killed her?"

"Did they believe you?" I asked, concerned.

"I think so." This didn't seem his main concern, as he continued, in some haste, "In any event, that's why I was there and why my fingerprints were on that paper Ibo wrote, *Things Truly New to Behold*, which I left with her. Before she died. Emphasis on before she died. She was alive when I left, I promise you that. And pissed. Seemed to think we'd all totally misread her." He narrowed his eyes. "She blatantly denied everything...Brought out the old 'I'm innocent as the driven snow' act."

"'Pure,'" I corrected him. I didn't want to hear his bitterness about the dead any longer. "What about later?"

"What do you mean? Oh." He stood still for a second, then resumed pacing, if anything more frantically than before. "That's what I wanted to talk to you about." He didn't look at me. He abruptly changed the subject: "That night. At Caffé Taci? Remember, with Christia and the whole Beltane fires story?"

"Of course." I waited, confused.

Nicholas finally sat down, on the edge of his bed. He squirmed. I felt nervous and impatient and I didn't do anything to make him more comfortable. "I was with Abdus and Kalinka."

"O.K. Um, what's the big deal?" Nicholas looked really guilty and I had no idea why. I was about to find out.

"The night Christia died was the first night we slept together. That's why I can remember the night so specifically."

Was I really that dense? "Who – slept together?"

"Um, all of us."

332

"Wow." I couldn't think of anything else to say. Then a wave of nausea swept over me. Sure, I was jealous – doesn't everyone want to think they are still the center of their ex's affections in some way? – but much more than that I felt betrayed. My best friend had lied to me. At length, and repeatedly. I'd almost fainted with the force of my feelings when a small but stalwart part of my brain told me to get a grip. Then I started to giggle: How could Abdus, who was so fastidious, and had a foot-fetish to boot, stand Nicholas' stank, carbuncled feet?

Nicholas looked at me. I'm sure he had no idea what to think, or whether I was sad, mad, or hysterical…Slowly, his features coalesced into a look of outrage. "I'm glad this is all so funny to you," he said coldly. "And that my having friends - lovers - to back up my alibi is so obviously a matter of no importance to you." His blue eyes were big with surprise.

My laughter turned to tears without my even realizing it. All I knew was that somehow I was suddenly sobbing and sad, no longer one bit giggly. "Friends," I sobbed, half to myself. Nicholas, doing his best to follow my mood swings and respond accordingly, tried to put an arm around me once he noticed the shift to tears. "No!" I shouted, and threw his arm off. "Don't even touch me," I said, much more quietly. I'd taken Nicholas' adoration for granted, and the clear revelation that it was no longer so smarted; but this was more a matter of trust. I kept my arm extended, palm out, to keep him away from me, and looked down at the floor, furious.

"You won't even look at me," Nicholas said indignantly. "I feel like some naughty boy whose mama's angry with him." I looked at him with disgust. "Let's be rational here," he implored.

Naughty. My stomach turned over. "Naughty? *Rational*? That's some motivated reasoning right there my friend. I don't care *what* you've been doing. Polyamory is frigging fine by me. The point is, you were *lying*! You've been lying to me for weeks!" I couldn't stop crying, which made me even more mad. I was terribly shaken – much more than I'd've expected to have been. Then again, who expects news like what I'd just heard? I'd clenched my jaw for so long that my mandibular joint was already starting to throb. Agony. I pulled myself together enough to ask one last question: "When did this start?"

He looked at me sadly. "The night we went to Taci. That's what I was talking about. When I left you talking with Redmund? Abdus had called my mobile and told me they wanted to talk, you know, as soon as possible."

"No, I don't know," I said disagreeably. "I do remember you thought it was important enough to interrupt me in a very important conversation about my dissertation and then ditch me."

"I came back."

"Yeah, without feeling the need to tell me a goddamned thing! Without so much as a different look in your eye after, oh, I dunno, starting a whole new relationship – *set* of relationships – without telling me. Me, who, by the way, has been feeling sorry for you and your fake heartbreak!" It occurred to me for the first time that someone who could hide something like that could be hiding a lot more, and I told him so.

He talked some more, trying to justify himself, I guess. I wasn't really listening. Outside, the day grew darker. We stared at each other. My eyes glowed feverishly - I could feel them burning. They bore into his as I walked backwards out of Nicholas' hole of an apartment. I couldn't abide the vulnerability of turning my back to him, even for a millisecond

Tuesday night was kind of a blur. I walked up to my neighborhood from Nicholas' place, and then I just kept walking. I needed to walk until my mental pandemonium subsided, and until tears stopped streaming down my face at semi-regular intervals. The world felt subtly psychedelic to me in my grief, as though anything solid was liable to shift at any moment. I walked and walked in the darkness. I walked until I began to feel numb and then I walked through that as well.

I found myself in Riverside Park, where I'd walked with Tomás. That evening's stroll seemed like years ago. A few late runners, mostly men, were out huffing and puffing in the cold night air. My own lungs were beginning to pain me, but I wasn't ready for home yet. From time to time I'd look up, searching for the few barely-visible stars we New Yorkers, with all our bright lights and skyscrapers, are allowed.

After Riverside Park's running path ends, around 120th street, there's a sidewalk that wends its way up past Grant's Tomb and beyond. In the low 120's, an old stone gazebo, covered in vines, sits overlooking the Hudson. It was one of my favorite places to think and I found myself there that night, mulling over what Nicholas had told me. I shouldn't have gone there alone.

I remember the rustling of the leaves on the gnarled vines, and the flowing, steady expanse of the Hudson alit in the night by the bright, wakeful city. I remember admiring the New Jersey Palisades on the far shore. I remember thinking that I might be able to learn an important lesson from what I'd been through that day. I'd learned that my gut instinct about Nicholas – that there was something slightly off about him, something *missing* in his character (if that term's not too old-fashioned) – had been on the mark. I resolved to trust myself more, especially when it came to my so-called love life! I remember that I was thinking of the people I *did* trust – Lark, my parents -- and then I remember little else, for someone knocked me over the head with something hard as a rock and I passed out.

Cold, cold, cold.

335

It was still dark when I came to. No one had found me, so I reasoned I couldn't have been lying there too long. I felt, understandably, quite chilly. Gingerly, I reached a hand to my head. There was an egg-sized lump above my left ear, and a wetness all around it in my sticky hair which I took to be blood. I still had my bag, with my wallet in it, and my omnipresent school books, so I surmised the attack had not been a robbery. This was all very strange.

I tried not to worry. I told myself that everybody knew head wounds usually bled and swelled-up more than injuries to other parts of the body. After mentally scanning myself and deciding I didn't feel too bad, I very carefully tried to sit up. Aside from a mild dizziness, I felt O.K., especially given the circumstances. It was then that a sensation that had been niggling at the back of my mind came abruptly to the fore: my feet were disproportionately cold. I didn't have any socks or shoes on.

Ugg: Just like Christia.

For the second time that day, I felt a wave of shock roll over me. I tried hard not to pass out again. Desperate, I mustered the modicum of sanity I would need to get out of there. I hadn't been sure if I would report the incident – New York City police have bigger fish to fry than searching for random mugger-types, albeit those of the non-stealing variety – but with the link to Christia's death I now knew I'd have to tell the police the whole tale. I was glad I'd met Tomasino earlier that day. I'd left my cellphone at home. If I could just make it out of that lightless, isolated gazebo intact, I would call him first thing.

I felt around in the darkness and recovered my tatty socks and my shoes, a pair of battered Birkenstocks. Boy, if this guy had a thing about shoes I was sure to have been a major disappointment.

Wednesday after lunch, I took the subway to midtown, Columbus Circle, to meet Theadora Harmon for afternoon tea in the Astor Court at the St. Regis.

She was sitting alone at a table set for two, her own personal china teapot in front of her. She arose to greet me, and as we shook hands, the rose-orange-labdanum scent of Chanel's Coco wafted gently around me. "So good to see you," she said. I'd only met her the once, but she was dressed in what I suspected must be her quotidian splendor. She wore a form-fitting red and black striped suit jacket with Edwardian sleeves. Chunky amber bead necklaces cascaded down the front of the hot pink blouse she wore underneath. On anyone else, the outfit would have shrieked "fashion victim," or worse, but on her it projected a level of confidence and élan that few of us can even aspire to.

"Thanks for taking the time." I replied and sat down. From my seat I could see the King Cole Bar, which was sparsely populated at that hour: men in suits, mostly. Astor Court, in contrast, was the province of women. With its impeccable service, and just the right amount of gilt and pomp crossed with an overall air of understatement, it conferred an aura of perfect propriety on all who dined there. Tasteful flower arrangements in muted colors sat in the middle of each table.

It was all a tasteful cover for culinary decadence.

Harmon looked at me more closely. "Annie, are you all right?" The lump on my head was still tender. I'd refused to have it examined, though. I knew I was fine, and they couldn't find any evidence in my scalp beyond the obvious: I'd been hit on the head, most likely with the very piece of stone they'd found in the gazebo with my blood on it. I recounted what had happened to me the night before. She was, naturally, totally shocked and sympathetic. When I told her about my shoes, she bit her lip in consternation. She asked me if there was anything she could do, and I said the police were looking into it.

337

"I actually think the head cop is a decent person," I reassured her. Between making my statement to the police the night before and, that morning, rushing to sit in on Intro.Comp.Lit. and then to Colonial Fiction, I hadn't spoken with anyone else about what had happened to me. I didn't plan to, either. It would have terrified some – my mother, Gretel, Brandi, Brenda – and it was nobody else's business, I thought, especially that scurvy Nicholas. It felt good to confide in Theadora.

"And after all that, you woke up and you just...walked away?" Her expression was incredulous.

"Well, I put my shoes back on first," I said, smiling, trying to make light of what had happened. "I'm sure it was all the adrenaline," I added frankly, "because I sure feel woozy today."

A waiter brought my teapot and a three-tiered silver tray with layers of finger sandwiches, scones, and chocolates. A separate tray, with clotted cream and pots of marmalade and raspberry jam was set down in front of us as well. Our attention was, thankfully, riveted by the food. We devoured what was in front of us in a matter of minutes and were served seconds – of *everything* -- without having to make the effort of ordering — or admitting to ourselves that we were eating a distinctly unladylike amount of food. I wondered how many social x-rays "accidentally" ate more than they'd planned in the same fashion as we did.

After a period of gorging, followed by a brief period of small talk, we admitted to each other that what we really wanted to talk about was Christia Thompson.

"This may sound strange," Theadora tilted her head and looked at me pensively. "Or maybe not, after what happened to you," she noted, licking a dollop of clotted cream from the end of her spoon, "But I've been fixated on the whole foot angle."

"You mean why was she barefoot?"
She nodded.

338

I shuddered as the image of Christia, dead, and – poor thing – barefoot, leapt, unbidden, into my mind. And then I shivered again: there was a more personal dimension to this discussion after last night's attack. Tomasino himself had admitted that he suspected a link with Christia's murder, although he was at a loss as to what the connection was, exactly. I, too, was at a loss. Before I'd found out about his betrayal, I would've dissected and analyzed the incident with Nicholas – and probably shared a bed with him for solace. For now, being alive and safe was comfort enough.

Unconsciously, I wiggled my feet under the table. They were warm and well-shod – qualities I was accustomed to taking for granted. I mulled over Theadora's query. "I guess I always thought with Christia that it was either a foot fetish thing or the killer was looking for a handy weapon." I paused, wondering how to phrase what I was about to say. It was all so gruesome. "But I think they determined that she was strangled by hand, not stocking, after all. The stocking around her neck was, ah, gratuitous."

"I was coming from a different angle." Theadora countered, placing her spoon on her plate. "I'm thinking maybe there was some religious or cultural significance to her being barefoot. At least for the killer."

"Hmm." I pondered her question.

"Hear me out." As she spoke, I took the opportunity to eat my share of the second pot of marmalade, plain, by the spoonful, while, of course, listening closely. "The bare foot, religion-wise, tends to represent purity and honor. It is, dare I say, even a symbol of virginity, or at least youth. That's in the West." She stopped to take a bite of a chocolate infused with rich caramel. "In Eastern cultures, it seems to vary more. Mind you, this is all off the top of my head. I'm gonna look into it more. But what I can come up with most obviously is for one, China. The foot, there, was bound to entice men, right? Everybody

339

knows that. But that bound foot was hobbling to women. All curled into itself and in need of constant cleaning and oiling to stay fresh. And painful? Whew. Can you imagine?" I grimaced. Theadora wagged her index finger at me. "Nothin' but the old oppression disguised as privilege, *à la,* 'You are too delicate and precious to even move, dear.'" I groaned. She looked at me sharply. "You think we're so far from that?"

I shrugged. "I guess not. In fact, I actually sometimes think Christia was killed for transgressing somebody's idea of the proper patriarchal mores. But – please, go on about the foot."

She had been nodding in agreement and took a minute to re-focus. "In India," she continued, "feet have twofold and contradictory significance. Given the climate, most feet are nearly-bare most of the time. Poverty plays a role too, I'm sure. In any case, this surplus of visible, available feet allows a lot of leeway for a mythology of the foot to emerge." This woman was so brilliant – just the way she talked extemporaneously was extraordinarily compelling. I listened with respect, sweets temporarily forgotten. "On the one hand," she continued, "When sitting or lying down, the soles of your feet are never to be directed toward someone. It's a sign of disrespect in a lot of Asian countries. This is especially the case with your superiors – elders, teachers, etc. But," she held up a finger, "*kissing* one's beloved's feet – be it a guru or a loved one – is considered the highest sign of respect." I thought of Western students at my yoga center kissing the feet of the (also Western) directors of the center. That was one mystery, at least, solved.

"Oh! I almost forgot! You are not going to believe this. Wait a sec." She reached into her red patent leather bag and brought out *The Golden Bough.* She flipped through the pages until a scrap of paper fell out. "Here it is. Page 283. '...the rule which prescribes that at certain magical and religious ceremonies the hair should hang loose *and the feet should be bare.'"* She looked at me, wide-eyed and proud. "I just opened it up to that page this morning!"

"Weird," I admitted. We smiled at each other, pleased with her lucky find. I thought of my recent paranormal experiences. "I've been pretty intuitive lately too – though nothing compared to these women I met the other day, who knew my name without my telling them." I was thinking of the three women of Intuitions.

"O-ho," Theadora burst into a big belly laugh. "Hocus Pocus, huh? Un-unh. Brace yourself." I pantomimed taking a huge swig of tea. "That was my sister, Adea, and her daughter, my niece Adoniah. The other one was Salima, a good friend of mine. They're part of the coven."

"Which coven?" I covered my surprise with one of the many questions flooding my mind at that instant.

"Puduhepa's Sisters! C'mon, you didn't suspect even a little bit?"

My jaw dropped.

"Don't let's be coy, now!"

"No, I really had zero idea." I took a moment to let her news sink in. "My brain's been a little fuzzy lately. I knew you were in Christia's coven, but that's it. I was trying to find that coven--"

Theadora smiled benevolently. "You saw all of us already, too. But for one."

"When?"

"At Christia's funeral." She looked at me intently. "Eleven women in red? Red – for celebrating the energy and spirit of Christia's life? I know you were looking at us – I saw you."

Of course. I thought for a minute, then said, "I didn't see you there. I definitely noticed the women in red, though. How could I not?"

"Well, that's us. Actually, I'm not surprised you didn't recognize me. I was wearing what my mother used to call 'a hat of stature.' I wasn't too keen on being recognized by people from Christia's department myself. Not afraid, mind you, just – why bother to explain to them?" She sighed. "They think I'm nuts anyway."

"No way," I argued. "It seemed to me like they all worshipped you that night at Caffé Taci. Those junior faculty guys especially, they *love* you: You're single, successful, beautiful…What's not to like? I mean about you. With them, uggh: *cave canem*."

She didn't respond to my attempt at humor. "Single?" She asked, anger suffusing her question. "Is that what they said? I'm not single." Her eyes blazed.

"Well, y-you don't wear a wedding ring," I stuttered a bit, feeling I'd offended her somehow. "No one actually said anything, as far as I can remember."

"Hey," she put out a hand. "It's not you, Annie, it's them. I don't deal with all that marriage palaver. If you're committed, you're committed, right?" I nodded eagerly. "And if you're not," she continued, "Ain't no piece a paper gonna keep you faithful. Or together." She popped the last bite of her crustless cucumber sandwich into her mouth and wiped her fingers on her cloth napkin. There were only a few crumbs left on our second (or was it third?) three-tiered tray. I reached for a petit-four I'd glimpsed hiding under a corner of a doily and offered to split it with her.

"You go ahead, Annie." She leaned back in her chair. "I am fully satisfied." She smiled a secret smile to herself. "In my love life too. After all these years I've found a happy, well-adjusted relationship."

I was impressed. "Details, please."

"A yoga teacher. Name of Ryan. We're gonna move in together."

"Wait! Is Ryan about 6' tall, almost shaved head. Ankh tattoo?"

"Yes," Theadora's expression was one of pleased surprise. "How did you know?"

"She's one of my yoga teachers!" I'd taken her class several times in the last month. "She's great," I said sincerely. "She's not all nicey-poo, but it's completely obvious that she is fiercely kind." I thought of the false politesse of academia, and the ostentatious piousness of many at the yoga center. "You know, that uncommon type of person who clearly has a big heart, but doesn't go around acting insipid, if that makes sense. That's my favorite kind of person." I concluded.

"Sounds about right," Theadora replied. "I aspire to be that kind of person too."

"Oh, absolutely," I assured her, though I am sure she didn't need to be told. "You are so totally that way."

"The way I feel is, I walk with spirit, not Emily Post. If manners make you feel comfortable, fine; if they make you – or anybody else -- feel like you're not good enough then forget it. So many people are just tryna make themselves look good." She excused herself, saying with a smile, "It's just about enough to send me to the ladies' room."

I sat at our round, sumptuously set table, observing the other ladies at tea. All around me, chic, elegant women in twos and threes – no men, save the service people – talked in hushed tones as they stuffed their faces with the dainty yet plentiful food. The trompe-l'oeil clouds on the ceiling lent the room a feeling of spaciousness and calm. I gave a sigh of contentment.

When Theadora got back from the bathroom, I smiled at my new friend. "My lord," I said. "I have to tell you: This has been immeasurably more fun than any meal I've ever had with anyone who actually *has* their Ph.D."

Theadora laughed, her long braids swinging with the movement. "Yeah well, they've mostly got their heads up their butts." Her eyes twinkled at me. "You gotta do like I did and write something that will put you out of the drudgery loop."

"Here, here," I said, raising my empty teacup in a toast; then I remembered the main reason I was there. "I've been having so much fun, I almost forgot: What about your coven? I'd like to meet with anyone who has time for me."

She closed her eyes for a minute. "I know." When she opened her eyes she seemed more serious. "We have all meditated as a circle and have decided you may question us."

"Terrific," I responded gratefully, "So what should I do next?"

"Well, have you asked me whatever you want? Because," she continued as I racked my brain for any possibly-missed details, "I think I've told you everything I can think of." She tapped her index finger on her temple. "There's only one other person who knew her as well as I did in the coven. We mostly met for ritual and divination, you know? Usually something more focused than your garden-variety conversation. Everybody's pretty busy otherwise…"

"I hear that." Living in New York, most of the people I knew were just barely getting through the day, financially, time-wise…romantically…"So, can you give me her number?"

"You already know her." I looked at her questioningly. "It's Brenda Fujiki."

I was in total shock. The thought of the slight, screwed-up, painfully shy Brenda as a self-actualized witch, an equal among powerful women, was as startling and refreshing as it was frightening. After all, I'd seen another side of her the day before. Like Christia, Brenda was becoming more and more fascinating to me. At least the latter was still alive.

I remained silent, bemused, as Theadora continued. "I talked to everyone about it after the meditation and nobody could come up with anything all that revelatory. Snake wasn't absolutely positive who you were until afterwards, but she did say she stands by her reading."

"Huh?" I was confused.

"When you went to Enchantments, did not a woman draw three cards for you?"

"Oh…Yeah." Monday afternoon seemed eons ago. The reading had been about pain and truth and justice. I guessed the pain part was the only element that seemed relevant at that point, but I still had high hopes for resolution with truth and justice.

"We decided that if anything came up for any of the individuals, they'd call you – I gave them your number. I thought that would be O.K.?"

"Of course."

"Or if you come up with any specific questions, you can let me know. Also, Brenda said to call her after we talked."

"But I saw her, like, yesterday, and she didn't say a *thing*!" I went over the bare bones of our conversation rapidly in my head. Not even a hint.

"Brenda is, understandably, our most secretive member. She didn't feel right, for example, sitting with us during Christia's memorial, it having been on campus and all. She has a lot of fear. I'm sure you've noticed that." Theadora paused, thoughtful, then added, "Nonetheless, she's stronger than she appears." She stood up, her long silk skirt floating around her.

I nodded and crumbled my napkin in my lap. "Thanks, Theadora. I'll call her." I pictured she and Ryan as a couple. Both were strong, frank, beautiful women. "And good luck on your move," I added, standing up and pulling my purse over my shoulder. "I think you two are going to be very happy. I just have a feeling."

She gave me a tight hug, long enough that I knew it was sincere. "Keep in touch," she said, taking her aqua faux-fur coat from the Maitre-d'.

We walked a few steps toward the arched exit, trailing the delicious scent of Coco. Theadora paused on the threshold to say one last thing: "There's a couple people I sure would like to spy on, if I could be a fly on the wall." I raised an eyebrow. "Everyone who visited her that last day had big, big issues with her. We sensed that. And we're also getting the message that you are vulnerable. I mean, before you got knocked out!" I'd sensed as much myself. Maybe it was because I had a passion for the truth. Still, I felt as if an even heavier weight was bearing down on my shoulders. Theadora Harmon looked right into my eyes -- to lend me strength, I think -- wished me luck, and then left.

Chapter Eleven – In Which Everything Starts to go to Hell

You Rang?
She rings so pure, a silver
Bell.
But we are never, ever sure:
Hell.

Philippe Perez-Throgmorton

After I spent some of Thursday morning crying cathartically (over Nicholas, etc.) and ruminating over having been clocked on the head (by whom?), what stayed with me was the possible significance of Abdus' thing about feet. How had I missed that before? Let's just suppose, I speculated, that Abdus had some reason for killing Christia, something that clearly had yet to be discovered by the authorities. Stroking Merlin's plushy black fur absentmindedly, I wondered: was there some way I could sort of…nudge things in the right direction?

"Guys, I'm gonna do it!" I said aloud to my always-supportive pets. They thought all of my ideas were fantastic. I set out for Abdus and Kalinka's house, armed with nothing more than my suspicions – and the excuse that I'd been in the neighborhood and wanted to – what, thank them for seducing my ex-boyfriend? Not appropriate. I was stopping by to thank them for inviting me to their long-ago party? Uh-uh. I would have to wing it.

I had one fleeting moment of panic on my way to Central Park West: what if Abdus and/or Kalinka locked me somewhere in their giant apartment and – immediately? eventually? – killed me, too? I'd told no one of my plans. So I called Brandi and left her a cryptic message that I hoped was just oblique enough as to let her know I was nervous without throwing her into a panic. It occurred to me when I hung up that they probably had no plans to kill me. After all, the killer(s) must've known I was alive while taking off my shoes in the old gazebo that night. I considered myself warned, but undaunted in my quest. Sooner or later I was going to be identified as the note-writer; and besides, I was starting to like the posthumous Christia.

Kalinka opened the door herself. Her expression was sullen, and in daylight, without make-up, her face looked lined. He thick chestnut hair was pulled back in a lackluster ponytail, and showing gray at the roots. She was older than I'd thought. I apologized for dropping in on her without notice, and she waved a hand dismissively.

"Ach, everything's a mess," she sighed, rolling her wide-set eyes. She looked like a very old child, I realized suddenly. A potentially dangerous one. I just barely stifled a high-strung giggle. She looked at me sharply, and then seemed to decide my strange behavior was par for the course. "Won't you come in?" she said with an achingly polite smile.

We went through a side door and through the kitchen to a breakfast nook. Nothing in the kitchen looked terribly clean. There were piles of dishes in the two big sinks, and pots and bowls with half-eaten food in them strewn about. Just inside the entry to the breakfast nook sat a vast Balinese carved daybed, upholstered in red silk jacquard with piles of Batik pillows in reds, purples and deep oranges. On the precious silk mattress sat a stack of dirty plates over a foot high.

She must have sensed my scrutiny, for she immediately explained with a shrug that Abdus had fired the servants. "He can't afford them anymore and he will not let me pay for them. It is beneath his dignity to be supported by a woman I suppose." I detected a note of bitterness in her voice. "He's not here, by the way," she added as she slid into a booth with cushy seats in the same richly-colored Batiks. The sunny table was situated under a large window with a view down Central Park West and the park beyond. She nodded at me to take the seat across from her. "Smoke?" she offered me one of hers.

"Thanks, no…" It was a little early for me.

She began to speak unprompted. "As you can see, I am in a very bad mood." Her stronger-than-usual German accent made her utterance sound even more ominous. She stood up and went back into the kitchen, emerging a minute later with a tall metal glass for me. "Here," she said, pouring mint tea from a matching teapot. I admired the tea set, which was fashioned of bronze with intricate, red-enameled grapes and flowers. I waited for her to elaborate. Another metaphor came to mind: she looked like a bleary-eyed alien. This time I was unable to stop a small chuckle from escaping my lips.

"It's because you think I am always so glamorous, yes?" Kalinka asked gently. "Now I am ugly and old. This is why you keep laughing?"

"I-I..I'm just nervous. I'm sorry. I've always found you beautiful, Kalinka." I'd never imagined her moping and unkempt.

She took a deep drag from her cigarette and blew the smoke in my face, perhaps unconsciously, perhaps not. "Why are you, as you say, nervous?" she asked, finally.

"Nicholas told me what is going on." There. That was certainly an adequate explanation.

She looked taken aback. "What *was* going on, you mean. I don't know what he's told you but I am no longer involved in the ménage. As for Abdus --"

Abdus walked in at that moment, naturally. He looked at lot more pulled-together than his girlfriend. His glossy hair was parted on the side, and perfectly combed. His lush lips were set in a slightly mocking smile. My, but he was an exceedingly attractive man. I couldn't blame Nicholas for wanting him, I mused. He'd always been unfriendly to me, yet I found myself – no glutton for punishment – strongly drawn to him. My eyes bounced from Abdus to the luxurious daybed next to which he stood, then back to Abdus.

"Good morning, Abdus," I smiled tentatively.

"Nicholas has told Annie about our little fling," Kalinka announced.

Abdus had evidently decided to be civil to me for some reason. "You must be hurt," he said, after taking a minute to absorb the situation. His voice was soft, sweet, sympathetic. "You're a good egg, Annie." Who else had called me a good egg recently? Nicholas. Grr. "I'm sorry for everything. For being jealous of you above all, I owe you an apology." The usual face of stone Abdus adopted around me was, inexplicably, gone. In its place was the open face of a normal, perhaps even nice, person. His chocolate-brown eyes exuded sincerity.

"You are quite mistaken." I said coldly. I was not ready to accept his change of heart without a good explanation. "Unless you wacked me on the head recently!"

"Of course not," he responded in honeyed tones. Then he looked puzzled: "Sorry…Did I miss something? Did you get hit in the head?"

I tried to shake my head no, but it hurt too much. "Let's not talk about that," I managed.

He nodded. "Annie, I simply want to express that I have long been unkind to you. Well, that is about to change. I no longer hold your friendship with Nicholas against you."

"Hey, thanks," I shot back. "That's great. Because we're no longer friends."

The look of sadness on his face seemed genuine. "You will not forgive him our affair?"

"Hah! I'm all for people following their bliss." I retorted. "It's boldfaced lying I don't like. And manipulation."

"So in principle you are not jealous, or angry."

"Not, in principle, jealous or angry about your," I paused, taking in Abdus' smoldering handsomeness, and Kalinka's exhaustion, and thinking of the golden, gorgeous, indolent Nicholas, "um, relationship, no." There was even a part of me that found the idea rather enticing. "Polyamory is a subject I've long been – interested in." Abdus had not taken his eyes off me. I felt my cheeks growing flushed. "Philosophically speaking, that is," I clarified. I lowered my eyes, avoiding Abdus' gaze. I was afraid he would deduce my thoughts.

There was a brief lull in our conversation, which suddenly felt more sinister as I remembered the original reason why I had shown up at Kalinka and Abdus' that morning. I tried to think of something to say that would change the course of our discussion, something that would give me some clue as to Abdus' role in Christia's life, beyond that of being one of "her" students.

"Do you think, then –" Abdus began, his level, friendly voice flooding me with relief. Given my muddled brain, I had remained at a loss as to where our conversation – the first-ever pleasant one between us – might proceed next.

"Be quiet." The words had come from Kalinka, who was completely still. Abdus and I both recoiled slightly in shock. I'd certainly never heard aggression in her voice; and from the look of him

351

Abdus hadn't either. "Now. You two listen to me." She was red with irritation. "Annie has come by for a surprise visit, so she will just have to hear this. *Und* since the two of you simply vill not stop chattering, I am forced to interrupt. Too bad." She turned her eerie gaze on Abdus. Such big eyes. "I was just wondering where you've been spending all this time away from our flat. Maybe you were with Nicholas?"

She didn't wait for him to respond. She went again to the kitchen, returning with a half-empty bottle of bourbon from which she poured herself a generous lashing, in her tea glass. "The one he's really in love with is Nicholas." She explained to me, in a confiding tone. "And so...Maybe that's why he did it." Considering my reasons for dropping by unexpectedly, it's hard to figure how it was that I had no idea what she was referring to; but such was the case, at first. My confusion made her even more angry. "Don't pretend you don't know what I'm talking about! You suspect him too, or you wouldn't be here. Look!" she exclaimed, carefully lifting her leg and placing a long, pale foot on the table where I sat. "You even kept your shoes on!" It was true, I realized, I hadn't taken my shoes off in the foyer. Had I subconsciously wanted to protect my feet from Abdus foot-obsessed gaze? Astonished, I realized she was accusing Abdus of Christia's murder.

His eyes were round pools of shock. "Kali – "

She swung around to face me. "Maybe you're next, since you're the one *Nicholas* really loves!"

Abdus exploded. "What will it take for you to believe me? I love you. You! I had some sort of odd displacement feelings for Nicholas. Admiration." Kalinka slumped over her drink, despondent. He turned to me, lighting a cigarette. "Look at you. The two of you are two peas in a pod. Fair maiden and fair lad." He shrugged. "How could I not desire him? The light to my dark?"

"You mean you felt you wanted to be like him? Or *be* him?" I asked cautiously. "But-but that's just the color of our skin – the melanin level in our bodies, for god's sake. It's a *stereotype*."

"You would not say Nicholas is more innocent than me?"

"No. Not now. What the hell? What century is this?"

"Well I would. Without a doubt. I have seen things that would break your pristine hearts. In Pakistan. In Peshawar…Hell, in the Meatpacking district." Kalinka stirred from her fog, and he directed his next words to her: "Yes, I had a thing about Mr. Perfect Scholar, the perfect American boy. But I got over that double-quick once we'd consummated things. It was all just - lust. Clearly," he glared at the stricken Kalinka, "you do not take me at my word." He stalked out of the room.

I was embarrassed for all of us, the fighting couple *and* myself, the unexpected guest. I didn't look at Kalinka. We two were silent, listening as Abdus' steps grew further away, then got louder again as he walked back into the kitchen. Kalinka and I got up wordlessly and joined him in the big kitchen. We were about twenty feet away from him, at the breakfast nook end of the kitchen when I noticed that he had something very odd in his arms. I looked more closely as we approached, determining that his arms were cradling a taxidermied armadillo, which, with great force, he threw down the airshaft to the cement, twenty-odd stories below.

"Nicholas gave us that!" Kalinka wailed. I should have known only Nicholas would give -- or have access to -- such a morbid yet unique gift.

"Oho – who's in love with whom now?"

"You know I cared for him, some." Kalinka's voice was resigned. She'd had her fit, and now was back to moping. She sort of wafted out of the kitchen into the spacious foyer, alighting on a priceless red and gold Kerman rug. "Oh, I forgot: your brother called," she told Abdus, who'd followed her. I was on the threshold of the kitchen, just out of sight.

"Bloody philistines!" Abdus sneered. "Trying to turn a poet into a businessman. I don't need their money anymore."

Kalinka was not having any of it. "Don't try to change the subject. I have the right to know where you have been!"

"Kali, love," Abdus said tenderly, even proudly, "I have got a job!"

Kalinka, rendered momentarily speechless, looked skeptical. Then her wide eyes filled, briefly, with wonder. After a pause she asked, "So...What will you be doing?"

In his warm, aristocratic baritone, Abdus intoned, "I shall be earning a living. For my family." Slyly, he gazed at her from under his thick lashes. "My wife."

As the significance of his words sunk in, Kalinka's face lost its tightness and was suffused with joy. I looked away tactfully, but, after I'd let at least a full minute go by, they were still holding hands and gazing into each other's eyes. Yech.

Making myself as inconspicuous as possible, I sidled into the grand foyer. "I really should go," I ventured.

They were in their own little bubble. Abdus did manage to dismiss me: "It has been awfully nice seeing you, Annie. You'll understand if we have other things to attend to." He gave me a placating smile, and draped an arm casually over Kalinka's shoulders. "My lady here and I, we have some shopping to do. Cartier," he said with a lazy grin. "For a ring." With this last, Kalinka had pepped-up considerably more. No longer listless, but glowing with happy pride, she took my arm, ready to escort me to the door.

I shook my head. "Wow, Abdus, you sure are in a new phase here. What happened to snotty, noncommittal you?"

"What a witch you are, Annie," he joked, half-seriously, a sliver of the old Abdus squeezing through his nice veneer.

"So can I ask you two a question?"

"Sure," Abdus answered for both.

"Where were you on Tuesday night?"

Kalinka looked at him in consternation. Abdus shrugged. "I was out to dinner with my employer, after I'd signed the contract. You can call him if you don't believe me." He wrinkled his forehead. "Why?"

"Oh, I got badly bumped on the head on that night. No big deal." Although the dinner could conceivably have ended by the time of the attack, I decided not to push him. I smiled. "Well, thanks for being so accommodating…"

"He's just being his fabulous self," Kalinka said, her voice husky. "Annie, you just don't know him."

Abdus turned to me expansively, saying, "It's all going to keep getting better and better, from here on in!" He shook my hand enthusiastically and strode out of the foyer.

Kalinka was still smiling a huge, and, I thought, slightly forced smile.

"Well," I said, "thanks for having me. 'Bye." I couldn't wait to get out of there and *think* a little, to process all that had happened far from the embarrassment, arousal, anger, and confusion I'd experienced in such a brief period of time.

Kalinka would not release my arm. "I am not in a bad mood anymore," she whispered quickly. "I did not know where Abdus was. Now I do." She looked imploringly into my eyes. "You understand?"

"Yes, of course." I disentangled myself as nicely as I could. "Probably you should go talk to him," I suggested. All I could think about, though, was the fact that Abdus had not denied killing Christia. Unfortunately, after all that, I was no further toward knowing his motivations.

I was, however, indisputably still alive.

Brandi and I arrived at the same time and took our usual seats side by side in Semiotics. Professor Svankmeyer arrived precisely on time, sporting a purple silk tie with red and yellow Eiffel towers. Matching socks adorned his feet.

Brandi raised her hand. "Professor Svankmeyer, is that tie from Paris?" she purred. He blushed and nodded. His worldly coolness had clearly been acknowledged by the hip young thing in red plaid bondage pants. I sighed. Brandi was going to do well in that class, being caught up in her work *and* having a well-established rapport with the teacher. I, on the other hand, was barely keeping up. Christia was becoming an obsession. I resolved to record and absorb every word of Svankmeyer's lecture. Toward the end of class, Brandi passed me a note, which read, "Didja figure out who did it yet, Lieutenant Campbell?" "It's Detective Campbell," I wrote back, "and no…But my main suspects for today are Abdus and Professor Redmund." Almost instantly she passed the piece of paper back to me. She'd written "Why???" in big block letters. Unfortunately, in her excitement, she'd forgotten to be stealthy. Svankmeyer gave both of us a dirty look and, for the rest of the class, I didn't feel comfortable responding.

After class, I explained to Brandi why I suspected Abdus, and told her I'd heard some things about Redmund – in strictest confidence – that added to my suspicions about him as well. We talked a little about our Thanksgiving breaks. She'd spent hers with her family in Rockaway. She asked me what Christia's brother had been like and I described him, adding that he reminded me of Tomás, "You know, my new bad-boy type?"

"Why aren't you suspicious of *him*?" she asked. "He definitely sounds like he might be resentful of his big sister's city-slicker success."

"He didn't even know she was dead until a few days after," I explained. I added a Southern twang to my voice. "He pretty much lives down on the bayou if you get my drift,"

"Not really," said the city-born and –bred Brandi, "But I can try to imagine."

In the hallway, we ran into Gretel. Brandi had to get going, but I spent a few minutes with my only other friend in the department. I thanked her again for watching Pepita.

"You betcha," she said. "Bite?" She offered me her bagel.

"Where's it from?" I asked. There's nothing worse than a bad bagel, be it light and airy, with the character of bread, or stale and cardboard-like, viable only if toasted into submission.

"Columbia Bagels. They're super." she replied agreeably.

I took a chewy, crusty bite. While I ate, I admired Gretel's ensemble of a tight black shirt with rhinestone appliqués in the shape of a guitar and tapered, front-pleated khakis. I also noticed that she looked remarkably happy. "What's up, Gretel?" I queried.

"Not me," she said, "I want to know how things are going with Tomás!"

"Oh," I groaned, "don't even ask. Total disaster." She was often skittish about Kirpal, so I tried to get at their relationship in a roundabout way: "So what's on your mind these days, love?"

"I still have that bad feeling I told you about," she admitted, looking around to make sure we had privacy. Her expression was serious. "You know my faith is very important to me." I nodded. "And as a modern Mennonite woman I've always had a bunch of things I found hard to reconcile. Pacifism and dealing with injustice. Modesty and self-expression. Humility and feminism…" After a quick, worried glance at my face, she sped up: "I know you need to go in a jif! I'm almost done!" Gretel was always congenial, almost irritatingly pleasant. It was startling – and refreshing -- to know she struggled with the world

357

like the rest of us. Seeing her sad and confused made her more human-seeming.

"Sweetie, please – we've never talked about this stuff, so please, if you want to take all afternoon –"

"No," she interjected politely, her demeanor so stiff as to be almost comical -- if not for the melancholy that had descended upon her since we began to speak. "It's Christia Thompson. That's what's up with me. I go back and forth with thinking she brought her death on herself." A tear escaped from the corner of her eye. "And in those moments when I think she 'deserved it' I hate myself more than you could imagine." She took a deep breath. "And please, Annie, don't tell me that thoughts like that are natural because who are we if not creatures who have gone beyond 'nature red in tooth and claw'? Every aspect of our educated lives is designed to civilize us and make us more tolerant, not turn us into judgmental idiots." She paused. "No," she said again before I could utter a word. "I know you and I know you will want to comfort me. Good of you, but I have my faith for that, if I can find it." She spent a moment lining up the edges of the books in her arms while I waited.

"Gretel," I finally said, "I think – I'm sorry but I have to say this – you're just at war with different viewpoints you've been exposed to. Small-town, traditional Wisconsin versus a particularly liberated section of what's already the wildest city in the world.

"It just so happens I know *you* as well – and I know you would treat anyone decently, no matter what they did. I mean, as long as they weren't hurting anybody."

She looked at me. "Who's saying Christia wasn't hurting anybody?"

"Oh, you know what I mean. Hurting someone innocent. Nobody who wasn't a consenting adult got hurt by Christia." My book bag was getting heavy. I began to set it on the hallway floor.

358

"I have to go too," Gretel said. I picked up my bag again. "Only, I wanted to say this: I have a pretty darn strong feeling that we're in danger." Not having told her about the attack on me, I knew Gretel's feeling was more on the mark than she suspected.

"I'm sure we'll be fine," I said in my most reassuring voice.

"If you know me so well, Annie, you'll know this is all really weird for me. I don't tend to be psychic or even to give credence to supernatural stuff."

I noticed she had a fine sheen of sweat on her upper lip. Steady, down-to-earth (boring) Gretel really was nervous. "I guess I'll try to be extra-careful then." I remembered my first observation of her that afternoon. "Well," I noted as we got ready to part, "something's making you look real purdy these days!" I smiled at her. "And I have my suspicions in this case as well." I wiggled my eyebrows.

"Aw," she giggled. "That's one good thing. Not that I know my feelings are cent-per-cent returned."

"C'mon. Kirpal's crazy about you. You have to admit it," I chided.

She shrugged. "I guess." I saw, however, that she looked happy again. That was good enough for me.

Although I was not looking forward to it, I thought I should check on Brenda before I went home. I'd told Theadora I would call her, and I hoped bringing up Puduhepa's Sisters would rekindle our connection. I found her leafing through a *Ms.* magazine with a murky glass of lemon water close at hand. "So I talked with Theadora." My words hung in the air. She didn't look up. "And she told me you would be happy to discuss Christia with me a little more. Or, I should say, not, er, happy, but, ah, willing."

"Oh," she said breezily, looking up at me with an ingenuous expression, "I haven't given her a thought lately. I've been so involved with my work." I'm sure I looked shocked, but she went on as if nothing were out of the ordinary. "I've been getting some help from other quarters and I've decided to continue with my Kassia research."

I'd done a tiny bit of online research and found out that Kassia only became a nun – and, ultimately, an abbess -- after being rejected as his bride by the Emperor Theophilos for being "forward." As the legend has it, his decision was based on her defending womankind when he publicly declared women the source of worldly evil. After Kassia's uppity outburst, Theophilos chose a more pliant woman; and Kassia, beautiful, strong and cussedly smart, threw herself into her faith and the discipline of composing liturgical chants still in use today. Legend has it, Theophilos regretted his decision, but – too late.

I wondered: Was Brenda drawn to the Greek Byzantine composer and nun because she felt in some important, primal way rejected? I was pretty sure Christia had – however gently – deflected any romantic overtures on Brenda's part. It was virtually impossible to imagine the sleek, sophisticated, attractive Christia Thompson being even faintly attracted to mousy, neurotic Brenda Fujiki. Still, I knew there was another side to Brenda. I'd seen her fury in person a few days before. Then there was her involvement with Puduhepa's Sisters, a coven of immensely powerful women. Here was something to reconcile: a kinship between Brenda Fujiki and Theadora Harmon. It was something to ponder, doubtless; but I hoped to reach Brenda before I went home to think.

"O.K.," I said insouciantly, "That's that. I'm sure the cops will handle it fairly and thoroughly themselves." I made as if to leave, sneaking a peak at her out of the corner of my eye. She looked nonplussed. I'd continued to walk away until I almost couldn't stand it when she said, "Wait."

I turned on my heel. "Yes?" I asked, my casual expression belying my inner excitement.

She sighed and closed the magazine. "I just thought you ought to know they didn't get a whole lot of information from the lab results. The DNA from the short hairs they found matched Christia's almost exactly. I guess you don't ever get an exact match because of deterioration of the sample or something." She scratched her head, "Must've been, you know, newer hairs that hadn't grown long yet."

"Could the hairs have belonged to, like, her brother?"

"I don't know. I don't think so, though. Someone said he had an alibi anyway. 'He was in the swamps of Louisiana with his good ol' boy friends' was what Nicholas said."

Her mention of Nicholas momentarily jolted me out of my willful moratorium on thoughts about *that* situation. I quickly distracted myself with thoughts about the lab results. I hadn't earlier, but I realized then that I'd pinned a lot of hope – for absolution, for resolution -- on those lab samples.

My disappointment was obvious to Brenda. "Weren't you hoping for something more concrete? I was," she said with a thin smile, "But beyond that there's no news. Probably just her own hair. I think there were just fibers from her own clothes, too. So no help there," she concluded, folding her hands on her desk. "Not," she added, "that I'm going to let myself get drawn into all that again."

"Fair enough," I said. "Thanks anyway. Good luck with your work."

Inordinately relieved to be home, I dumped my books and handbag on the living room floor and collapsed onto the sofa. After sitting there dazed for a few minutes, I reached into my bag and pulled out a stack of paper – drafts for Intro.Comp.Lit. papers, notes from Semiotics, sweepstakes-"winning" announcements. I sorted through my mail while Pepita raced around in circles.

I found a plain white envelope mixed in with the junk. There was no postmark, no address. I tore it open, immediately recognizing Nicholas' jagged handwriting, and read:

My Corpuscle,

These two days without you in my life have been hell. I love you. Won't you take one minute from your life to give a fellow a chance? I've been heartsick, truly.

Huh, I thought. What about me? Betrayed by my best friend. More than that, my ex-lover, for whom, to be frank, I still had some romantic feelings (maybe just because my budding relationship with Tomás had come to naught?). For better or worse, I cared a great deal about Nicholas...

But -- what was love anyway? I was beginning to think of love as potentially something quite dangerous. For instance, who'd loved Christia Thompson? The passage I'd read by chance in *Cremalgo's Companion,* about "invisible air-disturbances," had hinted that she'd been killed by a loved one. Philippe? No – he'd supplied a credible explanation for his whereabouts that night. Motte DuPree Thompson had loved his sister, and as far as I knew he'd been in Louisiana when she died. Brenda, too, had loved Christia, in her way. Had Richard Redmund loved Christia Thompson? Nicholas? Ibo? Abdus? Tomás? The only one of these I knew for a fact to have cared for her was my erstwhile lover, Nicholas. Yet I remained unable to conceive of Nicholas, howsoever imperfect and annoying he might be, in the role of a murderer.

It was entirely possible that each and every one of those men had loved her. Only they knew for sure. Perhaps more importantly: whom did Christia love? I'd never heard anyone say she'd loved anybody, although Philippe had said she and Nicholas (Nicholas again) were "mad about each other." Had Christia loved somebody especially?

362

"I know how you love this time of year," she said right before we hung up, "so try not to let Tomás get to you. After all, he's just a guy." I laughed. "Just focus on your work," she advised, "It's a good distraction – and the rest will come."

I set the telephone in its cradle and went to my closet for my small box of holiday decorations. I unpacked them and hung them along a garland of green tinsel I'd tacked up over my living room windows. I put the Christmas portion of Handel's *Messiah* on my stereo and hummed along. My radiators were going full blast, so I opened the windows a little to get some fresh air. Voices floated up from the Greek restaurant below my apartment. All around me, outside in the great city, Christmas decorations announced the season of joy and greed and generosity, of going into debt and trying to be kind to *all* of your relatives.

For me, though, it was largely about family traditions: twinkling Christmas trees, proudly laden with construction paper angels and play-doh animals, and waiting with my sister Alice on Christmas Eve for the sound of Santa's bells in the clear, starry night sky. There was never a Christmas where we didn't hear those bells some time in the night. I knew I was lucky to have had some measure of joy in my childhood. Christia's childhood, in contrast, struck me as largely tragic: abandoned by her father; her mother a suicide; a surely-depressing sequence of dead Aunts; being left to wander the bayou with her kid brother…Even her beloved Grandmere Luisah had – in her eyes – betrayed her. It was no wonder she had seemed cold.

I gave Pepita the last of my pasta and realized she hadn't gone out yet. I threw a big sweatshirt over my pajamas and slipped sneakers on my bare feet. I called Pepita over to me at the door.

"Good girl," I said as she ducked her head into her harness. "Let's go for a walk."

*

365

Tomás Bautista took his shearling coat off and slipped it over the back of his chair. He rolled up the sleeves of his black cotton shirt and looked over at the counter to see if his water was headed his way. The waitresses were so slow at the Hungarian. His coffee would probably be another twenty minutes, but in the meantime he was hot and thirsty.

Although he had arrived fifteen minutes early, he was not looking forward to talking to Annie Campbell. He had hurt her before and he did not want to do so again. He couldn't help his attraction to her, but he could certainly do something about his behavior. He opened his notebook and wrote, "Lust is a deadly sin." Then he had an internal laugh at his own expense. How very Catholic of you, Tomás, he thought to himself, but your efforts are misguided: doesn't sublimation make one's desires that much more vivid and perverse?

She came in with a burst of fresh, cold air. She was bundled up in a multicolored tapestry coat and a big faux-fur Russian hat. She waved and took off her hat. Her hair fell down in a bouncy, sun-streaked tangle. Tomás watched her as she ordered a hot chocolate and pointed to an almond horn, holding up two fingers to indicate how many she wanted. She was so thoughtful, getting him a cookie – his favorite, as it happened. Actually, she was too thoughtful.

She came toward him, looking shy. He hated when people were unsure of whether to be effusive or happy around him. He'd found that people often acted somber because he acted somber. Smile, he wanted to say to her, I can see that's what you want to do! Instead, he sat silently and watched as the woman he loved approached. He wasn't going to give her anything to smile about.

Annie leaned forward and gave him a peck on his cheek. Her scent, flowery, but not too sweet, made his nostrils flare and his toes curl devilishly. At the same time, he had the sensation of being in the presence of an angel. Pesky Catholicism again, he scolded himself. Remember: she's just a girl.

"What are you reading?" she asked.

"It's a book called *The Sacred Night* by Tahar Ben Jelloun. It's gorgeous. Intense." Tomás couldn't keep a smidgen of enthusiasm out of his voice. "Here, listen: 'Great pain affords me a lucidity that borders on clairvoyance.'"

"Ouch." Annie made a wry face and sat down across from him.

After a few minutes of awkward small talk, Tomás cleared his throat. "I'm going back to Miami with my parents for awhile, so I won't see you until after break."

"What about your work?"

"I can turn in my coursework from there. I only have one exam, take-home, and three papers." He kept his voice flat, low – emotionless. "I have some family business to take care of. Personal matters." Annie tried valiantly to smile. Tomás watched as she, at a loss, cast about for something else to talk about. He registered her pain and shock, and her immediate efforts to hide them.

Her solution was to radically change the subject. "Are you at all involved in the whole Christia scandal?" she asked at length, blowing on her hot cocoa. When he didn't respond, she continued, a little frantic. "It's just – I've never heard you say a word about it. You must have an *opinion*. Mine is that – well, I shouldn't say this, but then who cares what I think?" she laughed nervously, "My latest suspect is Abdus." Her eyes widened at her own audacity. "Only because he has a thing about feet," she explained, backtracking a little, embarrassed. "Today I visited him at his apartment and he was super-sweet to me, which," she concluded, "only made me all the more suspicious!" She picked up her cocoa for something like the tenth time and finished it in one gulp. She was such a nice girl. Tomás could tell she was ashamed to resort to gossip to fill the chasm between them.

He would have to be cold. It was the only way he could handle the situation. With what he hoped was a warning look he said, slightly disdainful, "I don't like gossip."

Annie looked utterly crestfallen. Her mouth hung open in surprise and her cheeks were a deep shade of crimson.

"How's your head?" he asked, to change the subject. All he could think was, I want her to stop talking, stop *thinking*, but I cannot hurt her. No more hurting. He crossed his legs, leaning away from Annie. He could see the disappointment and confusion in her face.

"F-fine," she managed. She was fidgeting with her silver ring. "So, Tomás, I just have to ask you…Why are you acting strange?"

"Everybody's acting strange, no?" Tomás retorted.

"You mean because of the foul doings in our midst?"

"Christia again?" Tomás shook his head. "You certainly are tenacious. Going to people's houses and interrogating them and so on. Could be dangerous. And, if I might ask, just who is it you think is going to benefit from all this, this *investigation* " -- his voice was mocking – "on your part?" He stirred two packets of sugar into his espresso. With pleasure, he took the thin curl of lemon rind from his saucer and chewed it slowly. Bitter.

Annie was not as docile as he'd expected. "I wanted to do something to help –"

His jaw clenched. "She's dead. You can't do anything."

"I can ask questions, can't I? For example, why did you go see her that afternoon? The afternoon of her death?" Annie's face was triumphant. She had succeeded in placing him at the scene of the crime.

Of all the imbecilic amateur-detective moves, thought Tomás. "I went to see her for a paper I'm working on. I play piano and I'm interested in different tonal philosophies. I am writing about polyphony just now, and she was an expert on Hildegard Von Bingen. Will that suffice?"

"Yes. And you can stop being so condescending."

"I'm sorry if that's how I seem to you." Tomás saw that her hands were curled into fists on the table between them. Of their own volition, his own hands reached out to unfurl her tight little fingers. Now he *knew* he had to leave soon. His strong inner resolve to put major distance between himself and Annie, for both of their sakes, was wearing thin. Her sincerity and her goodness of heart, in the face of his rejection and contempt, touched him in the deepest part of his soul.

"What's bothering me," she murmured, "is how much I like you despite all of this." She stood up, pulled her coat on and quickly twisted her hair to the top of her head, placing her hat over it. "But I'm gonna go anyway." Just as abruptly, she left.

Tomás ordered another espresso, this time with extra lemon. He ate one almond horn and carefully wrapped up the other to take home. The caffeine had made him jittery and he needed to blow off some steam. He resolved to go change into his workout clothes and go to the university gym for a good cleansing sweat. God knew he needed it.

*

"I can't get along with anybody," I whined to Lark. "And my head still hurts from Tuesday night. Do you think I might be damaged, you know, from the injury? Or mentally disturbed?"

"No! This guy is just a garden-variety jerk," said Lark, who was always very sensible. "Miami – hmph. And if there was something serious wrong with your head you'd know by now. What you need is something else to focus on, like, hey, here's an idea: your Ph.D.?"

"That's what my Moms said."

"So be it."

"Ciao. Love you."

Outside my windows, soft snow had begun to fall. Snowfall in New York transforms the city into a pristine, quiet place – if only for a short while. While many people hole up in their apartments, there are always a few who seek out the hushed atmosphere of near-empty urban streets covered with a fine white blanket. I went out into the enfolding storm.

There were Christmas tree sellers every few blocks, huddled under their tarps and blaring carols from the trucks they'd parked next to the curb. People walked with their faces down, some with umbrellas. It was getting late and stores were beginning to close. Although I knew it was reckless, I felt drawn to Riverside Park. I reasoned that I would be able to tell if there was anyone nearby by tracks in the new fallen snow. When I got to the edge of the park, I smiled to see my footprints were the first since the snowstorm had begun. How lovely – wholesome, even, like an idyllic country lane -- the sidewalks appeared, untouched like that.

Feeling safe and nourished by the beauty around me, I was able to more calmly review what had happened between Tomás and me. His cold behavior notwithstanding, I was powerfully drawn to him. I adored his broad shoulders, his green eyes, his slightly crooked nose. I loved the way the subtle motions of his nearly-black eyebrows revealed the movement of his thoughts inside. His mercurial personality, I reflected, was an integral aspect of his brilliance and inner strength. Then again, there was something wounded about him, and I wanted to throw my arms around him, nurture him, heal him. I craved his embrace, to hold and be held by him. I felt like I could help him through his all-too evident pain – if only he would let me in.

Isn't that what all co-dependent women say?

His leaving New York City made me sad, but, I reasoned, probably proved he wasn't Christia's killer. After all, the police wouldn't let him leave if he were a suspect. I'd heard they'd told even the remotest suspects (Brenda, Redmund) on no uncertain terms that they were not to leave the area. At least my crush wasn't a murderer, in addition to being erratic and mildly contemptuous. Small comfort, I sighed.

Dropping that thought-trajectory, I took some time for my monthly graduate-student-identity-crisis. I had my first comprehensive exams coming up next semester, and I had also decided to enroll in the year-long teacher training program at Ishwara Yoga. I had final papers due this semester in all of my classes, and would have over 50 papers and exams to grade for the class I was assistant teaching. My pulse began to race just thinking about the tasks I had ahead. With all my stress, I reasoned that thinking about Christia's murder was probably a relief for me.

I had come to the water fountain at the end of the path, and had no desire to revisit the stone gazebo in which I'd been clobbered. I turned around to head south, pulling my coat closer around me. The wind was whirling toward me now, distracting me from my racing thoughts. Flakes of snow swirled into my face, resting on my cheeks and eyelashes before melting into tiny water-dots. I had almost come to my block when I noticed that another set of footprints, large, probably male, snaked alongside my north-bound prints. The interesting thing was, they followed my peregrinations: where I'd veered off to examine a snow-covered stump or to the stone wall to look out over the Hudson, the other footprints mirrored mine.

Perhaps foolishly, I turned uptown again to discern whether I'd had company nearby on the way back down as well. I'd walked only about a block before I came upon the second set of footprints, headed downtown and similarly intermingled with mine. The person who was, possibly, following me had taken a sudden turn to their left – when I'd hesitated because I'd noticed the other set of footprints? – and from the skid marks in the snow it looked as if they'd been running. Presumably, they were gone now. There was nothing I could do but go home.

I stopped at the Korean market for a single red rose. When I got home I let Pepita out. She hates anything wet falling out of the sky, so that didn't take more than a minute. I drew myself a hot bath and sprinkled the petals of the rose into the bathwater. I also poured in a few drops of lavender oil for relaxation and some lemon verbena oil, for self-love. With my luck with men of late, I'd be needing it.

I drifted off to sleep an hour or so later, drowsy from my bath and an expired codeine I'd taken to stop my still-lumpy head from pounding. My last thought was of Christia: I had neither dreamt of her nor sensed her "presence" since North Carolina. I hadn't made the slightest pretext of following her instructions to stop my nosing around, and I was glad she hadn't concocted some horrible haunting as a punishment. Yet.

*

Friday night, Ibo was walking home from his job moving furniture. Before he'd taken on Christia's classes, his pay in the Department of Religion had barely covered rent. He'd gotten off the C train on 103rd street to leave himself a mile or so of walking on his way home. He walked briskly west, crossing the street to skirt the edge of Central Park, and then turned uptown. He so enjoyed the snow. As he passed the enchanting, crumbling old Towers nursing home on 105th street he fondly remembered his talks with Annie and Nicholas about turning the veritable castle on Central Park West into an artists' colony. Although they'd heard rumors that Columbia was buying it up and turning it into luxury condos, they'd fantasized about each taking a turret for their work space and all living communally below, in the giant, cavernous spaces that for now remained burnt out and abandoned. Gretel and Brandi and Kirpal had joined in the fantasy one night in Abdus' den; while Abdus and Kalinka had opted out, saying they'd prefer to stay right where they were. "Nothing would beat the views we get from up here," Abdus had explained, gesturing toward the rest of his apartment. How secure he'd been in his wealth and privilege.

Ibo felt a wave of resentment well up inside. To suppress it, he began walking even faster, deciding to make a loop through Riverside Park on his way home. In Ibo, anger and peace were at war. His heart yearned for the latter, but most everything in his circumstances steered him relentlessly toward the former. He attributed this interior split to his heritage. Is it, Ibo asked himself rhetorically, any coincidence that Istanbul's most deluxe hotel — the Four Seasons Istanbul — was formerly the site of the Sultanahmet prison? And the lemon trees that one finds anywhere there's the slightest chance a tree will grow in his hometown – is it any wonder the fruit is so sour? Liberation and imprisonment, the pretty and the painful, war and peace; never one without the other – and never, ever, just being somewhere neutral, balanced, for anywhere near long enough. Struggle was an intrinsic part of Turkish history, and as natural to Ibo as the air he breathed. What could change the country -- or its citizen?

He thought he knew. In his mind's eye, he envisioned the clay tablet he'd attributed to Puduhepa's handmaiden. Over three-thousand years ago, yet the main gist of her fragmented legacy was the statement that only a woman's continuing rule down through the years to come would save the world. How right she had been, he mused – and, with her comfy status under the protection of the powerful feminist queen, how far from even imagining what was to come.

If only, Ibo wished, I could wave a magic wand and change the course of history. The thought made him chuckle a little to himself. With his imagined omnipotence, Ibo declared his solution to the problems he was wrestling with. For all nations, Ibo prescribed the wise, gentle rule of womankind; for himself, the steady love of a good woman was all he needed to get through his ongoing crises.

Unbidden, the image of Christia Thompson popped into his brain, and he was thrown into a new reverie: imagining her as the woman in his latest fantasy. Christia had been a woman unlike any other he'd known. She'd certainly been capable of ruling nations; though he wondered whether she'd've been any less macho than a man. As a lover, she'd been fiercely passionate, and anything but steady. As far as he knew, no one had ever accused Christia Thompson of being good. He thought of her sharp, bright glance, the way she'd appeared so haughty, so rigid...until she melted in his arms. After a short while, though, she'd rejected him so cruelly that her death – murder -- was not as upsetting to him as it might otherwise have been. He imagined there were certain individuals who might have taken no little satisfaction from Christia's untimely death.

With this, his thoughts took another turn: What if you found out that you liked killing? It is not something we *try* as a matter of course. A killer might kill first by accident – and find to his surprise that he enjoyed the act immensely. What then? And if you found you could get away with it, like some human snowflake, just one among so very many, swirling gleefully away from a cloud of guilt, suspicion, and darkness, what then?

Unlike a large, dark man, society's fear-scapegoat, Ibo found that a small, dark-*ish* man could move through the city virtually unnoticed. He relished his anonymity, and sometimes took advantage of it. For example, his work. He'd been forced to find a job in order to have some money to send back to Turkey. It was not just any furniture that Ibo had been hired to move, but Ottoman antiques taken illegally out of Turkey. He prayed that his employer would agree to supply his alibi for the night Christia died. Metin Limonlu was understandably concerned with exposing his operations in the United States. But the police were pressing down on Ibo, harder and harder — and if Limonlu did not back his story up, Ibo would be screwed. He might be screwed even with his boss's support: how trustworthy, after all, was the word of a smuggler?

As he walked and walked through the snowy night, Ibo's mind was cluttered with these thoughts. A part of him, however, was soaring in the wind with the snowflakes, and in this way he found some peace.

*

I had been walking aimlessly when I saw Annie headed toward the park alone. I'd followed her without giving it a second thought. After a happy half-hour of snowy sightseeing, she'd noticed. I hoped I hadn't scared her too much, but I hadn't wanted to reveal myself. I didn't regret following her though, of that I was sure. One couldn't be too careful in New York City. I couldn't stop myself from caring about her and wanting to protect her.

Why hadn't she learned to be careful, after everything that had happened recently? A woman walking alone in dark, empty Riverside Park during a storm was just the sort of thing that criminal-types honed in on. Obviously, that overweight, donut-eating Tomasino character, with his thinning hair and bumbling-cop demeanor, could be doing a lot more to protect the women in the neighborhood instead of questioning a classroom's worth of innocent men and women.

Not that I cared particularly about what happened to anyone else. Not anymore. I knew that soon enough I wouldn't be around any longer; and Annie Campbell, with all her dangerous curiosity and zest for life, would no longer be an issue.

*

"Won't you stop your incessant *munching*?" The cat, Descartes, looked up at him with narrowed yellow eyes. He was probably starving. He'd been hiding for weeks – from the endless parade of visitors, from the change in his environment, the lack of his mistress Christia, the acrid odor of his master's grief.

375

Descartes had been Christia's cat. Philippe didn't care for the wily beasts. His mother, Philippa Perez-Throgmorton, had ended up one of those cat ladies after her landed-gentry façade had been exposed as a sham. Her siblings had voted as a majority against her, and sold the decrepit ancestral manor. It had then been converted into a mental hospital. Philippa's snobbery had been endured by English high society only as a courtesy to a fellow aristocrat. Once the country house was gone, so, too, were her "friends." Her only remaining companions were her coterie of inbred "Pusskins" and "Tommy-Kittens." He shuddered at the memory of his last visit. It might've *all* been better, he thought, if Mumsy had liked people half as much as cats.

Philippe returned his attention to the Saturday paper. He affixed his always-slipping spectacles to the highest point of the bridge of his nose and read, casually at first and then with growing urgency:

International Fugitive Found Dead

The body found in a midtown hotel room last Wednesday has just been identified as that of Paul Terwilliger, a.k.a. Rose. Mr. Terwilliger has long been sought for questioning in the death of Raphael Kavitaris, a Professor at Oxford University who died over a decade ago of acute acidosis brought on by an overdose of an antifreeze-like compound. Mr. Terwilliger's cause of death – an apparent suicide – has been determined to have resulted from the consumption of a similar, if not identical, chemical poison.

It remains unclear whether Mr. Terwilliger's suicide was intended as a confession of guilt or a final cry of innocent anguish.

Philippe let the newspaper slide from his grasp onto the spotless floor of his impeccable apartment. Descartes, startled, scurried back to his secret place.

376

*

Saturday morning dawned dark and gloomy. Accordingly, I lay in my bed and indulged in a little morose self-pity. The fellow I had a crush on was leaving town. My best friend was in love with me -- and making love with others to prove it. I'd written an incriminating note to a murder victim. And, incidentally, I was seriously behind on my studies...

The uneven yellow floors of my apartment creaked as Merlin and Pepita began to pad about, sniffing delicately to discern if any new and marvelous tidbit had materialized overnight. Unable to wallow any longer, I opened the book I'd left on the floor next to my bed – I was reading Christia's biography of Jeanne Marie Bouvier de la Motte Guyon – and began to read. Overnight, the snow had turned to rain, and big, fat drops splashed against the old and slightly warped glass panes above my head. The wind rattled my windowpanes, and the draft battled with warmth from the radiators

After just a few pages, I felt positively ashamed. Before the age of thirty, this woman had been through hell. Like so many of the other historical female prodigies – von Bingen, the Brontës, Plath -- she'd been a sickly child. Perhaps that protected her from her culture's hegemonic sexism, I mused. She'd endured the difficult: the death of her husband; and the unthinkable: the deaths of two of her children. Left a widow with three remaining children, she was at twenty-eight a woman whose life was, in effect, over. It was no wonder she'd sought something bigger than herself in which to entrust her faith. It was her tragedy that the proselytizing demanded of her by her "apostolic state" inflamed the wrath of certain important religious personages of the male persuasion. In her analysis of de la Motte Guyon's life, Christia intimated none too subtly that the popularity of this charismatic woman had been highly threatening to the patriarchal religious establishment.

At least she'd had financial freedom. And she'd had influential male advisors, like Père François Lacombe. She had male political allies as well. Ultimately, she had nonetheless been forced to refute her work, thereby perhaps compromising her integrity. Admittedly, her spirit had already been partially broken from having been imprisoned in the Bastille for seven years, a period described by Christia in harrowing, meticulously researched detail. Christia's narration and evaluation of these two seminal aspects of de la Motte Guyon's life – her self-betrayal and her imprisonment – had an astonishing degree of verisimilitude to them. As I read, I found myself wondering whether there was something analogous to these events in Christia's life.

I was also amazed by Christia's sensitivity in describing de la Motte Guyon's spiritual-mystical travails. I'd never sensed that side of her - it had only become a possibility with the discovery of her membership in Puduhepa's sisters — and so I was intrigued by the book's conclusion:

> In her model, spiritual practice culminates in the third and final stage of meditation, one that is only possible after the "mystical death" of the spiritual seeker. In this blessed state, the seeker becomes quiet, humble, attentive, and empty.

> In essence, these are Jeanne Marie Bouvier de la Motte Guyon's instructions to us: die as your "self," – and be reborn, devoid of will and ego, to serve as a receptacle for the divine. This credo apparently flies in the face of Feminist Theory; it threatens all of the inroads underprivileged, undervalued women have made into the established patriarchy; in short, it seems to tell women to submit – to whatever "higher" (probably male) power avails itself of their meek and willing subservience.

After long reflection, I have come to believe such an interpretation is far too simple. A woman of considerable personal power, Madame Guyon nevertheless knew what it was to endure adversity. After years of persecution, and only under the most wretched of circumstances, she buckled — and apparently forsook her better self. Yet her writings show this was only an exterior surrender. Further, most of us – male or female -- would have given in far sooner.

Scholars of history seek to expose and analyze the mental processes of their subjects; what I found was far more significant: an indomitable soul.

De la Motte Guyon's definition of the third stage of meditation seemed much like what I'd been instructed to aim for in yoga classes; that is, to strive to allow myself to be empty, in order to then be filled with the divine, which Guyon called God. I wondered if Christia had been convinced by her subject's arguments. Despite all I'd been discovering about her complex personality, including her intermittent kindness, I had a hard time picturing Christia as a humble vessel of God.

Chapter Twelve – Some Things Come Together, Some Come Apart

> "Forgive me, friends! I didn't reckernize you!"
> the Park Keeper called to the nothingness. "And I didn't
> reckernize meself, neither…But I know who you are
> now, all of you. And I know who I am…"
>
> P.L. Travers, *Mary Poppins in Cherry Tree Lane*

"Do you know who I am?"

"Yes."

"Why?" He was crying now, bitter, bitter tears. "Why…How could you?"

"What do you mean?"

"The…affection…" The yearning glances, he meant, then – and the clandestine touching: a brush of the arm, a meeting of fingertips…

"I love you so much, I didn't know how else to show you."

Silence. Two hearts beating hard and fast

"Besides, you're such a beautiful boy." Wait, she thought, bringing her hand to her mouth. It was too much. He seemed to think she was pulling her jokey-kinky thing with *him*.

*

I never meant to hurt her. I only needed something from her. I wanted her to love me.

But not like that.

*

He found his wife.

He went looking for her after she didn't come home for tea. They always had tea together, even after the nights she spent in other arms than his. *Always*.

At first he thought she'd fallen asleep at her desk, or that was what he told everyone. Bloody hell. He knew. The moment he saw her staring, plastic eyes. If eyes are diamonds, dead eyes are less-than glass. Plexiglass? Ah, don't think, he implored his own mind. Do not think: her bruised neck, stiff limbs, dull skin. Why was he not surprised?

Her cold, cold feet.

It was afternoon still, and plenty of people were about. They already found him foppish, so he knew he oughtn't scream and faint. How to bear this in a manly way…yet not seem – callous? He counted to seven, seven times. A course of action came to him. He had to compose his face. Shock, with grief the undercurrent. He would handle his wife's death with his usual meticulousness. Tell the right people, in the right order.

Wilson. Cyrus Wilson would know how to proceed.

And so it went.

Then, not two weeks later, Paul: dead. Beautiful, louche Paul Terwilliger, Philippe's school chum and his erstwhile refugee project – dead of the extreme acidosis that accompanies consumption of antifreeze. Suicide, apparently. Quite similar to the way Raphael

381

Kavitaris had died, to be frank; and this was certainly not lost on Interpol. The note read, "I'm tired of running." The next day, in the mail: "You were my angel." What the devil did that mean, Paul?

All the loose ends of his life tied up. One way of looking at it. Chin up.

*

Brandi put down her much-thumbed copy of Judith Butler's *Gender Trouble* and unscrewed the cap of her orange glitter nail polish. She swiped a second coat on her toenails and, after a moment of internal debate, dabbed the nail polish on her fingernails, which were bitten to the quick. She blew on her fingernails to dry the polish and then - carefully - returned to her book. She was feeling a little nauseous and wanted to give herself some time before beginning preparations for her party. She'd promised her guests food, but she didn't cook; she would have to buy some take-out. Oh, and she could make some fruit salad – she had a big can of fruit cocktail and some raisins somewhere. Her music mix was impeccable - heavy on the Bowie and Prince, for dancing, with plenty of slower and/or angrier stuff peppered in: Leonard Cohen, Patti Smith, PJ Harvey, the Bad Brains.

Tommy wasn't coming to her party, which was probably for the best. She'd run into him at the Abbey bar in Williamsburg last night and he'd been really drunk. In the end, so had she; and unfortunately she'd admitted to him that she had a crush on him "just like Annie does," and then accidentally they'd ended up making out a little, which she'd felt really bad about. She'd even asked him who was prettier, she or Annie, which showed she had been really lit. If she had been just a little drunker, she could've forgotten the whole thing: Tomás' crying over his family mess, her embarrassing admissions to him, their kiss, the ashamed parting that followed…the whole thing. Yuck. She would have to tell Annie - her friend was paramount, and honesty was the rule for real friendship. Double yuck.

She felt dizzy. Some of it was because she actually liked the guy. Brandi's thing for Tomás went back to the first time she'd seen him. She'd never told Annie because Annie had told her about *her* thing for him first. She never would have done anything about it either, if not for the coincidence of both of them alone and drowning their sorrows in the same spot. Anyway, there was no way he'd come tonight – apparently he was packing up his stuff and leaving New York City for Miami.

Between flashbacks to the night before and nerves about throwing a party, it was hard to concentrate on her reading. Brandi folded the corner of the page to save her place and placed the book in her giant, decorated armoire. After a moment's thought, she took out a stack of recent papers from a cubbyhole and placed them on a side table. She'd gotten A's or A+'s on every paper she'd ever written in graduate school and she figured it wouldn't hurt to have anyone who was prone to snooping through people's work during a party know she wasn't just some bubblehead.

Now, what to wear tonight? Brandi thought her gold glitter pants would look great with her clear Lucite spike-heeled sandals and her sparkly orange toenails.

On second thought, Brandi slid her papers back into the armoire: people could think what they wanted. It was their loss if they thought fabulousness and intelligence couldn't coexist.

*

"So what if I'm rather old-school," shrugged Abdus.

"Old school? Dude, that's old *testament*," Kirpal retorted.

From Gretel, who was standing quietly by Kirpal's side, I gathered Abdus had just told Kirpal about his intention to "make an honest woman of Kalinka." Before Abdus could get to feeling defensive, I jumped in with, "Hey fellas, how's about another round of drinks?"

Kirpal shook his head. "I'm just drinking orange juice."

"Champers?" asked Abdus, holding out his plastic flute. "Freixenet?"

"Fine." He handed me the glass, and then said, "On second thought, I'll come with you." He rushed after me, nearly tripping over one of Brandi's large white Persian cats.

During the short walk from Brandi's pink living room to her purple kitchen, he managed to apologize approximately forty times for his behavior since he'd met me. "I can't believe what a boor I've been. So jealous, so suspicious. Will you ever forgive me?" he concluded, a boyish smile on his handsome face.

I took a long drag from the Nat Sherman cigarette I'd bummed from him and composed my features for a brief diatribe. "In my experience you are sexist and overbearing, and possibly worse," like, a murderer, "but I believe you got caught up in the throes of passion in your own head for awhile there and feel bad about the way you treated me. I accept your apology, O.K.? Now let's just let it go." I passed him his filled glass and raised mine. "Cheers." Brandi collected vintage candelabras, which she'd filled with lit candles and placed all over the apartment. Our champagne glittered in the flickering candlelight.

We rejoined our friends who'd meandered over to stand next to a white fake Christmas tree decorated with blue glass balls. At the tree's base, grumpy and superior with their smushed-in faces, Brandi's two other cats lounged on leopard-print cushions. As cats and friends basked in the glow from the sparkling tree, I admired its unique decorating scheme. Brandi and I had painted stars of David on each ornament a few weeks earlier in anticipation of this very night. The tree was also festooned with several strings of red lights, adding a rosy blush to guest's complexions.

Gretel was telling Brandi how her Williamsburg neighborhood was "the real New York City, because it's really un-gentrified," and, "I

384

feel so *authentic* here with all your neat friends!" while Brandi looked politely horrified - especially since Williamsburg was getting more and more gentrified - and Kirpal, who was a little more with-it than his love interest, smiled indulgently.

Gretel pulled me aside to tell me that she and Kirpal had had their first official date the night before. They'd gone to MoMA, "and even though it was pay-what-you-want Friday night, he paid the full price! I mean, gosh, that's conscientious."

That's being supported by your parents, I thought, then I said, "That's great." I wanted to get her opinion about Abdus. "About what we were talking about the other day?" I saw she instantly knew what I was referring to. "Are you still feeling scared?"

"Yes."

"O.K. Not to make you feel more scared, but I'm thinking maybe it was Abdus." She raised her eyebrows, startled. "See," I explained, "he has a thing about feet, Christia's killer took off her stockings: voila!" I'd almost added that my attacker had taken my shoes and socks off, but caught myself just in time. No need to unduly frighten her.

Brow furrowed, she thought about what I'd said and then replied, "I don't believe it. That's a very precarious argument. I mean, it hinges entirely on the foot issue and any number of men like feet. Kirpal stares at my feet sometimes. That's why I've started wearing these a lot." She pointed a stiletto-clad foot in the air. "And, gee, Abdus is the most courtly man I've ever met. Sure he was jealous of you, but he's been super-duper nice to me. I'm sure he's totally innocent." She smiled apologetically and helped herself to a second plate of food and another glass of white wine. After a few sips, she asked, slightly reluctantly, "Is there anything more – concrete?" She was trying to be understanding, but her lifelong sensible nature was definitely prevailing over her newfound psychic openness.

I didn't mention the vague, speculative aspect of the fear she'd confessed to me mere days before. "Well, did I tell you about this tarot reading I got the other day?" She rolled her eyes. It was a very discrete, private eye-rolling, and I'm sure she didn't mean me to see it, but I did. I continued anyway. "This woman drew me the Queen and Prince of Swords, which represent people with negative energy, but the negative energy comes from what's around them." I tried to come up with a better way to explain what I was trying to convey. "Like, if you see injustice in the world, it makes you angry, right? But sometimes the solution is unclear. Like you were saying? About justice versus pacifism?" She nodded. "That's what these cards are about: decent people who are caught in painful situations. Oh," I added, my neck starting to get that ache that tells me I need to "relax," "and in tarot the suit of swords is associated with truth, which can be painful too."

"Um, what does this have to do with Abdus?"

"Maybe he's the Prince of Swords. I've seen him as an angry person the whole time I've known him. Until now," I admitted, "when he's starting to seem like a real pussycat. But I did just find out that his life is in turmoil over family stuff and money stuff, so there's a lot of outside factors that may be impinging on him. And Christia was the Queen of Swords. Obviously that's not too hard to imagine. And, bear with me here" — this was a stretch and I knew it since there was simply no evidence whatsoever for my theory – "somehow some kind of truth came out between them, I don't know what, and he killed her."

Gretel was looking at me like I was crazy, which was not entirely out of the question, and it was clear she had no idea how to respond to her raving friend. Lucky for her, Kirpal appeared by her side with a bowl of stuffed grape leaves. He offered us some with a bounteous smile. I took a grape leaf and excused myself. Nicholas had just walked in Brandi's front door. He was wearing a faux beaver coat over a three-piece tweed suit. He'd slicked his straw-colored hair back

386

away from his face and I could see his big blue eyes scanning the apartment. Looking for me, I imagined. Down, girl, I warned my leaping pulse. Enough with the roller coaster!

He hadn't seen me yet by the time I'd made my way back to Abdus and Brandi, who were still chatting by the tree. I intended to make it clear to Nicholas, once he found me, that I was going to be big about our falling-out, as well as about his affair with Abdus and Kalinka.

Brandi put an arm around me. "Happy 'Dirty Christmas,'" she giggled – her parties always had kinky themes -- and then resumed her chat with Abdus. The topic of conversation was Abdus' impending marriage. Kalinka had been unable to come to the party because she was out with her best friend, who was in for the weekend from Germany. Abdus was asking Brandi for her input on the notion of marriage, monogamy, "and all that." Since I'd never known Brandi to stay with one guy for more than a few weeks, I couldn't wait to hear what she would say.

"Hmm," she began, perching on a dresser and crossing her glitter-spangled legs, "I guess it could be really hot, if you did, like, a lot of role play and bondage and stuff."

Abdus looked uncomfortable. "Sorry – not, is it *hot*…" he corrected, "I guess I already know the answer to that. What I meant to get at was, rather: do you believe monogamy to be *right*? In the sense of being morally proper."

"Hell, yeah," she exclaimed. She lit a Kool and swigged from her wine cooler. Her eyes twinkled and she flashed him a dazzling smile. "Just not right now!" She turned to me. "Annie, hon, get me another drink? This guy's wearing me out!"

Ibo and Nicholas came over together. Nicholas looked ever so slightly contrite, and I gave him a peck on the cheek.

387

Ibo was as relaxed as I'd ever seen him. He flung a casual arm around Abdus' shoulder, saying, "We were just remembering our old idea about all living together in that magical castle on Central Park West. You, old boy, declined to join us as I recall. Perhaps now you'd be more willing?"

Abdus was taken aback. He shrugged Ibo's arm off his back and turned to confront him. "Whatever do you mean?" he asked.

"I've come out! You see, as I was just telling Nicholas, my family lost all their money. He explained to me I was not the only one and I guessed you." He pointed at Abdus. "Naturally. Who else has that much money to lose? So, now that you, like me, are broke," he began jokingly. At that point, he belatedly noticed the expressions of panic on all three of our faces. "Wait – isn't this common knowledge? Among friends? I was just," he looked around, saw that his words were not having their intended mollifying affect, but continued, more desperate now: "trying to make light of our mutual difficult circumstances."

This would be a moment of reckoning, I realized: I would see if Abdus really was as gracious as he'd been purporting to be. I looked around the room, avoiding meeting the eyes of my friends. This was something Abdus and Ibo – and Nicholas, the blabbermouth -- would have to work out on their own. The party had grown to almost fill Brandi's place, and was definitely in full swing. Someone had already knocked over one of the candelabras, and the air was full of all sorts of smoke. I saw, from a distance, Gretel taking a hit off what looked like a joint. Kirpal, standing behind her with his arm around her waist, was laughing and laughing. Definitely pot, I concluded.

"Yes, well," Abdus said. I held my breath. "Among friends," he continued, most tactfully, "I suppose it is not terribly shameful to admit that one is, relatively speaking of course, destitute!" As if with relief at his confession, the tension left his eyes and his mouth curled into a smile. Everyone was smiling now. "As a matter of fact, I've gone and taken a job!"

"So've I!" Ibo practically crowed. "Hey – I feel great! No more secrets."

"No more secrets," Abdus echoed. He caught my eye and his gaze was penetrating and clear. I could tell he, like Ibo, felt liberated to have admitted to no longer being a man of leisure.

Ibo inclined his head toward Nicholas. "That time, Nicholas, when you came to my office and I was rushing about?"

"Oh, yeah, I remember that," I said, "I was there too."

"Yes, well, I was late for work and had no idea what to tell you and I was so *angry* to be in that position." He looked remorseful. "I wish I'd just been honest in the first place."

"I'm sorry you even thought we'd care," I told him.

"It was more that *I* cared," Ibo explained. "Some people even gave me opportunities to 'fess up and I avoided them like the plague. I maxed out my credit card in Paris rather than tell Tomás and his cousins I didn't have a *sou*."

"That's too bad, old chap," Abdus said soothingly. His expression became more discerning. "But I have heard rumors that there's more in the works for you, no?"

Ibo's face brightened. "Right." There was an almost imperceptible hesitation. "I don't mind telling you all that I've got a major publication in the works. Several, actually!" Nicholas had inched closer to me and had taken my hand. I squeezed his hand to let him know everything was O.K. between us. We all turned to Ibo to listen.

"I've written a book about something I found when we were moving from our house in Istanbul. It's a three-thousand year old Hittite codex, an original, ancient text. I've written a book about it, as well as an article. It's going to make my name. You may all call me the Distinguished Doctor Heyreddin," he said, mock-pompously.

"You must be so happy, Ibo," I congratulated him. "I should say, Herr-Doctor-Majesty-Professor Ibo." We smiled at each other.

"Truly. It has been an amazing confluence of events – my being here at the university and beginning to study that time period and area; then returning home and finding it just in time…" Ibo explained that during his family's move he had discovered a clay tablet with cuneiform markings in a trunk that had belonged to his grandmother. He'd painstakingly translated the fragment as coming from a handmaiden to the Hittite queen Puduhepa. The artifact had been authenticated by no less than members of the staff of the Smithsonian; and its provenance was undisputed. It belonged rightfully to his family, there being no other claims to it, or reports of its theft. "The most wonderful thing of all, though, is the codex itself. It's from a time when there were so many new things yet to discover," Ibo said, rapturously. "By the same token, it was also a time when it was possible to know virtually everything there was to know in the human repertoire of knowledge, if one worked reasonably hard. Can you imagine?"

He told us he was considering selling the fragment to a museum, adding that such a sale would support his family in perpetuity, so valuable was the clay tablet. "That," he concluded, "might solve everything. The book will secure my academic future -- and the tablet, my and my family's financial future."

"I'm so glad for you, Ibo," I said. "I'm going to go get us another round to celebrate."

"Has Christia's death been at all helpful to you in this matter?" Nicholas' question – and icy tone -- stopped me in my tracks. "I went to see her on your behalf, as everyone here knows, but she seemed to think you were making the whole fracas up." His face was blank, but his voice had sounded slightly quavery, as if he were nervous or angry, or both.

Ibo had gone white. "Of course not! For God's sake, Nicholas, you know the whole story."

"I think I do," agreed Nicholas. "I simply asked whether you'd benefited from her death in the matter of publishing all of your forthcoming work as wholly your own."

"But –" Ibo sputtered, "It *is* my own work. Wholly my own! She was only helping me here and there! An adviser. A consultant…" he trailed off.

Abdus had been uncharacteristically quiet during this whole exchange. I was impressed once again with his diplomatic finesse when he said, mildly, "I think we're all a bit envious of Ibo's good fortune, but there's no need to be vituperative, eh, Nicho?"

Would Nicholas yield? To my surprise, he did, nodding sheepishly and muttering a quick "Sorry." I guessed I knew who'd been on top in *that* relationship.

I grabbed Nicholas' arm and dragged him over to the purple-painted kitchen, where most of the candles had burned down and the only remaining light came from a purple and orange lava lamp. I opened the refrigerator, hoping fruitlessly for more light, and groped around for more beer.

"This O.K.?" I held out a bottle of boutique lager.

He groaned. "That's what my parents drink." He took a step back, shaking his head. "It would make me feel immeasurably banal to even taste it."

I was exasperated. "Then get your own beer, Mr. Tantrum."

"Sam is here in the city. Did you know that? He's acting as my legal counsel in case the Christia situation deteriorates." He rolled his eyes.

"You're really lucky, you know."

"What – because I get to go to T.G.I. Fridays near his hotel with him for free?"

"You are incredibly ungrateful, Nicholas. It's really depressing." It was so kind of Sam to try to help his renegade stepson. "You're a grown-up now. Why do you have to be so critical of your parents?"

"Oh, I don't know, maybe because they raised me in a cultural vacuum, in one of the most vapid places on earth?"

"But they were always decent to you. You can't deny that."

"Isn't living in Palm Springs alone enough to indict them?" Nicholas pouted.

"I have news for you, my friend. Your mother, Janene, is a really, really good, sweet person. She wouldn't harm a fly. And have you ever actually talked to Sam? Did you know he was a civil rights activist and that he marched with Martin Luther King?"

"Darling, you're very kind, and you're right, as usual. I'll try to be nicer, I promise. But do let's change the subject," Nicholas pleaded. I started to protest, then decided Nicholas would have to work through his family issues on his own. I'd said my piece.

"How's this for news?" he asked with a glint in his eye, "Philippe's poetry book is being published. Some editor he met at the party for Theadora Harmon at Caffe Taci accepted his manuscript just the other day. In light of Christia's death, it seems a bit tacky, don't you think?"

I nodded in amazement. "Or sensationalistic," I suggested.

"According to Christia, his poetry was absolutely, mortifyingly bad. Of course, that can't be tested empirically but I've a mind to get my hands on it and see for myself!"

"I'm sure he'd share it with you if you asked."

"I don't know about that. He's been evasive lately. Again."

"Oh Nicholas, you're so solipsistic."

He grinned, and I couldn't help but smile back. "My little Betelgeuse," he said; and he grabbed me by the shoulders and kissed me hard on the lips. Then he leaned out the door and yelled to Brandi, "Have you got any absinthe in here?"

"Look in the cabinet to your left," she yelled back, "I forgot to take it out."

He took a big swig straight from the bottle, then offered it to me. I declined, citing fear of losing my mind. There were still masses of twigs and herbs steeping in the bottom of the bottle. "Wormwood," he confided, "so good for the spirit."

"You are so punny," I muttered as we went back into the living room. Someone had switched on the flashing function on the strings of red Christmas lights and the light in the smoky room was wavering in a slightly unsettling manner. At least I hadn't drunk any absinthe.

Kirpal, Gretel, Abdus, and Ibo were standing in a loose circle, talking about their shared favorite subject: religion. Don't these guys ever take a break? I wondered. A little too tired for intellectual sparring, I longed to find Brandi and engage her in some lighter talk. Nonetheless, I joined the gang.

"Considering that some of your cronies," Gretel jutted her chin at Ibo, "are working on women mystics, you'd think it would have come up – but I don't hear a whole lot about female religious leaders in Sikhism."

"Actually, you're wrong. It's no more sexist than any other religion, and in some ways it's remarkably less-so," Kirpal responded, his eyes dancing. These two loved to argue about religion – it was their first means of communication. "Yes, Sikhism is full of traditions – specific things to wear and do – but the religion itself is very inclusive. Guru Nanak, the founder, said – a half-millennium ago -- that God transcends religious distinctions; and most of us have taken that to mean that material distinctions – like gender or skin color -- also are irrelevant."

"I have to say, Kirpal," I told him, "that I've always seen you as someone who really does respect all people in a very loving way."

"I try," he replied, a little embarrassed. "That's just how I was raised. Sikhism actually springs from a combination of devotional love and mysticism; from *Bhakti* Hinduism and Islamic Sufism, respectively."

"And what does that have to do with women?" Gretel was not convinced.

"Uh, for one thing, Guru Nanak himself was married, with children. He went against a lot of the major religious trends in India to counsel his followers to ground their religious practice in the everyday, not in asceticism. Not *avoiding* women, as many *sadhakas*, religious seekers, were required to do. So," he concluded, "I think that's pretty revolutionary, and pretty tolerant and open and, yes, dear," he winked at Gretel, "loving."

"On the other hand, there's something to be said for more restrictive religions," Nicholas broke in. "They give people something to wrestle with." He certainly was in an argumentative mood, I noted. "Kierkegaard, for example: his father's overzealous, pious Lutheranism provided him with something to rail against for the rest of his life!"

"But was he happy? Did he lead a fulfilling life?" Kirpal asked, completely in earnest.

"No-o, but he did give the world something – quite a lot of things -- to think about for centuries on end." As usual, Nicholas came across as subtly condescending, but we all of us knew him well enough to know that wasn't his intention. "And he was the father of Existentialism."

"My point is you can have both," Kirpal countered. "The spiritual, or philosophical *and* the domestic, or personal."

"Perhaps," Nicholas agreed, "But only in moderation." He looked at me with intense focus. "Moderation in love is, essentially –

liking someone. And intellectual moderation does not a masterpiece produce!"

"May I say something?" Kirpal's tone was polite, but firm. "Listen to this. I think it speaks to what Ibo and Abdus have been going through, but also what we were just talking about: the conflict between a life of the mind and a worldly life: 'Truth is the highest virtue, but higher still is truthful living.' That's from the *Adi Granth*. Think about it, hoss." With that, Kirpal excused himself to get something to eat.

I didn't think Kirpal had been angry, but his words had been forceful. Everybody was quiet; at least some of us were moved by what Kirpal had said.

"That reminds me of something Theadora Harmon and I were talking about last week," I volunteered. "We were saying how some people talk a lot about being nice and act like they are really moral; whereas the people who often are the *most* decent might not be so vocal about what good people they are…You know, not tooting their own horns."

"Like me," Abdus smiled. I raised my eyebrows. "Just kidding."

"Are you going to become one of Dr. Harmon's sycophants?" That was pugnacious Nicholas.

"I seem to have managed so far not to get involved in any brown-nosing at school, where it might actually do me some good, so I should be O.K." I gave him a dirty look. "No, I think we are an example of your plain, garden-variety friendship." I decided to bring up what was on my mind. "Speaking of sycophants, any news about your Christia?" Nicholas flinched.

"Just that Redmund has been added to the list of suspects, but everybody knows that," Abdus declared.

Gretel, off in her own world during most of this exchange, was waving her finger back and forth in a candle flame. "Whoa," she said.

"You are so high," I informed her. Brandi appeared with a tray of brownies and Gretel grabbed two. I limited myself to one. On this pass.

"I know!" She began to giggle. "I'm not really used to – uh, what was I talking about?"

"Not much, baby," Brandi said.

"Oh yeah, I remember now! Kirpal and I had an idea." She looked around for Kirpal. Not seeing him, she continued on her own, "We think we should all stand in a circle and swear to each other that we did not kill Christia. Then, at least, we'd have, like, ten people we feel safe with."

"Hmm," I said neutrally.

"Do you really think you could tell if someone was lying?" Brandi asked, incredulous.

"Yes, I really do," Gretel argued, "Liars have a certain shifty look to them."

"Ha!" retorted Brandi in disbelief.

"I think I agree with her, mami," I said to Brandi. "Can't you just *tell* sometimes?"

"All right," she relented, "Let's do it. It sounds edgy anyway. Could be fun, and you know what the Cat in the Hat said, right? 'It's fun to have fun but you have to know how'!"

By this point, the party had clearly separated into two camps: the academics, my friends, who were congregated around the flashy tree in the living room; and the scenesters, people Brandi knew from her nightlife hijinks, who were mostly in the bedroom in various stages of undress. She went over and closed the bedroom door and then clapped her hands. "Yo! Everybody!" she said in her loudest voice, "We're gonna play a game! Everybody come over here by the tree." As people started to drift over, I exchanged a nervous look with Nicholas. I knew

396

he didn't like group activities – and I was concerned he might find this game particularly distasteful.

"O.K. Everybody get in a circle and hold hands. Close your eyes." She looked around the room. I knew because I'd kept my eyes open. I wasn't about to give Christia's killer an opportunity to compose himself (or herself) while I wasn't looking. Ibo, Abdus, Nicholas, Kirpal, and Gretel were bunched together on one side of the circle, to my left, while Brandi and four people I didn't know well from her comp.lit. cohort made up the rest of the circumference. I kept my eyes focused on the four men I knew well.

"This is the game:" Brandi announced, "We are going to go around the circle and each of us will explain that we did not kill Christia Thompson, and why."

In the split second after she spoke, I registered the following: a neutral expression on Kirpal's face, disgust on Ibo's face, surprise then delight on both Abdus and Nicholas' faces. Abdus was nodding mirthfully to himself. Brandi's four friends from the department simply looked confused.

"Alright," she said, "When I count to three, open your eyes. One. Two Three." She looked around the circle. "Annie, let's begin with you."

"O.K.," I said, "Um, I did not kill Christia Thompson."

"But, *why*?" Brandi urged.

"I, uh, didn't have any reason to kill her and I was nowhere near her on the day she died?" God, I'd been pathetic! As my mortification burned off some of my alcoholic fog, I was beginning to fear that this game was in execrably poor taste. I could only hope no one would take umbrage at our delusional idea of fun.

After I took my turn, Brandi shook her head, with its masses of dark curls, in disgusted disappointment. I'm sure she'd expected better drama from me.

397

Brandi brushed her hair away from her face and squared her shoulders theatrically. "I, Brandi Blumenthal," she intoned in a sepulchral tone, rolling her eyes back in her head, "swear to the gods and goddesses of grooviness that I did not kill Christia Thompson." Then she looked around the circle with a mischievous grin. "That woman was just too funky to die!" I couldn't help laughing at my brazen friend. She turned to the woman next to her. "Frida?"

"I never even met her and I have no idea what's going on," the woman giggled, as did her pals. Good, I concluded, they're probably all too drunk to care *what* we're "playing." The next three gave similar answers.

"I did not kill Christia Thompson," said Gretel. "I didn't so much as know where her office was."

Abdus looked guilty, "I didn't kill her," he asserted, "but there certainly were moments when I despised her, and I had every opportunity to do her in." He shivered. "May she rest in peace." Abdus was either a really good actor or a much better person than I'd long taken him for. The trouble was, I had no idea whatsoever as to which of these two mutually exclusive possibilities was true.

"She was a difficult woman," Nicholas admitted reluctantly, "But no – I did not kill her." I searched his face for some sign of prevarication and saw none.

"I didn't do it," said Kirpal. "No motive, no desire, etc."

We all looked intently at Ibo, the last player. "I don't think this game is very fun. Or funny," he said quietly. He dropped my hand and Kirpal's and went to get his coat in the smoke- and sweat-filled bedroom.

Ibo's outburst had put a bit of a damper on the academic faction of the party. Gretel and Kirpal left almost immediately after he did; and the rest of my gang held out only another half-hour.

To my surprise, Brenda walked in as Nicholas, Abdus, and I were leaving. I gave her a hug and told her to have fun. She felt like a scrawny child under her jacket, but she looked as if she'd made some effort to spiff herself up: she had freshly washed hair and was wearing drag. I thought she actually looked quite fabulous in her extra small (yet still too-big) tuxedo pants, lavender men's dress shirt and loosely-knotted tie. On the way home – Abdus had insisted we share a car service home – we discussed Brenda's transformation. I found it quite heartening, while both boys were convinced she was a hopeless case.

"Anyway, don't you find anorexia sort of jejune?" Nicholas waved a hand dismissively. "She's relatively innocuous, but far too tightly wound for my taste. I never know whether she'll give me the time of day when I go into the department."

"Nor I," Abdus agreed.

"Maybe you should try giving *her* the time of day," I scolded them. Upon reflection, I determined I was glad to be arguing with them: I would otherwise have found myself tempted to explore my own polyamorous fantasies – and I didn't think that was such a good idea under the circumstances.

It was almost two a.m. by the time I got home. Pepita was snoring and would not be roused for a tinkle. I, on the other hand, was unable to sleep. I felt afraid. I wondered if the queen of swords in the tarot reading could've been me. And what had the third card been? Ah yes, Judgment. Whose judgment? Could it have meant judgment by the dead? Depending on whether or not I was losing my mind, I had, it seemed, been experiencing multiple and various visitations from a dead person. Well, Brenda had sensed her too, but Brenda was kind of a kook.

The face of my clock glowed in my dark bedroom. Looking away from that faint light, I felt like the black night was closing in on me. Nonetheless, I turned away, willing myself to stop thinking in circles. I assured myself that the shadows in the corners of my room were no more dangerous than my own thoughts. I prayed for a dreamless sleep.

*

Tomasino had a fax on his desk in the precinct. The attached note from his partner read, "We found this email from Christia Thompson to a Raymond Solar in C.T.'s sent-mail files. We think he may be the perp.

Raymond:

I know this sounds crazy, and seems a silly excuse, but I am getting older. I thought I would've made my "greatest discovery" by now! I find in my restless mind there is only one thing I truly need. I know you've little or no respect for me. I have worked harder than you know to get where I am now and I am ready for the truth to be known.

I have discovered why I could not find what I was looking for before. I have, now, the name that eluded me for decades, no thanks to you.

I am not one to beg. If you will not give me the information I need, I will find the means to obtain it. My language is subtle now but my next step will be taken in no uncertain terms.

I will reveal what is rightfully mine. Be sure of it.
-- C.E.T.

D'Addario's note concluded, "This might be it. We're going through the usual channels to find him but no dice yet."

*

I wasn't sure quite what was different – maybe it was having everything out in the open with Nicholas – but I felt better when I woke up. Things seemed to be coming together for me. I spent a nice lazy morning lolling around on my soft, faded sheets, my hands behind my head, staring at the ceiling. I watched the dancing dust motes in the light from the window over my bed and my thoughts were led inevitably to Christia, as usual.

As a child I'd seen those numberless specks in the air as something that mattered, as information, as magical. I'd asked the adults around me what they were and no one knew what I meant by "the colored things in the air" -- until someone told me, "Oh, that's just dust." That didn't make me wonder any less, but at some point I stopped seeing them. I think it was because it was too much to take in. We train ourselves not to see everything because we cannot process every single piece of information that comes our way. So, regarding Christia: what was I not seeing? Another possibility occurred to me then: with so many millions of people in New York City, maybe I'd never even met Christia's killer. That shut my mind up for a few minutes.

I spent Sunday in the Village. I'm sure I got more studying done living in Morningside Heights, but I felt more at home downtown. I went to Friends' Meeting at the Quaker Meeting House on East 15th street, managing to keep my mind relatively calm for the duration. Then I took a yoga class a little further downtown at Ishwara Yoga Center with Brandi. After that, we meandered east to Kate's Joint on 4th Street and Avenue B for some tofu scramble. There, we relaxed for a good hour and a half on Kate's quirky, dingy sofas and rehashed the night before.

"What's the deal with Nicholas and you?" Brandi asked.

I busied myself with a knot in the drawstring of my yoga pants, buying myself some time to think. Finally, I sighed and admitted, "I have no idea."

"That's cool." Brandi leaned back on her lumpy sofa. "And Tomás?" she queried.

"Ditto." The only development there was I'd decided maybe *he* was the Prince of Swords – and he was running away to escape arrest. Of course, if I let myself think about it too much, I knew I might decide he was – for some reason beyond my ken -- running away from me. "I'm mostly over them both," I said, with bravado.

"Ah." She sat up. "Let's go to the Strand and meet boys."

"Do you think there will be a lot of eligible bachelor types there?"

"Probably. But the important question is: will they be able to resist our hung-over charms?" Brandi leered comically. "'Reply hazy. Try again.' That's stochastic science my friend."

"Whah?"

"The outcome cannot be predicted. Anyways, wanna go?"

"Yes!" I should introduce Brandi and Motte, I mused. They were the two most high-low people I knew. We gathered up our stuff. I went into the bathroom to change out of my yoga outfit and then we left. At the Strand, I wandered around aimlessly. I'd just finished re-reading my all-time favorite book, *The Idiot*, and was in the market for something to read. I am a compulsive reader, so I didn't feel the need to go to any particular section. My eyes fell upon a table with women's biographies. *Writing a Woman's Life*, by Carolyn G. Heilbrun, caught my eye because I remembered seeing it on Christia's bedside table. I vaguely recalled she'd left the book open to a section on Dorothy Sayers. I bought the book, resolving to read it later that evening, accompanied by tea, pets, and chocolate.

To that end (the chocolate part), I left Brandi and continued to walk west toward Magnolia Bakery, magnetically drawn along the tree-lined, cobblestone streets by the imagined aroma of freshly baked cupcakes. As I walked, I imagined the inhabitants of the stately red brick townhouses that fill the West Village. I'd never known anyone who lived there, and so I amused myself by picturing the luxurious lifestyles – daily flower delivery, personal trainers and chefs, 10,000 thread-count sheets – of the locals. I didn't feel envious; my life was really good. Plus, I reminded myself, money doesn't make people happy. *And* I was on my way to buy the most delicious cupcake in the city, possibly the world, as sugar therapy.

In one old home, the drapes were pulled back to reveal a view through to a private garden. I saw an elderly couple sitting inside, in chairs placed diagonally to the window. They looked so content, and it made me wonder whether there comes a point in life where we are able to be satisfied with the life we have lived; a time when we are able to say, "I have lived. I had a good life. Now it is over. Fine." I knew I was far from that, myself. Of course, I was a mere baby compared to that couple, who must have been in their eighties.

Still, I wondered: is it better to cultivate equanimity as we get older – or to nurture one's passions? Must these two be mutually exclusive? I thought of all the people leading what Thoreau called "lives of quiet desperation," compromising and compromising and finding their long-sought peace tainted with complacency; and then I thought of Christia Thompson, with her youthful antics and her slightly-desperate quest to stay cool and relevant as she got older. I was no closer to an answer to my question. I really needed that cupcake. Once there, I picked up a chocolate cupcake with vanilla buttercream frosting and a vanilla with chocolate frosting, *bien sûr*, and then hopped on the Uptown 1 train.

After a long day of class and writing, I had to stop by my department's holiday party on Monday night. They'd commandeered the graduate students' lounge for the event, and students and faculty huddled in nervous bunches, clutching wine in plastic cups and nibbling dried-out crudités. I knew as the night wore on that faculty and students would mingle more; heck, junior faculty might even get up the guts to converse with tenured faculty if both parties were sufficiently soused.

Winifred MacGregor, in a stunning boiled wool fauxchanel suit, and matching hat with a feather in it, approached me over by the punchbowl.

"Want the latest scuttlebutt?" she asked out of the corner of her mouth.

"Of course," I replied eagerly. I almost – almost! -- hugged her. I'd worried she might avoid me after having revealed so much in our recent conversation.

"They've informed Rich Redmund he's free to go about his business. No longer a murder suspect and all that." She gave a rueful smile. "I hardly see why he sought to involve me. Probably up to his old tricks in some way it's not given to me to understand." She shrugged. "*Tant pis.*"

"Do you mean to say they've figured out who killed Christia Thompson?"

"I *think* so. Not quite sure. Someone in the religion department, I think he said; mind you he wasn't *explicit.*" She laughed. "As if that rake ever was."

Thoughts of all of my friends in that department flashed in my mind's eye. I tried to keep my voice steady. "Should I, er, not know all this, what you've just told me?"

"Oh, la!" she said airily. "Why should he trust *me*? After all, I'm an ex-beau. Now I must be off. I'm meant to escort a prospective hire, introduce him to the important figures in the department, you know…"

Unable to focus any longer on chitchat, I went home and called Nicholas, who'd heard nothing about a change in the case, never mind an arrest. Between us, we called everybody else and determined that no one else had heard anything, either.

*

Cyrus Wilson, having called an informal meeting of certain members of his staff, sat in his office waiting for the people in question to arrive. Moments before, he'd heard two graduate students, Nicholas and Abdus, speculating about who'd killed Christia as if it were some kind of game they were playing. He'd been utterly furious.

"You'll want to watch who you accuse," he said to them, in a measured voice, but with his eyes as sharp as razors, "and how you act, as well. Honor still counts for something around here." Actually, he thought to himself as he stalked away, that's not true. Honor means nothing in academia, unless we're talking about the factuality of your research sources. Quite a depressing thought, but nothing new to Cyrus Wilson, a man who'd spent his life trying to be both honorable *and* successful. He'd sat down and, to steady himself, had directed his thoughts toward all of the good things in his life. He managed a small smile at the sight of the framed picture of his dog, Baruch, which was sitting in a prominent spot on his large desk.

Richard Redmund, Samuel Fleishacker, Ibrahim Heyreddin, Ruth Benda, Cole Wanamaker Biddle III, and Brenda Fujiki all came in at around the same time – he guessed they'd assembled in the department's office – and sat down in the chairs Wilson indicated. A few seconds later, Philippe Perez-Throgmorton walked in, surprising everyone but Wilson.

"I've asked Philippe to join us," Wilson explained, "as he is so inextricably involved in the death of one of our finest faculty members, who was first and foremost his wife."

Philippe coughed. "I wouldn't say that," he mumbled; then, more audibly, he continued, "as a matter of fact, her work was the most important thing in the world to her."

"Be that as it may," Wilson continued, "It is appropriate that you be here. My intent is to give a sort of briefing in the matter of the investigation of Christia's death. Detective Tomasino will be available this afternoon at the precinct to answer any further questions you may have. He may also have some questions of his own."

"Professor Wilson?"

"Yes, Ruth?" The petite Buddhism scholar had always reminded him of a monk. She kept her hair cropped very close to her head, wore wire-rimmed spectacles and tended to dress in monochromatic, flowing clothes.

"Why us?" her expression was curious but serene. Wilson knew others in the room were not feeling quite so mellow.

"It's simple." He ticked the reasons off on his fingers. "First of all, some of you were the people in the department who worked most closely with her or knew her best. Second, certain of you may have had reasons for wanting her dead and thus may have further information of relevance to the police. Third, and this is my own reason, I want the gossip around here to stop and have selected you as my agents." He looked around the room sternly. "Thus, I am going to, as it were, lay it on the line. I'm willing to share the facts in this case. Some of you have been the subjects of these rumors I'm talking about. This might be a good time to set the record straight." He winced. He was beginning to sound like someone in a potboiler. "Let's start with you, Heyreddin. Is there anything you'd like to share with the rest of us regarding your relationship with Christia Thompson?"

"Not *per se*," Ibo answered, slowly, "That is, I was working with her, and I've heard the rumors that I killed her because..." he paused, perhaps startled by his own admission, then commenced again, speaking more rapidly this time, "because she stole my work but it's just completely untrue."

"Well, what is the work whereof you speak? How come we've never heard of it? Through the usual channels, let's say." Wilson was curious. He knew part of the answer to his question, but he wanted to observe Heyreddin's response.

"Sir, I – I'm only just beginning to understand it myself." Ibo's forehead was wrinkled in concentration. He briefly explained his discovery and the ensuing work he'd done. "Originally, I didn't think my discovery was such a big deal; then, when it started to hit me that I'd fallen upon one of the most important discoveries of the decade, I started to get…superstitious. I didn't want to jinx my research by talking about it too much. So I asked Christia to keep quiet about my work."

"You asked her to keep quiet, and now she's dead. Doesn't that seem strange to you?" Rich Redmund's tone was sarcastic, and he clearly did not expect an answer.

The very well-mannered Cole "Coby" Biddle – a man Wilson had always perceived as incredibly stuffy -- stifled a gasp at Redmund's brash comment. His eyes, full of pity, flickered toward Heyreddin. Wilson took note of Biddle's compassion for future consideration in matters departmental. He'd be damned if he couldn't use such personal assets as part of his unspoken decision-making processes.

"Also," Ibo continued, haltingly, "My family has been going through hard times the last few years and I didn't want anyone to know just how much all this meant to me. Financially, as well as academically."

"I suppose that's fair enough," Wilson admitted.

Ibo nodded in assent. "The first step in my plan – publication -- has been initiated; the second, selling the codex to a museum, should be underway shortly. I hope this discovery will bring benefits to this department as well," he added.

"And what, exactly, does the codex consist of?" Wilson's tone was more kindly now, encouraging.

"Well sir," Ibo began, and looked around the room to include everybody. "It's the only known personal document from a Hittite 'commoner' – a woman no less. The actual artifact consists of Hittite cuneiform on baked clay. It's kind of a miracle that this fragment survived."

"What does the fragment say?" asked Ruth Benda, looking very intrigued.

"That requires a little background. The Queen, Puduhepa, had ordained that men and women participate equally in government. This was a condition of her marriage to her husband, King Hattusili," he explained. "All official documents required Puduhepa's seal, etc.

"Religion-wise, she and her subjects worshipped the goddess Ishtar and the lesser-known Lelvani. Her handmaiden, Tavanaliya, from what I've deciphered, agreed with her mistress's early-feminist leanings and, like Puduhepa, venerated a female deity."

"Sounds like a peaceful, mother-loving gang," said Redmund in a patronizing tone, that was softened slightly by a smile. Wilson noticed in Redmund the slight reddening of the nose that creeps up on pale-skinned drinkers.

Ibo turned on Redmund with a matching smile. "Ah, but there you err. These were not a gentle race, sir. War and imperialism were high on their agenda, much as we see in many modern nations such as yours. In Mesopotamia, Ishtar was a goddess of love; but for Hittites she was a warrior goddess. These were no weak, gentle, stereotypical females, but women who fully expected women to rule the world in perpetuity - as equals...or as superiors," he concluded. He turned to Wilson. "I shall certainly keep you fully apprised of my work in the future."

"Thank you." Wilson looked down at his much-lined hands. He found the role of inquisitor so tiresome. "Oh, Ibrahim?" Ibo looked up at Wilson, his eyes full of disappointment over still being in the spotlight. "One last thing: Can you tell us exactly what you saw the day Christia died? It's my understanding you were one of the last people to see her alive." Ibo was silent, thinking. Wilson rephrased his question.

"What I'm getting at here is: how can we be sure you were not the last person with her, that you didn't, in fact, return much later? Angry, let's say, that she was attempting to appropriate your work as her own? This is a rumor we've all heard?" There were nods all around.

"Of course he didn't kill Christia," Brenda burst out. Her skin was flushed. "Someone in this room did, though," she flashed a none-too-subtle glare at Richard Redmund, who sneered at her disdainfully as though her opinions were beneath consideration.

"Let's not get carried away." Wilson could see Brenda was unchastened, but she remained quiet. "Let Ibrahim answer for himself."

Thus pressed, Ibo admitted he'd seen Tomás leave the building long after his meeting with Christia should have ended. "I was in the hall with Nicholas Iverssen, taking a break from my research in the library. Any number of people can vouch for my being in one of those two places, but who can say where Tomás was all that time, between his meeting with Christia – *hours* earlier -- and his leaving? Come to think of it, I don't know where Nicholas was all that time either." Ibo looked ashamed. "I don't mean to suggest that either of them killed—" he glanced at Philippe, "were the cause of, er, what happened."

Wilson nodded. "We're not here to speculate, only to clarify," he said. The others might have seen Ibo's revelation as a last desperate bid to deflect suspicion, but Wilson thought he was telling the truth. He turned to Richard Redmund. "What about you, Rich? There have certainly been, shall we say, intimations in your direction."

"It's absurd," sputtered Redmund. "As if I would have to resort to murder to prove the superiority of my research and teaching." He slapped his hands on Wilson's desk. "My work speaks for itself!"

"Hmm," Wilson murmured, leaning back in his chair, away from Redmund and his impertinent hands. "Yours was one of the most convincing motives."

Redmund's eyes were on fire. "You mean to say you believe I could have killed Christia? That, perhaps, I'm not only some sort of violent madman, but a foot fetishist pervert to boot?"

"'To boot'....Oh, that's rich," snickered Wilson. "However, to answer your question, no. I never thought you capable of such an act." Too conniving, thought Wilson, to have left clues, a body, disarray.

Redmund loosened his collar. "Good." He cleared his throat and looked around with a half-smile. To Wilson's mind, it appeared he was ascertaining how to recover his standing in the group as a man of jovial equanimity. How exhausting it must be, Wilson thought, to be always trying to gain the psychological edge over others – while simultaneously trying to prove one's conviviality. Redmund gave a humble sidelong glance, and continued: "Because, obviously, as a lifelong Buddhist, I have been taught to honor all beings. When we all see each other as having been one another's mothers in past lives, how can we cause harm?" He turned to Wilson. "Even you, chances are, were my little baby in one of your past lives, and I was yours."

Wilson shifted in his seat. "Moving on," he announced. "Benda? Fleishacker? Fujiki? Any input?" He turned with a benign look to his new favorite teacher. "Biddle?" He waited.

Silence, and then that familiar affected whine. "I have little to contribute to the inquiry, but I wonder if I might, as it were, put my two-cents in?" Fleishacker's fake English accent was as thick as treacle, and his hunched shoulders belied his apparent boldness. "I must say, it would be nice to posit an omniscient god, and to discern a purpose in such senseless acts as murder and what-have-you. Just as, of course, we'd all prefer to endow each individual soul with its own perpetually re-manifesting *teleos*." Wilson imagined he wasn't the only one in the room to be wishing the man would speak in plainer language. "All this is just to say –" Fleishacker hesitated.

"Say it!" growled Wilson.

Fleishacker quavered, but held his ground. "Yes, ah – just to say, ah, perhaps we ought not impute meaning to this, ah, event, after all. Rendering Christia's a senseless death, even random, is not as satisfying; but may be the case after all."

"Point taken," Wilson replied.

"Poppycock!" Philippe exclaimed, looking around the room indignantly. "I shall have no more of this, this -- ech." He walked up to Wilson's desk and leaned over. "My dear Cyrus, if you are of a mind to include me in another of these-these…garish *gatherings*, do us both a favor and don't bother." With that, he left the office.

Wilson had recoiled slightly from the smell of liquor on Philippe's breath. He quickly wiped his face of a reflexive expression of distaste. "We seem to be touching some nerves here today. Let's commence the informative portion of this, ahem, meeting." He had to hide a smile at the thought of Philippe's phrase, "garish gathering." "Here are the facts in the case in question. I trust you will all disseminate them – and no other information, be it erroneous or simply gratuitous – as you see fit." He surveyed the room with his famous eagle eye. Satisfied, he continued, "All of the samples of DNA found around Christia were determined to match her genetic make-up. All documents found in her possession have, as of an hour ago, been traced. I have been informed that no one under the employ of this department is under suspicion any longer." He observed a mixture of relief and curiosity in the faces around him. He clutched the edge of his desk and drew himself up to stand, feeling every one of his sixty-odd years. "That's all," he told them and he waited until they had all filed out to sit back down again.

*

The next day, Tuesday, after I'd done some work on my final papers, I was determined to really sink my teeth into Heilbrun's book, the last book Christia had been reading in bed. Theadora called just as

411

I'd sat down, wanting to thank me for my company at tea. "I loved the clouds in the ceiling," I was saying, as a call came in on the other line.

I had been listening to Prokofiev's enervating yet exquisite 2nd Violin Concerto when the phone first rang. When the second call came through, the violin was just reaching its crescendo. It was Brenda on the line, asking me to come to Wilson's office, a.s.a.p. At that moment, the fraught music well matched my mood.

Walking down the hallway, I saw Brenda and several uniformed officers as well as my redheaded acquaintance, Tomasino. With him was another man, probably his partner I guessed, dressed in the kind of plain plainclothes that practically screamed "Detective." They were all looking at me. "Right this way, Ms Campbell," Wilson said grimly. Everyone followed me into the office.

Wilson gestured to the police officers. "They've figured out you wrote the note."

I sat down. "How?"

"Am I to take that as an admission of guilt?"

"Of writing a note, yes," I said carefully.

"It was a rotten thing to do, Annie." Wilson was right and I knew it.

"Especially given the circumstances…" I agreed. "How on earth did you find out?"

"You should have come forward earlier, Annie." Wilson's voice was stern. "I am to blame as well. I could tell something was going on with your snooping around. I take it you meant to find Christia's killer before the police did in order to prove your own innocence?" I nodded. "You may wonder how we know this?" I nodded again. "An acquaintance of yours thought we should know, being as we were wasting a lot of energy in that direction."

I was perplexed for about ten seconds, and then it dawned on me: Nicholas had told Abdus, and Abdus had told the police, or Wilson

412

– whichever. I found to my surprise that I wasn't angry with either of them. I felt as if a giant weight had been lifted off my shoulders. "I'm not actually under arrest, am I?" I asked in a small voice. I never thought I'd say those words!

"Of course you aren't," Tomasino said soothingly. D'Addario looked miffed, but kept his mouth shut.

I kept my arms folded over my chest. "How can I help you, then?" I asked in a neutral tone.

"Have you ever heard of a Raymond Solar?" Tomasino had rested his butt on the edge of the desk during my talk with Wilson; now he got up and began to pace around.

"No." The name was utterly unfamiliar. Tomasino continued his pacing, while I tried not to get annoyed.

D'Addario spoke: "It was a long shot," he said to Tomasino; and then, to me, "Do you have any information which you think might be of use to this investigation?"

"Not particularly." Both of the detectives fixed me with the same skeptical look.

"Not *particularly*?" D'Addario repeated.

I found I could not explain my choice of words in any kind of rational manner. I was on the verge of tears, and the adrenaline of the last few fearful weeks was pouring through my body. I looked at Wilson for help. He stayed silent, but there was enough compassion in his eyes to bring my voice back. "What I meant to express," I finally began, absentmindly rubbing the now-smaller lump on my head, "is that almost everybody I know has been high-strung since Christia was killed. For a lot of different, probably non-related reasons, from what I've been able to figure out. There's been a lot of fighting and drama and seemingly mysterious behavior." I looked down at the floor. "It's brought out the worst in everyone," I said.

The next day, after Colonial Fiction, I was of a mind to cook. Shirking any thought of homework or grading, I went to the winter-tiny Union Square Greenmarket and bought herbs -- thyme, mint and basil – and some wonderfully sour organic cherries. From there I went to Murray's Cheese Shop for fresh mozzarella and then to Balducci's, where I indulged in an artisanal cranberry-pecan sourdough loaf and some precious, completely out-of-season fresh peas. I'd decided to make fresh pea soup with herb dumplings.

I was walking up Broadway after leaving the subway, digging around in my bag for my keys, when I thought I heard someone say, "Tomás." I looked up and saw Tomás' parents just disappearing around the corner of 111th Street. The two of them were dressed all in impeccable white linen, the year-round uniform of the most elegant of Cuban ex-pats. I started to run after them and then I thought, why humiliate yourself? So what if they hadn't left yet. Maybe he'd gone south before them – or maybe he'd lied to me. What did I care? I was moving on. I went home.

As the hours passed, I continued to ruthlessly enforce my policy of not thinking about Tomás. I was alternating basil with an unconscionable amount of fresh mozzarella (for one person, at least) on a platter, and listening to Sarah Vaughn (at head-throbbing volume) when it struck me: How had Tomás known about my head? Because I knew for a fact I hadn't told anybody but Theadora and Lark. Oh, and Abdus and Kalinka, in a roundabout way…But Abdus and Tomás weren't, to my knowledge, particularly close. The question continued to trouble me as I ladled the steaming soup and tender dumplings I'd cooked into a big bowl, and as I ate my meal.

After a few phone calls and a nice walk with Pepita, my mind was clearer, and I no longer needed to remind myself not to think about a certain tall, dark handsome man. I finally sat down with the book late that night. As I read about Dorothy Sayers, I began to understand, if

414

only partially: I thought I might know why, but not *who* – and there remained plenty of unexplained details.

*

For Detective Tomasino, the call came through at 3 a.m.: they'd found Ramon "Raymond" Solar, and he'd confessed his relationship to Christia Thompson.

"I knew it," Marj said, from their cozy bed.

"What, that he was angry at her for getting rid of him that way?"

"Yeah, I guess I thought it might be something like that. But that wasn't the main thing."

"Well what was?" her husband asked. He kept the incredulity out of his voice: Marj's insights were based more on intuition than evidence, but they were often right on the mark.

"She loved him so much she didn't know what to do." She tucked the covers around Andy's shoulders and cuddled in close. "Like any mother," she murmured sleepily.

"We didn't think the feet were important," Tomasino muttered into the blanket.

"Huh? Feet?" Marj sat bolt upright. This, she hadn't foreseen.

Andy was already asleep.

Chapter Thirteen -- Goodness

Lelvani [the underworld goddess of the Hittites], in the domain of Hatti [the land ruled by Hattusili and Puduhepa], Tavanaliya/handmaiden to Queen Puduhepa, entreats you protect the widowed mothers [*utdati*: women with children, but without husbands] and the children/Long life to the family of Tavanaliya, your servant, your lamb/All glory to the great Queen, may her daughters rule for all time/else shall we all be sacrificed to you, Lady/and all we behold rendered dust.

Translation of entire text of the Tavanaliya codex, Hittite cuneiform on clay fragment, in I. O. Heyreddin's *Things Truly New to Behold* (forthcoming)

One of the messages I'd had on Wednesday night had been from Motte Thompson. I'd called him back, but he didn't return my call until late Thursday afternoon, just after I'd gotten back from turning in my last paper of the semester. I was mired in grading the Intro.Comp.Lit.

finals, all the while, I must admit, daydreaming about how nice it would be to visit Lark for the Solstice. I knew I was going to have to pull an all-nighter that night, but Nicholas and I would be able to leave Friday afternoon in time for Lark to pick us up on her way home from work. I couldn't wait.

Motte and I chatted for a few minutes, and then he told me why he'd called: his aunt, Marie-Rose, had called him from Paris to say she'd seen a ghost. He'd been "on the bayou" and hadn't returned her call until some weeks later, and he'd called me as soon as he'd talked to her. Apparently, he'd decided not to tell her about Christia's death until she returned from her trip – "She's the last one left of the sisters, and she's of a delicate constitution," – but she'd asked him right out on the telephone. "'Has something terrible happened?' she asked me. Lordy may! What would you have done?"

"I am incapable of lying, so…I dunno. Maybe I would've tried. It seems so harsh to have to give news like that over the phone." He coughed, a deep rumble. "Rough night?" I asked.

"You got that right, chérie!" I heard the sound of a zippo lighter, and a long inhalation, then more coughing. "Whew," he continued at length. "So, yup, I told her Christiane had died. But 'I knew *that*,' she says, 'that's not who I seen.' 'Then who was it?' I asked. 'Christiane's beau who died in Vietnam,' she informed me. 'As handsome as could be,' she said he was. 'Never aged a day.'" He paused. "Now, what do you make of that?"

"I don't know, Motte." If Motte and Christia's aunt wasn't batty (and what were the chances of that? Medium, I wagered) that made three people that I knew of who'd experienced paranormal sightings since Christia's death. On the other hand, it was all too possible that all three of us were bonkers.

"Sure you don't wanna move down here Annie? The food's real good." He was joking, but I could hear a tinge of wistfulness in his voice.

It was in my voice too. "Oh, Motte, you know I can't." Then, moved by a sudden impulse to be open with him, I added, "But I sure won't forget you."

It had snowed in the wee hours of Thursday morning, but by midday the streets were slushy and pebbly and dirty. I bought some peanuts from the roast nut guy on my corner. As I walked away, I remembered his simple advice to me the month before; essentially, he'd told me to just move on. Well, I argued with him in my head, so far there's no simple solution here. Someone is dead, a murderer is at large…Not to mention my love life is a mess and I'm in the middle of major grading. Although, I acknowledged to my imaginary companion, moving on is probably good in most less-than-perfect situations.

Satisfied for the time being, I turned my attention to the holiday decorations around me. Big colored lights – the old-fashioned kind – were draped on many fire escapes, more or less (generally less) symmetrically. In store windows, displays of color and richness to rival the pages of any illuminated manuscript were assembled. My holiday would be no less sumptuous, if much less commercial. In about twenty-four hours, I would be in Connecticut, by a lake, where the snow would still be white and the air pure and clean.

My friends had commandeered several tables at the Hungarian Pastry Shop and were variously writing, grading, and reading together in a tense, focused mass of end-of-semester duties.

I sat down next to Ibo because he was the only one who didn't look terribly stressed-out. He told me he had teaching assistants to do the grading for all of the classes – his and Christia's – that he was teaching.

418

"I can*not* hear that right now, if you want to remain on good terms," I announced, picking up the foot-high stack of exams I had yet to grade and thrusting it threateningly in his direction. "And I suggest you keep your voice down…Unless you want to help us?" I smiled hopefully. Then I picked up my red grading pen to return to my work.

Ibo put his hand on my arm, and I looked up at him. "I wanted to say again," he said softly, "how sorry I am that I was mean to you that time in my office. I was torn up inside over keeping my family situation and work life a secret, and I inflicted that on you." He smiled apologetically. "I know it was not a big deal to you, but I hate ever causing anyone the slightest pain. It's my father and the dead mother elephant all over again. I heard that story so many times growing up that other people's feelings are just not abstract to me. I simply cannot bear the thought of causing pain." As he spoke, he was rubbing the edge of a colored pencil back and forth on a sheet of white paper.

"I understand, Ibo. No harm done."

"I'm glad." He returned to his rhythmic drawing for a few minutes, and then turned to me again. I had been engrossed in a particularly egregious analogy perpetrated by a student who apparently had not even opened the books in question. "Sometimes pain is inevitable," he said in a sad voice. "With Christia, I became a little too – avid," he admitted. "Especially in matters of the heart, there is unfathomable potential for causing pain -- and in that case I hurt myself." He looked at me intently. "You probably do that too, Annie, where some people lash out and hurt others. But you *can* avoid it to some extent if you really apply yourself. You know, focus on other things, keep yourself busy…"

I wasn't sure what he meant. The comment was just vague enough to have applied to any number of situations in my life. I looked over at his drawing, but all I could discern was a monochromatic orange

419

color field, more saturated with color at the bottom of the page. "What are you drawing?"

"Hmm?" He looked surprised. "Oh, this. It's nothing, really…I guess you could say I'm homesick. Many days, there is an orangey haze in the sky over Istanbul, at daybreak and nightfall. This color reminds me of it." He held up his light orange pencil. He'd subtly imbued the orange with just the faintest hints of pink and ochre from the handful of pencils he had with him. "Speaking of Turkey," he opened up his backpack and offered me a square, wax-paper wrapped package, "I made a batch of Turkish Delight last night. I got tired of lamenting my family's illustrious candy-making past and got out the pot. I made rose-flavored. I hope you like it."

I opened the package and a sugary rose odor wafted up at me. "Mmm. How marvelous-smelling. It smells so sweet and fresh."

"The food of contentment," he said. "Enjoy."

"Thank you so much, Ibo. I was cooking last night too. Isn't it therapeutic?"

"What's that?" Abdus had set his book down and was sniffing in our direction.

"*Raahat Lokum*," said Ibo, "Turkish Delight. I made some for Annie because she's listened to me go on about Turkey so much."

"Puh-leese. I love to hear about the way other people live," I protested. "Maybe, if you're awfully good, Abdus, I'll share it with you." Pudgy Mahmoud was eyeing the candy too. I found myself wishing, selfishly, that Ibo'd given me the treats in private.

Abdus regarded me suspiciously. "In what sense…'good?'"

"Like, explain to me how the police knew I wrote that note."

Kirpal looked up sharply. "No," he said accusingly to Abdus, "You didn't." Obviously he, too, was in on my little secret – but then he was entirely trustworthy, as opposed to Abdus and Nicholas.

420

Abdus' remorse looked authentic. "Sorry about that," he said, his look encompassing both Kirpal and me. "I thought it might be helpful. I swear I meant you no harm, Annie."

"That's O.K.," I replied with feigned reluctance. "It all worked out in the end, I suppose." I wanted Abdus to know I was trying too. "I hear they got someone." I looked around the table for confirmation, but everyone seemed uncannily riveted by their work. Ibo, the only one not studying or grading, looked extremely uncomfortable.

"Um, do people know something I don't know?" Silence. "That's the feeling I'm getting here," I said brightly. After a moment of watching Ibo, Abdus, Mahmoud, Gretel, *and* Kirpal fiddle elaborately with their pens, papers, etc., -- and avoid my eyes -- I realized Nicholas was not at the table. After shoving the Intro.Comp.Lit. exams into my backpack, I ran outside without another word to anybody. My mind clear and urgent, I punched in Nicholas' number as I ran.

Unfortunately, he wasn't home. Part of me hoped against hope that he'd have a reasonable explanation of what was going on, but I was mostly terrified.

Planning can be very comforting, I told myself. I will walk to my street. I will turn the corner and walk down my street to my building. I will go home and get Pepita. I will take her to Nicholas' house and he will be home and he will tell me everything is fine. *Then*, I will go home and grade all night. No problem. The plan was rational. The voice in my head, however, was getting hysterical. Was *that* why nobody would tell me what was going on: they thought I was would get too upset? Or did they think I was in on the crime all along? It probably seemed that way, what with all my meddling.

Everything will be fine, I chanted to myself over and over as I went through the motions of my plan of action. After about half an hour, I found myself at Nicholas' door. He was home! He buzzed me in and I took the steps three at a time, with Pepita panting along behind me.

I grabbed him in a big hug. "You're still here!" I exclaimed.

"Why shouldn't I be?" he asked, perplexed. In Nicholas' tiny room, Nick Cave was singing some sickly beautiful religious-romantic song at highest volume.

I tried to catch my breath. "I-just-want you to know-I-support you – no matter what," I vowed, practically shouting over Cave's wail and his eerie accompanying choir. "You are my best friend and I love you. Whatever happened, I'm sure you had your reasons."

For a minute, he just stared at me. Then, solemnly, he went to the refrigerator, three steps from his doorway, and got out a Diet Dr. Pepper. He handed the cold can to me and I watched it perspire in my hand with disbelief: how could he be thinking about soda at a time like this? "I think you need this. Bad," he said. "You look like you've seen a ghost!"

I hadn't seen -- or dreamed – a ghost in ages. In a calmer moment, earlier in that hectic day, I'd been thinking about the sudden disappearance of Christia's ghost. I'd decided that Christia had been angry at first and then, much in the manner of live folks, becalmed herself and thought better of her hauntings.

I hugged Nicholas again. "No ghost, just – you." I squeezed harder. "You!"

He glared at me. "I have to go have dinner with Sam and some of his friends from law school at some Kosher steakhouse in a few minutes. As a lifelong vegetarian, I'm not too happy about it. *So*, as you might *imagine*, I'm not in the mood for tact and subtlety. What on earth is going on?" He enunciated his words very carefully, as if speaking to a non-native speaker – or a lunatic. "And please," he added, "start making sense quickly – I have about five minutes." As he spoke, he was fixing the cufflinks in his sleeves.

With great effort, I spat it out: "I was lead to believe you killed Christia."

"What?" He'd just taken a sip from his soda, and he almost choked on it. His face was awash in utter disbelief. "Who told you that?" he sputtered.

I realized no one had actually come out and said it. "No one."

He looked at me with compassion. "Annie, you need sleep my honey bear," he patted my head. "We all do. It'll be easier now that we all know what happened."

"*I* haven't the faintest idea." I rethought my statement. "Or, at least, I have only the very *most* faint notion about what may have happened," I amended.

"You mean you don't know yet who – barring me -- killed Christia?" I shook my head. He thought for a minute. "Do you remember the other day you told me Motte had called you – that cad," he muttered, then continued as if he hadn't said anything critical, "and said his aunt had seen a ghost in Paris?" I nodded. "Well, didn't you get the slightest bit suspicious?"

"No-o. Why?"

Nicholas pushed the phone towards me. "Call him," he ordered.

"Motte?"

"Yes," he barked, shoving a slip of paper bearing Motte's telephone number into my sweaty palm.

"Annie Campbell, why I declare!" Motte's voice, mocking but fond, came through the phone like a caress.

"Ask him the ghost's name," Nicholas urged in my other ear.

A few minutes later, I hung up. "I still don't get it. So, Marie-Rose saw a ghost of Christia's boyfriend Tommy – *and*?"

"Think about it," he said.

*

The halls of the Department of Religion were dim even in daylight hours. Outside, gargoyles watched over the windows and doors to Religion Hall. Inside, in the weak yellow-green light of her banker's lamp, Brenda Fujiki sat at her chair. Her desk was her fortress, behind which she would continue to sequester herself away from the petty machinations of her fellow human beings. Woe betide anyone who should try to engage her in a battle of wills. She would be moved neither to engage in conversation nor even in jovial repartee. *Particularly* the latter. She would accomplish her administrative tasks, and, in free moments, she would read her book. She would win by sheer apathy and slippery disinterest.

How oddly it had all turned out, she mused. She'd never have guessed the truth in Christia's murder. For all she'd planned the fiery justice of an avenging angel, she could no longer muster any rage. The story was just too sad and pathetic. Everybody's parents drive them crazy, that was common knowledge. Her parents called her gaunt and starved-looking and skeletal all the time. On her infrequent trips home, they tried to force her to eat, tempting her with her favorite dishes until she'd felt about to burst by mere proximity. She hadn't killed *them*.

Cyrus Wilson had been in and out of the department office ten times that morning – exceeding by eight or nine his usual amount of visits. Brenda knew something was up, but she'd be damned if she was going to approach the chair of the department with a wishy-washy question like, "Is something going on?" In her own time she would find out.

The next time he came in, nervously shuffling the papers in his hand, her patience was rewarded. He took a seat in the chair beside her desk and told her he had never suspected her. He'd been unable to defend her fully, he explained, because doing so would've forced him to reveal his hunch. He hoped she would forgive him.

Fine, thought Brenda. He is accepting responsibility for what he did, just as Mom said one should. She allowed herself to admit that maybe her mother had been right about something: it took a big person to take responsibility for their own mistakes. "That's good to know, Professor Wilson," Brenda said, "that you knew I didn't kill Christia." She waited for him to continue. Silently, she resolved to exercise an extra ten minutes at the gym that night. She would take responsibility for the extra saltine she knew she would have to eat just as soon as Wilson exited the premises.

Wilson rubbed his forehead as if to smooth out the furrow in his brow. He was lingering, had more to say: "She was Cajun and I'm Creole, but we understood one another, Christia and I. Not that she ever told me anything about it directly, but..." he looked at the ceiling and sighed. "I knew what really happened, sort of, but how could I explain anything about anyone's guilt or innocence – yours, Redmund's, you know -- to the authorities without revealing what I knew in the first place?" Brenda was confused. He sighed. "I have at times questioned my silence. I justified it to myself by reasoning that I could've ruined many peoples' lives had I been wrong. Also, I," he hesitated, searching for the right word, "hoped – I wish I could say suspected it in any real way – that I was incorrect. In my defense," he confessed, "I also surmised things would come out sooner."

Brenda was drawn into a dialogue despite herself. "Didn't you worry that he could've killed again?"

"Oh, my, yes, but *never* for the same reason!" With that, his mood turned more businesslike. He got up quickly and excused himself to attend a meeting, "a ten-minute walk from here, and," he looked at his watch with a wry smile, "beginning in five minutes." He waved as he walked out of the office. His step was measurably lighter.

Brenda fairly trembled with relief and saltine-anticipation. Human interaction over, she turned with ardent eyes to the book in

425

which she was currently engrossed. A few weeks ago, while doing some research for her current project, she'd come across a book on the Byzantine nun Kassia that she'd missed in her earlier efforts. Probably because Kassia's name wasn't in the title or subtitle. Her fellow Wiccan in Puduhepa's Sisters, Theadora Harmon, had written a book – ten years ago, for her doctoral thesis – on Kassia. Brenda couldn't believe she'd never known. She would have to talk more with Theadora, maybe pull her aside after the next full moon.

This was Brenda's tenth time reading the book, so she felt she was entitled to a little visual diversion. She turned to the inside back leaf of the dust jacket, to the photograph of a ten-years younger Theadora, in shorter braids and first-book-serious mien. She doesn't look a day older now, thought Brenda. She's always, always been a brilliant, powerful, captivating woman. Someone Brenda could look up to and emulate.

She dropped a salty crumb into her salivating mouth. Her emaciated fingers fondled the glossy portrait. Oh, my sublime heroine, Brenda crooned.

At the lake, snow was falling. There was a cheerful golden glow from the windows of the cabins inhabited by year-round residents like Lark and Ted. We stepped out of the car into snow-infused air, flavored with the homey smell of wood smoke. In the light from Lark's porch lantern, the snow sparkled as if it had been sprinkled with tiny stars. The winterberry bush planted by the steps nodded in the gentle wind, its red berries peeking out from under an uneven blanket of snow.

Lark's shoulder length auburn hair was sprinkled with snowflakes. She'd donned a vivid blue and green quilted Chinese silk parka over her office attire for the walk from the car to her front door. I scooped her up in a big hug. "God, thank you *so* much for having us here," I said with joy. Grabbing my bag, I took the path to her door in

426

big steps, once or twice kicking snow up into the air with sheer glee. Pepita ran to the door at lightning speed to greet *her* best friend, the Ruskin's pooch, Buster.

Nicholas and I were to share the guest room, generally referred to as "Annie's room." Lark had her altar, which was covered with Wiccan, Hindu, and Buddhist pictures and ritual objects, in there; and across from the altar sat a queen-sized futon, and a television -- with cable. Pure luxury, as far as I was concerned.

With a sigh of contentment, I put my backpack down and surveyed the room. It was one of my favorite places in the world, my safe haven. I noticed that Lark had added some striking new items to her altar: a Tibetan *thangka,* or devotional wall hanging, of the green goddess Tara, and a turquoise-encrusted silver knife – both from her recent trip to Sikkim, in northern India. Pepita had dug under the quilt on the futon, curled up into a ball and fallen instantly asleep. Lark and Ted's Springer Spaniel, the aforementioned Buster, was sniffing around our city-smelling accouterments. I pulled a stack of magazines out of my bag (I never had gotten to read them during the semester) to share with Lark, a fellow trash addict.

Lark was in the living room when I came out. "Annie-Fanny," – that was one of her many nicknames for me – "There are two messages for you. Your Mom's expecting you next week for Christmas. I think you knew that? But she called to tell you she's making not one but *two* pies, chocolate-bourbon-pecan and pumpkin custard, just so you can start getting excited." Lark and my mother went way back -- to Lark's and my teen years during which she, always more sensible and stable than I, helped my mother understand her flamboyantly rebellious daughter. "Also, someone from your coven called you to wish you a happy solstice."

"Which coven? I don't *have* a coven." I was a solitary then, celebrating the seasonal holidays and the moons alone or with Lark.

427

"Puduhepa's Sisters. You know, as in the ancient queen I researched online?" she peered up at me curiously from underneath her bangs.

"I never gave them this number…" I said, shaking my head in wonder.

Lark's eyes twinkled. "More mysteries, huh?"

Nicholas was lying on the rag rug in front of the fireplace. He'd partially laid the fire, but hadn't lit it. He said he was just too worn out.

"That bad?" I asked him, guessing he hadn't slept any more than I had.

"I'm just flat-out *tired*."

"I hear it. Just stay there. Peace-out," I comforted him. "I'll light the fire." I looked at my ex-boyfriend supine on the floor in a cashmere cardigan and gray moleskin trousers. He was dashing, even in his exhaustion. "You have a whole month to unwind before you leave for Berlin." Nicholas had won a Fulbright to study 17th-century metaphysics in Germany.

Together, Lark and I managed to get the chimney to draw, and then all three of us took our places facing the fire to wait for Ted to get home. We'd planned a leisurely evening of cooking, eating, and talking. The firelight flickered on the big room's cabin-style wood paneling and on the faces of my two best friends in the world. In a corner, the scrawny Christmas/Solstice tree Lark and Ted had cut down themselves – "We picked it because it looked so forlorn, like the tree in *A Charlie Brown Christmas*," Lark had told us on the ride home – lit up the room with multicolored lights and colorful ornaments from lands far and near.

Lark broke the silence. "Help – I forgot the rest of that message! It was kinda confusing. I'll just play it for you." She got up and pressed the play button on her answering machine and then sat back down.

I didn't recognize the voice: "Lark, this is a message for Annie. Puduhepa's Sisters wanted to wish her a happy solstice. Blessed be. Oh, and about Christia's killer…We *are* sorry to have kept you and Brenda in the dark." I sat bolt upright. They must've known all along who had murdered their coven-sister. If they could find me at Lark's place, hey, why not use those powers to scry into other more serious matters? "But," she went on, "we know you will understand why we had to let things unfold as we did." And then the mechanical voice: "End of messages."

"O.K., That's it!" Lark burst out. "I have to know the full story of what happened in the big scandal at the University of New York, you guys." We hadn't spoken since the day before, Thursday, and I'd learned a lot since then.

"It's a little tender for me still," I admitted. "I can't believe how stupid I was."

"Nonsense," Nicholas said generously. "You were enchanted by the fellow."

"Basically," I began, "the guy I was sort of seeing –"

Nicholas and Lark interrupted me simultaneously: "The one I warned you about?" Lark asked; whilst Nicholas sneered, "A fling. A diversion from *moi*," little knowing he was more wrong than he could have imagined. I had truly cared for Tomás Bautista.

My eyes flickered back and forth. Lark looked merely surprised, while the patronizing smile that had replaced Nicholas' fleeting sneer held more than a hint of jealousy. "Yes, yes," I placated them both. "So, as I was saying, Tomás murdered his --" – I couldn't help but flinch at the word – "his mother, Christia Thompson."

"I didn't know it was *him*!" Lark was aghast. "And…his *mother*? Oh, Annie, I am so sorry – but *this* I've got to hear!"

"Well," I said slowly, "we don't know the full story yet, but people think he was angry at her for deserting him. I mean, it's all anyone was talking about — even though at the end of finals and grading there's precious little time for gossip — but I feel we'll never know the whole truth. A few people have said maybe he had seen her behaving like, um, kind of a slut, and it infuriated him. I'm not sure what the facts are there. We don't even know if she knew who *he* was…What's strange is that what I read in *Cremalgo's Companion* was right. Remember I told you it seemed to be somehow telling me she'd been killed by someone who loved her, or who she loved?"

Lark nodded, wide-eyed.

"Well, dears, it's all behind us now." Nicholas gave a bored yawn. "Personally, I *much* prefer the kind of story you find in *Vanity Fair*. You know, where a sordid but elegant *bon vivant* murders a tipsy socialite; or, how's this: 'International Playboy found in Compromising Position with Cabin Boy by Wife; Butler Slays Both at Wife's Behest'?"

I gave Lark a look to let her know we'd talk about Tomás in-depth later, just the two of us. "You're morbid. And salacious!" I chided.

"Why not?" he argued. "Aristocrats and murder go well together: 'The gleaming mahogany railing of the yacht's starboard deck was slick with blood,' and so forth."

"Nicholas had his own little scandal recently," I snipped. "Maybe you'd like to tell Lark about your little fling this fall," I suggested, squinting at Nicholas half-heartedly, too relaxed and comfy to muster much sarcasm.

"Yes, ahem," he cleared his throat. "And maybe not."

"Aw, c'mon," Lark pleaded. "Give me a little thrill."

"I had a brief, three-way, ambisexual, polyamorous-type incident with my friends Abdus and Kalinka," Nicholas explained.

"Kids these days," Lark said, laughing.

I grinned at her. "Hey, he's older than us, Devi-ma," I said. The nickname was a combination of her (Sanskrit) middle name and a Hindi endearment for women. "Plus, he admitted he did it all just to get my attention!"

"Yes, and look where it's gotten me. You won't commit to more than a weekend with me," he complained. "Never trust a woman," he intoned, and swiped at me with a magazine. "Don't you know the story of Samson and Delilah? The archetypal example of womankind as the downfall of man? I'll tell it to you! With my own commentary." He tented his fingers and assumed a scholarly expression. "Oh, no, wait." A giant grin covered his face. "I've got something even more entertaining, if you can imagine that...It's a nature poem from Philippe Perez-Throgmorton. He kindly offered me a copy of the manuscript for his new book. Listen to this. It's a haiku:

My wife and me

I am the bear. Roar.
My nature is your horror!
She is the sweetmeat.

I dissolved into a fit of laughter. "You have *got* to be kidding. That's getting *published*?"

He nodded. "Care to hear more?"

"Lemme see that," Lark said. "It sounds like Spock's poetry. Classic."

"Leonard Nimoy," he corrected, handing her the sheaf of papers.

I looked out the big picture window at the snowy night. Just a few big, fluffy flakes were falling, signaling the end of the storm. The sky had cleared up here and there. Far in the distance I could see a mountain, bathed in moonlight where the moon's rays made it through the clouds, framed in the window like some photographer's idyll. I was so happy to be there. I thought of Philippe, imagined him all alone in his cold, impersonal apartment. I felt a wave of guilt wash over me for all my bad thoughts about him. In my mind, I had deemed him guilty due merely to his strange, erratic behavior following the death of his wife. Who was I to judge his grief? At least my judgments had remained unexpressed, verbally speaking. To be completely honest, although I'd never been convinced about Brenda's being involved, I'd had plenty of bad thoughts about almost every other potential suspect. This included the man right now curled up by my side, and Richard Redmund, and Abdus, and Ibo, and even – reluctantly – Tomás.

As Lark and Nicholas went through the manuscript together, emitting almost-constant howls of laughter, I watched the peregrinations of a brown house-spider along the lip of the stone fireplace. Spiders were long associated with Athena, and have been called "the Witches' friend." I silently entreated the spider to lend me a little of her wisdom so that I could learn to avoid being impetuous – writing ill-timed notes, and falling in love with damnably inappropriate men. The spider crawled off of the fireplace and into a crack in the wall. Mesmerized by the fire's warmth and dancing flames, I drifted away in my head.

In the now-roaring fire, a log popped, and I jumped. I'd been worlds away, daydreaming about Tomás. I knew full well I could have loved him. He saw me with my fists clenched and opened up more than my hands. In retrospect, it dawned on me that it had been in that very instant that I'd simultaneously both fallen in love with him and realized he was forever gone to me. I must have sensed something at the time, somehow, on some sub-subconscious level – but all I remembered feeling at that moment was despair. What will happen to him? I wondered sadly.

432

Ted arrived in a flurry of wind and snow, and a racket of happy dogs. He was dressed in his usual Casual Friday outfit of a flannel shirt, jeans and Topsiders, and had his arms full of packages: wine and gifts and a big birch log for our Solstice celebration. There were hugs all around, and then we made room for Ted and canines on the rug.

"Hey Ted," Nicholas began, a sly smile on his face. He and Ted were very fond of each other, but they did like to engage in manly ribbing together. "Have you heard the latest about John Ruskin?" Ted usually let it drop within a few hours of meeting anyone that he was distantly related to John Ruskin, the Victorian English architect and author.

"No, I haven't, Nicholas. Perhaps you'd like to share this interesting tidbit with us?" Ted's cheeks were still rosy from the cold, and his light-brown hair was mussed in the outdoorsy way that big-city stylists try to emulate for exorbitant fees.

"Ruskin almost had a heart attack on his wedding night, because he didn't know women had pubic hair!" We all laughed. "But," Nicholas continued, "it makes sense if you think about it: look at classical sculpture and the other publicly-displayed art of his time in general. Even though he wrote about art and morality and spirituality, think of what he was exposed to…How would he have known?"

"Good point," I conceded. "However, what *I'd* like to know is, how the hell do we know this? Who on earth did he tell this to?" Laughter again.

"All joking aside," Nicholas tone was sincere, "I can see his principles have been passed on through you – and I see it in Lark, too. He wrote a lot about how moral and spiritual comfort were interrelated and could be cultivated. He invented the notion of 'domestic architecture' to encompass these comforts." Nicholas reached out to tap them both on their arms, then spread his arms wide. "You two have the coziest home in the universe."

After a few minutes, Lark stood up and stretched. She turned to me, offering her hand for a boost up. "Let's get the Yule log prepared for the solstice," she said. We went into "my" room and gathered candles and oils from her altar and set about preparing the log. We'd kept the custom – we'd learned years ago from *The Golden Bough* that it was a very old and widespread one – of saving a piece of last year's log with which to light the new. We nestled the log in dry moss, grasses and leaves to ensure prompt burning. The longest night of the year was fast upon us and we planned to kindle the warmest, brightest light we could to symbolically entreat and welcome the sun's return in the morning.

Once we'd just about finished our preparations, I heard Nicholas talking about Tomás with Ted. "I have to hear this," I informed her. "Let's join them?"

"Annie," Ted said, "Nicholas told me about the attack on you, the threats…Weren't you worried that you were in danger yourself?"

I blushed. "Yes… Though I was more in shock than scared. I guess if I'm honest with myself, my so-called beau did bash me over the head with a rock. Which kind of gives lie to some great attraction to me on his part." I sighed heavily. "It's something I've been trying to avoid thinking too much about."

Lark nodded compassionately, and then turned to Nicholas. "Did you tell him about the ghosts?" She was one of the few people in whom I'd confided about my visions.

"Ghosts, too?" Ted looked shocked.

I bit my lip. "Look, I don't want to think about all of that right now. I mean, I can talk about the end of the story in a rational way…but not every little detail."

Lark nodded compassionately. "You've been through so much lately."

434

"O.K. Just one more question?" Lark gave Ted a warning look, but he continued. "Didn't you ever have any suspicions about this so-called boyfriend of yours?"

"He was not her boyfriend," Nicholas interjected. Again, my eyes met Lark's.

"I had some idea of what might have been the root cause of Christia's death – but zero idea who would fit into my suspicions, if that makes sense. It could have been any number of people – her husband, an ex-lover, a would-be lover, her brother..."

"Her brother. Why?"

"...Jealous, I guess," I ventured. "But somehow I never really thought he was involved."

"So how did you figure it out?" Lark asked.

"I looked up the last book Christia had been reading in bed, and the exact page she'd left the book open to, and it got me to thinking," I explained. "The section she was reading was on Dorothy L. Sayers, and how she turned down this major award, an honorary Doctorate of Divinity from the Archbishop of Canterbury. It's generally accepted that she did so," I paused, "because she didn't want anyone to find out she'd had a son she'd abandoned. She bore a child out of wedlock. That was a really big deal in those days. A child she was, or certainly *felt* she was, forced by circumstance to abandon. Greater renown might have led to discovery and scandal and shame..."

Ted had brought all of us a glass of red wine, and a seltzer for himself, and taken a seat on his recliner behind Lark on the floor. She was resting her head on his lap. Nicholas looked intrigued by this line of reasoning. I took a sip of my wine, momentarily mesmerized by the crystalline surface of the snow that had accumulated on the windowsill outside. "So then I was thinking: who looks like Christia? I didn't know for a fact that it was someone I knew, but out of the people I could come up with only Ibo and Tomás fit the bill." I sighed. I'd guessed the

435

truth back then, but still hoped I was wrong, for obvious reasons. I supposed I'd never fully understand what had happened between the central figures in this terrible mother-child tragedy. "The funny, or, not funny but *touching*, thing is," I continued after a few minutes, "this is something she actually talks – talked – about at some length in her biography of de la Motte Guyon, who often left her children for years at a time to pursue some religious goal. She referred -- not infrequently -- to the '*mater abscondita*,' the, I dunno, *escaped* mother?"

"Better to say, 'the mother who has fled,'" Nicholas corrected, from the couch. He'd stretched out lengthwise and completely encased himself in a quilt.

"Yes, but she has fled with something -- *absconded* – with her child's heart, and his or her security in the world."

"How can you say that in this case? Tomás must've been days, even hours, old when he was adopted!" Nicholas was indignant.

"Yes, but Dahlia and Orlando never loved him 100% for himself. They loved him, Dahlia especially, as a sort of reincarnation of her beloved brother, Tomás Solar. On some level he must've intuited that." At least, this was how I'd reasoned things through, with what limited information was available to me.

"You know what really gets me?" Lark's tone was thoughtful. "None of this would have happened if women were in charge!"

I nodded. "You got that right! Even in early '70's Louisiana, mothering would have been venerated -- not a death sentence to her reputation and aspirations as it would be in the 'real' world!"

"Exactly," Lark said, "You've got a scared, small-town girl with a lot of dreams and potential who's stuck pregnant, broke and alone…What are her options?"

"And her family never knew?" asked Ted, looking amazed.

"Nope," I replied. "Basically, Tomás Junior's grandparents - that would be Christia's boyfriend's parents - along with his adoptive

asleep next to him after I'd felt so inflamed, and now I was awake again. This time, though, there was no ghost, no danger, no confusion – only the sounds one hears in an old house once everything else is quiet.

Around me, everyone in the house slumbered peacefully. Outdoors, the house was cradled by the softest, whitest snow, and the heavy-limbed pines loomed silent and protective around the cabin's log walls. I soon fell back asleep, lulled by the soughing of the wind.

The wee hours of the first day of the new year found me repeating to myself: "I will never be a dumb-ass again," which resolution, much like "I will never eat chocolate again" was perhaps one of tempering – more than the actual eradication of -- natural tendencies. My love life couldn't've been any worse. That meant it could only get better, no? I had Merlin and Pepita and good friends and a decent life. And a great apartment.

I only wished, quite naturally, that I hadn't fallen for a mixed-up killer. I knew it would take me awhile to get over him.

It was another snowy night. According to the weather report on the radio, snow was coming down heavily upstate, too, where, somewhere, Tomás Bautista was expected to be in prison for at least the next decade. The verdict was expected to be voluntary manslaughter, or worse. His sentencing was a priority for the university, and thus, indirectly but significantly, for the judge involved, who was a devoted alumnus of the University of New York. Tomás Bautista Junior would not contest the D.A.'s version of events, nor would he plead temporary insanity as most people expected he would.

Me, I'm not sure what I expected. I do know I had hoped to have a lot more figured out about my life by this year, so it was one of those times where I needed to call upon every ounce of my long training in yoga in order to be able to chill out enough to fall asleep. I consciously relaxed every part of my body, head to toe. I visualized a violet light at my third eye and a calming, protective halo of golden light all around me. Just breathe in, and then breathe out -- that's all you need to do, I reminded myself over and over. Finally, I drifted off to sleep.

One night, weeks later, Nicholas and I attended a concert together at the Miller Theater. The program was avant-garde classical music, performed by a cellist in Goth garb with waist-length crimson curls, and a virtuoso/bad-boy double-bass player, with tattooed wrists and a pierced nose. The latter was an old friend of mine, and we'd come as his guests.

It was a nice break for me. I'd been spending my post-holiday vacation studying for my comprehensive exam in February. Other than that, I'd invested my scarce free time in taking yoga classes, gearing up for the spring teacher training at the Ishwara Yoga Center. Nicholas and I had been spending a lot of time together, most of it at the library. We'd had a few dinners with Gretel and Kirpal, now an official item; and once, at Caffé Taci, we'd dined with Abdus and Kalinka. This last was surprisingly enjoyable now that Abdus wanted to be my friend. I'd always felt that Abdus looked down on me, and had never quite grasped that he was jealous. He'd told me he'd taken comfort in being mean to me. He hadn't felt guilty because he'd never thought it touched me at all: I'd seemed so "above it all," so "inviolable." He'd felt terrible when I told him how much it had hurt. We actually had a fantastic time as a foursome.

Nicholas and I did give in to our lust a few days after the solstice, and repeatedly thereafter. As long as I knew he was leaving shortly for a year in Germany, the pressure was off to define our relationship. That worked for me. After our long days of studying and procrastination, we'd eat fiery, garlicky Korean food at The Mill, or take long walks when it wasn't too cold; occasionally we'd share an artsy outing on the culturally rich Upper West Side.

After the concert at the Miller, I told Nicholas I needed to go home and study some more 18th-century literature. He went back to his apartment to do some online research into apartment availability in Berlin. He'd be staying with his friend Klaus until he found a place.

I got my mail and went upstairs. Pepita was dying to go out as I hadn't been home all day. It was only by chance that the pile of mail I'd plunked thoughtlessly on my kitchen table caught my eye when we got back inside. I was looking for something to aid my goal: procrastination. A thick envelope marked Eastern New York, followed by a series of numbers, was sandwiched between two bills. It was a letter from Tomás. "*Querida*," it began. "Forgive me. Not for hiding my terrible act – or for that act itself – but for caring too much for you."

I sat down. I was shaking. I felt so dizzy I had to hold my head in my hands for a long time before it stopped spinning. I would have to fortify myself if I planned to make it through this letter – I could see there were several more pages – with my sanity intact. I looked at the clock: 11 p.m. It was too late to call any of my friends except Brandi. I put the letter back in its envelope and picked up the phone. She answered on the first ring, and I told her I'd gotten a letter from Tomás and that I might need to call her again after I read it. She had a guy over, but agreed to answer the phone if I was absolutely desperate. She explained that I should start talking – loud -- on her answering machine so's she would know it was me...

"Can you believe it, though?" I asked before I hung up. "A letter from prison."

"Outrageous!" Brandi exclaimed. "He really cared about you, baby. He told me so." Her words were slightly slurred.

"Oh?" I didn't know they'd ever really spoken.

"We ran into each other out here, in Williamsburg, one night. The night before my 'Dirty Christmas' party?" I was quiet, wondering why she hadn't told me anything about the encounter. "Didn't I tell you?"

"No."

"Yeah, he was really maudlin, cryin' into his beer about being adopted and all that…I thought I told you…" In the background, I heard a male voice whispering something. "Listen cookie, I gotta go!" She was giggling as she hung up the phone.

So I was on my own with the letter. I fixed a cup of chamomile tea, for relaxation, adding some mint for my upset stomach, and lots of honey. I picked up the letter and read the end of the paragraph I'd begun a half-hour earlier: "For myself, I shall never forgive my never having been quite brave enough to let you go entirely." The tears began again. I agreed with him – he should've left me alone – but imagining his turmoil was painful nonetheless. "I suppose there are a lot of things you'd like to know," the letter continued:

> …since you are one of the few people around who might care for anything other than the basest of reasons. And I am the only one who knows most of the story.
>
> It took me many years to figure out that I was adopted, and, once I did, many more years to find out who my mother was. Once I had finally located my mother, I began to make plans to join her at the University of New York. I planned to meet her and get to know her before revealing my identity. I wasn't sure how she would take it after almost thirty years.
>
> As an undergraduate, I had gone to Juilliard and Columbia to study piano and philosophy in a joint-degree program, so I had most of the credentials to

attend a good graduate program. I'd always been interested in religion, too, so it wasn't too far of a stretch.

My grandfather, Ramon Solar, offered to pay for my graduate education out of remorse for having hidden the truth from me for all those years. He never told me my mother had been looking for me, only that he should have told me I was the son of his beloved son Tomás. I'd always known I was named after him. He never told me he'd kept his address and phone number unlisted so as to avoid my mother, or that he'd kept my adoptive mother Dahlia's married name – Bautista -- from my mother in order to keep her from finding me.

My parents told me that my birth mother never asked after me. It was all they knew, according to what *Abuelo* Ramon had told them. It would have made them terribly unhappy to know she'd searched for me with no success for years. Adoption records were, first, legally sealed; then, they were found to have been tampered with. My grandfather is an important personage in Miami, and he went to great lengths to keep secret what he thought would only harm his family.

In my family, I've always been called "*el bravo*" – because I'm seen as not just courageous, but sometimes bad-tempered and reckless. My parents instantly feared I was involved when they heard about Christia's death. They rushed to New York for damage control.

My mother, Dahlia Cordelia Solar Bautista attacked you in the park. Please understand: she was trying to make it seem as if there were some sort of serial

443

foot-baring maniac on the loose. She risked her own
safety (on many levels) to deflect attention from her son
– and this was before she was even sure I had killed
Christia Thompson. She did call 9-1-1 (anonymously) –
and you did survive, thank god.

It was almost, but not quite, impossible to imagine the
immaculate, aristocratic Dahlia clubbing me over the head with a rock,
and methodically stripping off my socks and shoes. She'd been as
ferocious as a lioness defending her cub, but I felt quite sure she'd also
made sure I was alive before fleeing the scene of her crime.

I don't remember killing my mother, but I
must've done it. I remember before and after so clearly –
why not that? There is not even a blur. We were talking
and chatting. Oh, and Nicholas came in while I was
there. Believe it or not I was hiding in the closet because
we were drinking. When he knocked, I ran in there with
the glass and bottle in-hand. They were as usual both
angry and flirtatious together. Christia told him he
smelled "gamy," I remember; though why one
remembers such things, I've no idea – especially when
one cannot remember one's most tragic moments…In
any case, as I've written above, we were talking and
chatting and then it was time for me to go.
When I left her office in the religion department,
I felt - do I have the right to say this? - devastated.
Everything was in slow motion. I saw everybody else
who might've had reason to kill her. Brenda was bent
over a file cabinet, her butt in the air like a scrawny
baboon. Philippe was slipping into the men's room, or at

least I think it was him. Who else wears bright pink shirts? Nicholas was still there. He and Ibo were talking at the end of the hallway, by the stairs. They were engrossed in their conversation and I don't think they saw me leaving. I heard Redmund banging around in his office as I waited for the elevator downstairs.

I had with me her copy of the adoption papers, releasing me into my grandparents' guardianship, and her journal. For all I know, she could've given them to me willingly. I have enclosed a photocopy of the pages of her journal I thought you might like to see. Of course, they don't let me keep it in here, but they were kind enough to copy it for me....I wish to God I'd read it before I did what I seem to have done.

All this time, there was precious Annie, with the innocent eyes.

I rang your doorbell before Thanksgiving…

Yes, and I remembered I'd had a visitation from Christia shortly thereafter, just as I had when he'd walked by in the rain, talking with Gretel and Kirpal, near the Hungarian Pastry Shop. Funny that he, like Abdus, called me "innocent." I certainly didn't feel innocent. If anything, I felt like a naïve idiot – and, at the same time, like the last few months had aged me inside.

I wanted to tell you everything, and have you offer me some kind of absolution but then I ran away, knowing there was never to be peace for someone like me. As you'll see, my mother felt the same.

Don't worry, Annie -- my childhood faith, Catholicism, taught me the usefulness of guilt, confession and repentance.

445

It is so, so quiet here. With the snow the silence only becomes more profound, and a little softer. The hush. Quietly, softly, I remain shattered. I do not ask for pity. In the deepening sky, filling with stars there is a coldness as vast as that in my heart. It's no use wishing on these stars. The thousands of other prisoners have already used up all of the wishes. What would I wish for, anyway – to turn back time? Better to forswear wishes, and admire mother moon, millions of miles away. (The moon always reminds me of something I read once: "...endlessly weavin' garments for the moon/wit my tears/I found God in myself/& I loved her/i loved her fiercely..." Ntozake Shange wrote that, but these days it makes me think of my mother and all her lost dreams and quests.)

Yesterday, in the sunny daylight, this snow was already falling, and I saw something I'd never seen before: the sun was shining through the snow. The very air was *sparkling*.

Do I write too much of the snow? I know you enjoy snow, Annie. And then -- here I have nothing but time. I find it almost liberating, to have my senses and activities so confined. I am finally reading *Don Quixote*. Next, I shall read *Swann's Way*.

I am sorry this letter is so long. Mostly, I am writing because I knew you could have loved me too...

"You could have loved me *too*..." There was a seemingly endless stream of tears washing down my cheeks. When I started to feel like I was starring in my own soap opera, I returned to the letter.

446

…and I would've brought you down, further than anyone should go, Annie. And that was wrong.

Solange visits me. She and my mother come every Sunday. It's only two hours from the city and my parents have relocated there, perhaps permanently. They do hate the cold, but I hope that in time they will acclimatize. That is my one selfishness now, the bottomless need for their unconditional love. I flatter myself by thinking they're glad I'm still alive.

Oh, and you might be interested to know I had a visit from my uncle Motte Thompson. He felt like family from the moment we met. He's dark and light and funny and kind. After I found out I was adopted, I always wondered why I looked so much like my dead uncle Tomás; and I felt that same tremor of recognition when I saw Motte. My face is practically an exact amalgam of the two men, the man I now know to be my father, and my maternal uncle. I'm surprised you didn't see the resemblance between Motte and me. Or perhaps you did?

I wonder: Why didn't you ever tell me about him? He's a little in love with you, too, and so we both thought it better that he not contact you while he was up in "the land of northern aggression."

In prison, as everywhere, there is a hierarchy. Those who have hurt children are the lowest of the low. To my surprise, I have been grouped among them by my fellow prisoners. There are the normal criminals – drug dealers, gangsters, thieves – and then there are monsters like me. (I think wife-beaters and –killers are in the middle?) We (such a "we," I refer to!) are ostracized or

447

worse. So, I live in my own head. I sleep a lot. The nights pass, tender sleep, merciless dreams, with never a hint of the crucial moment.

Except -- Do you know what syndactyly is? It means "together-digits." Commonly known as webbed feet. I have them. It's something I had always been ashamed of, but not anymore. Thirty percent of the time they are inherited from a parent, but no one in the Solar or Bautista families has them. Christia did.

That explained why he'd been the only person wearing shoes at Abdus' party. I had only half-consciously registered what had appeared at the time to be only a mild breach of etiquette.

I don't remember any violence. The only thing is, I do have this flash of taking her stockings off. When I saw her webbed toes just like mine I kissed them and cried on them then dried them. Was she alive then? I wish I knew.

Dahlia, the woman who raised me and swears she couldn't possibly love me more had she given birth to me (now, I believe her – I do wish I always had) brings me her home-made guava cheesecake, and books. Such goodness. I'm no longer under suicide watch, but they do x-ray Mama's cakes…

How should I sign this? (Happy New Year?)

And — goodbye. Be good.

Yours truly,

Tomás

I carefully re-folded the pages Tomás had sent me. I didn't trust myself to get through Christia's journal with my equilibrium intact. I would finish reading in the light of day.

Epilogue (Sweet)

A woman like that is misunderstood.
I have been her kind.

Anne Sexton, "Her Kind"

Here, below, are the journal entries Tomás sent me. They are excerpted from the weeks between June and November of ----.

When I woke up the morning after receiving Tomás' letter, it was a fresh and promising Saturday morning. I'd invited Nicholas, Abdus, and Kalinka over for dinner. After a moment's thought – realizing I wasn't that ballsy, after all – I'd called Brandi, Ibo, Gretel, and Kirpal and invited them as well. It would be a farewell dinner for Nicholas. I would miss Nicholas, but in a sense I missed Tomás more. Nicholas would always be in my life in some fashion, while I guessed I'd never see Tomás again.

I never responded to his letter. Why perpetuate a doomed love affair? He knew how I felt.

450

That morning, I showered and dressed and walked Pepita around the block before I read the journal entries. I'd promised myself I would go grocery shopping – distracting, and one of my favorite things to do -- immediately after reading the dead woman's innermost thoughts.

Christia's handwriting was cramped but precise. The first entries were willfully opaque, perhaps out of some fear of bringing shame upon herself, or causing a ruckus. (Aside from this one circumstance, when had Christia Thompson ever avoided hoopla?) Then, as things progressed, she became more and more exuberant and open:

> I told R.S. I'd discovered the name. It was such a coincidence: All day yesterday, I was flustered over a petty department imbroglio. One of the several flighty things I did in that state was to accidentally run a search for "Tomás + Solar" in the school search engine rather than the web search engine I'd intended to use. To my astonishment, I came up with a match! Tomás Bautista, enrolled for the fall semester in the religion department (?!), tuition being paid by his grandfather, Raymond Solar. I emailed "Raymond," the man I'd always known – and searched for – as Ramon, and discretely gave him one more chance to give me a way to contact Tomás, since he may not arrive in New York City for another two months. There is no contact information for him in the city or anywhere else. Just "Raymond's" email address. Courteously, deferentially (within reason), I contacted him. What will he say?
>
> ...
>
> Only in this I have never wanted to cause a scandal or maybe I never wanted anyone to know what I'd done or what *it* had done to *me*, irrevocably. None of this had to happen. Thousands of years ago, in

451

Puduhepa's court, there would have been a place for me to be both a young, single mother and a scholar. Why not in late-twentieth-century Louisiana? How had we regressed so far, we women? Why do I fear we have continued to regress, despite all the trappings of liberation?

For all I write and rave about power, who feels weaker than I?

...

I have not allowed myself so much as a comfortable chair in my own home, or a view from my desk at the university. I have practiced a lifetime of such sacrifices, to atone for my actions. I have denied my husband the pleasure of knowing I knew he was the bear in the Beltane fires – even after I read his puerile poem...Why? Because it would have brought me pleasure too, to bring all that was wild and pure that night into our dry marriage.

...

I was so good before my double tragedy and since then my punishment has been that the only pleasure I permit myself has been power, in career, and in relationships. I reckoned it was within my grasp at least to mete out my own judgment - yes, both a punishment and a prescription for the avoidance of future pain.

My own mother died young of a broken heart. Almost all of the DuPree women did. Such LOSS. So I, of all women, should have known better than to fall in love! After my mistakes – my foolish, ill-fated love affair, motherhood, non-motherhood -- I resolved that

452

everyone should hate me as I hated myself. I would become bad, mean, cold. But I never could quite bring myself to be cruel to the downtrodden; and it has always been hard to resist being good to the good…And so many are good, aren't they?

Annie Campbell. Maybe she would've understood? She seems kind and strong. My beloved sisters in the coven would have taken my pain into themselves, never imagining how rotten it is, or how endless. I believe it would have destroyed some of them. Brenda, at the very least. She is brittle on the surface, but there's steel beneath that. Then, though, brittleness again inside of that. My friend, Cyrus Wilson, sharing the knowledge of what it feels like to be a redneck bayou baby in the big apple. I could have told him instead of letting things fester inside of me.

I've always said there would never be peace for someone like me, a woman who knew full well that a women from her family should never fall in love and yet fell -- headlong; a woman who sold her own baby for what she thought would be passage from hell to purgatory. But I think now there is a chance.

Would I ever have judged any other woman who acted as I did, much less a child not yet twenty years old?

Never.

But each of us must find her own peace and – dare I dream? – I think I have found the path to mine.

As I become infected by hope, my armor crumbles, so that I find myself smiling – even at those I have fit into the category of those-who-should-hate-me,

those to whom I should act like an ice goddess. Those
who aren't too tender or too good to suffer for my
mistakes. Like my wickedly irresistible Nicholas (who
only wants the love and acclaim he will surely some day
garner from the whole world a tiny bit early from me)
and his adoring, adorable (and much softer than his
arrogance suggests) Abdus – or the imperious (secretly
vulnerable) Rich Redmund.

I marveled at her astute observations about everyone, and at
how deeply-buried her sweetness lay. What a tormented, twisted soul
she was. She reminded me of so many women who came before her,
who suffered greatly for being fertile – whether in body or in mind, not
to mention in both...What wrenching we endure in this mixed-up world,
I thought – and how it distorts us all.

I'm sorry, I said to Christia with all my heart, but it was too late.

Something struck me today, as I waited to catch a
glimpse of Tomás coming out of his class. My
"creation," my "discovery" – is so beautiful...Why have
I spent my whole life associating him with shame?

We academics always joke about how
sociologists are all social failures. Similarly, I am a
religion scholar who is spiritually inept! I should never
have punished myself as I have. After all, forgiveness is
one of the central messages of all religions. Starting
today, I will learn to forgive myself, and to be satisfied
with the life I have lived.

...

Leo Tolstoy said, "Everything that I understand, I
understand only because I love." How true, how true.

454

My tall little son, you are my light, my everything, just as Maddalena was to her mother in *Andrea Chenier,* my husband the bear's favorite opera.

After all this so-far wasted life, I have my child within my reach. And, praise the universe, to quote *cara* Maddalena *"Vivi ancora,"* I am still alive to savor this long-awaited day.

...

Dear goddess, I don't know how to be a mother after all these years of burying it! I will smile and reach out to him and even if he recoils it will have been enough to know I have a wonderful boy, my son, my sun.   It must be enough.

I don't care if he finds me compelling or intelligent or accomplished or attractive or respects me. I just need to see his face when he learns that his Mama loves him, only but once. Then, one last thing: I need to know he won't die on me like his Daddy did, even younger than he is now. I want my baby to stay alive.

Made in the USA
Lexington, KY
27 September 2018